Ace Books by Philippa Ballantine

GEIST
SPECTYR
WRAYTH

WRAYTH

Philippa Ballantine

ACE BOOKS, NEW YORK

THE BERKLEY PUBLISHING GROUP
Published by the Penguin Group
Penguin Group (USA) Inc.
375 Hudson Street, New York, New York 10014, USA
Penguin Group (Canada), 90 Eglinton Avenue East, Suite 700, Toronto, Ontario M4P 2Y3, Canada
(a division of Pearson Penguin Canada Inc.) • Penguin Books Ltd., 80 Strand, London WC2R 0RL,
England • Penguin Group Ireland, 25 St. Stephen's Green, Dublin 2, Ireland (a division of Penguin
Books Ltd.) • Penguin Group (Australia), 250 Camberwell Road, Camberwell, Victoria 3124, Australia
(a division of Pearson Australia Group Pty. Ltd.) • Penguin Books India Pvt. Ltd., 11 Community
Centre, Panchsheel Park, New Delhi—110 017, India • Penguin Group (NZ), 67 Apollo Drive,
Rosedale, Auckland 0632, New Zealand (a division of Pearson New Zealand Ltd.) • Penguin Books
(South Africa) (Pty.) Ltd., 24 Sturdee Avenue, Rosebank, Johannesburg 2196, South Africa

Penguin Books Ltd., Registered Offices: 80 Strand, London WC2R 0RL, England

This is a work of fiction. Names, characters, places, and incidents either are the product of the author's imagination or are used fictitiously, and any resemblance to actual persons, living or dead, business establishments, events, or locales is entirely coincidental. The publisher does not have any control over and does not assume any responsibility for author or third-party websites or their content.

WRAYTH

An Ace Book / published by arrangement with the author

PUBLISHING HISTORY
Ace mass-market edition / September 2012

Copyright © 2012 by Philippa Ballantine.
Cover art by Jason Chan.
Cover design by Lesley Worrell.
Interior text design by Tiffany Estreicher.

ISBN: 978-1-937007-75-1

ACE
Ace Books are published by The Berkley Publishing Group,
a division of Penguin Group (USA) Inc.,
375 Hudson Street, New York, New York 10014.
ACE and the "A" design are trademarks of Penguin Group (USA) Inc.

PRINTED IN THE UNITED STATES OF AMERICA

10 9 8 7 6 5 4 3 2 1

ALWAYS LEARNING   **PEARSON**

To all the librarians in my life.
You opened up a world of knowledge
and adventure in my mind
that helped bring these stories to fruition.

ACKNOWLEDGMENTS

Thanks are always necessary when a book is finally birthed, because no author is an island, and no story is written in a vacuum. To Danielle Stockley for helping to shape Arkaym and keep Sorcha under control. To my agent, Laurie McLean, who held my hand as I ventured out into the publishing world. To Jason Chan, who has always brought my thoughts to life with his amazing covers. To all my kind, generous and supportive podcast listeners—these books wouldn't have happened without your backing. To my wonderful, talented husband, my captain who helped me set out on this adventure, and keeps me paddling. Finally, to my daughter, who might find writing "boring" but hopefully will enjoy these books when she's older.

ONE

Taken in Shadow

In the time when the earth bucked and heaved, many secrets were revealed—some were for good; some were most definitely for ill.

As Caoirse followed her partner into the darkness, she could only wish that the situation they were walking into was the former. It had already been a long day for both her and Klanasta. Against the moonlight he was only a gray shadow on a horse before her, but they shared much more than moonlight. In her mind, her Active burned like a warm ember—something to hold on to, something to put all her trust in when surrounded by a perilous world. It was the real joy of being a Deacon: never being alone. It couldn't make up for the dangers of hunting geists, but it came awfully close.

She tucked damp curls of her reddish hair away from her face, pulled her green cloak tighter and shivered. Her mount, Tilin, was a Breed horse, and a fine creature to ride, but she'd been in the saddle going on three days now. It was enough to make anyone tense, so Caoirse kneed him up to walk alongside Klanasta's horse.

"How much farther?" she asked with a sigh.

Klanasta's long nose was the only real detail she could make out in this dark and fog. "The tunnel isn't far away, and Goine and Leontis should have a nice stew waiting for us."

Since they were two young lads just out of the novitiate, Caoirse had severe doubts about their abilities with a pot, but she stayed silent on the matter. Instead she opened her Center and spread it out all around them, looking for their compatriots.

Caoirse frowned. Everything was laid before her: the snake sleeping in its underground lair, a vulture with his head tucked beneath his wing and a vixen snuffling her way through the undergrowth.

She didn't need to tell Klanasta what was missing; they shared the Bond and her Sight.

"No Deacons," he whispered. The Active Deacon's hands instantly sought out the Gauntlets he kept tucked in his belt. When he slipped them on, Caoirse felt better. Her partner was no wet-behind-the-ears novice. If there was a geist waiting for them, then it was the undead that should fear, not them.

She did her part too. As the Sensitive Deacon in the pair, she probed deeper into the mist and swamp with greater focus. All she uncovered were more hungry predators and frightened prey. No geists and no Deacons.

It was only when Tilin's large hoof clattered into a tin plate that she realized that they were at their fellow Deacons' camp. The fire was long dead. At least two days of rain had dampened the area considerably.

Together she and Klanasta slipped down off their horses, landing with a wet slap in the mud. Her partner did not have to ask. Caoirse brought her Sight to bear on the camp. Activating Aiemm, the Second Rune of Sight, she let her mind run back in time, back to when two Deacons were sitting at this campfire talking about the things young men talk about—even those from the Order of the Eye and the Fist.

She did not listen in to their conversation until they rose to their feet. Certainly their expression said they'd heard something, but it wasn't something that she could perceive. Very odd.

The lads gathered up their cloaks and the foci of the Order, the Gauntlets for the Active and the Strop for the Sensitive.

"They heard something," she said to Klanasta, "and went this way."

He followed her, as she in turn retraced the path that Goine and Leontis had taken. "They went down toward the temple."

Her partner groaned with ill-concealed frustration. "They were told to wait for us."

A chill ball of dread made itself known in Caoirse's belly, but they went on. The temple was not much to look at, a scattering of old rocks covered with faded writing. No one had ever been able to decipher the language of the Ancients, but that didn't stop scholars of the Order from trying.

An earthquake a month ago had opened up the side of a hill, near the temple. On hearing of it the Mother Abbey scholars had almost frothed at the mouth. Maybe there were untouched artifacts or unmarred writings down there, they clamored. Through weirstone communication, they demanded someone be sent to investigate. Goine and Leontis were the closest, being Deacons of the nearest Priory, and their mission was only to secure the site. Caoirse and Klanasta had been sent for, from further afield, to make the actual examination.

"This way," she hissed to her partner as she pushed aside branches and followed the path the foolish young Deacons had taken.

A large part of the small hill had indeed broken away and revealed an ancient tunnel.

"I've yet to meet a lad who can resist a tunnel." Klanasta rolled his eyes. "It was bound to happen."

"They should have sent someone with more experience," Caoirse agreed, "but it is what it is. Come on."

They scrambled up through mud and broken vegetation to the entrance. A lantern was perched on a nearby rock. Klanasta raised an eyebrow. "Looks like they expected us." He opened the lantern, struck a match, and lit the wick.

He went first though, a faint shimmer coming off his Gauntlets, as if to remind Caoirse that she was safe.

The tunnel dipped down, and Klanasta jumped back in irritation. The rain of the last few days had collected in the depression, making a wide pond of the passageway. It was impossible to see the other side, or if the tunnel rose up again.

Then suddenly that became the last thing on the Deacons' minds. It was as Caoirse feared; the bodies of Goine and Leontis floated facedown in the water.

Klanasta shook his head. "I suppose they were trapped down here when it flooded. By the Bones, when will the young learn some sense!" Bunching up his cloak in one hand, he began wading out to them, grumbling all the time. Deacons deserved a proper burial—even if they were fools.

Caoirse didn't have any real desire to see the boys die, but some sense of duty propelled her to watch the rest through Aiemm.

Klanasta reached the first body, and rolled it over. "That's strange," he called as he began to pull it back toward her. Caoirse's eyes widened, as the image of what had been laid over what was currently happening.

"Klanasta!" she screamed, while her Center wrapped around him. At the same time, something exploded toward him out of the water.

It was not a geist, and she would have sworn her Center had not seen it until a moment ago. Her partner was hampered by the body and slow moving in water. To her horror, she caught a flash of legs, long and sharp like a crab's, but much, much larger, dart out from under the water. They wrapped around Klanasta and jerked him off his feet and into the seething pond.

Drawing her sword, she leapt into the murky pool after him, but she didn't need to see the blood in the water to know he was dead; the abruptly severed Bond told her that. Caoirse gasped in horror, but plunged deeper—even if it were just to wrestle her partner's body from this foul creature.

She had little regard for her own safety, because it mattered so little to her in that moment. When she dived down under the water she thought briefly that she had got hold of Klanasta, until her fingers locked on something harder. The claw twisted in her hand and grabbed her in turn.

The Deacon thrashed wildly for the surface, but more of those nightmarish things closed around her, jerking her down. Caoirse kicked out hard, gasping in a mouthful of dirty, bloody water.

Whatever these things might be, they were strong. Their pincers and legs formed a cage around her, and carried her below the water, down into unseen depths.

Her last desperate thought was outrage that she hadn't seen them coming.

✦ TWO ✦

Life of a Moth

If there was any worse thing in the world than being conscious and unable to communicate Sorcha Faris did not know of it. She lay on her back, propped up on pillows, staring at the ceiling of the Mother Abbey's infirmary and counted the dancing moths by her bedside. It was the only thing she had to keep madness at bay.

She could feel Kolya's hand on her wrist, but she could not pull it away as she wanted to. Her oh-so-nearly-former husband only ventured in to sit with her when Merrick was out of the room. At first he had spoken falteringly of his sadness, his regrets. He had been wrong. He should have let her in, should have trusted her.

It's too late for that, had been her unspoken, unheard reply.

Yet despite herself she started to listen. Sorcha knew she had not been the best of wives. It was easy to admit that in the quiet of the infirmary, with nothing to do but think.

But Kolya, he was not without fault—even now. She could feel him trying to renew their withered Bond, the magical connection between an Active and a Sensitive

Deacon. Sorcha shared an exceptionally strong one with
her younger partner Merrick Chambers. What Kolya was
trying to do was immoral and highly illegal within the
strictures of the Order of the Fist and the Eye, and she suspected that he was acting under Arch Abbot Rictun's command. Not that she, lying mute and incapacitated, was
capable of telling anyone. Even with Merrick, she could
not manage to send words along the Bond as she once
could. He could feel her emotions and that was it, and it
was hard to reveal Kolya's duplicity with just those. She
had probably given Merrick more than his fair share of
headaches by trying. Sorcha might have felt sorry for
that—but trying was all she had left.

If she cared to strain her eyes to the left she would be
able to make out Kolya's head bent over her hand, pressing
his forehead against it. She could feel the low tug on the
remains of her Bond with him, like an unpleasant tickle
that she could not scratch. Deacon Kolya Petav was wearing away her strength. Sorcha resisted as best she could.
She bent her will to keeping the Bond with Merrick alive,
and burying the one she had once shared with Kolya.

She'd fought and defeated the geistlord Hatipai, but
she'd overstepped her bounds as a Deacon. Now, this was
her life—and what a miserable life it was.

By the Bones, Kolya, don't bother. I'm not worth it . . .

"Deacon Petav?" If Sorcha had believed in gods at that
moment she might have let out a shout of exaltation. The
curly, dark head of her current partner appeared around the
door frame. "To what do we owe this unexpected visit?"
Ever the diplomat, he didn't let out a curse as she might have
done in the same position. Still, his tone was accusatory. On
the inside Sorcha cheered. It was delightful to see the young
Deacon taking the situation firmly in hand. Watching from
her bed, Sorcha realized her partner had grown up.

Kolya, as always keeping his demeanor cool, stroked
the back of Sorcha's hand. "I am still her husband, Deacon
Chambers."

It's not about that is it, Kolya?

Merrick stepped through the door and carefully placed a tray down on the table. From this angle Sorcha couldn't see what was on it. In the good old days, two months before, she would have hoped for a cigar or a spot of hard liquor—now such bodily pleasures were beyond her. Instead, she settled for watching the two men spar over her prone body.

Her real partner took his place on the other side of her, and his voice was calm but sharp. "Only because she was not capable of standing at the final reading of the dissolution. It was merely a formality that Sorcha could not unfortunately attend."

"Still formalities are formalities," Kolya said, and it was the first time that Sorcha had ever heard real steel in his tone. She knew him well after years of marriage, and Kolya could be stubborn—beyond stubborn in fact.

Straining her eyes, Sorcha could make out Merrick's tight expression, and observed him swallow hard. Without the complete Bond, she had to hang on every little nuance and expression. Funny how she had once been so annoyed by the leaking of words and thoughts between them—and now she missed them terribly.

"Brother Salay said we must leave her to sleep, and I believe Presbyter Mournling is leading a discussion this evening on the latest findings on geistlords." The Sensitives faced each other from opposite sides of the bed, and even Sorcha, trapped in her body, could feel the tension. If they had been Actives it would have already devolved into a brawl, but Sensitive Deacons were different creatures altogether. In point of fact, Sorcha had no idea how they settled arguments.

Kolya was the first to break. "I've been looking forward to that discussion." He turned, caught himself, and swung around to plant a brisk kiss on Sorcha's cheek. "I will see you later."

Don't come back. Just let it go. She concentrated on moving her arm, just a little bit—just enough for a small gesture. Yet there was nothing.

Then she and Merrick were alone, and she turned her attention to the Bond; funneling all of her frustration into it. Merrick took a step back, and pressed his fingertips to his forehead. "I know, Sorcha. I know—but there is little I can do. I can't keep him out of here since his status as your partner and your husband has not been tidied up."

Sorcha immediately felt guilty. For the last two months she had leaned heavily on their Bond. By dumping all her feelings to her partner, she had managed to hang on by her fingernails to her mind, however in the process she had strained the young man to that very same point.

I just want to get better. A wave of despair washed over her, and when it drew back she was not the powerful, stern Deacon—she was just a woman trapped in her body and terrified that it was going to be that way forever. *If so, just kill me now Merrick!*

He couldn't hear that plea, but he could feel the emotion it rode on. Merrick sat on the bed next to her and took her hand in his. "It'll be all right. Think how much better you are than when we brought you back from Orinthal. You really are healing! Brother Salay says your muscles are responding to the exercises they put you through." His brown eyes sparkled dangerously with something close to tears. "Please, don't give up, Sorcha."

Sorcha wasn't embarrassed when one of her own leaked out and ran down her cheek. Merrick wiped it clear and smiled. "I won't tell a soul about that. Now I want to hear what Presbyter Mournling has to say as well. I'll see you tomorrow." He was lying to her—that much she could tell from the Bond. However she would not deny him his secrets.

Her partner got up and snuffed out the wicks on all but two lamps in the room. The sound of him closing the door behind him was bleak indeed. The moths were altering their dance accordingly, with the change in light, but these new patterns held no magic for Sorcha. She was alone. The small hours of the night were quite the worst.

Dimly off in the corridors she could hear lay Brothers about their work, the whisper of hushed voices, and the occasional sob from relatives come to visit their loved ones in the infirmary. Then the door creaked open again.

Maybe Merrick had changed his mind and was coming back to sit through the night with her as he had when she'd been first brought back to Vermillion.

"She's in here." Sorcha recognized the voice, and felt even better than if it had been Merrick. It was one she had sorely missed these last months. Her partner before Kolya, Garil Reeceson was now a retired Sensitive—old, battered, but still one of her best friends. As a trainer at the Abbey he was busy, so she had understood his infrequent visits.

He came into view at the foot of her bed, but his face had changed since he was last there. Sorcha knew Garil; knew his strengths, his fears and his weaknesses. She had seen him when he was in pain, in fear and in triumph. Yet, she had never witnessed this expression from him before. Great guilt lingered about his eyes, but his mouth was set in a hard determined line.

Just as she was trying to puzzle out what that might mean, she observed he was not alone. Sorcha could not have been more surprised to see Aachon appear at his shoulder than if the Prince of Chioma had. He was the first mate of the *Dominion*, Raed Rossin's friend, and someone she had not seen since the attack in the ossuary in Vermillion. When she had met the Young Pretender in Orinthal he had described how he had left Aachon and most of his crew on the *Dominion*. He'd planned to rendezvous with them later after finding his sister. Could this mean that the Young Pretender was close by?

Sorcha's heart surged. If there was one man that she wanted to see in the world it was Raed Syndar Rossin, the Young Pretender. Despite her current condition, she'd not stopped thinking of him. Often in the dead of night, she dreamed of their brief moments of passion, imagined his skin against hers, his breath in her ear . . .

Probably not best to think about that at the moment however. Sorcha flicked her eyes side to side desperately searching, but the first mate was alone. Though Aachon had shown no particular fondness for her in the past—which could have something to do with her getting his Prince constantly into trouble—now he too looked guilty. Two men with that same look could not bode well.

Garil? By the Bones, what is going on?

She sent the question as a last ditch attempt, but their Bond was long dead—as broken and shattered as his body had been by street thugs. When she caught the glint of a knife in his hands, for a second she was relieved. Maybe Merrick couldn't find it in himself to finish her off—but Garil was made of sterner stuff. She was about to experience the Otherside for herself, and terrified as she was she didn't want to exist in a body that had become a prison.

The knife swept down. No pain reached Sorcha, only a strange pressure. Garil pulled the knife back and it was clean of any blood. For a moment the three of them stared at the blade.

In that silence Sorcha was remembering the Prince of Chioma, part human and part geistlord. In preparation for her battle with Hatipai, he had gifted her with his invulnerability. He had said it would be only temporary. That had been weeks and weeks ago. His concept of temporary must be very strange indeed.

"Now that's what I call an impressive demonstration," Aachon rumbled, taking the knife and holding it up to examine in the faint light.

The laid-out Deacon couldn't lever herself up to see if the knife had cut and then she healed, or if the blade had bounced off her skin.

"One of the lay Brothers said he noticed last week that when leached the animals would not feed from her." Garil sheathed his knife with an abrupt gesture. "Now I see that in fact they couldn't. The real problem is revealed."

"An invulnerable Deacon?" the first mate of the *Dominion* replied. "I would have thought that would be a cause for celebration."

"It's an abomination!" Garil's voice was filled with such anger and bitterness that it was impossible to guess that he had once called Sorcha friend. "Such a blending of geistlord and Deacon powers can only bring horror to the world. It must be removed."

Her stomach tightened into a pit of ice, but she could not move to tell him what had happened—to explain herself. The runes that the Deacons used were essentially the same as those wielded by the geists; moving through walls, seeing through another's eyes—but no one had ever tamed the greater powers of a geistlord. Garil might have been her friend, confidant and mentor for years upon years, but his training as a protector of the realm still held true. In his eyes and those of all members of the Order, she was revealed as something else. Something alien.

"You must take her far away from the Mother Abbey." Garil spoke softly, rubbing his forehead as if in pain. "The path is dark, but it is the only chance for her to be free of . . . this."

"But the lay Brothers must have tried." Aachon leaned down to stare at Sorcha. "What makes you think the cure is beyond these walls?"

"The Order do not have the answer to this. Only those that gave her the gift can take it back." Her old partner let his breath out slowly, as if centering his being as best he could. "Her healer is waiting for her out there somewhere."

"And so I must carry her around until one of these creatures appears?" Aachon did not appear pleased with this plan.

"Since it fits nicely with your own goal . . . yes." The old Deacon smiled crookedly. "I have something to help you find who you are looking for." Garil reached into his pocket and produced a stone on a chain. It was a weirstone. He spun the unusual swirling blue and white globe over Sorcha's chest. Out of the corner of her eye she saw the object twisting, and then abruptly turn and tug westward. It looked exactly like an eager dog sensing its master.

Aachon held out his hand, and Garil laid the weirstone in it. The first mate clenched it and raised one thick eyebrow. "Another impressive display, old man. You haven't lost your touch with these things."

"The weirstone uses the Bond between Sorcha and your Prince. It should lead you right to him." The elderly Deacon dipped his head. "And please do not try to alter what I have done with the stone. I recall it was one of the reasons you were ejected from the Order. Now, your skill may be put to some real purpose."

"I shall resist the temptation." The first mate draped a coarse brown cloak over Sorcha. "If she can lead me to him, then all shall be well."

The Deacon's hand clamped down on Aachon's, and he fixed him with a look that could have melted iron. "Watch your back, old friend. You will be sailing into danger—more than you ever have before."

Aachon clapped his hand on Garil's arm; a surprisingly gentle gesture. "What have you seen ahead?"

The elder man stared down at Sorcha. "Blood and shadow, Aachon. So much chaos and so many choices that I can barely make out what is coming." He touched her head, but she wished she could feel it.

Don't send me away, Garil. Not without Merrick. Get Merrick!

Her old partner couldn't meet her eyes, and Sorcha suddenly realized he was about to toss her out into a sea of possibilities.

Then she panicked.

Merrick! Merrick, come back!

He couldn't hear her of course, but she hoped that wherever he was it was close and that he could feel her distress. Everything was wrong. Garil had not only been her partner—he had been her mentor and her friend. How could he be sending her out into the world in her state? Perhaps this was part of some delusion and she was still lying helpless staring up at the ceiling?

Neither of the men took any note of her wide staring eyes, indeed Sorcha's old partner was taking great pains not to look too closely at her. Instead, he handed Aachon a scroll. When the first mate opened it, the seal of the Presbyter of the Sensitives was revealed; a thick slab of wax with a swirl of ribbons. He stared at it for a moment. "Garil," he said with a shake of his head, "this is a tremendous risk for you."

Garil sighed. "You think I stole the seal for this? No, old friend, this is the genuine article. Presbyter Yvril Mournling did indeed sign and authorize this. You will have the full use of whatever airships you have need of. I recommend the *Autumn Eagle*—and I believe she is in port at the moment. Her captain Lepzig is a good man that knows the value of not asking too many questions while on Order business."

Sorcha, still terrified by the situation, nonetheless paused for a moment. Active Deacons sometimes whispered about the Sensitives—that they held things back, and had their own agenda. She'd always thought it was mindless gossip by bored novices. Yet, the look in her old partner's eye was somber and deep. Why would Mournling do such a thing, and for those wanted by the Emperor himself?

Aachon nodded. "He concurs then. Very well, I shall requisition the *Autumn Eagle*."

While she screamed and struggled inside her head, Garil bent, gathered up her Gauntlets and placed them on her chest. "It is a blessing that the fires have burned so low in her." Touching another's talismans while they still lived, even for a Bonded partner, was a dangerous action. The thick leather gloves, carved with terrible runes, were now no more dangerous than any other lady's adornment that might be found in a market. While her old partner stared down at her from his scarred and battered face, Aachon gestured and two hooded figures entered the room, bundled her up in a blanket and hoisted her between them.

The logical part of her brain, which miraculously was still functioning, was wondering just how they planned on smuggling a Deacon from inside the Mother Abbey. In the end it turned out to be remarkably easy.

Her powers were indeed very far gone. Unable to even reach her Sensitive, hanging on the edge between life and death, she appeared nothing more than any other patient. As they approached the gate, she could see out of her eye the duty Sensitive talking and laughing with one of the lay Brother guards. A small stream of traffic was heading out of the Mother Abbey; merchants come to deal with the kitchen staff, workers and labors returning to their homes beyond the Imperial Island, and many family members, taking home their loved ones from the infirmary.

Aachon and his small band of men, accompanied by an old Deacon, blended right in. Nothing in the ether said that they were passing an Active Deacon out under the noses of her compatriots.

Stop them! I'm in here . . . get Merrick!

Her howls only echoed inside her own head. The Sensitive didn't even look up as they filtered past him, and the gate to the Abbey was shut tight behind them.

"This isn't how I imagined things," Aachon murmured in her general direction. "If it makes a difference, I am sorry Sorcha."

It didn't matter. For the first time in her life, Sorcha was cut off from the Order, and truly alone.

THREE

Rare Feelings

Grand Duchess Zofiya did not like the company her brother was keeping. Not one little bit.

She stood with her eye pressed to the peephole and observed the dark corridor with the intensity of an owl waiting for a mouse. Except, she was positive this man was far more dangerous than a mouse. The width of his shoulders leaned toward brawler rather than dandy, while his long strides spoke of a man on a mission. Zofiya felt something else about him—something that she was very well acquainted with. Danger.

Ever since the Emperor's sister had lost her faith, she had deliberately tried to steer away from superstition in all its forms. After her goddess was exposed as a fraud in a violent public display that nearly killed her, Zofiya had decided a new path was the best course. Huddled on the Imperial Airship the *Summer Hawk*, she had determined that from that moment on she would only believe what her eyes would bring her. Yet, this newcomer to the Imperial Court, one who had in the last few weeks been spending an increasing amount of time in her brother's private chambers, had an aura of menace about him she could not nail down to any one glaring attribute. The only feeling she could go by was a deep-seated sense of unease.

Lord Vancy del Rue did not live up to his slightly comical name. He was tall, with a gray beard and hair, but a face that looked much younger. He wore the thinnest of calfskin gloves, and never removed them—even in the heat of the palace. He was the newly appointed ambassador from Ensomn, though he did not look to be of that western principality. Zofiya had never personally spoken to the man, but he had certainly caught her attention.

A soft knock on the door meant an end to her covert and definitely frustrating observations. Moving down from the step at the peephole, she quickly exited the wardrobe, replaced the false back, and retook her seat in her privy chamber. It was a private and intimate space that she only let people she trusted come to, so consequently it had very few visitors.

At her command Deacon Merrick Chambers entered and made a very proper and well-executed bow. As he did so, Zofiya couldn't help smiling. The Deacon just had that effect on her. However, she would never tell anyone— especially him—about it. By the time his dark head rose, she had succeeded in secreting the expression away.

"Your Imperial Highness." Merrick might have got over his initial nervousness around her, but she could not shake him of the habit of addressing her so formally in private. She had decided to look on it as an endearing trait. "You summoned me?"

She had found quite a few reasons to call Deacon Chambers to her in the months since their flight from Chioma. At first they had been real ones, concerning his mother, who had birthed the heir to that principality within the Imperial Palace. But after it became apparent the Emperor would not support an immediate return, to claim Chioma for the new infant Prince, she had found other excuses to bring the young Deacon out from the Mother Abbey. She was worried that the Court gossip would become unbearable, that maybe her brother would ask her questions—or worst of all Merrick himself might notice. Yet, despite all that she persisted.

"I need your help, Merrick."

The Deacon's brown eyes widened and an expression of vague confusion darted across his face. Zofiya wished she hadn't been so foolish as to use his first name, as if they were friends or even more intimately acquainted. "Is it about my brother?" he blurted out.

He was always most concerned about Lyon's future, but perhaps he was starting to guess her brother's intentions. She did not want to disappoint Merrick by telling him that the Emperor had no intention of raising another Prince in Chioma. Recently married, he hoped to have his own son and immediately make him ruler of that realm. For all intents and purposes the quasi-independence of the south was done.

Zofiya did her best to hide her emotions while rearranging her skirts. Perhaps there was a use for women's fripperies after all. "No," she said smoothing the lace with one hand. "It is something else entirely."

"Whatever service I can offer is yours, Your Imperial Highness." He paused, and drew in a careful breath before continuing, "Providing it does not go against my vows as a Deacon."

"Naturally." She got up, placed her hand daringly under his elbow, and drew him over to the window. A small enameled tea set was already laid out as per her instructions. The insulated teapot had kept the brew at just the right temperature, and as the Grand Duchess sat down, she could smell the apples of Delmaire. It was a perfume that brought back beautiful and painful memories of her birthplace. "Please join me, Deacon Chambers. I have this tea shipped in from my father's capital city, and it is a pleasure to share it with someone who I know is not out to seek advantage."

After a moment's pause, Merrick flicked his cloak back

and took a seat opposite her. The slight twist in his mouth made him look about as happy as a cat dunked in water. He was making a polite attempt to conceal it—but was not very good at it—at least to the Grand Duchess' eyes. Unfortunately for him, Zofiya was very good at spotting such things. Growing up surrounded by intrigue and aristocrats out to ingratiate themselves had taught her a thing or two. Since he seemed incapable of knowing where to begin, she did it for him.

"I know you Sensitives see things that others cannot," she said pouring the tea, and sliding the delicate cup over to him, "and I have need of such a person. A very great need."

"The Order is always ready to fulfill the requirements of the Emperor and his family. The Sensitive Deacon assigned to your brother, Deacon Lolish, is very good, but if you aren't happy with him, I am sure you could request someone from the Mother Abbey to—"

He remained as dedicated to his work as she remembered, but Zofiya had to stop him before he got completely the wrong idea. "That's true. But a thing like that would be noticed in the Court—and I wish it not to be." She fixed him with a hard look. "Have you heard of Lord Vancy del Rue?"

After a quick sip of his tea, Merrick shook his head. "You'll have to forgive me—I am not very well versed in the comings and goings in your brother's palace. Deacons generally do not involve themselves with politics."

"A wise decision to be sure." Zofiya stirred her drink with a tiny brass spoon and considered how much to tell this Deacon. It was a very long time since she had trusted anyone with her thoughts. Even Kaleva, her brother and Emperor, did not know every concern and dark musing that passed through her mind, and though she'd taken lovers within the Imperial Court, nothing of greater substance that a groan or a sigh had passed between them.

Yet as she looked across the table at the young Deacon, she was reminded how well he had kept the secret shame of what had happened in Chioma to himself. The riots in the distant principality were generally considered to be just another bout of civil unrest. She had heard no whisper that any suspected that the goddess Hatipai had in fact been a geistlord. Those followers of hers who had gone to the desert temple had heard the call, even seen some things, but they had not been close enough to observe the true nature of their goddess. In all respects Zofiya realized they were luckier than she.

Only the Young Pretender Raed—whose whereabouts were unknown—the comatose Deacon Faris, and her partner, now sitting opposite the Grand Duchess, knew the real truth. As she contemplated that, Merrick pushed back his cup and fixed his steady brown eyes on her face with the sort of intent she'd only seen in the most accomplished warriors. "You have been kind and generous in your care of my mother and brother, Imperial Highness. You have done your best to see to it that their claim to the Chiomese principality is not forgotten—and most of all, you have been careful not to recall these kindnesses as any kind of debt. So even if I were not a Deacon, I would certainly want to help you in whatever way I can."

Something about the honest way he delivered that little speech brought an unusual rush of blood to her cheeks. Luckily, she was no pale maid on which such a thing might be called a blush. "I was born into a scheming Court, Deacon Chambers. I've known knaves and backstabbers since before I could walk, and yet this Lord del Rue unnerves me in a way none of those ever did." She fiddled with the now-empty cup, rubbing the bottom back and forth on the saucer. "He is admitted often to my brother's presence—but in private. I have been introduced to him, as he dines and dances with the rest of the Court, and he is the very image of a polite, respectful courtier, and yet something here," she went on, placing one hand over her stomach, "rebels against his nearness. Every single time I feel ill, and several times

I imagine there is a smell about him—like something rotten. I admit I have actually been ill several times on his account."

It was an embarrassing admission, but Merrick sat up straighter in his chair, and she noted his hand went to the length of leather tied to his belt—the Strop that was the focus of a Sensitive Deacon's power. His frown was deep, making him appear so much older, and he pressed his lips together. Finally when he looked up, his eyes scanned her enough to make her think that she was some insect under scrutiny. "It could be," he finally offered, "that your closeness to the geistlord Hatipai has woken an awareness in you that has lain latent."

Zofiya could not stop the words escaping her. "You think I am some kind of Sensitive?"

Merrick grew suddenly bold, taking her hand and tracing a design in it. She let him, because his hand was warm, and she wanted his touch rather badly. "No," he leaned back, placing the Grand Duchess' palm once more on the table. "There is a glimmer there, but nothing that could be trained up to the level of Deacon. It seems you just have had your inner eye opened to certain things." He smiled reassuringly. "In your position, Imperial Highness, it could prove quite useful."

"Well, having to excuse myself and rush off to be sick while at a state dinner is quite inconvenient. Rumors get started that way."

Now it was the Deacon's turn to blush. "I will try and find a way to bump into your Lord del Rue and see if there is something deeper to these feelings. It may be that he was merely the target of an unliving attack sometime in his life. Such things do leave scars." He stood up. "If you could arrange for me to mix with the Court tomorrow, I am sure I can put your mind at rest."

She looked up at him and smiled. "I will tell the seneschal that you will attend as extra security when the Prince Gyor arrives from the west. The Emperor has arranged a state ball for him, and that should give you a chance to run your eye over del Rue."

The Deacon bowed. "Until tomorrow then."

Just as he turned to go, Zofiya found another way to prolong his visit. "How is your partner faring?"

Merrick's eyes dipped away from hers. "No better and no worse, Imperial Highness. No one has been able to penetrate the coma—not even myself. All I can feel is her frustration and anger. The Presbyters are almost on the verge of assigning me a new partner, and I can only put them off so long."

Zofiya felt a twist of jealousy at his concern. She knew the Bond between Active and Sensitive was a powerful one, but Deacon Faris was a woman. Still, she managed to conceal the stab of resentment. "I'm sorry to hear it. I imagine you are heading back to sit vigil?"

He shook his head. "I did when we first returned from Chioma, but after a couple of weeks her emotions bled so much into my own that I could not sleep."

"I am sure it is not deliberate on her part," Zofiya murmured. "I will look for you at Court then tomorrow."

As he bowed once more and withdrew, she was able to consider the rashness of her actions. She was used to taking risks, with blood and body, but she wondered if the young and handsome Deacon Merrick Chambers might be a risk of a totally new, and more dangerous kind. Still, what was life without risks?

FOUR

Dealing with Shadows

As he crouched in the shadows of buildings looking across the lake to the fortress of Phia, Raed heard the rumble of his burden.

She is in there. The traitor. The vermin.

"She's my sister," Raed replied under his breath, "remember that." He was fully aware how bad it would look to be found talking to himself on the street. He couldn't risk another incident like the one yesterday with the bounty hunter.

Tracking his sister, far from friend and family, he'd had to rely on the Rossin, but that didn't mean he liked it. With Fraine and her collaborator Tangyre Greene stirring up rebellion in every principality they could find, the Emperor had raised the price on Raed's own head. Things had gotten that much more difficult—and without his crew he felt as vulnerable as a turtle out of its shell. Bounty hunters were coming out of the woodwork left and right.

Which was why he had turned to the Rossin. Somewhere in the humid jungles of the west, he had lost all hope—and fallen back on the one resource he still had.

Inviting the geistlord to occupy the upper portions of his conscience was a risk, but it was what the Rossin was willing to accept in return for his help. As much as it pained the Young Pretender to the throne, he knew that he would have died on the street yesterday without the fell creature's warning. Only months before, the idea that he would be bargaining with the creature he had despised for decades would have been laughable. Now it was a grim reality.

The town was quiet at his back. The death of the bounty hunter had been swift, but plenty of citizens had seen the huge, agile shape of the Rossin on the rooftops. If Fraine didn't know already, she would soon hear that her brother was nearby. What she would do with that information was a mystery. The uncomfortable fact was he didn't know his sister very well. Evidenced by the fact he'd never suspected she harbored such hatred for him, and that she was capable of slaying members of his crew in cold blood.

Snook's face as her throat had been slit and her blood had poured down to the sands of Chioma still haunted his dreams.

Fool. Don't think of the past. Think of what you must do.

The Rossin's voice was seductive again; a velvet wash across his senses, reminding him how good it was to be strong and mighty. It was an effort of will every day to not just give up to the geistlord. He couldn't yet—not when Fraine was in danger of bringing the Empire to its knees.

If Fraine succeeded in launching a revolution, countless thousands of citizens would be swept up in civil and regional wars, as old feuds and rivalries were released with the death of Imperial control. It would be generations before the continent would know peace again—they would all be plunged into another time of darkness—as when the Otherside broke through into the world. While few written records had survived from that period, stories and dark legends had been passed from parent to child. The light had very nearly been extinguished in Arkaym. His family had rekindled that flame. Raed would not let them be the ones to now blow it out.

First, he had to reach Fraine within the fortress. The ruling family of Ensomn, the Shin, were renowned for their paranoia, cunning and ambition. It was said their shadow guards were trained in four hundred and thirty ways of killing in silence, and that their homes were mazes fraught with deadly traps. All of these things had helped keep the Shin monarchs of this principality for hundreds of years.

They were also well-known for their hatred of the Emperor—who lived on the east coast of the continent and taxed them, in their opinion, far too heavily. No one ever liked taxes, though they kept the roads safe, and petty wars from breaking out. Provinces far from the bright heart of the Empire rarely saw Imperial Dirigibles or the Imperial Guard, and so tended to forget they existed.

"Nothing to offer then?" Raed whispered, as he slipped closer to the river. "No great geistlord insight about the Shin?"

The wash of malice made his jaw tighten painfully. *Trapped in your bloodline for generations, I know little of the petty doings of humans. All I know is the taste of their blood.*

So all he had to rely on was his own teaching about the Shin—and that had not included knowledge about the internal layout of the fortress. Luckily there were still some people here who remained loyal to the Rossin family. Not everyone had been delighted with the Conclave of Princes' choice to bring a foreign Prince in to take over as Emperor; some still remembered or held tight to "the good old days" when Raed's grandfather had ruled. That was how he had managed to find someone in town willing to give him basic information about what he might find in the fortress.

It was for these same reasons that his sister had found her way here. In their grandfather's time, the Shin had been allowed far more latitude to rule their own kingdom. She was undoubtedly reminding them of that. Every minute that she was left to negotiate with them was another step closer to civil war. Unless he could prevent it.

The Emperor sitting back on his warm throne in Vermillion would never know he owed his rival such a debt. Perhaps though, Sorcha would hear of it.

Raed inhaled sharply, recalling the last time he had seen the Deacon, hanging limply in Merrick's arms, like a discarded puppet. The Young Pretender wondered every day if the Sensitive had held to his promise to save Sorcha. If only there were gods to honestly pray to for that.

Weak mortal. The Rossin growled. *You think of her at a moment like this?*

For once the creature was right. He had to focus on the here and now, not on the what could never be.

The sky above was clear and warm, and the stars bright and sharp with no clouds to hide their beauty. Before he could lose his nerve, Raed quickly stripped his clothes and boots off, and shoved them into an oilskin bag. Already the bag contained the maps he had secured the previous night, his sword and his pistols. The satchel was the kind sailors used to keep their belongings dry while on deck. He had one too many times found himself naked in the wilderness, and he didn't want to be that vulnerable in the fortress.

"I'm ready," he whispered more to himself than to the Rossin. Nude, he crouched by the water's edge for a moment, running out the waxed cord that secured the bag's mouth. "You remember the deal?" he asked the geistlord as confidently as he could. Raed knew it was useless to try to hide his real emotions from the beast, but it made him feel better.

I fly. You break in. I feed.

"We find my sister first—then you feed."

Unless we are discovered.

It should have been impossible for another consciousness in his head to sound so cunning—but the Rossin did. Raed was becoming aware that his lifelong assessment of the geistlord as merely a beast running on bloodlust was quite incorrect. It was convenient to think of the geistlord as an animal, but they were more tightly connected than ever now, and Raed was catching glimpses of something else; an immense patience, and a fearful delight that all was coming to fruition. Just what that might mean however was still wrapped in shadow. Not for the first time Raed wondered what the beast had gained by allying himself with the bloodline of Raed's ancestor, the first Emperor-Deacon.

"Only if we are discovered," Raed said as he stood tall by the lake edge. "Then you may have at it, and see how the dice roll—but if you break our agreement, back into the depths you go, and I will never call you out again. It is as we agreed."

Something about the pact they had made bound this creature of death and mayhem. Raed was not going to question how it worked—but perhaps a Deacon would know more of it than he did.

Previously, whenever the geistlord had taken control, the Young Pretender was always subsumed. He awoke from the Rossin's rampages with only a scattering of memory, the taste of blood in his mouth and terrible guilt. However, since he had drawn the beast into his own consciousness—they shared an awareness. This was, Raed reasoned, a fair cost for the Rossin's help. Just how much control he had over his passenger in this state, he had never tested. Sooner or later he knew he would have to.

Pain. That was another change. He felt a deeper pain as the Rossin bent and twisted his flesh to make its own shape. Bones snapped and were remade. Every nerve and sinew was severed and spun by the geistlord's will. He wanted to scream to release some of the agony, but even his throat would no longer obey. He had nowhere to hide from the agony.

The Rossin took his flesh and snarled in hunger. The head of its aerial form was that of a great eagle, while the body remained feline and huge. A pair of long feathered wings snapped angrily in the air. The beak was curved and wicked and could carve human flesh as readily as the teeth of its other forms. The Rossin was beautiful and deadly. Magnificent—if you were anyone else but the Young Pretender. He was carried along like an unwilling rider on a runaway mount.

After snatching up the bag in its beak, the beast leapt into the air. Flying was something that many people dreamed of; being carried aloft, leaving the world below, and touching the ultimate freedom. As the Rossin sprang into the air, Raed felt elation, but he tried to repress the emotion. It was wrong to find any enjoyment in anything the geistlord did.

Lying in his arms, Sorcha had spoken of the giddy rush of power a Deacon felt when wielding the Gauntlets, and how she had to fight it; how it was a constant struggle and a deadly temptation. He now understood what she had meant.

Deacons should be destroyed, not loved. They are liars and manipulators. We should kill them all.

The Rossin naturally loathed the Deacons; not only did it hate the first one that had traded with the geistlord, but Sorcha, who had put controls on him with the Bond. The beast did not like restrictions of any kind.

Raed wanted to think about Sorcha some more, but he dare not. The geistlord hated her so, and she was a complication in his already broken life. He didn't expect to see her again. He didn't expect to live very much longer.

The air was cold up here, in the clouds, but the heat of the Rossin was greater. Birds scattered from the great shape, like pebbles thrown across the sky. The natural world was always so much better at sensing the unliving than humans.

It was not far to the stronghold of the Shin, but the Rossin wheeled above it, careful to keep himself low and away from the sliver of the waxing moon. It was a good night for dark deeds. The feathers that lined the wings of the Rossin

were like owls', soft and silent. In all his forms the creature
was a predator. His eyes were sharp too. He could make out
details of the fortress and its defenses; a collection of low,
curved roofs capped the towers that jutted sharply out into
the clouds. All in all a very unwelcoming sight.

As the Rossin turned and banked away he could make
out a handful of human shapes moving atop the curved
roofline. They smelled of steel and gunpowder, but now
they were fodder for the geistlord. Folding his wings, the
Rossin dropped down from the dark skies and aimed for a
guard leaning against his polearm and looking down
toward the city. He never saw his end coming, until it was
upon him. The Rossin knocked him to the ground, wrapping his wings around the guard, and plunging his beak
into the man's unprotected throat. The taste of blood flow-
ered in Raed's mouth; thick, rich and terrifyingly satisfying. To his horror he found he was enjoying it.

The geistlord fed on flesh, blood and bone until he was
sated. Having gorged on the bounty hunter only a few days
ago it did not take long. As the geistlord sucked down the
last of the blood, Raed reasserted control. Its hunger satisfied, the beast gave way without any hesitation and retreated
into the depths of the Young Pretender's soul, much as he
used to before they had made their new pact. Then he was
on the ground, covered in blood and with the foul taste of it
stuck to the back of his throat. Raed lay there for a moment,
steeling himself to get up and do what needed to be done.
He rolled over, opened the bag, pulled out his clothes, and
slid them onto his stained and fouled body.

Every part of the Young Pretender ached, like he'd been
trampled by a horse, but Fraine was close now—closer
than she had been since their meeting in the desert. She
had led him into a trap, sold him out to a geistlord masquerading as a goddess, and killed five of his crew members in cold blood.

Raed could understand why Fraine had turned on
him—her childhood had been marred by the death of her

mother in the jaws of the Rossin. What, if any, affection
she had retained for Raed after that had then been twisted
by Tangyre Greene's lies. That did not mean he would let
her rip the Empire apart. Whatever feelings he had for his
sister, guilt, love and anger, didn't really matter. The entire
Empire was at stake.

The map, obtained at so much risk in the city, was still
not complete—it showed only the upper and outer levels of
the fortress that was constructed like some elaborate puzzle box. At least that was how it looked on his first examination of the map. The mapmaker had even struggled to
draw it, but had settled on three layers, like a peeling away
of an onion.

Raed strapped on his pistols and sword and went to the
first door. Opening it, and stepping inside, he immediately
understood the mapmaker's dilemma. Everything inside
the fortress was designed to confuse the eye and befuddle
the brain. The corridor he walked down was tilted at an
odd angle, and wound its way deeper in the fortress. Along
the way, there were doors that opened straight outside
again. Others were set in the ceiling, or half-buried, and
only passable by a child.

The map saved him from going mad in the first instance,
as Raed quickly lost his bearings. He found a shaft indicated in red, and by virtue of wedging his legs against one
side and his back against another, shimmied down through
it and to the next level. This all seemed a very useful way
to hold off intruders and stymie assassins, but he couldn't
help but wonder how on earth the Shin traversed their own
fortress in any comfort at all. Even if they memorized the
passages and odd doorways, it would not have been com-
fortable. On the first level he had not seen a single guard,
and he understood why—surely they would have been
driven mad by the illogical and crazy layout.

Raed's feet touched down in a new, deeper layer of the
fortress, and for a moment he stood there swaying. This

looked like any number of corridors in any number of palaces he had visited: stone walls, lined with tapestries. However there was a deeper hush on this place than anywhere else he'd ever been. He stood there contemplating which way to go and examining the map. It had marked out a straight path to the right and then deeper.

As he walked the corridors Raed contemplated how much better this would be if Sorcha and Merrick were with him. A couple of Deacons would have been most useful at this point. But that wasn't all. This was the first long stretch of time he'd been alone in his entire life. As a Prince and then as a captain, he'd been surrounded by servants, soldiers, crew and friends. Though he had been the one to make decisions, he'd always had someone else to confer with.

You have me. I will never leave you.

Raed had never before considered if the Rossin had a sense of humor—not that it was one that he appreciated overly. It was merely a distraction that he didn't need since reading the map was becoming harder and harder. The designer had drawn a series of strange red circles on the map, but the map had no key.

Raed was just contemplating what they could mean, when the floor slid out from under him. Reflexes far beyond a normal mortal being kicked in and Raed managed to catch hold of the lip of the trap before he fell, though his shoulders were nearly wrenched from their sockets.

The geistlord was awake now, ready to take over. "Not yet," Raed gasped, as he flexed his fingers against the stone. He didn't want to lose his clothes and gear if at all possible. Though the beast had no respect for such trivial things, as a man, he preferred not to enter dangerous situations naked. With some effort he managed to get the edge under his armpits and from there haul himself upright.

So he had his explanation of the red dots on the map. As he followed the path he took careful note and edged around them. It certainly explained why there were no people on this level either. The Shin were obviously master trap makers, which cut down on how many guards they had to have.

He was just contemplating how many of the Shin themselves must have fallen into their own traps while distracted, when a sound pierced the suffocating silence.

It was laughter. Female laughter. It was so unexpected and delightful that Raed stopped. In his life, there had been precious little female company let alone merriment. If he concentrated, he thought he could recall his mother and sister giggling—but perhaps that was merely wishful thinking. On the *Dominion* the women had occasionally had cause for amusement. Snook had been most cheerful—the most likely to see the fun in any situation.

Snook. Now dead at his own sister's command.

Frowning, recalling why he was here, Raed went to find out what was so funny in the lair of the Shin. He had a feeling he would not like it.

FIVE

Alone in the Abbey

Merrick made his return in the tail of evening to the Mother Abbey. It was only a short distance from the Imperial Palace to the home of the Order of the Eye and the Fist, and it was a walk that he had taken often since returning from Chioma. Though the Emperor himself had shown little interest in returning Merrick's mother and his half brother back to that southern province that they should by rights be ruling, the Grand Duchess had been most considerate of their care. She had seen to it that Japhne was given a wing and the best doctors when the time came for her to give birth. She even visited her so that the older woman would not be so alone. Apparently they had many things in common, and despite Zofiya's reputation, his mother found her a great companion.

As he looked up at the stars he found himself considering Her Imperial Majesty the Grand Duchess Zofiya in quite a different light. Everyone at the Abbey thought he was studious and quiet, but he noticed the fairer sex like any other normal man. Since he had traveled back in time and stolen a few moments with Nynnia, he had been more

at peace with his lost love. The mere fact that she still
existed—even if he could never be with her again—had
allowed him to come to a certain acceptance. Nynnia had
given up her body in order to save the world from the
destruction of the terrible geistlord the Murashev, and she
seemed content with that. It would be churlish of him to
remain angry for her choice.

So his refreshed eyes and soul had perceived immediately that the Grand Duchess was very beautiful. Even to
have thought that a season ago would have been ridiculous,
but in their time together, he had seen beyond the intimi-
dating cover she presented to the world. She had lost her
faith and her goddess had proven to be a horrible fraud. In
a way, Merrick and she shared a loss.

Naturally, these thoughts were idle ones. Deacons could
indeed have sex, love affairs and even get married—
however Imperial sisters had to be far more cautious. He
could tell by the expression in her eyes that she liked the
look of him—he'd learned that much in the past year—but
in her position, she would have her pick of lovers from
among the Court.

Still it was pleasant to wonder about some things, such
as what would her lips taste like? What secrets of her inner
heart would she reveal after they kissed? How would her
skin feel against his?

Merrick shook himself free of these idle thoughts as he
reached the gates to the Mother Abbey. Between intrigue
and duty he allowed his imagination free rein—but once
back inside the walls of the Order he had to return to reality. The lay Brother opened the postern gate and let him in
without challenge. Most Deacons were ensconced in the
dormitory, but others were on patrol, or doing the business
of the Order.

As his step passed over the lintel, Merrick stopped,
for a second frozen comically there, head tilted to one
side. Everything was quiet and in its correct place. The

Presbyters tucked in their presbyterial chambers. Arch Abbot Rictun was awake working on some paperwork, the light flickering in his antechamber behind the stained glass. The lay Brothers were either asleep in their quarters or moving quietly about their duties. Deacons, Sensitive and Active were the same, but lying in their cells in the dormitory. The powerful and beautiful Breed horses shifted in their stalls, but signaled no distress. Injured and addled citizens and Deacons were sleeping or cared for in their rooms. All but one.

Merrick set off at a run in that direction—his senses now focused on the infirmary with the intensity of a hawk searching for a field mouse. Their Bond had gone so quiet that he had almost forgotten it was there, and now he was kicking himself for that carelessness. She was dead—by the Bones she was dead and he had not even noticed!

Bursting into her room, Merrick ran to the bed expecting to see Sorcha's still corpse lying there—but there was nothing. Nothing at all. Her bed had been stripped and a lay Brother was in the corner bundling the sheets away.

"What happened?" Merrick grabbed the poor man by his shoulders and gave him a sound shake. "Where have they taken the body?"

"There is no body." In the confusion the young Sensitive had not noticed Sorcha's retired partner Garil in the chair in the corner of the room near the door.

He spun about. "What do you mean? They can't have buried her so quickly!"

"She's not dead . . . at least not yet." Garil raised a hand and gestured the bewildered Brother away. He shut the door behind him in a manner that suggested he was very grateful to get out of the line of fire.

Merrick sized up the older man. Something in his tone set the young man's teeth on edge. He did not know a great deal about Garil's personality, and only a little more of his life. Sorcha had told him once, since it was no secret, that he had been badly beaten by some thugs, years ago, and taken off active duty. She had retained a genuine affection for him, even after their Bond had been severed, and trusted him implicitly.

Indeed, at one time both Merrick and Sorcha's lives had been in his hands. When they had ventured to the Otherside, where geists came from, they had shucked off their bodies and ventured there in spirit. It had been Garil who had brought them back. Yet now, every hair on Merrick's body was standing on end and his skin ran with an uncomfortable prickle. Cautiously he stepped away from the bed. "Deacon Reeceson, I need you to explain yourself. And now."

It was awfully impolite to address an elder of the Order in such a way, but technically Merrick outranked him since he was still a practicing member and Garil was not.

The old man sighed, and levered himself out of the chair. That was when Merrick went far beyond the boundaries of propriety and possibly into the realms of illegality. He opened the First Rune of Sight, Sielu, and attempted to see through Garil's eyes. It was a bold move that should have outraged the old man.

Instead he laughed—not in a mocking way, but gently as if he had caught a child out at a silly prank. "Don't bother trying that on me, Deacon Chambers. I may be elderly, but I am not without my faculties."

"But apparently quite without your loyalty," Merrick snapped back, at a loss with what he should do. "Sorcha trusted you, loved you as a father—and you let her die."

Garil's eyes dropped away. "I did what was best."

Suddenly Merrick was reminded of the one other thing he knew of Deacon Reeceson—the other thing, apart from Sorcha that they had in common. A wild talent. A secret gift that was quite outside the Order, the runes and the rules. Now both Sensitives shared a hard look. Deacon Reeceson's talent was for prescience. The ability to see into the long future—something even the rune Masa did not allow a member of the Order.

"What have you done with her?" Merrick asked in a whisper filled with dread.

"She is gone to a distant Priory, one that can deal with her particular illness. One that might be able to heal her."

His words were clearly spoken, but through his Center Merrick could feel a murkiness to their meaning. "She is still my partner," he countered. "I should have been informed—gone with her."

When Garil shook his head, the young Sensitive's heart sank. "That can be quickly fixed in Presbyterial Council—you are far too great a talent to be lost to the Order. They will find you—"

"Enough!" Merrick could take no more of it. His eyes burned as if he might shed angry tears, and he did not want to do that in front of Garil. "You are a retired Deacon—no longer fighting geists, no longer a real Brother. I will speak to the Arch Abbot himself on this matter." Then before the old man could stop him, Merrick darted out of the room, and blundered out of the infirmary. He caught glimpses of the concerned faces of lay Brothers, and a few scattered visitors, but none of these things registered.

His brain was too full of concern for Sorcha and outrage that anyone would ask him to sever the Bond with her. It was unlike any other he had ever read of, and when it had been in the fullness of its power, before Sorcha had been stricken, they had worked as a seamless pair. It had been beautiful.

They would not take the chance of its restoration from him. They would not. He charged through the silent Devotional building. Bereft as it was of Deacons, he could not help glancing up at the carved images of the Native Deacons that occupied its soaring ceiling space. They had been hacked about their stone faces, destroyed in an act of mindless vandalism generations ago. It gave them an eerie appearance, and it took very little imagination to think that they were glowering at him, or perhaps laughing. Many years had passed since the last of that old Order had died.

The Order of the Eye and the Fist had come only recently to take on the geists in Arkaym, but before them there had been others. Others who had been thought extinct.

That was until Merrick had had that assumption crushed. Beneath the Chiomese palace, he had run into living, breathing examples of that old and corrupt Order. They had made their intentions perfectly clear—to use geists, rather than to fight them. To take the power they thought they deserved. Even the remembrance of it made his stomach clench like he'd been punched there.

The young Deacon paused for a second under the defaced and hacked final statue. The angry populace had left it one piercing eye under a stern brow. It reminded him of the nameless leader of the Order of the Circle of Stars—which had to be impossible. And yet—Merrick swallowed—many impossible things had been proven since he had left the novitiate, and been Bonded with Sorcha.

As he stood beneath that frightening gaze, he recalled how his report on the Chiomese affair had still not been dealt with by the Presbyterial Council. They had taken it, had assured him it would be given the greatest weight, and then . . . nothing.

Clenching his teeth, he spared one final glare for the one-eyed stone harbinger, and then ran on to the back of the Devotional to where the Presbyters and the Arch Abbot slept. No guard stood at the door, since this was the heart of the Mother Abbey, and so he passed on, unchallenged.

The Arch Abbot was unlikely to be asleep, but Merrick knew that his receiving hours were well over. Still he banged on the door. The tiny sparrow of a woman named Drale who served as his secretary answered Merrick's rabid banging on the door. She was a lay Sister of the Order—one who had gone through the trials and yet proven not powerful enough to be trained with the runes. Still, she was due some respect. Her eyes were bleary, as she undid the door and peered out.

"Deacon Chambers?" she whispered, glancing over her shoulder. She was well aware, like most of the Mother Abbey, that Arch Abbot Rictun was no friend of Sorcha's, and that, by association Merrick was also tarred the same. Still, he and Drale had spent a lot of time in the Abbey library together, and had become, if not friends, at least friendly.

"The Arch Abbot has retired," she said, narrowing the gap in the door. "His chambers will be open just after lunch tomorrow. He has—"

"I must speak to him *now*," Merrick said, pushing forward, his knee pressing against the smooth, ancient wood of the door. "I cannot wait until morning!"

"Deacon!" Drale hissed, not quite pushing back, but looking horrified as the young, quiet Deacon she knew turned into something far more like his partner. "You will make no friends on this course. Please, go back to the infirmary!"

"You think I care," Merrick shot back, his voice rising. "Deacon Sorcha Faris is missing—and as far as I am aware she is still one of our Order. We do still take care of our own don't we?"

"Do you doubt the morality of the Mother Abbey?" Rictun finally pushed open the door and stood facing his younger colleague. The Arch Abbot was a young man to have reached such lofty heights, about the same age as Sorcha. He had golden hair, and the kind of handsomeness that would have brought women flocking to him had he had another occupation. He still could have married, because there was no injunction against it by the Order, but he had the kind of personality that tended to repel most on long acquaintance. Still he was the strongest Presbyter in both Active and Sensitive powers, and amid the chaos of the previous Arch Abbot being killed and revealed as a traitor, he had been the best choice at the time.

Now, Merrick was beginning to think it had been a very

wrong decision, because there was a set to Rictun's
mouth that suggested he was not surprised to see him at his
door.

"Do not worry, Drale." Rictun stepped back and gestured to his audience chamber. "I am always open to all
members of the Order, day and night."

The frightened secretary scampered to her own tiny bed
in the corner of the entrance chamber, all too happy to get
out of the way. Merrick stormed after Rictun, not feeling
an ounce of his rage dissipate. Sorcha was still gone.

Rictun slipped into his chair behind his desk, but Merrick did not sit. Instead, he began to pace, trying to compose his thoughts, while a hundred angry words clamored
to get out of his mouth. The small audience chamber was
lit by flickering candlelight, and the way it danced over the
ancient stained glass disturbed him. This place must have
been the home of the Arch Abbot of the Order of Stars.
Perhaps a part of those that had gone before still lingered
here.

This thought outraged Merrick further. He slammed
his hands down onto the desk and glared at his superior.
"Deacon Sorcha Faris has been taken from the infirmary
without my knowledge, and Deacon Reeceson says she
is bound for some distant Priory—but I know this cannot
be. The Bond is sacred. She should not have been sent
without me."

The Arch Abbot shrugged. "If I remember Deacon
Faris' Bond is still under review. You and Deacon Petav
are still disputing your right to be called her partner. Such
decisions take time, and Deacon Faris needs help now."

"But the Mother Abbey's infirmary is the best facility
the Order has!" Merrick growled through gritted teeth,
leaving the question of their Bond aside for the moment. He
knew Rictun had thrown it down to distract him. "Where
can she possibly go to get better help for what ails her?"

It was then that the man on the other side of the desk

smiled. "I do not believe, Deacon Chambers, that you are
versed in the healing arts. Deacon Reeceson, since his
retirement from his trials as a Sensitive has made a study of
them in the infirmary. He suggested Prior Ellan in Aber-
felck might have the experience and skill to treat her." The
Arch Abbot cleared his throat. "What's more, I think I
should remind you of your place in the Order."

Merrick swallowed. Ever since his father had been
killed by a geist, he had only ever wanted to be a part of the
Order of the Eye and the Fist. He had found sense and a
peace that he had not expected to. He had fought geists,
freed people, and saved the city of Vermillion itself. His
mind raced, thinking over what his choices within the
strictures of the Order were now. He had studied harder
than any other novitiate in the class, but now he could find
no other avenue. Even if he protested to the Presbyter of
the Sensitives, the best that Yvril Mournling could do was
take it to the rest of the Council. Everyone knew that Rictun had the sway of the vote there.

Once the ideas of what he could do within the Order
were all run out, Merrick began instead to think through
what his other options were; all of this while under the
stern gaze of the Arch Abbot. That moment of consideration seemed to stretch forever, but really it didn't take long
for Merrick to make up his mind. Sorcha was his partner,
and despite his love of the Order, he had seen its darker
side. Corruption was not something alien to it, and Arch
Abbot Rictun was no example of the best of their Order.
Sorcha was. Maybe his partner was not perfect, but she had
always been his back. No other Bond Merrick had ever
heard of, or read of, had ever been as strong as theirs.

Quickly, he stifled these thoughts and decisions down.
While it was entirely inappropriate for one Deacon to peer
into the mind of another, he didn't trust Rictun to not do
what was inappropriate. While he did so, Merrick bowed—
not too deep, lest the Arch Abbot suspect it was coming too

easily—and sighed his regret. "Yes, Reverend Deacon. I am sorry, I guess I have just been confused by the last few months—and now this."

The Arch Abbot stared at him with his jaw clenched—and there it was—the subtle probing of Merrick's thoughts. Really an Arch Abbot, the only Deacon to be able to hold both talismans should have been better at this covert intrusion. That he was not, steeled Merrick's determination that he was on the right path.

Merrick wondered what the punishment for daring to breach the mental defenses of an Arch Abbot would be. As he threw up a subterfuge of contrition tinged with an edge of outrage, he traced the lines of the rune Sielu and pressed it toward Rictun.

The Arch Abbot's mind was a pit of unexpected fear. For a second Merrick teetered and almost fell into it. Everything was dangerous in the world. Everywhere in the Empire of Arkaym was danger and menace. Rictun was quite the consummate actor, the younger Deacon found. So much terror about what could be waiting around the corner was stuffed deep down inside him it really was amazing he didn't just panic there and then.

His surface thoughts were easy to read: Rictun was relieved to be free of Sorcha and the trouble she always seemed to carry about with her. From her earliest days within the Order she had been a problem. A powder keg rocking on the edge of a great fall. The Deacons in charge at the time had foolishly accepted her, and for a while Rictun had been forced to deal with her. Now she was, with every moment, moving away from Vermillion and the Mother Abbey. Never had a thing been better done.

It was a tantalizing look into Sorcha's past—a glimpse of something Merrick had in idle moments contemplated. Every Deacon had a past. Most were brought to the Order as children, and some of those children had been traumatized by geists before even getting there. Those that could best wield the runes were also the best focus for the unliving to attach themselves to, so the various Abbeys and Priories were used to dealing with problem children. Yet in Rictun's mind Sorcha stood out.

Merrick was tempted to probe deeper, but the thought that she was moving away with every minute spurred him on. As quickly and efficiently as possible he let Sielu die away. After this, he would look differently at the Arch Abbot—but since he planned never to come back to the Mother Abbey that really did not matter.

"There is one other matter," Merrick said, folding his hands into his cloak, just in case they shook a little. "Grand Duchess Zofiya has requested my presence tomorrow night at the Imperial Palace."

"The Council are going to weigh the matter of your new Active partner." Rictun smiled. It was as condescending and vile a smile as Merrick had ever seen. "I want you Bonded with someone more appropriate before the new moon. The Order has much for a Sensitive of your capacity to do—however it is the Emperor's sister. I suppose the matter can be deferred until the day after."

"Thank you, Reverend Father." The title stuck in Merrick's throat, but he comforted himself by thinking he would not have to choke it out much longer.

"You may go." Rictun waved his hand. He paused and eyed the younger Deacon. "I can only apologize for you being paired with Deacon Faris. A more inappropriate pairing I cannot imagine, but as you know, that was my predecessor's decision."

Merrick nodded slowly, bowed, and made his exit. As he strode back to the dormitory he knew that the one thing he needed, but was unlikely to get this night, was sleep. After tomorrow, once he left Vermillion he would be a renegade, hunted down by every Deacon and Imperial Guard. If they considered him a real threat they would most likely form up a Conclave of Deacons and set them after him.

With those odds stacked against him, he would need a very good ally—a very powerful one. He would wait one night, because fortunately he knew where he could find one of those. Tomorrow night, he best dress the part.

SIX

Unholy and Unhappy Choices

Aachon did not like flying one little bit. He had not enjoyed it on his first occasion when traveling from Ulrich to Vermillion. That had been a mission of deadly importance—just like this one. Only grave matters would get the huge first mate of the *Dominion* on board a flying deathtrap.

Not that he said as much when he handed over his documents to Quent Lepzig, the captain of the *Autumn Eagle*. He was a small, neat man, with a ruddy mustache and the gleam of command in his eye—the same look Raed possessed. That at least made Aachon feel marginally better and he took it perhaps as a sign of good luck.

Captain Lepzig glanced up at Aachon and frowned slightly. "It says here I am to go wherever you need to. This is a little strange; to have no destination is dangerous for an airship. If we need to refuel and there is no station . . ."

"Would you care to pop back to the Mother Abbey and ask the Presbyter himself?" Aachon rumbled sternly. "I am sure he would not mind being woken up at this hour."

The captain swallowed and glanced up and down the length of his deck, perhaps checking that none of his crew were near enough to hear. No man in command liked to be dressed down, especially on his own vessel, but Aachon could not afford to let this captain think he had the upper hand. "I understand the needs of the Order come above anything but the Emperor himself." He straightened as he spoke, but it was a pointless exercise against Aachon's height.

As they stood awkwardly to one side of the gangplank of the *Autumn Eagle*, the half dozen crew of the *Dominion* he had brought with him appeared from the darkness. Most were only lightly encumbered, their covert methods of traveling to reach Vermillion had seen to that. However, Serigala and Arriann were not so lucky; they carried Sorcha between them wrapped in a blanket. They were both strong lads from the isles and hefted her as easily as if she were a bundle of laundry.

Captain Lepzig flicked aside the covering and stared at the comatose Deacon for a moment.

"This looks like Deacon Faris," he said with a raised eyebrow. "I had heard she was struck down, but what use is she to you now?"

Aachon folded his arms in front of his barrel chest. "What use she is to us is quite frankly no business of yours, Captain. Now where shall we put her?"

Lepzig's mustache fairly bristled. "The aft cabin is available. May I be permitted to ask what direction we should head, since we have no destination?"

"Cast off and set course for west for the moment, but I will give you course corrections as they need to be made." Aachon stared down at Lepzig and realized that they could be stuck together for quite some time. Taking that into consideration he decided to soften his approach. "I apologize that I cannot tell you our eventual heading." He jerked his head in the direction the lads were carrying Sorcha. "She will tell us that as we go."

Lepzig's brow furrowed at that, but he was part of the Imperial Fleet and used to obeying orders. Aachon knew how lucky they were to have the right papers as this man did look the sort for protocol.

"The *Autumn Eagle* is at your command," he muttered, and then strode away to hurry his crew to their tasks.

Aachon set off after Sorcha and her bearers. Serigala grunted and called out to Arriann, "Hold on a moment!"

The two lowered the Deacon to the deck. Serigala bent over and rubbed at his arm with his face contorted in pain.

Aachon caught up with them. "What's the matter, lad?"

"It's nothing," the young man grunted, but held out his arm revealing a nasty and quite deep bite. "Some damn Vermillion dog took a disliking to me." He twisted the wound back and forth in the air, but was careful not to touch it. "Hurts like the bloody blazes."

That was all they needed right now. The crew were few in number as it was, and all were committed to finding their captain; Aachon knew he would require every one of them.

Taking Serigala's arm in a not quite gentle grasp, he held the weirstone over the wound, and peered at it. "A dog you say?"

"Yes, a huge brute of a thing, rushed right at me while we waited for you outside the Mother Abbey." The crew member winced as the first mate poked at the edges of the bite. "The others pulled it off me, but it got away."

"Frothing at the mouth at all?"

"Thank the little gods, no."

Under weirstone light, Aachon could detect no inflammation that looked out of the ordinary. It would probably take a while to heal, and be painful, but with the right treatment Serigala would survive. "Get some of Aleck's healing salve and keep it clean," Aachon growled.

Serigala nodded and took up his burden with Arriann once more. Two men was more than enough to carry the Deacon. She was a deadweight but not a great deal of one. Her long time in bed, unable to move had whittled her

curves down to sharp lines. Aachon had thought her beautiful once—now she was a shadow of that glory. Once they
got her into the cabin, he dismissed the crew members and
took care of her himself. As Aachon tucked her into the
bed, he couldn't help feeling a little sorry for the Deacon.
To be sure she had caused a great deal of trouble for his
Prince, and had dragged Raed Rossin into more scrapes
than were necessary—but she had also risked much to save
him.

Garil had given him the details of her flight to save the
Young Pretender in the soaking heat of Chioma. Her partner Merrick had relayed them to the lay Deacon, and it was
quite a tale. The desert principality was not a place Aachon
would have cared to go—but like Sorcha he would have for
duty.

He looked down into her face, and all belief that the
Deacon was merely a sack of meat was lost. Those open
blue eyes had lost none of their power, and even though her
face did not move, her eyes flicked back and forth—focusing
on him with the kind of baleful intent he had only ever seen
on the face of a geist-possessed person. It must be terrifying and frustrating to be trapped in your own body, and
then whisked away in the dead of night.

Aachon did not consider himself a cruel man. With a
sigh, he squeezed himself into one of the chairs by the bed.
The tight confines of an Imperial Airship had not been made
for a man of his size. The engines of the *Autumn Eagle*
began to thrum, and outside he could hear the shouts of her
crew making ready to cast off.

Dipping into his coat pocket he withdrew a swirling orb.
The weirstones were illegal, dangerous the Order said. No
one should deal with them but their Deacons.

Aachon had never made secret his dislike of the Order
of the Eye and the Fist. While most sane citizens were cautious of them and the power they wielded, they were mostly
just grateful to them for ridding Arkaym of the geists.

The first mate of the *Dominion* had another opinion entirely. He had wanted to be one.

"I will tell you a little tale, Deacon Faris," he began resting his arms on his knees, and staring into the orb swirling in his hands. "And you will have to do me the service of keeping quiet."

It was a foolish joke to break the tension, but he could see by Sorcha's eyes it was not one well taken. Aachon cleared his throat. "When I was a lad, my father sent me across the ocean to Delmaire to train with your Order."

It felt so long ago that it was like telling the story of someone else entirely. "I was lucky to have a tutor by the name of Garil Reeceson." Aachon tilted his head back, and closed his eyes, smelling some of the musk of cigar smoke that had even then lingered around the Deacon. "Back then he was rather handsome, and I was smitten with him immediately, but it wasn't until I was just about to take the final tests that we became lovers."

The flames died in Sorcha's eyes as realization spread there instead. Aachon looked down at the weirstone again, feeling old regrets beginning to bubble up. "Perhaps we would have become Bonded partners." He let out a short laugh. "Then you and Garil would have just been colleagues. What might have been is now lost however. Instead, my research on weirstones offended some people, and then when I tried to defend myself . . . well let's just say I had to quickly return to Arkaym."

He glanced across at the still Sorcha before continuing. "When you brought us here to Vermillion chasing the Murashev, we met again," the first mate of the *Dominion* went on, his fingers tracing patterns on the surface of the weirstone. The swirls of water in the deep blue orb mimicked his motions. "He told me of his wild talent—told me of a dark shadow that lay ahead for you and my prince.

"Then when I lost Raed in the heart of Chioma, where he went looking for his sister, I came here to get Garil's help locating him. But my prince's path had fallen into such chaos that even he couldn't discern it."

Aachon leaned across and touched her hand. "We both knew that because of your Bond with my prince you could be the only one to track him—Garil has had a vision of you well again and with my prince. I know not, however, how this will come to pass."

He sighed. "You must know that the ability the Prince of Chioma placed over you should have been temporary and faded at the next sunrise. No mortal creature can hold on to a truly geist power as you have done. Not without some kind of foci." With one hand on Sorcha and the other cupping the weirstone, Aachon looked down. He did as Garil had tried, to see into the flame-haired Deacon's past. His was a much more blunt instrument than the Order's Rune of Sight Aiemm—but he should have been able to see more than he did—only her time within the confines of the Abbey. The moment of her first hesitant kiss with another initiate under the bowers of a flowering jasmine. The time she passed the test and carved her first rune into her Gauntlets—the pride swelling in her chest. He caught glimpses of her running as a child through the infirmary garden, smelled the lavender in her nostrils, and heard the squeal of excitement in her mouth.

Yet, if he tried to push back further there was nothing but a void. Aachon closed his fist about the weirstone. When he looked up, a tear had trickled free of Sorcha's eye, so he carefully wiped it away with the edge of his sleeve. "How anyone let you into the Order with such a nothing for a history even Garil doesn't know. Any Sensitive could look back and see this hole in your past if they cared to."

The *Autumn Eagle* began to lift beneath them, and the thrum of the weirstone engines could be felt running through the ship. So many wonderful uses for them—and yet every one exposed the population to danger. Aachon looked deep into his own stone. Without access to the runes that the Deacons used, it was his only way back to power, but he'd accepted that danger long ago.

With a sigh, he put his own weirstone away, and exchanged it for the one Garil had given him. He moved it closer to Sorcha. Her eyes blinked rapidly, as if she were trying to tell him something. It was a nightmare he would have spared anyone the living of, but there was nothing he could do about it.

Best to think of her as a compass—a compass that he needed to keep a cautious eye on. "My prince," he muttered, and narrowed his eyes, looking at Sorcha through the weirstone. Through her, and to his friend and charge.

The Bond was so powerful that it was confusing, deep and wide, so as to almost swallow up the rest of her. Aachon felt the strength of it, like a magnet stone drawing him. In that moment, a stab of jealousy hit. Something like this could have been his if the past had run differently.

He had to get past that. Focusing his etheric vision on the Bond, he traced where it ran back to Merrick; disappearing behind them in Vermillion.

Sorcha! Sorcha, where are you? The lad's voice was so strong, that for an instant Aachon was sure that somehow the young Deacon had found a way to smuggle himself aboard the *Autumn Eagle*.

The first mate took a deep breath and tried again. While Merrick was a powerful Sensitive—stronger than the last time he'd seen him—he was not the target. Besides, a powerful Deacon like that would find another Bond soon enough.

His captain was in far more deadly danger. Pouring all of his concentration into the weirstone, strengthening it with a lifetime of care and friendship, Aachon saw beyond the looming part of the Bond between the two Deacons.

Far away and to the north his Prince was in danger. Alone, angry, guilty and with the Rossin riding very close to him. Aachon caught a glimpse of the great leonine head turning to him. A snarl of rage and victory echoed in his ears and the connection was abruptly severed.

The first mate sank back on his heels and stared blankly at Sorcha. She was staring right back at him. Both of them had seen where Raed Syndar Rossin was, and how he was surviving.

The *Autumn Eagle* could not go fast enough for Aachon, and had he the power and the right paperwork he would have insisted Captain Lepzig burn all the weirstones he had to reach his own captain. However, at least now he had a direction. "North," he whispered, "and then west to the land of Ensomn."

He levered himself up, and glanced down at Sorcha. "I give you my promise I'll find him and bring him back."

She couldn't utter a word in reply, but instead she closed her eyes: a mute acceptance of his terms. It was, after all, the only thing she had to offer.

SEVEN

Dancing with Royals

There were no two ways about it; Merrick knew that he was going to stick out like a donkey in a horse sale at this ball—no matter what. The Order's plain clothes and cloak harkened back to the style of at least a hundred years ago, and so it was not as if he were going to make some incredible statement that would set the Court aflame with his fashion sense.

And yet . . .

Merrick swallowed. He had made up his mind, but the prospect was still daunting. He was about to turn his back on the world of the Order—the place he had journeyed across countless miles and a wide ocean to find. It would give anyone pause, but still he knew in that uncomfortable place where his conscience resided that it was the right thing to do.

"It will have to be this then." He seized up his best-kept cloak, shirt and trousers.

Charming the Grand Duchess was uncertain territory that no Order teacher had ever instructed him on. A young man his age should have many conquests under his belt, a

few notches on his bedpost—but while the Order did not
demand celibacy of its members, it did not exactly provide
normal social relations either. Deacon Merrick Chambers
had only ever had one lover, and through a strange set of
circumstances she had been taken from him. She now lived
on the Otherside, surrounded by geists and quite without a
body.

This thought propelled him from his room out into the
hall. The tall mirror that stood at its end was etched with
the mantra of the Sensitives; SEE DEEP, FEAR NOTHING.

He stared at himself in the mirror. He knew the Duchess liked him—he was not that much of a fool as to not be
able to spot her eye lingering on him. He wouldn't be much
of a Sensitive had he failed to observe that.

He knew he was not an ugly man, but he also realized of
late he'd been more likely to frown than to smile. His curly
brown hair was unruly, but at least the diet at the Mother
Abbey and their vigorous training regime had kept him
trim.

Staring into his own brown eyes, he tried one final time
to think of another way to get to Sorcha. Another way that
did not involve Zofiya. It was not the path of an honest
man, and he liked the Grand Duchess too much to feel
good about this. Yet he had been unable to find one all day,
and no other struck him now. Before he could change his
mind, Merrick turned and raced down the steps.

His walk to the palace was brisk, but with each step he
took he thought about how much farther Sorcha was getting away from him. He barely took in the finery of the
Imperial Island anymore—the bustle of important people
to and fro simply did not register—yet as he approached
the palace, Merrick did glance up.

The palace and the Mother Abbey were the oldest buildings in Vermillion, and bore the scars of many years and
many owners. However there was a grace to the low, ram-
bling structure that covered the highest points of the island.
Carved representations of geists and geistlords served as

water conduits on the parapets. However no real geists could cross the water to this spot, and the Deacons made sure every soul that died here was sent to the Otherside before it could make trouble.

The only danger on the Imperial Island was the living.

Merrick was expected and indeed a little late. The guards at the gate nodded and waved him through—just as they had all the other times. If they wondered at his invitation to a party rather than coming during the day, they did not show it. Gossip however, he was sure would be hard on his heels. He tried not to show his nerves by scampering up the main path, and instead slowed his steps.

Impatient as the Deacon was, he could not afford to let anyone know it. Also, he must perform the task Zofiya had set him. Thinking all this, steeling himself to be as he was not used to being, Merrick let the rest of the partygoers filter past him. Immediately he knew he was proved right—he was a crow among hummingbirds.

Certainly not every Prince in the vast Empire was here tonight, but ambassadors and their entourages were—and in greater number than the pigeons perching on the crenellations. Every one who had a beautiful son or daughter appeared to have decked them out with pearls and gems, and the latest fashions. Merrick couldn't help blinking and staring about as the youthful best of the aristocracy sailed about him. Men wore stiff collars and sharply tailored suits, while ladies in tight-fitting bodices trailed next to them, their skirts considerably shorter than would have been dared on the streets.

Merrick was still young enough to remember the fashions when the Emperor had first come to Arkaym. It appeared that Emperor Kaleva had brought a new level of restraint to the trends of the day. The Emperor did not like to see money spent idly, and so the yards of fabric a woman once wore had been consigned to the history books.

He was just musing on that as he walked up the stairs toward the ballroom, when he heard his name called.

"Deacon Chambers!"

He turned and there stood Grand Duchess Zofiya, sister to the Emperor and second in line to the throne. For a second, all thoughts of Sorcha and his cunning plan evaporated. She stood in her finery, one gloved hand holding an ivory fan, the other extended toward him in greeting. Her evening gown was the color of fresh green leaves, standing out against the fine polished bronze of her skin. It was cut low and square across her bosom, embroidered and beaded so that it appeared pale pink peonies trailed down across her right breast over her hips, and fell across the small train at her feet. It did indeed have little fabric, but it in no way could be considered austere. Meanwhile her thick, dark hair was piled up in elaborate braids that only served to accentuate her elegant neck and shoulders.

Merrick had never seen the Grand Duchess like this. She was known for her martial nature, for being a crack shot, and for pruning out the members of the aristocracy who disagreed with her brother. None ever really dared to comment on her beauty.

In that moment Merrick was struck by even greater doubts. Maybe he had misread the situation. Maybe Zofiya was in no way interested in him—perhaps she only thought of him as a friend and confidant. She was a highborn lady, sister to an emperor, and daughter to a mighty king. Though he had some aristocratic blood in him, it was very minor compared to hers. What's more, she was a dazzling dark star who could have any man in the Empire. What would she possibly want with him?

All these things ran through his head as he stood gaping up at her. Never had the Order's archaic dress felt so dowdy. In his confusion he sketched a bow—a far too deep one. The Deacons were not exempt to showing deference to the royal family, but the form was the most fleeting of any rank. She smiled at him, and the look of it quite washed away the memories of her stern past.

On the airship back from Orinthal, they had both had

their perceptions and attitudes turned all upside down—
some for the better.

Then the Emperor Kaleva himself appeared at his sister's side. With him was his new bride, the once Princess of
Chioma, Ezefia. They were scarce a month married, and
already everyone was looking to her belly for a child to
secure the succession. She was a beautiful enough woman,
darker of skin than the Emperor, with eyes of deep blue—
but there was also a deep scar in her mind. It fairly blazed
in the ether, so that even those not of the Order could see it.
He had seen such things before; the result of a traumatic
event. The new Empress had certainly suffered not just
one—but many—of those. Her father had been killed and
his principality had been lost along with him.

Fortunately, or unfortunately depending on the point of
view, Merrick had larger things to worry about. As long as
his new brother, Lyon and their mother were safe he really
didn't mind that they could have had more. In his experience such jockeying for position only ended badly for the
families.

"Deacon Chambers, indeed!" The Emperor's smile did
not reveal any ill will. "A pleasure to see you once more in
our halls." He shot a sideways glance at his sister. "We have
become quite used to your presence."

Zofiya did not move, but Ezefia flicked open her fan and
began to wave it back and forth. Her eyes were fixed on
Merrick with something that might have been a baleful
look. "His presence did my father little good."

The Emperor glanced at her and Merrick sketched a
brief rune of Kebenar in his mind. It was another advantage of being a Sensitive Deacon—most of their runes did
not require their talisman to be activated or even touched.
Actives were considerably more flashy and less subtle.
Kebenar unrolled before him, laying out the strains and
stresses, the structure and the curvature of the situation.
The russet air between the Emperor and the Empress spoke
of a not entirely content marriage. Kaleva still had both of

his favorites within the Court, and the lines that stretched between them were a fiery red of passion. His bond to his sister looked strained also, though still the soft, rose pink of affection. Hers in return was thicker, but the pink was slightly stained with green. A change was coming over her.

Merrick closed his eyes, dropped them away from Ezefia, which neatly concealed him pulling back his Center and letting the rune fade in his mind. "Forgive me, Your Imperial Majesty, but my partner and I tried our best to save the Prince of Chioma. He made a valiant sacrifice for his people—but it was a path he chose willingly."

Zofiya turned on Ezefia. "Sister, you should honor his choice, and hold his memory dear. He did what all sovereigns should be willing to do." The words were said pleasantly enough, but the look on her face was as sharp as a blade. The Grand Duchess was never unarmed, even when she carried no weapon.

"Ah, Little Wolf," the Emperor interrupted, "you have such a sharp bite—even on the defenseless."

His sister glanced at him, a flicker of a frown on her brow. She did not reply, but instead, turned to Merrick and held out her hand. "I have been told that the Order does not prohibit dancing. Do you know how, Deacon Chambers?" Then before he could answer, she whisked him away from her brother, up the stairs to the ballroom.

The largest and most ostentatious room in the palace, it looked even more so tonight. Exotic flowers were crammed in every vase, and filled the room with a cacophony of scents. Gaslights, so unlike the candles used at the Mother Abbey, reflected off every polished window and gleaming brass surface, while an orchestra of beautifully dressed musicians played on a balcony above the dancers.

Merrick found himself out on the floor with the best and brightest of the Empire, moving as agilely as he could to the Drevense quadrille. It was lucky indeed that the Order had taught the basics in Court etiquette for those living and working at the Mother Abbey. This had included two days on the favorite dances of the Court. He'd thought it quite the most useless class in the novitiate—but now he was extremely grateful for this passing acquaintance with dance. Even so, he was in deadly peril of squashing the Grand Duchess' toes at every move. The strange thing was she was allowing him to lead—a totally unexpected turn of events.

"I never used to wear anything but my uniform," Zofiya whispered, and smiled somewhat sadly, "but many things have changed since Chioma—my fashion and my brother for example."

Her voice was so melancholy that Merrick couldn't help pulling her a little closer. "He still loves and cares for you, Zofiya." Her name just slipped out over his tongue.

It was the kind of error that she'd challenged men to duels for in the past. When she pulled back and stared at him, Merrick felt his throat grow a little dry.

Her smile was dazzling, but her eyes still darted around the room.

"Do you see him over there?" she whispered in his ear, as she danced a circle behind the Deacon. Aside from the words, the feel of her breath on his neck was quite distracting.

He had in truth almost forgotten her mission, in the turmoil of thinking of his own. As he turned to face Zofiya he managed to catch a glimpse of the person who had her so worried—and instantly his vague interest sharpened to something else. It was a face that he could not forget.

In the tunnels beneath Orinthal, Merrick had faced a group of people who wore the insignia of the Order of the Circle of Stars—the native Order of Arkaym. They had tried to take his mother from him, and he had only managed to recover her by using his own shameful and hidden wild talent.

The face of the other Deacon was burned into Merrick's mind. He was not wearing the cloak of his Order, but the finery of a minor lord as he chatted amiably to an older lady over by where they were serving wine on a damask-covered table. Merrick did not know his name, but he knew one thing—that he was here in the center of the Empire boded ill.

He glanced down at the Grand Duchess and feverishly considered his options. Should he tell her? Should he shout and point the finger at this man right now? What would Zofiya's reaction be if he did anything like that? Merrick realized it would be his word against that of a member of Court.

So instead he spoke as calmly as he could manage, "I shall have to speak to him to find out." Then, with his heart pounding in his chest, he worked his way toward the so-called del Rue. His coming did not go unnoticed. The gray eyes lifted from the woman and fixed on the young Deacon.

The older man stepped forward to greet him and raised his glass. "Why Deacon Merrick Chambers. I did not expect to see you here—but I can say it is not unpleasant to run into you like this."

It was just as it had been when they had "run into" each other in the tunnel. Merrick could feel his rage begin to boil again. He sorely felt Sorcha's absence at his back. However, thinking of his partner helped him keep a hold on his anger. Yet only just.

"What are you doing here?" Merrick managed to keep his tone soft, but not necessarily civil.

"I should ask you the same question." The man, whose real name was most likely nothing like del Rue, smiled and took a long draft of his wine. "After all, I am not the one with a darkling shard in my soul." That piercing gaze narrowed—in an instant going from charming to razor sharp.

Merrick jerked back, feeling his skin grow suddenly cold. In Ulrich he had been forced to take a sliver of the soul of a slain Deacon into himself to unravel a conspiracy within a Priory. It had been his only choice, and he thought to outrun any consequences from it. Yet here was this man pointing it out like it was a red letter painted on his cheek.

"It does make you rather stand out my young friend." Del Rue picked up one of the tiny cups filled with candied fruit and began to nibble at it. "As does that wild talent of yours. Quite the conflicted little bundle aren't you?" He tapped his spoon against the bowl. "Still I am not surprised anyone in your Order missed it. They are as near blind as to make no difference."

It was unnerving that the man was able to place verbal jabs into the most vulnerable places. However Merrick was not going to show how well they were hitting home. "Maybe I am conflicted, but if I turn around and tell everyone here how we met it is *you* that will be reduced to a little bundle."

The man's eyes narrowed, and he put down his little half-eaten cup of fruit. He smiled. Then he laughed. It was loud enough to draw the attention of the glittering folk nearby. Undoubtedly they were wondering whatever a dour Deacon could possibly say to get such a reaction.

The older man's expression was now ice-cold. "Tread carefully, Merrick. I am a close confidant of the Emperor. He trusts and values my opinion, whereas you are merely a Deacon—a Deacon with a terrible reputation." He leaned forward. "Who will believe you—the Emperor? Or perhaps your Arch Abbot who hates you?"

Merrick felt his throat close up, words deserting him. Yet he opened his Center and examined the older man through it. Nothing. Despite what he had seen in the tunnels in Chioma, and the sly smile on the Native Deacon's face, not a trace or hint of power could be seen. It was impossible. Merrick knew himself to be one of the strongest Sensitives in the Order, and yet this man was a blank slate—no more talented than the servers whisking away their used dishes.

All he could tell—and that was by looking—was that

del Rue was amused. He flicked his fingers at the Deacon. "Now go on, scuttle away. I have more important matters to attend than yours."

He turned away from Merrick.

As the young Sensitive made his way back to the Grand Duchess' side, his mind swirled chaotically. His first thought was of his mother. She was kept largely away from Court life, and had Lyon to look after, so she must not have ever run into del Rue; something that her older son could only be grateful for. Yet, if he tried to use her as a witness, then perhaps she would be a target again. He wasn't even sure how clearly she had seen her abductors in Chioma. Too much had happened in one night, and it would take a few moments to come to any kind of decision.

Zofiya smiled at him as he approached and a horrible possibility leapt into his mind. Del Rue knew that he had the ear of the Grand Duchess. She could be in danger as well.

However, he realized he was in the more dangerous position. Whatever the Native Deacon was up to, he was surely not yet ready to risk murdering the Emperor's sister—who besides everything was much harder to kill than might be supposed. Even though right now she looked like merely another Court beauty.

So Merrick let her take his arm and lead him out of the flow of the party.

"Merrick," Zofiya whispered, her fingers tightening around his wrist, "you have gone frighteningly pale, which I am not taking as a good sign."

The Deacon could feel her; not the woman at his side, but the woman he shared a Bond with. His Active was getting farther and farther away from him. She was his responsibility, they were Bound tightly together—closer than siblings or lovers—and yet she was not his highest calling. The vows he'd taken, along with every other Deacon, echoed in his head like uncompromising drums.

I promise to protect and shelter Imperial citizens from

*all attacks of the unliving—even to the end of my mind,
body and soul. I shall never lie down before the geists and
give up a mortal while they have soul or breath.*

The Order had never lectured on this particular choice,
but they did school them that every Deacon was dispos-
able. As a student, Merrick had nodded and agreed—but it
was quite different when faced with the reality. With a
start, he glanced up and saw that the Grand Duchess had
guided him toward the edge of the partygoers that lingered
in the hallway outside the ballroom. The guests were chattering on—completely unaware of the dangerous currents
that flowed around them.

Zofiya, despite her beautiful form, was not so blind. Her
eyes, clear gray against the darkness of her skin, fixed on
him. "What is it, Merrick? Do you know this man? Is he a
danger?"

The Deacon opened his Center. Once again he could
feel nothing in the air. It was more terrifying than anything. A blind Sensitive was worth nothing.

"Not here," he whispered to her. Now he was the one to
take her hands and pull her away. Together, they moved as
quickly as they could back deeper into the palace where
hopefully even Sensitive ears could not overhear them.

EIGHT

Blood Ties

The Rossin was whispering in Raed's ear. Cruel, unpleasant things. Things about his sister, and how she would not turn from her path. They would have to kill her. Ahead he could hear the echo of familiar laughter. His mother had laughed like that once. Long ago.

You cannot trust her, you know that. You'll just give her another chance to kill you. The Beast growled into the back of his skull. *She'll succeed this time and then the Empire will be ripped apart.*

Raed did not answer—mainly because he had no answers to give. All he had was the now, and this eerie puzzle box of a fortress. The Young Pretender did not like the fact that this palace had no windows and no guards on these deeper levels.

He would have given anything to have Aachon, or Merrick, or most especially Sorcha at his back.

"Instead all I have is you," he impotently whispered to the Rossin, "and a rather piss-poor companion you are."

The minute he spoke, Raed realized that it had been a bad choice to do so. His voice slithered and echoed in these corridors for far too long. He came to a halt, his heart racing in his chest until the reverberations stopped. Only then did he move, treading as fast and silently as he could.

Reaching a dead-end corridor Raed paused—but now in confusion. He could still hear the laughter, but there was no door or window it could be coming through. Dropping to his knees he discerned that there was a grate in the floor, where the faint breeze and the laughter emanated from. The Rossin sensed something else though. It was not any sound that caused the beast in his head to rage; it was a smell.

Kill them. Break them. Take what is theirs.

The words sounded so loud in his skull that Raed had to stop and draw in several long deep breaths with the kind of concentration that probably only should have belonged to a Deacon. Then, slotting his fingers into the grate, he pulled it loose and stared down into the vent. It was going to be a tight fit.

He was not frightened of narrow spaces—years of living on a ship saw to that—but he was a little nervous about being down there if the Rossin should break loose. Still, it was not like he had a choice. Luckily, months of harsh travel had whittled his frame down considerably, and he was able, with a significant amount of wriggling, to get himself into the shaft.

This was the most curious of palaces for a Pretender to the throne to find himself. The air was warm and uncomfortable as he tried his best to keep his breathing low and quiet. Raed passed three junctions, and at each of them paused to listen for the sound of laughter. It didn't take long to locate the source.

It was Fraine, but she was most definitely not alone. Raed peered down through a grate into another level of the fortress and saw a most strangely beautiful scene. Below, three women were lounging on reclined benches, while another three stood nearby. He recognized two of them

immediately—his sister and his old friend Tangyre Greene.
His instant reaction was to feel a flare of unreasonable happiness, though both of them had passed him into the hands
of a geistlord that wanted to kill both him and the Rossin.
Hastily, he quashed those feelings. He reminded himself
that they had also ordered the destruction of the small portion of his crew that had followed him. The Young Pretender forced himself to recall the hard look in his sister's
eyes when she had done it.

Yet all his struggles to get from Orinthal to here were
suddenly worth it. Raed had, in truth, feared that he would
never find them. They looked to be well, and no different
from when he had last seen them, as he was held in the
sand and his crew was massacred.

Next he examined the other women in the room with his
sister. The Shin women were creatures of beauty—Raed had
read about that before—but nothing had prepared him for
the aura of strange lethargy around two of them. He was,
however, the only one to remain calm; the Rossin was almost
apoplectic with rage on seeing them. The Beast flooded the
Young Pretender's brain with images of slaughter.

It was, perhaps, because the women were still laughing.
Certainly their appearance would have been enjoyed by a
huge number of men in the Empire, even if the geistlord
was raging about it.

The pair reclining were pale to the point of eeriness,
their white hair spread out on their couch. The hair was
however the only covering they wore. Their breasts were
exposed, nipples painted with ocher, and around their
waists were looped strings of pearls and lapis lazuli. It had
been months since Raed had seen any kind of naked
woman, but he found no excitement stirring in his trousers.
He had seen napeth users in the islands, and those empty-
eyed beauties left him as cold as these Shin women.

Sorcha, all flame and passion, leapt up in his recollection in contrast to these chill beauties.

Behind the supine two were another pair, also white

blonde in coloring, but they were more clothed. Flowing silks were bunched around their waists, but their breasts were bare, and there was nothing lethargic about them; they had the coiled power of a jungle cat, and they paced backward and forward. These were the two that the Rossin was focused on, particularly when he noticed their nails. Curved sheaths of bronze extended them out far beyond normal length, and gave them the unsettling appearance of claws. Upon seeing these two, the Rossin flooded the Young Pretender's brain with images of slaughter.

Now the Rossin's rage crystallized into actual words.

Enemies. Blood drinker. The Wrayth. Kill them all.

Raed let his breath out slowly and carefully. Yet the Rossin's constantly running thoughts were bleeding into his own. It was warm in this narrow space and he could not afford to panic now.

"So, Fraine Rossin," one of the standing women said, taking a seat at the feet of her supine companion, "have you had a chance to consider our terms?"

Raed's stomach clenched. It appeared he was too late. The Empire was about to come undone.

Below, his sister shifted on her chair, and glanced up at the silent Tangyre. "Lady Iuhmee, if you join our rebellion there will be plenty of benefits to the Shin and Ensomn itself. I don't understand why you need—"

"If you don't understand," the second woman broke in, "then our business is done here. Your rebellion will founder without us and you know that very well."

Above, in the vent, Raed frowned. He knew the Shin were influential among the Princes, but not so that they could have such a deciding vote.

They have moved while you slept, foolish mortal. They are more stealthy than you can possibly imagine.

Raed was beginning to feel his own anger rise. He had most certainly not been sleeping while tracking down his sister. Also he was suspicious that the great Beast in him knew something it was not yet sharing. Raed had only felt rage this great twice before, in the ossuary and in the desert of Chioma. He could only conclude one thing: the Shin were in league with a geistlord.

His sister glanced back at Tangyre. "I will not become your peon." She waved her hand at the pale-haired women, still reclining on the couch and about as noticed as a piece of furniture.

Iuhmee's gaze remained fixed on Fraine while those sharp bronze fingers danced along the girl's pale skin, causing her breathing to come in tiny gasps, before one flicked at her throat. The thin line of blood oozed from the cut, shockingly red against her almost chalky flesh, before Iuhmee bent and licked it clean. Both drinker and supplier let out the slightest of groans: the kind that might be heard from a contented lover after long hours of play.

The Rossin, for once, had been speaking literally. Blood drinkers indeed. Summoning geists through from the Otherside, luring them with the spilling of blood in terrible ways, was something that only the mad and the foolish dared.

If ever he had seen a threat demonstrated more clearly, Raed could not think of it. Fraine blanched, and Tangyre's hand went to the younger woman's shoulder. "You have made your point," the captain said, actually stepping between the Shin and her companion, "but that does not mean Her Grace will be tying herself to you as a peon. How dare you! She is of the greatest line of nobility in Arkaym!"

The Lady Iuhmee lifted herself from the peon's throat, and wiped delicately at her mouth, for all the world like some aristocrat at a state banquet. "If she were a peon, she would hardly make a decent leader for the rebellion, would she? No, that is not what we ask." She snapped her fingers, and a fourth slave appeared from out of the shadows of the room. She was carrying a tray with a curved silver bowl on it, from his position it was impossible to make out the nature of the symbols carved into it, but he did catch the gleam of tiny weirstones embellishing the rim. Not good.

Get out. The Rossin growled, angry and frustrated by the inability to take shape in the narrow stone confines of the shaft they were in. *Get out of this place now!*

However Raed was too transfixed to move. He wondered if his ancestors had known this about the Shin, or if this was a recent development. The west had always been a place of terrible legends and wildness—but he had never heard of anything like this. Blood drinking was the ultimate dark path to power, and had been one of the first things the Order of the Eye and the Fist had stamped out. How could they have missed all of this?

Now here was Fraine about to indulge in it. From all the threats he had faced in the ossuary under Vermillion and the temple of the false goddess Hatipai, Raed Rossin knew the power of his blood. The blood he shared with Fraine. He cast about for a way to get down there quickly, but the vent was made of stone, and all his shoving against it didn't move it any discernible amount. The restrictions of the shaft meant he couldn't swing his sword or anything else.

Fool! I cannot protect you forever. Get out!

His mind ran to the weirstone bullets he had taken off a bounty hunter in his travels across the west. Made by the scarlet witches, they were thought to be most useful against geists who had taken flesh. The bounty hunter had thought to use them on the Rossin. Now they could be put to better use. With frenzied wriggling, Raed was able to pull out the pistol and slide it between the grating. He knew what the consequences would be, but he could not merely watch as his sister aligned herself with these blood drinkers.

Raed pulled the trigger. His aim was off, thanks to the tight confines of the shaft, and the limitations that the grate afforded him. The bullet instead of striking Iuhmee, punched a neat hole through her reclining peon's head.

The Princess of Ensomn screamed however, as if it had been she that had been struck. At least he presumed she was screaming, since the retort of the pistol had set his ears to ringing. She collapsed to her knees, and when she turned her face upward in his direction, it was a totally different one, with burning eyes and a mouth full of fangs.

She pointed at Fraine who was looking as pale as a Shin peon. While Raed yelled through the grate, since stealth was now abandoned, three slaves appeared and wrestled his sister to the ground. Two held her, while the third slid Fraine's sleeve back, and sliced the softest part of her forearm. Her blood seemed to drip into the bowl the peon held beneath for a very long time.

When he had been a young man, Raed had seen his little sister do many foolish things, but coming to this nest of evil was an awful kind of grown-up idiocy. However she was no longer a little child he could warn away from open flames and sharp objects. The worst bit was that Captain Tangyre, supposedly her friend, stood by as she was forced into giving up her blood.

Finally it was done and Tangyre handed Fraine a towel to staunch the flow. She held it tight for the younger woman and whispered something soothing to her. Anger toward his once friend was catching up with Raed. He blamed all of his sister's missteps and foolish dreams on that poisonous captain. She'd been dripping lies into the sheltered girl's ear for years. He would make her pay for that disservice.

His ears were clearing, and he saw Iuhmee climb to her feet. Her momentary outrage at her peon's death was replaced with a cruel smile, aimed in his direction. Raed knew he should move, and yet he found he could not. Dimly he could hear the Rossin howling at him to flee rapidly.

Raed made to wriggle away from the vent when his sister stood and drew his attention back to the activities below.

Fraine was visibly shaken, but she stood before the Lady Iuhmee. "So we have our pact?"

The Shin woman took the bowl from the slave and peered down into it. Her face was alight with avarice, so that even Raed could see, so much so it was as if she was holding a bowl of priceless gems. That made him even more sure that his sister had done something terribly wrong.

In his head the Rossin had gone silent, but the man could feel him watching with infinite cunning. Raed found that far more disturbing than when the Beast was roaring in his head.

Iuhmee smiled at her, a smile that made Raed's skin crawl, and should have, if Tangyre was looking after Fraine's best interests, caused the other captain to yank her charge out of the room immediately. Then, the Shin lady raised the bowl and drank deeply. The sound of her gulps turned Raed's stomach.

However, the Young Pretender was not able to see her expression after that, because pain flared white-hot deep in his core. All he felt was his body screaming in pain. His throat clenched around a howl while his fingers spasmed tight on the vent. Nothing else mattered but this instant.

When it retreated he was left gasping and nauseous in its wake.

Too late. The Rossin snarled in outrage. *Too late for anything.*

In the room below, Tangyre was helping Fraine to her feet. Apparently both siblings of the Imperial line had experienced the excruciating pain. Lady Iuhmee was grinning like a wolf as she placed the bowl, quite empty of anything, upside down on a nearby table.

"Now we have an accord," she said conversationally. "We shall give you our support for your rebellion, and once you have overturned Kaleva, you will turn out all the other western Princes, and give their kingdoms to us. We will make this coast our playground."

Fraine nodded. She nodded, and then let herself be gathered into Tangyre's arms like a complete child.

Iuhmee curled the fingers of one hand together: the brass of the fingernail guards rattling together like the unpleasant skittering of some many-legged insect. "But first,

we shall have to deal with our little vermin problem." Her
eyes darted upward, and Raed realized with a start that she
had not forgotten the shooting of her peon—she had merely
had more pressing matters. The other Shin, and even his
little sister Fraine, followed suit.

He understood now that an enemy who could be so calm
and focused when being shot at, was not someone to be
taken lightly. He frantically wriggled and pushed with his
knees and elbows out of sight of the vent and away down
the shaft. He comforted himself that once beyond that, the
Shin would not be able to locate him—though there was a
sharp knot in his stomach that insisted he was perhaps
being a little optimistic.

The Rossin's growl felt as though it was rumbling in his
own chest.

I cannot help you here. Get free of these narrow places.
Let me run free!

"Doing my best," Raed hissed. His muscles were pro-
testing at this unwelcome and unnatural form of locomo-
tion, and it was damnably hot in here. Sweat ran down his
back and along his neck. The worst of it was he couldn't
easily wipe it from his face. It stung his eyes and obscured
his vision.

However he also soon realized that the Shin were not
done with him—not by a very long mark. Something was
behind him in the ventilation system of this mad fortress. It
didn't sound like whoever his pursuer might be was having
nearly as tough a time of it as he was. It sounded instead as
though they were running, like animals in hot pursuit.

Raed turned himself around in the confined space and
managed with more than a little swearing to work his pistol
once more out from his side. Primitive fears of being
chased and trapped were beginning to rise, and he could
hear his own heartbeat in his head—louder, even, than the
Rossin's thoughts.

Holding the pistol trained between his thighs in the
direction of the ominous sounds, Raed pushed with his

legs, sliding on his back farther away from the pursuit. It was slow going, and he was wondering what exactly he was going to do with the pistol. If he fired it in this position, he ran a good chance of shooting himself in the thigh, as well as blowing his own ears out.

Either, however, seemed preferable to facing whatever was closing rapidly on his position.

"By the Blood, I'm not dying like this," he hissed, all the time working his way in some unknown direction. The Rossin, impotent in this particular, unexpected turn of events, was silent.

He smiled grimly, though his legs ached, and he could barely see with his sweat-blinded vision. "Not exactly what you planned is it, my old friend? I think you've become just a little cocky after gobbling up that Hatipai."

If the beast made a reply, Raed was too occupied to notice, because his pursuer was actually visible, only feet away, and coming at him through the gloom of the shaft.

She must have once been human. The face was a wreck of former beauty twisted in rage. Lips, that could have been full and lovely, were held back from sharpened teeth, and eyes under perfect brows were now bloodred and bulging. Beyond that however, the creature had no resemblance to anything human. Long, jointed legs braced it in the tight space, and carried it forward much faster than Raed could manage. He could not get a good look at the rest, but had the impression of a thorax and segmented body similar to a scorpion. The odor of it, this close up, was almost choking. It smelled like it had bathed in blood and guts—and perhaps it had done that very thing.

It was a transformation, but only halfway—so unlike the one he had to endure on a regular basis. Raed was abruptly glad that he had never had to experience a terrible in-between state like that.

Apparently however, his sympathy to it meant nothing. The creature surged forward, hissing like a snake. The Young Pretender didn't want to find out if the creature bore poisoned fangs. He fired his pistol between his knees and directly into the onrushing thing's face.

The scream it let out was most likely terrifying, but Raed couldn't hear any of it because the retort of the gun in such a tight space set his head buzzing. Everything developed a murky strangeness to it after that. Through the smoke he could make out the shape of the Shin monstrosity, twisting and flailing around. So it seemed a gunshot to the face was at least painful.

Not planning to linger and find out, Raed dropped the pistol onto his chest, and kicked out with his feet and hands even more furiously in a scramble to get away. He passed a junction where three shafts met the one he'd been traveling in. Craning his neck from side to side, Raed determined two things: the passage to his left was the only one that tickled his face with the possibility of fresh air, and the others brought him only the sound of more skittering pursuit.

It wasn't a decision he had to think long on. His pants were wearing through on the stone, and his fingertips were bleeding where they grasped at the unforgiving edges of the shaft. He was leaving plenty of scarlet drips behind for the Shin to follow, but he didn't care. They already knew he was here, and they already had tasted the blood of his family.

The hisses and growls behind him said that the other monstrosities were catching up just as their companion had. Raed had to decide if he was going to stop and make a stand, or scramble on. He had only four regular bullets left, and he couldn't be sure he'd even injured the halfling beast. The terrible truth was, he didn't know exactly how many more of these things were after him.

The breeze on the top of Raed's head was like a siren song now, and he wriggled harder, bracing his elbows, hands, knees and feet. He blocked out the pain as best he could and tried to also ignore the sweat mingling with his blood on the surface of the pipeline he was trapped in. If he could get out, then he would give those Shin peons a decent fight. He'd have a chance to unleash the Rossin—then they would pay.

So determined was he, that Raed shoved and thrust himself out of the horizontal shaft and half into the abrupt drop of the vertical one without even realizing it. With a lurch he discovered his sudden predicament, but much too late. He couldn't brace himself with his legs alone as his chest and arms flailed.

To the sound of gleeful laughter and chattering, Raed Syndar Rossin tumbled into the unknown depths of the Shin fortress.

NINE

In the Sanctuary

Zofiya's fingers tightened on Merrick's as she drew him with her down the corridors. Most of the folk, both high and low were busy celebrating, yet her heart was pounding harder than any of theirs.

Her head was full of concerns for her brother—for the Empire itself—but she was also exhilarated by the nearness of the Deacon. Still, she told herself, she had good reason to bring him to her chambers. Good reason, yes indeed.

Her few maids had been dismissed to enjoy the evening, and as usual there were no sentries on her door. She was the head of the Imperial Guard and, as was her habit, had no one watching her apartments. If danger was coming to an Imperial sibling, she would rather it came to her than her brother. Now this worked to her advantage.

"Quick," she said, tugging Merrick into her privy chamber. "This is the only place where I am sure it is safe to speak." She pressed shut the redwood doors behind them. The room was quiet and lit only by two flickering sandalwood-scented candles in the sconces. None of her ladies had really been expecting her to return so soon. They were alone.

The doors on the other side of the rather sparse privy chamber were ajar, providing a glimpse of the far more opulent bedroom. Pride of place was a vast and silk-shrouded bed carved to resemble a ship. It was a ridiculous indulgence, but it was one of the few Zofiya allowed herself.

The young Deacon glanced around, his eyes slightly wider than usual, a sure sign he was using his Sight. "We do indeed appear to be alone."

Zofiya shivered. When the Order used their powers so flippantly she was reminded how little she understood what they did. Certainly, they were invaluable in maintaining the integrity of the Empire, and giving the ordinary folk some reassurance that their grandmother was not going to vomit acid, but they were also a dangerous power. As the Grand Duchess circled the room, trailing her hand over her trinkets, she watched Merrick Chambers out of the corner of her eye. The Order had done things that the Empire could only be grateful for, but she had always been cautious around them. Zofiya did not like how much power they wielded. Merrick was the only Deacon she actually had learned to trust.

"Tell me what you know about del Rue," she commanded. Her hand now rested on an onyx box, but she did not reach in to take out what it contained. Not yet.

The Deacon took a breath, and his eyes darted away from hers. He was not a very good liar—even his expression gave him away.

Zofiya's finger traced the sharp edge of the box. "Tell me," she repeated, but this time not in her Grand Duchess voice. Instead, she whispered it—almost like a normal woman.

Merrick cleared his throat. "I am sure you know the history of the native Order that was here before my own."

She tilted her head. She had been expecting something else—something related to a minor nobleman seeking advancement, or a Prince of the Empire annoyed at some petty oversight by her brother. When the Deacon mentioned history she was surprised, intrigued and just a little worried. Although the mysteries of the Order and its kind were not unknown to her, she was not foolish enough to believe that she knew everything about them.

When Zofiya did not speak, Merrick paused and glanced up. His eyes were dark pools in the half-light, and they were so very earnest. "We thought they were gone, wiped out and stricken from the records. Stranger still, there was no remnant in the oral tradition, and several of my own Order have suggested this was . . . deliberate. We knew they existed, but that is all."

The concept that anyone could remove memories from the entire population of Arkaym was a terrifying one. And yet she had seen far more terrible things; recollections of when a geistlord had taken residence in her body welled up. She swallowed them back. "But you don't think they have gone at all, do you?"

"I know they have not. I saw them beneath Chioma—they tried to take my mother from me." He swallowed hard. "That man was leading them; the man you know as del Rue."

While he talked in a calm, flat tone she flicked open the box and looked in. The shiny pendant inside gleamed back at her, almost mocking. It was the sigil of Hatipai—her greatest mistake. It was a reminder not to fail like that again. Her brother and the Empire were at stake.

"That is a concern," she murmured.

"I'm sorry," Merrick replied, and despite everything Zofiya smiled.

"How is that your fault, pray tell? The Empire is under constant attack every day. There is always someone trying to destroy my brother, unbalance the Princes, and cause mayhem."

"Arkaym was not perhaps what you expected when you came over with your brother." The Deacon took a step toward her, a rather telling step.

"No, and neither was finding a Deacon as an ally." Zofiya flicked the onyx box shut with a snap. "I do confess facing another Order like your own is something I didn't expect. I am not quite sure how to fight back against them."

Merrick tucked his hands into the sleeves of his rather plain cloak. "I think we should take this to the Mother Abbey in the morning. They may have more knowledge of the Native Order than I am aware of. Unless you think we should try and talk to your brother about this?"

Zofiya pressed her lips together. "I have already tried asking about del Rue, and he tells me nothing. It is as if my voice no longer matters." It hurt to admit that. She and Kal had been as close as twins when growing up. They'd weathered the storms of their father's Court in Delmaire together, and she could never have imagined a time when he would take no notice of her counsel. Yet, that time was upon her.

She could not have pinpointed the exact moment when that had changed. It had been gradual, and so subtle that it had snuck up on her. And so had loneliness. She had few friends in Vermillion and none close enough that she could share these fears with. The Court was a cesspit of intrigue and backstabbing. Those that she chatted with daily, even her Imperial Guardsmen, or her body servants, could be working for any number of factions and being paid to bring them information.

When Merrick's hand touched her shoulder, the Grand Duchess did not flinch away. He rubbed gently, and whispered, "I am sure we can get him back. These rogues cannot have that deep a hold on him that he would forget his sister. Everything will be all right in the end."

It was such a ridiculous statement that Zofiya should have laughed, and most definitely should have pushed him away for his temerity in daring to touch the Grand Duchess.

Those are the things she should have done. Instead, she found herself leaning into his touch. The moments where she allowed herself to feel weakness were few and far between, but something about this earnest young man had already breached her defenses and perhaps, if she was truthful with herself, she had just been waiting for a chance to let him in.

Everyone in Court would have been truly amazed at the next words that came out of her mouth. "Don't leave." Her voice was soft, yearning, and utterly alien even to herself.

With the little light in her room Merrick's eyes were hard to read, but as a Sensitive he had to know what she wanted. They were not a celibate group she knew, and though inviting a Deacon into one's bed was not forbidden by anyone, it was a little rash. If the gossips in the Court got wind of the Emperor's sister bedding Merrick Chambers, it would be the talk of the season. Yet, at the particular moment, she didn't care. She was sick of weighing every move, every person, and considering how it would affect her brother's Empire. He had taken a little-known aristocrat into his trust after all. It was time she had something for herself too.

Merrick stood silent, a still, dark shape against the faint starlight coming in through the window. "Zofiya, I don't think it is wise for me to stay. People will get the wrong impression—"

He wasn't going to make this easy for her—either that or he was quite without a clue. That was the problem with being the Grand Duchess; everyone was always so damned afraid to approach her. "Perhaps they would get the right impression," she growled, and cupped his face in both of her hands. He was taller than her, so it was a strangely penitent gesture.

He did not pull away. "I would not want you to think I was taking advantage—"

That was the last thing he got to say, as she got on the tips of her toes and shut his mouth effectively with her lips. Merrick kissed her back with a surprising passion. When they parted she looked into his eyes. "Tomorrow we will root out this poison from the Empire. Tomorrow I will take back my brother. However, that is many hours away, and I would have something sane in my life before the insanity begins."

"That would be most wonderful," he agreed, and deftly pulled the pins out of her hair. It tumbled over her shoulders and abruptly she was not the Grand Duchess, just a woman with a man she had admired and desired for months. It didn't matter that he was a Deacon, and technically her subject. She wanted him. He wanted her.

They kissed again in the half-light, and with their mouths still locked she guided him over to the bed, shaped like a sailing ship. It was certain no Deacon of the Order slept in anything so magnificent. Not that she was planning on allowing him anything like sleep.

Still there was the business of her rather ornate ball gown. Members of the Order had surprisingly little experience trying to unlace a lady from such a garment. Zofiya giggled as Merrick swore and fumbled with the lacings. Finally, she yanked open her bedside drawer, and passed him a stiletto. "The lacings aren't worth a thing to me." When she presented her back to him, Merrick did not hesitate.

"Who am I to argue with the Grand Duchess," he chuckled, slipping the blade between the leather laces and slicing them away.

The sound of them parting was delicious and arousing. Zofiya spun back to him, letting the confection of lace and satin drop to her feet. With only faint starlight and dipping candlelight to illuminate her, the Grand Duchess stood quite naked before Deacon Merrick Chambers.

His indrawn breath was quite satisfactory. His fingers

brushed her skin, making her shiver with anticipation, but she stood still and let him examine her. Merrick's hands traced the line of scars and bruises her training left on her. Some were old and some relatively new.

The long scar that curved from her back around her hip was the one that made her flinch when touched.

She didn't really think about it anymore, having successfully shoved the darkest of her times in Delmaire firmly to the back of her mind. However, sitting on the bed, holding and touching her, Merrick looked up at Zofiya.

"Your father did this?" She'd been a fool to forget his powers. It was so much easier to do with a Sensitive than with an Active, but she did not move his hand away.

"I was not exactly what he expected in his children—especially his girl children," she said as lightly as she could manage. "Finally, he had enough. So you can understand why I decided to come with my brother." She shivered when Merrick laid his lips to the silvered line, licking it gently with his tongue.

"Our scars are part of us," he said, placing his hands on her hips and pulling her backward onto the bed, "but you are more than the sum of them."

He really was the most strange, extraordinary young man, and Zofiya felt her mood slide from the need for anger and sexual release, toward wanting to explore him more deeply.

She stripped off his clothes as he lay on her bed, kissing her, and traced the lines of his body. He too was not without his scars, though they were smaller than hers. "Most of mine," he confessed, "were in the practice yard at the Abbey."

Straddling him, Zofiya pressed her naked length against his, and tucked her hair behind one of her ears. "Is it a strange thing," she whispered, "for a Grand Duchess of the Empire and a Sensitive Deacon of the Order to be together like this?"

While his hands ran over her body, Merrick smiled back. "For a few hours, let's not ask such questions. Let's just be two ordinary citizens, about the business of pleasure and togetherness."

Then they needed no words after that.

Maybe Zofiya had been expecting meekness from the man, but that was not what she found. Merrick was gentle when she needed him to be, and passionate when that was required. He matched her movement and desire, something that she realized must come from his training at the Abbey. If any of the women of Arkaym knew of the benefits of bedding a Sensitive Deacon then they had kept it from her.

He had control and passion—something she'd never experienced in such perfect balance in a man before. Merrick Chambers knew where to lay his hands merely by listening to the Grand Duchess' sighs and soft groans. It was as if he were a master musician and she a willing violin.

Later, when she lay resting in his arms, looking up at the moving silk hangings around the bed, she felt exhausted but stronger. Merrick had drifted off to sleep, his face nestled against her neck, one leg hooked in hers.

The daylight had not yet crept in through her open windows, and it was easy to imagine the fight before them was a long way off. She would allow herself that illusion for a few more minutes.

She glanced to her right and at the sleeping Deacon. He was about her age, but there was still a strange innocence about him that she had never been able to afford in the palace at Delmaire. Sometimes it felt as though she'd been born world-weary and conspiracy alert.

Zofiya sighed, turned her head and pressed her face against Merrick's curled head. It felt good to have an ally— even one with divided loyalties outside the palace. Despite her doubts, the Deacons had always fought bravely for her brother and now she hoped one of their number would fight

just as bravely for her and the Empire. It could get very
ugly very quickly for both of them.

Just as she felt sleep tugging at the corners of her own
eyes, a tiny sound made her slide cautiously out from under
Merrick. It was so soft and gentle that it might have been
mistaken for a mouse running by the wall, but Zofiya
knew every noise in her private domain. This one was not
familiar.

Her eyes darted to the door that led into the privy chamber, and then to the only other entrance to her bedroom, the
one that led to her balcony. It was that place at least three
assassins had tried their hand at reaching. Two had fallen
to their deaths without a handhold on the sheer wall, while
another more agile one had met his fate at the end of her
sword. If this del Rue was going to try a similar thing then
she would be only too happy to oblige him. Once she had a
dead assailant to show her brother he might well view her
concerns more seriously.

Taking up her weapon, she slid naked from the bed and
padded toward the balcony, but when the sound came again
it was not from that direction. It appeared to be coming
from the large grandfather clock that stood in the opposite
corner. It was one of Kal's rejected pieces, so it didn't work,
but she had always admired the detailed carving on it. Now
it made a decidedly odd creak—almost as if one of the
gears had come loose.

She knew every inch of the palace, and was certain
there were no secret doors or passages behind this section
of wall. However as she leaned forward, brow furrowed,
to examine the clock, a hand, covered in a fine leather
glove that shone with the light of a rune shot out of the
solid oak paneling and grabbed hold of her. Then another,
with an encircling wreath of green flame closed over her
shoulder.

The Grand Duchess abruptly had no strength to lift her
sword. It was suddenly heavier than an anvil. As it dropped
from her strangely numb fingers, a hooded face appeared

out of the woodwork, phasing through it as only a Deacon could manage. It did not surprise her that it was del Rue, or that he was smiling.

Then after that, all was darkness.

TEN

A Vast Enemy

The Rossin fell and, snatching control of Raed's body from the weak mortal, transformed in midair. The human's clothes were ripped away, and the pack he carried tumbled down the shaft. None of that mattered. An eagle's scream sounded in the nest of the Phia and he didn't care. Raed had called on him again, a deep desire to survive might have driven it, but he had still done what was required. With every change he was one step closer.

The Beast was careful to hide his thoughts when the mortal wore the flesh, but when his royal host was subsumed it was liberating in all ways. He had tried to keep them away from the land of Ensomn, but he'd not been able to stop the fool. Apparently sibling bonds ran very deep.

Now, they were in the lair of the Wrayth and there was nothing to be done except get them out. The Shin was a name they had taken to hide their true natures, and it appeared to have worked well for them. A fortress. Ruling over a stupid population of people. It was an old trick, but still a good one.

The Rossin twisted his wings and surged upward toward freedom and the open sky. Only the narrow slice of moon gleaming through the steel grate stopped him crashing into it. He twisted midair like a falcon, and slammed his curved talons into the barrier. Then opening his wings wide, he heaved. The only thing that snapped however was his beak in rage.

Hanging there like an enraged bat was not his happiest moment in this realm. The Wrayth were cunning and so numerous that they were in fact a far more dangerous opponent than even Hatipai. The Rossin's avian form was meant to fly, meant to dominate the air. It was not meant to be caged like this—but what was the other option?

His head twisted around, as he peered down into the darkness. He could smell the Wrayth below. He knew there would be a way out down there, for the peons to come and go. It was the only way he was going to get free of the Wrayth.

Folding his wings about him, the Rossin released his claws from the grating and dived into the darkness.

The smell of the Wrayth was stronger the farther he went; the reek of blood and flesh combined with the sharp odor of the geistlord itself. He transformed a moment before he reached the ground, and dropped to the dirt in his feline form. It was his most powerful shape; a thickly muscled cat the height of a human's shoulder, with spotted fur and teeth made to rend. It also meant that he was silent and deadly—useful things in this situation.

As he moved forward, the Rossin crunched over the broken remains of Raed's pack, and paused to consider. It was humiliating to even have to think about his host, but should they be trapped in a position as they had been just recently the weak creature would need his weapons and clothing. With a derisive snort through his nose, the beast took the pack in its mouth and padded on.

The heat down this deep into the Shin fortress was

terrible, especially to a huge beast covered in fur. It was the mass of flesh his fellow geistlord commanded that created such a hot, humid atmosphere. The Wrayth were not known for their kindness to any creature—even among other geistlords, but the Rossin was ready to hurt them in return. They had fought in the chaos of the Otherside, a battle of survival, and now it appeared they would continue it in this realm.

The Rossin moved deeper into the hive, his ears flicking back and forth seeking any movement. The smooth walls of higher up in the fortress had devolved into rough stone passages, but his massive padded paws took them with ease, though his mortal host might have had problems with the darkness and uneven terrain. Mortals often had problems with many things. When his plan came to fruition it might well be a relief to his Young Pretender.

The Rossin paused and inhaled. The stink of the Wrayth was now overcoming every other scent, and he knew that there would be many of them ahead. He clenched his claws, their creamy length puncturing the earth. A growl remained deep in his chest and largely unvoiced.

Shoulders scything, the Rossin eased himself still deeper into the Wrayth hive.

Many geistlords used humans as tethers to this world; from his own ability to hide within the bloodline of a family, to Hatipai's method of actually birthing a half-geist child of her own to act as a link. The Wrayth's method combined a little of both; as was immediately apparent when the great cat climbed through a breach in the earthen wall, and peered down into his fellow geistlord's breeding chamber.

It stank of humanity—a lot of unwashed, highly sexed humanity. At least his own host did not reek as badly as the Wrayth's—but mainly that was to do with sheer numbers. He had found his enemy's breeding pit. Women, all of them with their belly's swollen in various states of pregnancy, wore very little except the brand of the Wrayth. A pair of claw marks on the shoulder. Their eyes were vacant and staring. Their skin white from lack of sun.

Moving among them were drones, males with the same mark upon them. All of them stank of the blood ties the Wrayth used. This geistlord was vast in number and the most dangerous of the Rossin's enemies and kin. The great cat's eyes narrowed, and his head sunk between his shoulders. He could charge down now among all those peons of the Wrayth, but there was a chance they could overwhelm him. He had rage, but they certainly had numbers.

The Rossin bathed in blood, grew strong from it, but for the peons and their geistlord blood was more than that. It was a web that bound them together in a vast network of people. Each child born here became another peon and carrier of the enemy. This was one opponent that the Rossin could not easily destroy—even with all his strength.

So instead, he chose to leave them. His host would have been greatly surprised; but the Rossin was more than a mere Beast. He had his own plans and means, and when he was sated by blood he could think and act as clearly as any of the other geistlords. It was the restriction of being tied in blood. The Wrayth had found their own way around it, and that rankled.

Still they had to breed constantly lest the geistlord within them weaken. It was a vulnerability that the Rossin could not yet think of a way to exploit.

Letting a little huff of annoyance escape through his gaping mouth, the Beast padded around the room of silent and pale-eyed peons. The Wrayth's attention was not here—not yet. The Rossin could feel it above him, flitting about among other higher-level peons.

Deeper into the hive, the warmth was now so extreme that the great cat felt it laying like a blanket on him. He let his mouth droop open and began panting. New noises filtered from below, sounds that drew the Rossin; the echoes of human pain. Despite his caution, the geistlord found himself caught by curiosity and followed the sounds.

That was how he found the cells. Swinging his head from side to side, carefully placing his massive paws down as delicately as a house cat, the Rossin peered into them. These were pregnant women too, but not happy in their servitude to their Wrayth overlord. Even the Rossin felt something close to pity for these scraps of humanity tethered to the wall, their swelling bellies attached to wasted and wretched bodies.

The smell of them was strange; not merely just the reek of shackled humanity, but an odd mixture of Wrayth and something else. The cat stood at the bars of a cell and tilted its head, regarding the woman within, for a moment confused. She carried a Wrayth child, but was not of the Wrayth herself. She was something more trained, more powerful. She looked blankly back at the geistlord, broken inside and out, but there was a flicker of her past in there.

The Rossin's growl was deep and threatening as all trace of pity was wiped away. The prisoner's head jerked upright. She'd been a Deacon. Though she had no Gauntlets or Strop anymore, she still nursed a tiny spark of the Order within her. Many Deacons were presumed killed by geists, but obviously not all of them had been. Intriguingly enough, it appeared the Wrayth was occupied in some kind of breeding program—though to what end the Rossin could not tell.

If they had met in different circumstances he and this Deacon would have been enemies, now they were the same; trapped in the Wrayth hive. On the Otherside the geists consumed each other and the souls of the dead, but they did not shackle each other in such a way. The Wrayth had obviously learned some new skills in this realm.

The woman lurched forward, wrapping one hand around the bar while reaching out with the other toward the great cat. "Kill me," she gasped, her voice a rasp of horror. "Take my blood. Take me!"

The Rossin flinched back with a snarl. However other women in the row of cells had heard their fellow prisoner's call. Soon a dozen hands were thrust through the gaps, opening and closing in supplication.

"Take me!" one howled.

"No, me," other unseen women screamed.

"Have pity," the first woman said, and her fingers actually brushed the fur of the Rossin.

Despite his love of blood and violence, there was something repellant about what had been done to these women. He backed away, hissing and growling in disgust.

Then, from down the corridor, came the sounds of many people coming toward him. He could hear feet slapping on the stone, and smell the Wrayth coming toward him.

It damaged his pride to turn around and run, but on the Otherside the geistlord had learned to do what it took to survive. The Wrayth were coming, and the Rossin fled down the corridors in huge bounds, yet he snarled all the way.

He burst out into another main room, and realized immediately that this was where the Wrayth wanted him. The cat spun about growling and roaring at the surrounding peons. They reeked of the geistlord, and they held sticks and polearms. Every one of them was pale and blank-eyed, but there could be no mistaking their intentions.

"Welcome, mighty Rossin." A voice high in the vaulted ceiling caused the cat to jerk his head up; the female creature his host's sister had been talking to. She was beyond even his reaching, leaning out to talk to him from a balcony of stone, decorated with lapis lazuli.

"Thank you so much for visiting." The peons below bent like wheat in the wind at her voice, responding to the whims of the Wrayth.

The Rossin crouched, and even though he knew the pointlessness of it, sprang among them. He bit and raked his claws through their flesh. He broke bones and tore muscle, and even while he did, they did not scream. It was like cutting grass or biting water, and just as fulfilling.

Even though their blood flooded his mouth, it offered him nothing. Humanity should not be like this, and every part of the Rossin was disgusted by it. No strength came to him; the Wrayth's power slipped out of the peons before he could absorb it. Finally, he stood shaking bits of rent peons from his jaws, blood splattered on his patterned fur, and a growl emanating from his mouth.

"Are you done?" the Wrayth above asked, her voice stained with amusement. "As always you are limited, and as you can see, we are not."

The peons that were still capable formed up another circle. Some were dragging broken limbs, or their own eviscerated bowels, but they still moved to the controls of the geistlord in their bodies. At the same time, fresh peons from the rear came forward. They were carrying polearms, and on the end gleamed weirstones.

It was always this way; geistlord competing to devour geistlord. The Wrayth would have him and all the power that remained from Hatipai. However when the woman spoke, the words she let loose were not the ones that he expected.

"You will make an excellent experiment. Once you return to your host, we will find out what new lines he can form with our female peons. What interesting creatures might be made with your power and ours."

She turned, and his host's sister appeared on the balcony as well. She looked down on the snarling cat with such hatred that even the Rossin felt it.

He would not change. He would not surrender himself to that. He would breed nothing for the Wrayth. Then the peons were on him, pushing him with the weirstones, and where they touched, they burned. In this way they drove the Rossin out of the main hall and down into the hive.

Though he battered at them, charging, snarling, ripping an odd one or two down, they kept coming in a relentless fashion that he could not match. Eventually they pushed him, just by sheer numbers and determination, into a cell, much like the one their female prisoners occupied.

It was a tiny space for the massive feline, and he could barely turn around. The door was slammed shut behind him, and the Rossin let out a roar that shook the vile nest of the Wrayth. Yet, he would not release the form. If he did, then his host would become like the women, used for their breeding.

"How long can you wait?" a peon spoke. His face was slack, his eyes unfocused but the voice that came out was high-pitched and unnatural. "How long can you burn before you have to give us what we want?"

The Rossin snarled and crashed against the bars, but they were built strong—stronger than anything a human would make.

"Eventually you will give us what we want," the peon intoned, and then stepped back away from the bars.

Soon all of them departed and the Rossin was left to the sound of weeping and screaming women. His roars of outrage merged with theirs of despair.

Zofiya drew in her first conscious breath, and felt her body react with violent disagreement to this event. If her stomach had contained anything she would have thrown it up immediately. She twisted about, spitting and choking on her dry mouth. It was then she realized that she was tied, tightly and effectively, in place.

"Yes, unfortunately the phase effect on simple folk is rather unnerving." A voice to her right gave her reason to open her eyes. "However in your case I think it is something else as well." It was a voice she recognized, and her stomach clenched. Lying on a simple iron-framed bed her bones ached, her mouth was parched, and she knew she was in great peril. It was not the peril she was used to: a blade in the night, a conspiracy of minor nobles or an angry servant.

Del Rue, or whatever his name was, smiled at her. He was crouched down, hands on his knees, grinning at her as she lay bound more tightly than a spring roast. "Very interesting. Something about you is more . . . open shall we say . . . than your average plain stupid human. I wonder how that happened." He sounded genuinely curious.

She ran her tongue around her mouth to loosen it, since it was as dry as a pile of Orinthal sand. "Keep wondering," she replied as tartly as she could, "and while you wonder, I shall enjoy, as my brother executes you in front of the whole Court."

"Now, why would my good friend do that?" The older man spread his hands as if in great shock. "It was those pesky Deacons of the Order of the Eye and the Fist that kidnapped you. Why one of them was even in your bed." He waved a finger at her. "You naughty girl, I hadn't expected that, but it nicely took care of that Merrick Chambers. It was very helpful of you."

Zofiya swallowed hard, her eyes darting around the dark chamber. It looked like a cellar somewhere, perhaps in the Edge section of Vermillion—the damp smell clogging her nostrils suggested that. Surely they couldn't be farther away than that. She was certainly grateful that she'd not been conscious for the portion of the journey that involved phasing through walls. She was no coward, but her experiences in Orinthal had made her leery of anything that involved runes or undead powers. It seemed that she was going to have to deal with them now.

The man crouched down next to her oozed a terrible charm. From what Merrick had told her, del Rue was quite willing to sacrifice anyone to get what he wanted. He'd wanted to murder Japhne del Torne and her unborn child—and she was sure that was not the end to his foul deeds. The idea that her brother had been locked in his privy chamber for months with this man left her raging beyond sensible thought. Yet, she had to be sensible and calm as well.

"I am not prone to kindness," she replied conversationally, "and I suspect neither are you. Since you have my brother wound around your finger, you don't need me. Therefore you can dispense with the formalities altogether and get to the killing."

Del Rue smoothed his mustache, and stared at her before letting out a little laugh. "My dear Grand Duchess, if I wanted to murder you I would simply have left you embedded in the walls of the palace."

Despite her inner strength, Zofiya shivered at that. The idea of becoming part of Vermillion forever was not a pretty one. She'd seen strange creatures and bones trapped in rock, and despite her outrage, she would have not wanted to end up like that.

"I won't help you destroy my brother," she blurted out as bravely as she could.

"Oh," he replied mildly, "we don't need your help at all since we have him quite in hand. Your brother is not as strong willed as you." He wagged his finger at her, as if it were Zofiya's fault somehow.

Then something moved just out of her line of sight, and she flinched, straining. Hooded figures slid out from the shadows of the room, bearing a device she could not quite make out.

Del Rue touched her hair. "So many uses for a little royal like you. Blood, breeding or leverage. You didn't imagine you could be so useful did you, Grand Duchess? All that time trying to guard your brother and you never really thought about yourself."

His gloating was cut short by one of those figures throwing back his hood. "Are we getting on with it?"

Del Rue glanced up, a flicker of annoyance passing over his face. Zofiya saw at once that he was a man that both enjoyed his moments of power and did not like to be interrupted while having them. "Yes Master Vashill," he hissed, "I believe we are."

The other hooded figures stepped back once more into the shadows. Del Rue pushed himself up from the floor and

made way as the machine was rolled forward. The Grand
Duchess ran her eye over it. Immediately apparent was the
gleam of a weirstone seated within the gears and cogs of its
inner workings. It sat there with blue and white light flickering over its surface. The Grand Duchess had been privy
to many curious and wonderful devices brought into the
Court for her brother to admire, but she had never seen
anything like this.

The man called Vashill let his fingers trace the device,
and pride shined from his face. "My mother said that it
could not be done."

"I am glad we could prove her wrong, but do not forget
this would not be possible without my assistance," del Rue
growled. He turned and stage-whispered to Zofiya. "He is
quite mad you know, but the results of combining our
runes, raw geist power and his tinkering have been most
impressive."

Vashill opened up the side of the device and Zofiya
could see several tall vials of liquid within. He was not
comforting her with his rabid muttering. She'd also seen
her fair share of madmen in her time—she just didn't like
them this close.

She wetted her lips. "What exactly is it you plan to do
with me? I assure you torture will not break me; you would
be a rank amateur compared to my father. If I can take his
years of abuse—"

"Yes, yes, I am sure." Del Rue waved his hand dismis-
sively. "Compared to him I imagine I am almost a . . .
saint." He seemed to find some amusement that she did not
in the statement. When he finally recovered from his own
private joke he went on. "It is not my intention to break you
merely for my own amusement."

Vashill was apparently satisfied with the inner workings
of his machine, because he closed it up. "All is well."

Del Rue shot him a withering look that he completely
ignored. Yes, Zofiya thought, completely mad.

"You brother is easily swayed. Too soft, really, for an

Emperor." Her captor brushed hair out of her eyes. "You are quite another story: strong, determined and far more charismatic than Kaleva."

The Grand Duchess did not like where this was going in the least.

"If you can be taught, you would make an excellent Empress."

"Why don't you just sit on the throne yourself?" she spat.

He laughed at that. "Perhaps . . . perhaps I will. However for the moment I will be occupied in other ways, and besides, first we must tear down the Empire, and then rebuild it. If need be, your brother will go with it. Then when the Circle arises out of the ashes with a new Empress to offer to the people, we will be fully accepted."

"A puppet? For you?" Zofiya felt the kernel of worry begin to grow, but she would not let it show to this man. "You are as delusional as he is." She jerked her head.

Del Rue's hand rested on her forehead in an almost paternal gesture—not that her own father had done any such thing. "It really is a shame you are so strong, but never fear . . . we shall get there in the end." He nodded to Vashill, who from behind his back produced two long thin needles.

Zofiya closed her eyes and turned her head away; she would give them no screams or tears.

ELEVEN

Bargaining with a Coyote

Sorcha existed in her bubble of silence and stasis, cut off from the world and mortal cares. It was awful. The crew of the *Dominion*, even Aachon now that he had his compass, ignored her. These were people that knew her—at least a little from their time in Ulrich—and yet soon enough they regarded her as they did a piece of furniture.

Thanks to the Prince of Chioma she didn't even have the mortal discomforts of the privy to worry about. She was as perfectly preserved as a bug in amber. So on the morning of the second day, when someone new entered the cabin and sat at her side, Sorcha was hungry for company and distraction.

Straining her eyes to the right, she was able to make out the shape of a man at her side. Her brain, as always teetering on the edge of utter madness, believed for a moment that it was Merrick or Raed; her beloved and dear, come to free her from this invisible prison and punish his crew.

However when she discerned it was not, she was able after a moment to identify him as Serigala, the man who had helped carry her aboard. He was young, with blunt features that matched his rather large frame. At least, that was his physical appearance.

Cut off from her powers as she was, there were still some that remained unaffected—namely her latent Sensitive Sight, and something about this man sitting beside her set it all aflutter.

Her gaze drifted to the wound he had talked about, a dog bite he had said.

"Ah yes," Serigala rubbed at the spot on his unmarked flesh where it had been. "Quite amazing how a little salve cured that." The grin he shot her was wide, full of teeth, and not at all comforting. "I am joking of course, but let's not waste time on words—especially if they happen to get overheard."

He grabbed hold of her arm, hard, and despite her condition she felt it clamp down on her flesh like ice. She wished she had a scream to let loose, but before she could mourn that, the real world flared white and disappeared.

Sorcha blinked. She was standing on a shifting stretch of sand, and she knew this place. The kingdom of Chioma—where she had battled a geistlord masquerading as a goddess. The place she had stretched her powers too far without her Sensitive and been lost.

Slowly she raised her arm and stared at it as if it were a great prize. Movement—after so long. She squeezed her eyes shut and drew in a ragged breath, trying to calm herself.

"I wouldn't become too excited if I was you." The voice made her start and spin around. A coyote the size of a large pony stood eyeing her with sharp intelligence. It had long shaggy beige fur, the brightest green eyes she'd ever seen, a sharp muzzle and frighteningly long bone-white teeth.

Her abrupt joy at this returned freedom froze in an instant. "Where am I, Fensena?"

Yes, Sorcha knew immediately that this was no place on the mortal plane, and she even recognized the geistlord.

Certainly there were precious few of them to know, and their names were drilled into the initiates of the Order. His name stood out: the Fensena, also called the Oath Bender, the Widow Maker, the Broken Mirror. No one had seen him for a hundred years, and yet here he was standing before her.

"So generous of you to remember me." The coyote's head tilted in a frighteningly human way. "I would have thought by now mere mortal memory would have forgotten my name."

Cautiously she circled around him. She was wearing her clothes, but was stripped of weapons. "Believe me, it was written down and every initiate memorizes it faithfully."

"Very kind, I am sure." The geistlord sank down onto his haunches and watched her intently. "As to where we are . . . why, inside your mind; the plain of your inner self, if you will. Not the most elegant of settings, but it will do for my purposes."

Purposes. The way the geistlord just threw out that word made Sorcha break out into a cold sweat. It might only be an imagined one, but it felt very real. She had experienced the might of the Rossin, been humbled by his strength, and now here she was with a geistlord inside her very own mind. Her immediate reaction would have been rage, but several things held her back from that; she was still cut off from her power, and she was without Merrick.

"Yes, quite a shame he has abandoned you." The coyote's huge tongue lolled out of one corner of its mouth. "I thought you were supposed to be Bonded and all that."

He wasn't just a projection inside her mind—he was reading it too! Across the vast plain, walls suddenly erupted, shoving their way out of the sand with a staccato hiss narrowly avoiding the geistlord. The coyote leapt nimbly back, landing only feet from Sorcha. She might be immobile, but she still had her training.

The Fensena's eyes flared abruptly red, but his voice

continued on calmly enough. "Why would I want to read your mind, little pup? Everything that I need know about you I can see already." The coyote paced around her in a tight little circle.

Sorcha held her ground. She was damned well not going to run away from the creature in her own mind. Besides—where could she go? This moment in her head was the most she'd moved in long weeks. "What exactly do you think you can see?" she said, slowly and softly. It was hard not to approach this creature as she would a rabid dog.

The coyote's head tilted. "A foundling child with a broken past and a terrible future. A frightened little girl trapped in her body by something she doesn't understand. And to top it all off, you were born in for a reason that you cannot yet see."

"I do understand," she shot back. "I went too far with my runes and without my Sensitive. That is all."

The Fensena's tongue lolled out of his mouth as he considered her. "You really know nothing? How intriguing—but never mind, where you are going there are plenty of answers. I wish I could be there to see your face though."

Sorcha could feel her anger begin to boil up, and she knew that was a foolish emotion to have around a geistlord—even one that looked like a coyote. She'd always rather liked dogs of all shapes and kinds, but she was rapidly changing her mind. "You don't need to make fun of me! I am not the first Active to damage themselves without their Sensitive."

Now the coyote let out a sigh and flopped down on his haunches by her feet, his huge fluffy tail covering his paws. "That was part of it, but by now you should have recovered. That cloak that the Prince of Chioma gave you is rather getting in the way, don't you think?"

She thought of the moment that she had taken his gift—one that he said would be only temporary. Then she thought of Garil stabbing her and the result. "Are you saying without this gift I would recover? It worked fine for the Prince. He moved around perfectly well."

"There are differences. Important differences," the coyote replied enigmatically.

"Do you want it for yourself?" she blurted out as the possibility suddenly dawned on her. The image of an invulnerable geistlord was not one she wished to contemplate.

The Fensena licked his lips. "It does not work for my kind. If it had, do you not think Hatipai would have used it herself? You really are an extremely foolish Deacon!"

She may have been lying on her back for weeks on end, but her brain was still fully functional, and if there was one thing Deacons were taught it was that geists—and particularly geistlords—could not be trusted. Among all those powerful unliving creatures, the Fensena was known for being the most slippery and cunning. Now he was sitting before her offering her salvation.

It was enough to give anyone pause—even someone who had been slowly going mad inside her own brain. Yet, as much as Sorcha wanted to give him an emphatic no, another part of her craved conversation and company. "Why would you help me, a Deacon?"

The great coyote yawned, showing a huge line of fangs, and then stared at her with his once again green, implacable eyes. "There are some among my kind, that have lived peacefully in the human realm. You are most likely not taught about us in your tedious lessons, but not all geistlords live on chaos and pain."

Sorcha frowned, but did not quite believe his words. Tricks upon tricks.

A low rumble ran through the ground, a sound of the Fensena's anger transmitted even in this landscape of her mind. "Tricks I may have, but even you must see the truth of it. How else would I have survived so long without drawing the notice of your, or another, Order?"

In the last year, Sorcha's faith in the Order of the Eye

and the Fist had been strained. She had seen corruption at the highest level, and so a crack of belief opened inside her. "But you take a host like the Rossin does . . ."

"Do not speak to me of the Beast!" the coyote leapt to his feet. "I too live in the blood, but I no longer do my host harm. The most they suffer is a dog bite. I have learned to move on before the body becomes strained." The geistlord stood and circled her, his long, broad snout pressing against her waist, inhaling. "You I would not touch—but I will do you this service. And you should not think it is for my own gain."

A geistlord overcome with empathy and good-heartedness? Sorcha was not yet so far lost to madness that she would believe that. "Who is to gain then?" she asked tartly.

"There are those that would use the geists and the geistlords." As he sat before her, the great coyote's voice dripped with menace and anger that would be hard to feign. "They would take our power for their own, and break the world to make it how they want it."

A chill knot began to develop in the Deacon's stomach, though she knew that was impossible. Her stomach was somewhere completely different. "You speak of the Order of the Circle of Stars, the old Native Order."

"They have many names, but that is the one they currently wear." The Fensena got up and turned toward the distant horizon. Against the ink blue sky, Sorcha saw a line of stars pull themselves free from their fellows and form into a circle that glowed brighter and brighter. The light hurt her eyes and made the great coyote flinch away.

"It is true," he went on, "that every Order of Deacons in this world draws its power from the geists they fight. All of your runes come from our powers. What you call the Native Order would seek to take that one step further. They would harness the geists themselves. That, geistlords like myself could not allow."

Sorcha blinked. "You want me to stop them?"

The Fensena growled, low and deep and deadly. "This is my world now. The Otherside is a place of great hardship to many of my kind. I have made a place—a peaceful place—for myself here. I do not wish to see the Circle of Stars destroy it."

It was fine talk, but Sorcha was not totally taken in. She'd had more experience than most with the geistlords, yet this one did seem more capable of talking rather than destroying. "Why me?" she asked cautiously.

The canine grin flashed again, an uncomfortable lolling of tongue over razor-sharp teeth. "So many questions, but these are ones I cannot answer. Some things are forbidden to me. The real question is, do you want to live again, or remain in half death?"

Sorcha thought of the possibility matrix she, Merrick and Raed had found beneath the Mother Abbey. She could have done with one of those now. Instead, her poor scattered mind had to decide. Certainly none in the Order had been able to help her, and her oldest and dearest friend had given instruction to have her done away with. Then she had to consider that without it she was cut off from Merrick and Raed. Both would need her. Maybe it was hubris to imagine that she was that important, but she was also the most powerful Active the Order had.

The Fensena regarded her, seemingly unmoved about her decision, but she was not fooled; deep in the coyote's eyes, bright fire burned.

"You will take this mantle of impermeability from me as a favor?"

"Well, not completely—you will of course owe me one in return. Something at my own time and at my own choosing." The beast now got to its feet and stood muzzle to nose with her. She could feel his hot breath on her imaginary face. "After all, without my help you shall never be able to reach your partner, your lover or your runes in time."

"In time?" she hissed. "In time for what exactly?"

The only reply was a widening of his jaws. This then

was how it would be. Once again, she had to roll the dice and trust in her own instincts. Sorcha could only hope that someday soon she would not regret this, or end up having Merrick chide her to death.

"Do it then." She stood straight and tall, but kept her eyes open just in case. He needed no further urging. The coyote lunged forward, mouth open, teeth gleaming. And then—and then she felt his tongue on her. It was smooth and gentle at first, but then after a while he began to nip at her with the front of his teeth. That did not hurt as much as the Prince's gift turned around and did.

Sorcha was no stranger to pain, but this felt as though hooks were buried in her flesh and were being tugged reluctantly free. She clenched her jaw shut on the pain for as long as she could, but soon enough she was howling and screaming into her own mind. It had to stop, or something had to break. She hung there, suspended between life and death, broken and remade for what felt like a tormented eternity.

She went to the darkness willingly because of that.

When it finally let go of her, Sorcha's eyes flicked open and she found herself staring at the roof of the cabin aboard the *Autumn Eagle*. All she could hear was the sound of her own breathing, shaky and shallow in her ears.

She hardly dared to try to move. The possibility of disappointment was huge, and she feared it more than anything else. Then, taking hold of her tumbled thoughts and pressing them into a cohesive mass, she found her bravery once again. Sorcha turned her head and looked at the man with the coyote eyes sitting next to her. She did not need to ask him if it was gone.

In a rush of excitement she jerked herself upright in the bed. The resulting wash of sensation in her head and muscles was overwhelming, and she barely kept herself upright. Yet, she would not lie down again. Her hands, far more sinewy than she remembered, clenched onto the edges of the cot.

The Fensena smiled, still managing to be very coyote-like despite now wearing a human face. "Yes, I would take it easy for a bit. You have been protected from the worst atrophy by the Prince's gift, but you will still need to eat a great deal to regain your strength."

"The favor I owe you . . ." Sorcha croaked out, already concerned about what the geistlord would ask of her.

The coyote in man's clothing waved his hand. "Let's not be mercenary about it. The time will come when I will ask for your help." He looked her up and down with hardly concealed dismay. "However that time is definitely not right now. You have some way to go before you are of any use to anyone."

He stood. "And a little piece of advice," he said leaning in, so that once again she could feel the heat of his coyote breath on her face, "I wouldn't try any of your Deacon tricks on me . . . you are far too weak to take on a poltern let alone a geistlord."

Sorcha blinked at him, feeling her anger rise to the occasion, but also realizing that he was completely right. Banishing the Fensena would just have to wait for another time, when she had her Sensitive with her and was feeling stronger. She smiled slightly. Perhaps that would even be the favor she did him.

Taking her smile for completely the wrong thing, the man stepped back. "Good then, we get off this airship and go our own ways. You go to save the world from your own nefarious kind—and I will set off to enjoy the pleasures of the flesh." He made for the door and then, pausing, turned back. "I do hope my confidence in you is not misplaced, Mistress Deacon."

Then with that he was gone. Sorcha slumped back on her cot. Unused arms and sheer determination had only just held out long enough not to make a fool of her in front of a very dangerous beast. Now she could concentrate on doing what needed to be done: find Raed, stop the Order of the Circle of Stars, and then get back to the Mother Abbey.

After working her jaw a little, she began to gather the strength to summon Aachon to her side. She couldn't wait to see the expression on his face.

TWELVE

For Services Rendered

Merrick's dreams were a confused tumble. He held Nynnia in his arms, but she crumbled to dust, and he could not hold her together. She sifted through his fingers and was lost.

Zofiya danced away from him covered in blood and cradling the Emperor's severed head in her arms. The dead Arch Abbot, Rictun's predecessor, Hastler wrapped himself around Merrick, whispering of conspiracies and murders still unfolding. The flames of war covered the Empire and Merrick was carrying a water bucket with a hole in it. Finally, he heard Sorcha call his name, but found his mouth stitched shut so he could not call back to her.

Yes, Sorcha was calling him.

Merrick lurched upright in the magnificent bed of the Grand Duchess Zofiya and for a moment had no clue where he was. Looking around he realized morning light flooded the bedroom and sparkled on all the treasures of an Imperial sibling. Calming his breathing, he closed his eyes and put aside the residual panic of the nightmare. Then the Deacon opened his Center and felt along the Bond.

She was there. His partner, Deacon Sorcha Faris was

distant, and growing more distant by the moment, but he
could feel her once more as a presence. Wherever she was,
his Active had gotten free of the affliction that she had suffered from ever since Orinthal. Just how she had been
healed when all the best minds of the Mother Abbey's
infirmary had been left baffled remained unclear.

Merrick let out a long, slow sigh of relief, and closed his
eyes. It was true, he still felt guilty for not being there, and
he was sure Sorcha was annoyed he was not, but at least he
knew she lived. However, if she lived, she would find her
way back to him. Deacon Faris was many things, but helpless was not one of them.

Hurry back. We need you. He sent that along the Bond,
but the distance was too great for him to tell if she heard
him or not. For a moment he sat poised, waiting for a
response, but was not surprised when there was none. Even
if she had heard his message she was probably not able to
send one in return. There were a few things Sensitives
always remained better at: diplomacy and messages were
merely two.

The young Deacon pushed aside the fluttering sails of
the canopy, and opened his eyes for the second time. He
was ill equipped to be meeting this very important day,
being both sleep deprived, and uncertain how the Grand
Duchess would treat him.

As it turned out, he did not have to worry that Zofiya
would treat him as a plaything or a marriage prospect,
because she simply wasn't there. Merrick laid his hand on
the spot where she had collapsed after their exertions of the
previous night: it was cold.

As a Grand Duchess she undoubtedly had many duties
to attend: with the Imperial Guard, and her brother. Yet, he
could not help being a little disappointed that she had not
lingered. It would have been very pleasant to wake to her
touch, and steal a few more kisses before the serious business of the day began.

As Merrick opened his Center once again, and sent it

questing through the corridors for Zofiya, he found some-thing else interesting. A large group of Imperial Guards was striding down the halls. They were accompanied by the Emperor himself, so something was surely afoot. It was not his concern, but it would be something that his new lover should be aware of.

With effortless ease, Merrick opened his Center wider and let it travel the length of the palace to find her. It dived down to the dungeons and the kitchens where people toiled. It scampered through the rooms of the powerful and aristocratic where they lay recovering from a surplus of wine. It twined through the ballrooms and card rooms that were being tidied by tired servants. Every man, woman and beast in the palace of Vermillion was accounted for.

About the time that a frown creased Merrick's brow, at the exact moment he realized he could not sense the Grand Duchess anywhere in the palace, that was when the group of armed Imperial Guards burst through the privy chamber and charged into the bedroom itself. At their head was indeed the Emperor Kaleva of Arkaym himself. Unlike many who he had entertained the previous night, there was not a hair out of place on his dark head. He was dressed in the white uniform and sash that he wore when at state occasions—though why, was impossible to say. The other thing he wore was a very angry face.

Merrick was not at all used to the situation. He was more adept at helping rid the world of geists than at being caught in a young woman's bedroom by her very angry brother. However why the Emperor would be so furious was inexplicable—no one could think the Grand Duchess a virgin; she'd taken other lovers in the Court before.

However, any more ruminations on exactly what was happening were cut short when the Emperor pointed at Merrick. "Seize this traitor!"

The Deacon forgot to breathe. Perhaps he was still enmeshed in those extraordinarily strange dreams? No

Emperor or King could possibly ever call one of the Order a traitor. Rictun's mad laughter as he summoned the Murashev was not a recollection he wanted to have at this moment. Yet that was the only example he could think of.

Merrick didn't know how to react—however he was sure of one thing—he did not want to face his Emperor with not a stitch on. Quickly, before the Imperial Guards could reach him, the Deacon slipped into his trousers. "Your Imperial Majesty," he began, but got no further.

"Bind his tongue," the Emperor barked, "and then bring me his Strop!"

Two burly guards grabbed hold of Merrick and pinned him facedown on the bed before he could protest further. Another man appeared and what he carried made the young Deacon begin to struggle. In the old days, when a Deacon went mad and his brethren felt he might harm the innocent, a device called a brank was used. It was a large metal mask, with eyeholes cut out, and a strap underneath to prevent its removal. However its worst feature was a curving line of metal that was meant to run from each side of the prisoner's mouth and hold their tongue still. Rows of spikes meant that any who attempted to talk paid a bloody price for it. To make it extra secure for the containment of a Deacon, a circle of weirstones was embedded around the crown.

They must have had to bring that from the palace dungeons, because he had not seen one except in a history book. He'd never thought to see one, and now that he had, the Deacon wished it very much gone.

It might not have been very dignified, but Merrick was not going to have his chance to talk to his Emperor before being taken away. Twisting, he managed to land a blow between the legs of the guard to his left, and then swung around, wriggling free of the other.

He only managed another "Your Imperial Majesty" before reinforcement guards surged forward and brought

him crashing to the floor. Primitive instincts kicked in, and
the Deacon still tried his best to get free, despite the pum-
meling he took for it.

It was a game he couldn't win, and eventually with a
great deal of swearing and hair yanking from the guards,
they managed to manhandle the brank around Merrick's
head. They jammed it on with such force that it cracked the
corners of his mouth and raked his tongue. The Deacon
gagged on his own blood, while struggling to retain his
consciousness. He could see only the carpet in front of him
and a lined mass of Imperial Guardsmen feet. This was
one terrible nightmare. This had to be what this was.

One more kick to his side rather destroyed that hope.
No, it was real, and he was bound. Alone. Cut off from that
which mattered most to him.

Out of the corner of one straining eye, he spotted a
guard gingerly rifling through his bag lying on one of Zofiya's velvet chairs. The investigator was clever enough not
to pick up the Strop directly when he found it. Instead,
using a pair of long-handled pliers, the guard pulled out the
thick strip of leather, decorated with Merrick's sigil and the
Runes of Sight, and placed it in a silver tin. This too was
studded with weirstones.

They had certainly come prepared. He had been anything but. Merrick could have kicked himself for underes-
timating del Rue, but surely the Mother Abbey would sort
this out. Bedding a Grand Duchess was against no Imperial ruling or Order stricture. He had done nothing wrong.

The guards, now assured that he was neutralized, bound
his hands behind his back, and hauled him to his feet. The
Emperor still looked furious. "Where is she?"

Merrick shook his head to clear it, but stripped of his
Sight and his voice, he was befuddled. How did the Emperor
expect him to answer with the brank on? This was utter
madness.

Then the enormity of what the Emperor had asked settled over him, and he was able to connect it with the dis-

covery he had made just as they burst into the bedchamber. Zofiya was missing.

Now this situation became more than just a ridiculous reaction to his bedding a Grand Duchess. It became something far more sinister. Despite the pain it caused him he managed a muffled, "I don't know!" Then gulped back the mouthful of blood that was the result.

The Emperor's hands balled into fists. Merrick had never seen this side of his ruler before. It was frightening to see him so unhinged. "We all saw one of you damned Deacons with her, phasing through the wall. You took her, and by the time my torturers—"

"Your Imperial Majesty, I am here as requested." Yvril Mournling, Presbyter of the Sensitives, stood in the doorway of the bedroom, his hands folded into the sleeves of his green cloak. His face was as serene as if he were having tea with Kaleva rather than interrupting him threatening one of his fellow Brothers.

Mournling's gray eyes flicked over the brank and the wide-eyed Merrick trapped within it, but he did not flinch.

"I most certainly did not request your presence," the Emperor growled. "This man is involved in the disappearance of my royal sister, and I will have answers."

"This Deacon," Mournling emphasized, not moving an inch, "looks currently unable to answer any questions. Also, the Mother Abbey is the only one equipped to deal with his interrogation."

"And how," Kaleva said, his eyes darting around the room, "did you come to arrive here so quickly since no one sent for you?"

The Presbyter remained unmoved by the tone of his Emperor's voice. "We are Sensitives, Your Imperial Majesty. He is our brother and our responsibility—as when we first set out with you from Delmaire." It was so close to a slap in the face that Merrick could scarcely believe it. The Order of the Eye and the Fist swore an oath to the Emperor himself, and it was generally accepted they were part of his government. Deacons could requisition airships, command troops and enter and leave the palace as they saw fit.

After the Native Order was thought to have been destroyed, the geists came back. Everyone knew that without the new Order, Arkaym would have been overrun with the unliving and impossible for the Emperor or anyone else to rule effectively. Before their arrival with Kaleva the once-unified continent had devolved into petty principalities on the verge of losing control. Trade had dried up, and that had been what forced Princes to send for a new leader from Delmaire.

Stunned and injured as he was, Merrick suddenly saw how precarious a thing the relationship between the Emperor and his Order was. It looked vulnerable as it never had before, and as he swallowed blood he thought of the man that called himself del Rue whispering into Kaleva's ear for all that time. He began to realize the damage that could be done with words—far more than if the Order of the Circle of Stars had stormed the Abbey with Gauntlets blazing.

Perhaps Zofiya's disappearance was the kind of punctuation mark del Rue needed with the Emperor.

Both men waited as still as statues: the representative of an Order that had brought Arkaym back from chaos, and the Emperor who had been called from Delmaire to rule it.

A tiny muscle twitched in the Emperor's jaw, but finally he spat out, "Very well, take him before your Council—for now—but my Guards will escort you back to your Abbey. I will expect your Arch Abbot to appear before me before midday."

Merrick found himself yanked to his feet and bundled from the room. Mournling led the way, his hands still tucked in his sleeves. The Emperor could be heard behind them, yelling at the remains of his Guard. Despite Zofiya's voiced concerns that her brother had been pulling away from her recently, he sounded quite unhinged.

Still the fact was the Grand Duchess was gone, and if

the Emperor had him killed, Merrick would never be able
to find her and get her back. He'd lost far too many women
in his young life. He certainly was not going to lose another
one. First things first; he had to get out of this dangerous
situation.

The young Deacon was still in the brank, and Mournling was not making any attempt to have it removed. Merrick kept his head bowed, and tried to hold his tongue flat
enough that it didn't hurt.

They passed through the hallways, which were lined
with members of the Court. He didn't need his Sensitivity
to tell him what they were thinking. Their pale faces, and
the way they wouldn't look directly at him said quite
enough. Maybe it was a good thing Sorcha was gone.

They filed out of the palace, and through the courtyard,
standing in two silent rows, were twenty pairs of Deacons.
The line of grim hooded figures awaiting him made
Merrick more fearful than he had been back before the
Emperor. The Order was not without punishments of its
own.

The Imperial Guards handed the young Deacon over to
his brethren, and just as quietly they turned and took him
from the palace grounds. Presbyter Mournling was at his
side, and now apparently felt free to talk. "The brank," he
spoke softly to Merrick, not turning his head to address
him, "is an unfortunate device, but we dare not remove it
until we reach the Mother Abbey. You should be lucky that
the Emperor's Sensitive was watching the ether so closely
last night. For now, please try your best not to talk, Deacon
Chambers."

They marched on farther downhill from the palace and
the short distance back to the home of their Order. Merrick
felt as if he were in the middle of an armed escort, though
none of his fellow Deacons were actually carrying any
weapons. It was a most odd sensation. As they approached
the gates, he glanced up and noticed that for the first time
ever there were hooded shapes also lining the walls.

The Mother Abbey was built within a great wall which
had a portcullis and gates, but it was only manned at the
entry—well, it had been. It looked like things had changed
since he had left last night. Usually, even at the gate it was
lay Brothers that took sentry duty. However those above
were not in the gray. It looked like there would be no Feed-
ing of the Poor today. That kindly ritual would have to
wait. This all had to be on his account.

Merrick's heart sank at seeing that, and he began to see
the scope of what had happened in such a short time. He
should perhaps have gone after Sorcha after all. Perhaps
del Rue would not have moved so quickly if he hadn't been
there. Perhaps if a Deacon had not been in the Grand Duchess' bed he would have taken more time to reveal his plan.

"You are beginning to see," Mournling continued, "the
consequences of what you have done, but you cannot possibly imagine them all. The Emperor has sent his Deacons
back to us. For the first time since setting foot in Arkaym,
Kaleva is without our protection."

Worse and worse. Merrick couldn't believe it was only
half a day since he'd left the Mother Abbey. As he entered
it again the angry stares and whispered comments followed
him. At that moment he was almost glad not to be able to
see into the minds of his fellow Deacons, or taste their contempt. All of them wore their hoods up, which mostly hid
their faces and turned them into a rank of strangers. Except
for one. Deacon Garil Reeceson stood to the rear of the
crowd by the gate. His face was serious, but not angry.
They shared more than just the Order and a history with
Sorcha. Maybe he had come to make sure Merrick would
not use his wild talent on the Deacons, or maybe he was
there merely to give support. Merrick was not afforded the
opportunity to find out.

"Take him to the Silence Room," Mournling ordered
once the gate was fastened. "Remove the brank once he is
there."

He stood before Merrick and looked at him; an odd

mixture of compassion and distaste in his gray eyes. "The Presbyterial Council is in urgent session, and then Rictun will attend the Emperor. For now, this is the best I can do for you."

Then his hand clamped down on Merrick's shoulder as he repeated the mantra of the Sensitive, "See deep, fear nothing." It was almost cruel to say such a thing, since both were impossible right now.

His fellow Deacons were however not unkind to him as they took him into the Devotional. The soaring walls, great vaulted ceilings and awe-inspiring stained glass windows had never felt anything but beautiful to him before this. Now, he feared where his colleagues were taking him.

Once, during his time in the novitiate, he and his class had been brought to the Silence Room. It had partly been to shatter any rumors and partly to serve as a warning. It was the Deacon equivalent of a geist horror story, since Deacons were not encouraged to fear the undead. Merrick had come late to the Order, but it had still frightened him.

All but two pairs of his escorts left him at the simple wooden door in the asp of the Devotional. One of the Actives removed a silver key etched with unfamiliar runes from her robe, and unlocked the door. When she turned and glanced at Merrick he was finally able to recognize her.

"Ofrior," Merrick gasped out, before the brank reminded him he was not yet free of it. The pain had subsided to a dull burn, yet ranking his tongue against the spikes brought fresh waves of it back.

His friend from the novitiate winced, and held up her hand to the other Deacons about them. She glanced down into the darkness behind the open door and shook her head, then pulled him aside a little. While she dabbed gingerly at the fresh blood with her cloak sleeve, Ofrior Karli whispered to him. "Be strong, Merrick. The Abbey is in an uproar, but I heard old Mournling talking with Troupe just before we left. They said they have to be sure—it is their duty to keep the Emperor safe."

"Ofrior!" Vermon, her Sensitive, gestured toward the door. "Now is not the time to disobey the Council." He shot a slightly ashamed look in Merrick's direction. "Sorry."

The young Deacon couldn't really say anything in reply, but he just nodded and gently pushed Ofrior's hands away from his mouth. That she had used the sleeve of her own cloak to do it was enough kindness to get him through this.

However she would not go away. Her green eyes were wide, and she grabbed his shoulders and pulled him tight. "He also said something about the Pattern. I don't know what that means Merrick, but he sounded . . . he sounded scared." The two friends stared at each other for a moment.

The Pattern was a phrase he had never heard before, though he suspected he'd soon have ample time to mull it over.

Then he found himself whirled around. Vermon had lit a lantern and led the way down the spiral stairs down into the earth. Ofrior kept her hand on Merrick's shoulder, which was just as well; with the brank still clamped around his face it was impossible for him to tilt his head down to see the steps. He would have stumbled and fallen several times without her assistance.

When they reached the bottom there were the rows of cells; four in all and every one empty. For the moment. They looked similar to any cell that might be found at the palace or in the office of the sheriff, except for one thing, the lining of the walls. Tiny slivers of weirstones were embedded in the stone of the walls, gleaming blue and beautiful. It was an expensive thing to do to control a Deacon—however the cell would be far more pleasant than the Emperor's barbaric methods.

As carefully as they could Ofrior and Vermon took the brank off him. Merrick's tongue was swollen and bleeding, and the corners of his mouth were not much better. Aside from the physical pain, he was still reeling from shock. He had no Strop. He was for all intents and purposes a normal citizen of the Empire—at least for his time down here.

"It won't be long," Ofrior said, as she guided him forward into the cell. That was the best she could offer as she first slid the bars shut and then pressed her hands against the weirstones.

That was when Merrick howled. He'd thought the brank was terrible, but in fact the room was worse. Instead of containing his powers, it flowed over them and ripped them from him. It was as if every nerve ending was set aflame, burning and cutting him to the bone. He lay on the floor, twitching and wide-eyed for a long time. Long after the other Deacons had left the room.

It took many hours for him to become used to the sensation of quiet that was buried in him. Eventually, he levered himself off the floor and made it to the hard bed of stone, covered with a thin blanket. Merrick sat there shivering, and tried to hold on to his sanity. The Bond was gone, the ever-present drone of life around him was gone, and most of all his awareness of self was badly bruised.

However, with all that extra noise gone, Merrick became aware of something else. A whisper in the corner of his mind, one that he'd been too busy to ever really notice.

And as he became slowly aware of it, the Deacon came to the horrifying conclusion that del Rue had been right. Beneath the Priory in Ulrich, on his first mission with Sorcha, he had taken a darkling into his soul. It had been a decision made in a desperate moment, and it had been instrumental in uncovering the rot in the town, but it had also exposed him to a little sliver of the undead.

Now, all alone in the Silence Room, she could be heard. A thin whisper of a life lost to conspiracy and treachery. One who had been taken by the machinations of the Order of the Circle of Stars.

He longed for his other partner. His living one.

"Sorcha," he whispered into the silence, "I need you."

THIRTEEN

Dropping from the Clouds

Sorcha wished she could have recorded in some way the expression on Aachon's face when he entered the cabin to find her sitting up—albeit shakily—on her bed. He could not have looked more surprised if he had walked in to find Raed there.

Calling his name had quite taken all Sorcha's strength, and she had to make several urgent gestures for water, before the first mate came back to himself enough to understand. He had plenty of questions, but she decided that despite his loyalty to her lover, he had also participated in kidnapping her from the Mother Abbey, and that meant he needn't be privy to everything that had happened. So she kept quiet about the geistlord who had removed the cloak. Instead she made up a tale about how getting away from the Mother Abbey had revived her. Aachon was no great lover of the Order and swallowed the lie easily. It was a performance worthy of a Sensitive, and one she did not think the Fensena would interfere with.

In fact, the next morning after her revival, it was found that Serigala had disappeared. Even though the *Autumn Eagle* was searched thoroughly, he could not be located. The other crew whispered that he must have come down with a fever from the dog bite, and fallen overboard. However it was Lepzig who pointed out that one of the landing ropes was unwound, though how anyone could survive a fall into tall jungle was impossible to imagine. Sorcha remained silent on Serigala, but then why would they suspect a Deacon who had just climbed out of a coma would know anything?

The next few days were spent trying to get used to walking again. In a normal patient, such as she had seen many times in the infirmary, this process would have meant months of gradually easing herself back to normality. However, her limbs had not atrophied at all, though she had lost some weight and had to double her belt around her waist to keep her pants up.

Captain Quent Lepzig took time from his duties where he could, and helped Sorcha circumnavigate the airship holding on to his arm. Aachon, despite using the Deacon's abilities to direct their course, seemed unwilling to spend time with her. Sorcha suspected something within him was warning of the unnatural nature of her recovery. He was not, however, a fully trained member of the Order and so his concerns remained unconfirmed.

Sorcha would work to keep it that way.

So instead she started off dragging her arm over the shoulder of the surprisingly strong captain, and took her exercise like a good little recovering invalid. In another day, she had moved to just holding on to the crook of his arm. While they walked, the two of them talked, and despite their age difference and their different professions, it was a pleasant way to spend the time. Captain Lepzig, it turned out, was quite the wit, and several times had Sorcha in hysterics with his dry humor. One would never have suspected it from a member of the Imperial Fleet.

Three days after her recovery, Sorcha was making another tour of the *Autumn Eagle*, first thing in the morning. It was almost becoming a habit.

Sorcha no longer needed Lepzig to hold her up. He merely hovered nearby just in case she should fall. The Deacon would not normally have liked such mothering, but the captain was a kind man, and it would have been humiliating to fall on her face.

However as she felt strength returning to her legs, she was also feeling her concerns mount. Having successfully managed to shove aside the fact she owed a favor to a geist-lord, she began to think of finding Raed and bringing him home. Wherever that might be.

She missed him. Standing upright, she could face that. She had missed Raed Syndar Rossin in all those months, and now she wanted nothing more than to see him again. Her memory kept reminding her how good his skin on hers had felt, how his smile made her feel. When she found him, she would not let him out of her sight again—no matter what the Rossin or the Order did.

Sorcha leaned on the gunwales and smiled. The land below was hidden by a mass of thick white clouds, and for some reason this made her unreasonably optimistic. In this stillness, she heard voices talking beyond the stack of barrels on the deck. It irritated her for a moment, until she recognized the voice of Captain Lepzig and his first mate.

Haltingly, she walked toward the voice, ready to reveal herself and share how much she was enjoying the day sailing above the skies, until she heard the tone in his voice and the word he whispered. "War."

The Deacon stopped, the moment of joy draining away. Instead of revealing herself, she hitched herself into the shadows, folding her cloak about her.

"Surely not, Captain . . ." Sorcha could see the first mate of the *Autumn Eagle*'s head flicking around, but she was good at hiding when she had to be.

From her position she observed Lepzig's magnificent mustache ruffled by the breeze. "Think about it, Melso. You can almost feel it in the air."

The first mate was silent a moment and then muttered,

"I did find it mighty strange when we hailed the *Sunrise Dove* last week, and she didn't reply to our signal. We were at the same altitude even."

Sorcha glanced forward to where great lanterns with shutters were hung. Next to them, two large scarlet flags would take care of communication during the day. An Imperial Airship not communicating with another—strange but not a reason to think of war. She wondered if all this lonely toing and froing around the continent was getting to Captain Lepzig and his crew.

Lepzig however nodded. "And think of what we've been ordered to do of late. Shoring up the garrisons, bringing in troops—and all the time not to speak of it to anyone."

Now he really had Sorcha's attention. Troop movements could only mean that the Emperor was feeling vulnerable. The Princes in the most isolated kingdoms were always prone to delusions of grandeur. They grew complacent far from Vermillion, and forgot the benefits of the Empire in their desire to keep all the wealth of their area. Also, it helped that the Deacons had brought more stability to Arkaym. They were also quick to forget how it had been before the Order came with the Emperor. They might even labor under the assumption that the geists would never come back.

The Empire could not afford a civil war. It was something that the geists would take full advantage of—not to mention, the spilling of blood could bring on a new wave of undead activity.

While she pondered that, Lepzig tugged his first mate closer. "The soldiers weren't nearly as tight lipped though . . . were they?"

Melso shook his head slowly. "No, they were all far too young to keep secrets; all too eager to tell anyone that would listen how important they were. Still, I confess, I thought it was all just talk."

Sorcha thought of the eager young men in the Imperial Guard she'd been in charge of briefly in Vermillion. Where were they now? She'd seen no war herself, but she'd studied the past ones enough. The outcomes had been terrible—not just in terms of lives lost, but also in numbers of geists created.

She pressed a hand over her forehead. As if they needed more troubles. If what Merrick had talked about all those long nights in the infirmary were right, then the Order of the Circle of Stars could have something to do with it. They certainly would want revenge, and bringing down the Empire would give them ample opportunity.

"Then think of this Deacon business," Lepzig continued. "What are they doing heading west in the dead of night?"

"Sorcha?" Aachon's voice boomed somewhere farther aft, and she just about leapt out of her hiding place. He wasn't actually visible, just shouting for her, but immediately the captain and first mate ended their discussion and went back into the belly of the ship.

With a sigh, Sorcha moved out of the shadows, and caught hold of some nearby rigging. Her legs felt like string, and her head was pounding with effort.

At last Aachon appeared. When his gaze fell on her, she knew immediately that he wanted something from her. The usual something.

Raising her hands in surrender, she gestured him over. "Your compass awaits," she said sweetly.

The large man's eyebrow shot up, but he withdrew the small weirstone from his pocket. As he swung it on the chain over her, she dared a further comment. "You know you can just ask me now which direction to go."

He glared at her.

"Do you think I would steer you wrong then?"

Having ascertained the westward pull of the stone, Aachon tucked it away and fixed her with a dark look. "I lost a crew member in mysterious circumstances around you, Deacon Faris, so I am double-checking everything."

"You have my word I had nothing to do with that." It

wasn't a lie, though she would have lied if needed. She tilted her head and regarded him. "You don't much like me do you, Aachon?"

"I don't know you well enough to say," came his gruff reply. "I only know that things seem to happen when you are about. Sea monsters rise, deadly geistlords appear and my prince is constantly in danger."

Sorcha appreciated his loyalty to Raed, but she was feeling more than a little on edge. Shoving back her cloak, so that he could see her Gauntlets tucked into her belt, she leaned forward. "It is a dangerous world—you know that as well as I. I've been trapped in my own body for months, and your Prince has been lost for that long. That isn't my doing either."

"Danger follows you—"

Sorcha didn't let him get any further. She surged forward and grabbed Aachon by his collar. Where the strength to thrust him back against the gunwales came from was an utter mystery, but she did it. Holding him, back arched over the void, she put her face only an inch from his. "Danger follows Raed too. None of us are saints in this, but I want you to know something . . ." She released him enough so that he would be able to tell she wasn't about to shove him to his death. "I love him."

For a moment they stood toe-to-toe. Aachon's dark eyes searched her face, no doubt trying to find a lie etched there. Finally, he shook his head like a wounded bear, and slid away from her, raising his hands.

Now Sorcha recalled Garil's words to him. Perhaps nearly dangling the first mate of the *Dominion* over the edge of the ship had not been a good choice to convince him of her intentions.

Still, she was surprised when Aachon began to laugh. It was a low deep sound that he appeared reluctant to let loose. "I do believe I have never heard of a Deacon in love," he gasped.

It was a ridiculous comment for anyone to make, but

Sorcha shook her head. "You nearly went into the Order, you know it is possible." She fixed him with a sharp look of her own, "You loved Garil."

The big man's laughter stopped. "Yes, yes I did."

What Sorcha didn't share was the fact that she didn't even know if she would still technically be called a Deacon. She'd left her partner behind, and was most likely considered dead. She still had her cloak and her Gauntlets, but that was about it.

She could feel the Bond with Merrick, a faint tugging on her conscience from the east, but he and the Mother Abbey seemed a long way off. She missed him and his sensible ways. Still, he was safer behind her than ahead where she was going. Ahead was a stronger tug on her. The Bond with Raed, leading her on like a lodestone.

As if in echo to her thoughts Aachon muttered, "Love seems a long way off in this world." He was very melancholy for one with such a tough appearance, and Sorcha wondered if that was because of what he had seen in his travels.

The two of them slid down the gunwales, and sat on the deck in silence for a while, watching the sun flicker above them. It was beautiful and serene—at least for a moment.

"He's not dead," Sorcha eventually offered. "Whatever mess Raed has got himself into, I know he is not dead."

"But war is stirring." Aachon's words on the heels of Lepzig's made her shudder, but she did not offer comment. Even when he got to his feet and looked down at her. "Come what may, we will find the Prince and the rest will fall where it must." With that he turned and left her.

It was another two days later that they finally saw Phia off the starboard side of the *Autumn Eagle*. They arrived just as evening was taking over from day and a full moon was beginning to rise. Even in the evening, it was a beautiful-looking town with tiled roofs, and the buildings stacked down toward a deep blue black lake. Aachon and the rest of Raed's crew came up behind Sorcha. The first mate moved forward and joined her, looking toward the city.

"What do you know of Phia?" he asked, his hand clenching on the rigging.

Sorcha shrugged. "Not a thing. Merrick would have been the one to ask, and he would give you an encyclopedia's worth of an answer." She tried to sound offhand about it, but even saying his name gave her a pang. It hadn't even been a year, but she had come to rely on him, and being separated from her partner felt unnatural. She'd lost him for a time in Orinthal, and she hated this even more.

Sorcha turned her face east, and even though she knew he couldn't possibly hear her at this distance she tried. *I'll be back soon. Look after yourself.*

Then she faced Aachon. "Now we find Raed, and for that I will need your help." At the far end of the lake was a huge, strangely windowless fortress. She'd seen enough palaces of Princes that she could spot one immediately, however this one gave her a chill. It was typical of Raed that he would bring her to this sort of place. He really was the most awkward, dangerous man. Unfortunately he was also charming and good-hearted. Still, when she saw him again, she was going to certainly have words with him— among other things.

She cleared her throat, and focused her thoughts on what needed to be done. "I can tell he is in that direction, but I will need you to act as my Sensitive." The words were almost choked out, because just one year earlier she would have never imagined saying such a thing. Her loathing for weirstones was legendary among the other Deacons, and she'd often complained to Merrick about the weak minds and foolishness of those that wielded them. How he would have laughed if he'd been standing on the deck of the *Autumn Eagle* right now.

The tall first mate inclined his head, gestured for the crew to stay back, and withdrew his weirstone from the bag hanging from his belt. Now that she understood Aachon's training within the Order, Sorcha felt a little better about him handling it—but she was not going to tell him that.

Captain Lepzig strode up behind them. "What are your orders, Deacon?"

Sorcha took a breath. Now was the moment she wished she knew something of Phia, because there could be repercussions. "Take us in close to the fortress. I want to have a look at it."

Lepzig didn't question, he snapped a salute and returned to the bridge. As the *Autumn Eagle* turned into the wind and the engines began to spin the propellers, Sorcha opened her Center. She'd formed a Bond with Merrick and even Raed with ease, but she was not willing to do that with Aachon. Instead, she would use the weirstone to enhance her own nascent Sensitivity. It was dangerous and tricky, but there was nothing left but to do it.

With eyes half-lidded she whispered, "Open the stone."

Holding it in the space between them, Aachon did so. Weirstone power was something Sorcha had never sampled before. She was not one of the Deacons who had ever worked with them, and it was so strange that she was knocked back, distracted for a moment. Whereas Merrick was warmth and gentleness, like smooth cream over her own sharp characteristics, this tasted almost medicinal. It contained not an ounce of human emotion or connection—which was the thing that made the Bond. She took another breath, unclenched her hands and reached out for the stone again.

Underneath the chill indifference of it was a well of power. Touching it, Sorcha realized why those who used them were so drawn to them; the power was clean like a river from a glacier. It was totally without the complications of a partner, but then it was also not as deep a well of strength either.

"Are you all right?" Aachon's voice seemed like it was coming from a great distance, and it took some time for her to find her voice.

Her tongue seemed to be stuck to the roof of her mouth, but she managed to mumble, "Yes. Fine."

"Then look for the Prince," Aachon snapped in return. He'd probably forgotten about the first time he reached for a weirstone's power.

Still, Sorcha managed to ignore his rudeness. She turned her Center away from the *Autumn Eagle* and toward the fortress of the Shin. To her altered Sight, it was like looking into a cube cut from the night itself. A window into nothingness. The only thing she could discern was the Bond disappearing into it.

The airship circled low over the fortress, so that she could pick out the glow of people standing on the parapets, but apart from that she could not see beyond the walls. She felt sick to her stomach just looking at it.

Aachon grabbed hold of her arm as it seemed she might topple. She shook him off. "I can't see past the stone walls. It must have its own cantrip defenses. We're going to have to get in somehow."

She let go of the weirstone power and sagged back against the gunwales with a shudder. The rest of the crew shuffled their feet.

"What now Aachon?" one of them asked, but she could not focus on who it was who spoke. She was struggling to reel in her Center. Still, she did not like that they were asking the first mate and not her. Sadly Raed's crew had completely forgotten anything like real discipline.

"Now"—Sorcha heard the dark tone in Aachon's voice—"we go and get our captain back."

Recovering herself a little, the Deacon smiled. It would be good to do that. Just as long as she could keep her feet, everything would be fine.

In the dark and silence Merrick woke. He had ceased to be able to tell what time of day it was. He couldn't even be sure whether it was day or night beyond the stone walls.

He thought of Zofiya and wondered if she was dead or alive.

He knew he should have been thinking about Sorcha and where she might be, or del Rue and what he was up to, but the Grand Duchess' wide eyes and smile kept coming to him. It seemed impossible that she had been taken. Merrick had only ever known one person that was as ruthlessly efficient and competent as the Grand Duchess in his time, and that was his partner. Yet in one season he had seen his partner laid low with a mysterious illness and now Zofiya taken.

He sighed and rolled awkwardly onto his back. He was not a broad man, but even to him the bunk was incredibly narrow. They had not built the Silence Room for comfort.

The strangeness of the place was starting to get to him. For the longest time he thought he heard a voice repeating the word "Ratimana" over and over. What it meant was impossible to say. It was strange what the mind could conjure up when left to its own devices.

So he stared up into the blackness and thought dreary thoughts. It felt like from the first moment he'd stepped out of the initiate and become a fully functioning Sensitive, the Order had been under attack. The Murashev had tried to destroy Vermillion, and now he was certain that Arch Abbot Hastler had been working with the Circle of Stars. Hatipai had tried to return to the world, and he had hard evidence that they'd aided the false goddess there too. Now one of their number was in the Imperial Palace, spreading poison and arranging for the Grand Duchess to disappear.

"I have to get out of here," Merrick said aloud. It was mostly to hear the sound of his own voice before he went mad—however once he had let the words out, he wished he had not. The room ate his words. No echo, no sound reached his ears. It was a horrible effect that gave him chills.

He decided immediately that he would keep his thoughts to himself.

However, they kept rolling around to Zofiya. It was maddening not knowing if she was dead or alive. Surely they would have come down and fetched him if she had been found murdered. That sort of deed would demand immediate retribution from the Emperor, and even the Presbyterial Council would not be able to stop him.

Merrick struck that eventuality off his list. They had not come for him, therefore Zofiya must still be missing. And if she was missing, then she was of some use to the Circle of Stars. The Sensitive ground his teeth together. One fact kept rising to the surface. She was the second in line to the throne.

When the King of Delmaire had sent one of his spare sons to rule over Arkaym, the deal had been that his unwanted sister went with him, and should Kaleva produce no heirs . . .

The young Deacon swallowed hard as he considered the implications of that. Implications that also included him. By the Bones! What if he'd gotten the Grand Duchess pregnant?

That thought made Merrick sit bolt upright in his narrow, mean-spirited bed. All the other quandaries paled in comparison to that one. No, no, Zofiya had been no maid. She would have taken the powders to keep that eventuality from occurring. Still . . . he had slept with the Emperor's sister.

He would see her again. If the Circle of Stars had her, and thought she was useful enough to keep, then there would be a way to get her back.

Only the darkling in his head whispered to him.

You could not save Nynnia. You could not protect her.

The idea that the same thing could happen to Zofiya was too horrible to contemplate—and not just for the Empire. Despite all his control and all his training, the thought chased around in the back of his brain, and would not let him sleep for the longest time.

FOURTEEN

Entering the Nest

"There is always a way in to a fortress," Aachon muttered to Sorcha as they tramped through the thick, humid night-time jungle, with only the light of his weirstone held aloft to guide them. "You only have to think about the needs of the place. Food, water, effluent . . ."

Sorcha was listening to him, but mostly concentrating on keeping upright. She supposed that she should be glad that her legs were still working. The *Autumn Eagle* had circled into the wild a bit, and let them down via rope ladder. It had been a relief that Captain Lepzig did not argue with the instructions to avoid the Imperial Airship port. Seemingly something about that strange fortress stilled any concerns about protocol he might have had. Sorcha shared his unease about the fortress.

"It just depends how desperate you are to get in," Aachon went on talking, pointing to the towering destination beneath the full-bellied moon that they could glimpse through the rare breaks in the trees. "Have you noticed something about this palace?"

Sorcha wiped sweat out of her eyes and glared at it,

while the half dozen crew members walked around her not wanting to engage in any extraneous conversations. "It looks bloody impregnable."

"You think that's what the lack of windows says?" Aachon laughed. "It doesn't make for a welcoming appearance, but I don't think it is for the benefit of outsiders. I think it is to make the inhabitants happy." He swung a machete, knocking down a section of bamboo.

"They must be very strange inhabitants," Sorcha grumbled as they moved on again.

"The west is very strange," Aachon agreed, battering at the swarming mosquitoes with little effect.

They went on a little farther before she could take no more. The first mate obviously knew something, and their link through the weirstone was giving her no clue what that might be. It was frustrating, because with Merrick she wouldn't have had to ask. "Aachon, if you have information about what we're going into then I would appreciate you sharing it with me."

The big man shrugged. "I don't know much about this kingdom except a few things: it is far from the center of the Empire, it has fewer Deacons than anywhere else, and the land is wild. The stories of this land are full of danger."

Sorcha pressed her lips together. The man was infuriating, and it was no wonder he had not been able to continue in the Order if this was how he was prepared to share. "Such as?" she urged.

"Blood. The west is soaked in blood they say. And there are rumors of rituals and creatures that dine upon it."

Sorcha shook her head. Residing in Vermillion there was a tendency to think the whole of the Empire was like the city, but the truth was the capital was the most civilized place on the continent. It had the most Deacons and was therefore the most free of geists. It was important—but hard—to remember that vast tracts of Kaleva's dominion were wild and untamed.

"Who do you know that would build a fortress without

windows?" Aachon tilted his head and regarded her from under his shaggy eyebrows.

She pondered that question, while staggering after the crew members ahead. Her training was extensive, and she ran through the different geists it could possibly be, but none were quite right. There were plenty of undead that preferred the dark, but most were simple, hungry beings that would not have the control needed to build a whole fortress.

"I can't think of any, but—" She stopped suddenly, as she made the connection. "You mean not a geist . . . a geistlord?"

Aachon nodded somberly.

"But this is the capital of the province? A geistlord for a Prince?"

"A Princess in fact," Aachon corrected her. The first mate turned and raised one eyebrow in her direction. "From your experience in Chioma is that so hard to believe?"

The recollection of the Prince, willing to die for his people, yet part geistlord, gave her a pang. She had been struck by him and his tragic fate. "He was not a geistlord," she snapped.

"As near as makes no good."

Sorcha swallowed a response and wished once again Merrick was at her side. She began wondering about the Abbey here in Phia. It certainly couldn't survive with a geistlord so near—not unless it was corrupt. She'd seen far too many of those kind of outposts of the Order lately, when even just a year ago she'd wouldn't have thought there was one.

"I am beginning to wonder what the Arch Abbot was thinking coming to Arkaym," she said, pressing the back of her hand to her forehead.

Aachon did not reply to that, but she already knew the answer; the Order was dedicated to rooting out unliving in all the places it had grabbed a hold. It didn't matter if it was geist or geistlord, they were set against. Even if Sorcha was uncertain of her status in the Order, she'd dedicated her life to the same goal.

The buzzing of insects and the slap of damp foliage kept them all busy for the next hour—far too busy to bother with words. Animals moved in the jungle around them, but luckily they were all moving away from them. Still it was hard not to imagine that the whole native world of Ensomn was against them.

Sorcha felt as though at any moment she might collapse in a damp bundle on the jungle floor, but she called on all her reserves to keep putting one foot in front of the other. She reminded herself that with each step she was getting nearer to Raed.

"I won't let him get away this time," she muttered, batting aside an umbrella-sized leaf that threatened to slap her in the face. She was thinking how good it would feel just to be held by him. One little goal at a time.

By the time they reached the narrow clearing around the fortress, every one of them was thoroughly sick of the jungle. They were all sweating like pigs, bitten by ravenous insects, and were covered in mud up to their thighs; not exactly the best-looking group of invaders.

Aachon wrapped his main weirstone in the sleeve of his jacket, and ordered all the lanterns they'd been using doused as they stepped from the trees onto the rocky ground. He still held the stone's connection alive for Sorcha, and she was impressed at his casual control of it.

However the sharp tang of its power was making her head ache, and her eyes burn. Aachon might be able to hold his grip on the power for a long time, but she doubted she could.

Cautiously Sorcha put on her Gauntlets. "I hope you have control over that thing, Aachon. It would be a shame to recover from a coma just to fall into another one."

"Yes," he said, fixing her with a piercing look, "that would be most unfortunate. One can't count on two miraculous recoveries."

Serigala's disappearance had raised some issues for the first mate—that much was certain—but Aachon's connection to her was not as powerful as a Bond, and so he couldn't possibly be able to read what had actually happened from her mind. He was most certainly not Merrick.

"What's the plan, sir?" Naleni, short, bitter and utterly contemptuous of Sorcha, would not address the Deacon, and most certainly would not ask for directions from her.

Aachon jerked his head toward the place where the fortress, tall, black and imposing, met the scrubbed earth. "I don't care what sort of creature you are, if you have flesh you have to deal with the effluent of living." He pointed to where a small stream ran out of the base of the stones. "We're going to follow that up into the fortress, find our Prince, and then get out." He turned and smiled at them grimly. "I suggest you all learn to keep your mouths shut. It's going to get messy, but we have Deacon Sorcha Faris on our side."

The crew members shared worried looks, while others began tying back their hair shooting doubting glances toward the Deacon. Frith whispered something to Naleni under her breath that made the other woman shake her head emphatically.

They could look as skeptical as they like, Sorcha was busy being glad of the power that flowed through her. It gave her Center a wider reach than it would have otherwise. The Deacon closed her eyes, and dipped once more into the strength of the weirstone. It was unpleasant, but it meant she could see.

Sorcha reminded herself that, despite the fact that the vision provided by the weirstone was not as precise as it would have been with Merrick, she wasn't looking for much, apart from Raed and keeping an eye out for this geistlord—in whatever form it might take. Taking a long, deep breath the Deacon now focused it on the fortress. Immediately, she could tell that Aachon's hunch was unfortunately correct. The place reeked of geist activity, but of a kind she'd never seen before.

"It's like the whole place is undead," she whispered to herself. After opening her eyes, and flexing her head from side to side to relieve a little stiffness, Sorcha refocused. Nothing changed. No particular place in the fortress flickered with the telltale signature of the undead; the entire building did. It was entirely unprecedented. For a time she was quite dazzled by it; dazzled, confused and just a little bit frightened.

Aachon pulled Sorcha aside, his hand tight on her forearm. She flinched back in surprise as he barked at her. "Do you feel it? Can you hear the Rossin in there?"

He must be able to see the same thing she was seeing, but he said nothing about the all-encompassing geist presence. Aachon was nothing if not dedicated to his Prince, and he would ignore everything else until the Young Pretender was safe. Since he wasn't going to bring it up, stubbornly Sorcha decided that she wouldn't either. This close, she could feel Raed like a splinter under her skin; a constant distraction from reality. But more precisely, she could feel the Rossin, as Aachon could. The geistlord was there, right along with Raed.

He burned through her bones, and reminded her of the power that could be hers if she merely reached for it. She'd felt that before, but there was something else. The Rossin's flame was far hotter than she ever recalled it being—even in Chioma, when faced with the geistlord Hatipai, the beast had not felt like this.

"Yes," she finally nodded. "It has him, but it feels like the Rossin has been present for a long time." She felt along the Bond. It remained intact, but the whisper of Raed was very faint.

"The Rossin has always abandoned my prince after it is sated," Aachon said, glancing over his shoulder, "but if things have changed, then we cannot be sure we can get Raed out. Not without being killed by the creature, that is."

Sorcha pressed her lips together, remembering the last devastating time she'd been face-to-face with the Rossin. It had begun with the death of two innocent women, and rapidly gone downhill from there. "What are you suggesting?"

"While we go in through the sewers, you use some of those runes of yours, phase through walls and get to the Rossin. Only you have any chance of pulling him back and reclaiming the Prince."

Her desire to see Raed again, to hold him tight, even if just for a moment, was intense, but she had to be careful. She pushed her tangled and sweaty hair back from her eyes, and nodded tightly. "All right, but you better hold that connection open. I was lucky in Orinthal running through walls without Merrick. I don't want to push the fates any further than I have to. Without you I could be some very pretty wall decoration."

As expected Aachon did not laugh, instead he turned and bellowed at the crew; they were used to it. Only Arriann made any kind of grumble, the rest quickly scattered to their tasks.

Sorcha adjusted her blue cloak, one that she might not have a right to anymore, and ran toward the dreadful-looking fortress without looking back. She would have been far more grateful for a Hunter's Moon than the gleam of a full one; it made her feel very much exposed over this open ground.

As she ran, stretching her legs to the greatest strain they had encountered in months, she thought, *By the Bones, it is good to be moving again.*

Her body had made a remarkable recovery thus far, but she didn't know if she trusted it enough to believe it wouldn't fail her at an important moment. Her legs were shaky and her vision uncomfortably blurred in and out if she turned her head too fast. Sorcha couldn't be sure it was the weirstone that was keeping her upright. She most certainly did not like relying on it.

Still, she was committed now, so raising her Gauntlet she summoned Voishem. The world shimmered and became a shadow of itself: unreal and sketchy. It resolved itself down to the basics: stone and gaps in stone. She staggered on through it, holding the rune before her like a talisman. Once the Deacon stumbled and fell to one knee awkwardly. She hadn't tripped on anything, she couldn't in phase, but it was confirmation her strength was limited. After taking a quick breath, she lurched to her feet and went on.

It was impossible to say how long Sorcha staggered toward the burning Rossin presence. It seemed like forever, and with every step she missed Merrick more and more—though he would have chided her for this rash dash.

However, finally she emerged gasping into the same space as the Rossin and was able to drop Voishem. It was like having a huge load removed from her shoulders.

For a long moment, Sorcha rested her hands on her knees, drawing her breath as slowly and evenly as she could and trying to control the spasms in her legs. If the Beast had wanted to devour her then, then he would have had no better time.

He did not. Slowly the Deacon raised her head, and took in the Rossin. Every time that she'd been near the great cat she'd been in awe of him. He'd demonstrated tremendous power and bloodlust whenever she had seen him. She'd been a witness to him ripping Deacons and citizens apart, and been a grateful observer to him destroying another geistlord. However now, he looked capable of none of those things.

The Rossin lay on the simple stone floor, his eyes half-lidded, his massive head propped up on his outstretched paws.

Sorcha was able to observe all this because she was jammed into the tiny cell with him and was only a couple of feet away from his heaving flank. He was hot—so hot that she could feel it on her exposed skin as if she stood near to a bonfire.

Despite everything she had seen the Rossin do, and people he had slain, she dropped to her knees and touched him with no thought to her own life. Aside from a flinching of the muscles beneath the skin, the creature did not acknowledge her presence. She slid around him, placing herself behind the great bulk of the geistlord, just in case his captors were nearby.

Captors . . . of the Rossin? It seemed impossible, but there it was. Someone or something in this fortress had imprisoned the terrifying geistlord. Why was he even still here? The Rossin devoured, sated itself on blood and then retreated, leaving Raed in charge of his own body once more. However it seemed this time was different.

The creature was burning both himself and his host up. A geistlord gained many things from claiming a foothold in a human, but it remained a complicated relationship. No one frail human body could contain the power of a geistlord all the time. Even a common geist could burn out the flesh of their host, and that was what it felt very much like the Rossin was perilously close to doing to Raed Syndar Rossin.

But why would he do such a thing?

"Raed," Sorcha whispered into the soft fur of the Rossin's ear. "Raed, it's me. Come back."

The Beast stirred, opening one of his eyes. His characteristic rage was indeed burning low, because she saw nothing of the hatred and hunger in him that she had seen all the other times they'd encountered each other. A low growl was all there was, and even that was felt through her hand rather than heard.

The Rossin swung his head about and inhaled a breath, tasting the air with all the intensity of a predator trying to smell a piece of prey. Then he turned awkwardly on his back and closed his eyes once more. The fur around his thick neck twitched and spasmed. Sorcha knew the signs and stepped back. Her heart was hammering far too fast, and she clenched her hands tight.

The change took a long time—much longer than she had ever seen. The outline fluctuated between man and beast in drawn-out madness. She was completely unable to do anything to assist but felt the helplessness deeply. It must have been painful because both Raed and the Rossin were wracked by spasms. They arched their backs, their mouths stretched in silent screams of pain—but somehow they managed not to make any noise. It was an impressive feat.

When it was finally over the Young Pretender was left curled up, naked on the floor, his skin pale and waxy looking. He looked thin and very vulnerable—and her breath caught in her throat at the sight. Finally, the Deacon unclenched her hands, letting her breath out in a long gasp. Part of her couldn't believe it was him and dared not touch him least he evaporate and spin away from her like mist. At last, gathering up her courage, Sorcha bent and wrapped her cloak around him.

Under her fingers his skin was chill but somehow still covered in a layer of sweat.

"Raed, please get up," she whispered, cradling him in her arms, and rolling him over gently. For a long few heartbeats she was afraid he was dead from the strain of the change, but then the Deacon discerned his chest moving slightly. Sorcha couldn't help it; she bent and kissed his cheek. "Come on, please Raed. We have to get out of here."

He groaned and opened his eyes. They were the same beautiful hazel eyes that she'd craved seeing for months. All Merrick had told her about him leaving after the disaster at Hatipai's temple did nothing to remove her feelings for him. He must have had his reasons. Now holding him in her arms, she just wanted to protect him and make him smile again. It was strange to see the normally strong and brash Raed as weak as a newborn kitten.

"Sorcha," he managed to croak out her name through parched lips as she took off her cloak and draped it around him. It was not the first time she'd done so.

"Yes." She smiled and pressed a hand to his cold skin. "What trouble have you got yourself into, foolish man?"

He blinked at her, and then that handsome mouth

twitched upward a fraction. "Oh you know . . . the usual business where I need you to help me out of it."

She tried to glare at him.

Raed Syndar Rossin's smile broadened. "Now," he whispered, wrapping his fingers around hers, "why aren't you kissing me?"

It didn't matter the situation, there was none so dire that she could deny him a kiss. Sorcha pressed her lips against his, and for a second that was quite enough. Once again, she told herself this time there was no way she was letting this man out of her sights.

When she'd quite thoroughly kissed him, stolen both of their breaths, she pulled back. "No more cross-country jaunts for you," she growled. "I don't care if I can't move . . . next time take me with you!"

Raed's eyes went distant for a moment, then he looked back at her. "I stand . . . or lie . . . corrected. I won't do it again."

Taking him at his word, Sorcha helped him to his feet. She dare not use Voishem on him in this weakened state for very long; that rune was a terrible strain on anyone, let alone a person under strain from the change. She would need to find Aachon and the others and get him out that way. Along the fragile weirstone Bond, she pushed the image of a hurt but alive Raed to him. Hopefully he received it and understood.

Then Sorcha wrapped her arms around him and pulled Raed through the bars of the prison. Even just that small moment caused the Young Pretender to wince in pain.

"Hold on," she whispered to him, while keeping her shoulder under his arm. Sorcha glanced left and right up the corridor. It was hot and it stank down here, and it was a smell she was familiar with: the wretched odor of unwashed and uncared-for humanity. It often came with the presence of geists. They were not able to control human bodily functions very well.

Holding Raed up was proving difficult too. At full strength

it would have been awkward, but as she was currently, it wouldn't be long until they both ended up on the ground.

"A little help please, Raed," she grunted, maneuvering him as best she could down through the cells, in the direction of where Aachon and the crew were.

"Sorcha," he stumbled over her name and shuffled his feet, desperately trying to get them under himself, "where are we going?"

"To safety," she said, hauling him higher. "Haven't you heard? Wherever you are, I need to be. Some call it fate." Despite the whole sorry situation, she squeezed his arm. Hopefully it conveyed reassurance.

He worked his mouth a few times, gathered some strength and pressed on. "You seem to be short one Deacon. Where is Merrick?"

The Young Pretender was always one for the questions. "We got separated, but I have Aachon with me. We're using a weirstone so I can see, and we're going to get you out of this."

That got Raed's attention. His head rose fractionally, and his face shifted into something that was a strangely concerned expression. "I have to get to Fraine."

She'd had quite enough of him throwing his own safety to the wind so that he could chase his twisted sister. "She's lost, Raed. You can't save her."

"No"—the Young Pretender tugged on her arm—"I know I can't—but she is getting ready to start a rebellion. It will tear apart the Empire."

Sorcha swallowed. This was just the kind of news she really didn't need to hear, but it was also the kind she could do nothing about right now. As a Deacon her area of expertise was the unliving—not Pretenders to the Imperial throne.

So she murmured, "We'll see, Raed, once we find Aachon."

As she moved down the corridor supporting him, Sorcha saw they were not alone. She stopped, stock-still.

The rows of cells that lined the corridor were not empty. Her gaze locked with a woman in the cell next to the one the Rossin had been in. Sorcha had seen plenty of dead-eyed people in her time in the Order; it was pretty much a standard for the possessed souls who were the prey of geists. This was nothing like that. She could see no sign of the Otherside in the woman. All that despair and hopelessness was very real and very human. The way her twiglike hands clutched onto a far-too-swollen belly was not a protective gesture; it was almost a pleading one.

"Deacon," the woman's voice was barely a whisper. "By the Blood, a Deacon." She gave a little laugh, one that sounded like a mockery of amusement. "I waited for a fellow Deacon to find me. I dreamed about it, and now here you are—but far too late."

Sorcha stopped dead still in her tracks. "You . . . you're a member of the Order?"

The woman glared at her, taking a step back from the bars and standing up as tall as her condition allowed. "I was. A Deacon of the Phia Abbey, only a year ago I was brought here, and now look." Her trembling hands sketched the devastation of her body. "I dreamed of being an Abbot one day. All the women here like me had dreams."

"All the women?" Sorcha swallowed hard, turned and looked up the line of cells. Around each doorway, she could see other thin hands wrapped desperately around the bars.

At Sorcha's side, Raed levered himself upright, away from her. He looked as frail as a newly hatched bird, but none of the other women were any better. They were all trapped in a real living, breathing nightmare. Each of them had the tattered aura of members of the Order, and each of them had the dead eyes of a long-term prisoner.

"We can't leave them here." The Young Pretender staggered, holding himself upright as best he could. That was the trouble with Raed Syndar Rossin; in his presence

Sorcha found herself doing things that weren't particularly sensible.

She tilted her head, and closed her eyes for a second—not to reach out to Aachon—but to consider her options. Usually she would have gone to the nearest Abbey for support, and to clean out this damn nest of undead horror. That was not a choice she had here. The logical part of her mind said that they couldn't possibly get all these emaciated, pregnant women out of this place—not when she was weak and underpowered.

Then she looked at Raed. In those hazel eyes she wanted to be better than logic permitted. Sorcha sighed, "Yes, you are completely right." Activating Voishem once again, she thrust her Gauntleted fist through the bars and toward the woman. The once Deacon however stepped back, shaking her head. "Too late. I told you too late!"

"Don't be a fool," Sorcha hissed waving her phased arm. "Come with us."

The woman folded herself into the dank corner of the cell and continued to shake her head violently. "You don't know how powerful they are. There is nowhere you can go where they cannot." She jammed her tiny fist into her mouth as if to block out any more words that might escape her.

Sorcha pulled her hand back and turned to Raed in despair. "I can't make her come, but I can . . ." She shook her head in frustration. "This is so—"

"Then we move on." The Young Pretender clasped her hand. "Find if there are others."

Merrick had spent hours with Sorcha when she was locked in her own body, telling her what had happened to him when he'd gone missing from Orinthal. He'd also spent a bit of time talking about Raed, and how he had left her. Merrick had emphasized how he suspected Raed's disappearance had something to do with the Young Pretender's sister.

Sorcha heard the crack in his voice, and didn't need to be a Sensitive to understand how important it was for him to save a young woman—even if he had given up on his sister.

"Raed," she said as gently as she could manage, "we can't force these women to come with us. We can't save everyone . . ."

"I know that," he snapped. "Fraine's different—she's trying to start a bloody civil war. I have to stop her." His expression was so tormented that Sorcha reached out to him. "We have to take her," he repeated, and she knew that look. Raed could be funny, jovial and gregarious, but when he put his mind to something that was it.

"Fine," she whispered, "then let's get moving."

Like two old men after a hard night drinking, they staggered farther up the hallway, heading gamely in the direction Sorcha could feel the tug of Aachon. As they went, they passed more women in the same state as the previous ones, all of whom turned away and hid their faces when Sorcha reached for them. It was by far the most ghastly thing the Deacon had ever seen in her time hunting geists, and yet she found herself walking past her colleagues with a masklike expression.

We'll get them later. We'll go back to the Mother Abbey and bring a contingent of Deacons back here to clean this nest out. We're not abandoning you.

It was the best she could do, but it didn't make it any easier to walk past these fellow Deacons—these fellow women.

They reached the end of the cells with people in them. These last few were only full of shadows. When Sorcha propped Raed up against one of these, she leaned back to take a few breaths herself.

Darling.

The chill voice ran up her spine and made her spin around.

"What is it?" Raed's fingers brushed hers. "I hate it

when you see things I can't." He was trying to be amusing, but it fell flat in the darkness and shadows of the hive.

"I heard someone's voice. It sounded familiar, but . . ." She stopped, uncertain, and peered into the empty cell. Was it truly empty? She narrowed her eyes as shadows flickered in the rear of the cage.

Beloved.

"We should go." Now it was Raed tugging at her, but she resisted. The voice was feminine, soft and pleading. It broke with longing and sadness. A part of her twisted when she heard it; a deep primal muscle that jammed her breath in her throat and brought tears to her eyes.

Daughter!

"Sorcha?" Raed turned her head so he could meet her eyes, and flinched back when he saw her crying. Though she choked back sobs, the tears kept coming. Such a visceral reaction caught her completely off guard.

Her training told her that some tiny shard of a person remained here—most likely a rei. It would have taken nothing to dismiss such a tiny geist. Rei were the least kind of shade. While shades could sometimes be seen by normal folk as they repeated what their human selves had done, rei were emotions. They reflected a specific feeling that a person had felt when they died. They were in essence little capsules of the moment of a person's passing.

Their effects were limited to an icy feeling on the back of the neck, or a touch of sadness for no reason. Most Deacons did not bother to dismiss them, since there were many worse kinds of geists in the world that were far more important to get rid of.

As a member of the Order, Sorcha should have been able to brush its effects off easily, but instead she was almost unable to see out of her eyes for the tears. Reaching out, she pushed against the cell door and it opened with a slight creak.

Raed tugged her cloak tighter about him, and stepped in after her. "It's very . . . chilly in here." Even he could feel

it, the difference to the oppressive heat in the rest of the
fortress. "But shouldn't we be going?"

Sorcha didn't answer him for a moment, but cautiously
examined the room. It, like all the others, had a small
benchlike bed, and a waste chute. It also contained a set of
shackles, though these were rusted and ill cared for. Standing over the bed, Sorcha examined it. This was the seat of
the rei. She could tell by the great well of sadness that was
threatening to choke her.

She was certainly getting an appreciation of what Sensitives dealt with every day. It was no wonder that they had
to train just as hard as Actives. Sorcha was having difficulty understanding her own reaction to this one room. A
rei should not have had this effect. She had no Runes of
Sight to rely on, but she did have her Center.

It told her there was blood on the bed, and that knowledge made her feel quite ridiculously ill. Her hand hovered
above the marks for a while—trembling in fact.

"Raed," she whispered over her shoulder, "I have to
experience this rei. It's . . . it's like nothing I've felt before."
She thought back to what the Fensena had said on the
Autumn Eagle; he had promised answers ahead. The odd
thing was, she hadn't really had questions . . . until this
moment.

Now her hand was only a few scant inches from the
ancient blood on the stone. She was deathly afraid, but it
drew her nevertheless; blood to blood.

"Is it dangerous?" Raed asked, touching her back
lightly. She appreciated that he wasn't stopping her, trust-
ing her judgment. Just as Merrick would have.

"I don't think so." She glanced back at him, having great
difficulty holding back her tears. "I have to do it though."

"Then don't hesitate on my account." He smiled, a
memory of his wicked smile that had undone her in the
first place. "I'll watch over you."

Spreading her fingers wide, Sorcha placed her hand
on the blood. The effect was like no other rei she had

ever known. It jerked her beyond thought, and into the memory of flesh. It took her away, until she was a person she had never known, but sometimes wondered about in idle moments.

FIFTEEN

Finding a Cradle

She was lost and alone. Frightened. Pregnant. Caoirse curled up in the cell they had placed her in, and remained very, very quiet. It took every ounce of her self-control. As long as she didn't cry out when the contractions came they would not know she was in labor. Not yet anyway.

The sweat was running down her back as she crouched in the corner, straining to both hold back her groans and give birth to her daughter. She knew it was a daughter. She'd heard her tiny thoughts; mostly thoughts of comfort, warmth and desire for life.

Her mother, long dead, had been a midwife in their village, and Caoirse was now grateful for all those births she'd witnessed, however unhappily, as a child. She'd never thought she would have to use the experience she had gained on herself, alone and in the shadows. However the daughter she'd never wanted to have was coming soon. As a Deacon, few expected to have children, but as a captive she'd had no choice.

No, she couldn't afford to think of the drone who had taken her into the cell, his blank stare, his unnatural strength, and how she'd been unable to resist either. Not today. Caoirse couldn't afford to think of anything but what lay ahead. Her plan.

Luckily it was night, and the Wrayth were elsewhere, terrorizing the population of their kingdom no doubt. Though which kingdom or province she was in she'd never found out; there was only so much she could get from the terrified women that occupied the other cells. All of them were Deacons, and all of them had similar experiences. Unfortunately the Wrayth were clever. The cells were carefully crafted with thick walls to keep the woman from touching and forming a Bond.

By the Blood, she missed the Bond. She missed her old life, and her partner—even if he'd been the lucky one.

She'd been in Sousah province in Delmaire, exploring a strange ancient temple with her partner. An earthquake had revealed a new section of tunnels beneath the temple, and they'd been sent to investigate it to see if there were any geists lurking there. Delmaire was mostly a tamed continent, but old places were still feared. Rightly so as it turned out. What they had found was a twisted creature of flesh, lurking in the water. The creatures that boiled out of the tunnel when they approached she had not been able to sense. They had killed Klanasta immediately—having no use for men. And they had taken her Strop. She was a Sensitive, alone in this place, with no Active to help.

Except the one she was birthing.

Caoirse breathed deeply but as quietly as she could, and pushed. Reaching down, she felt between her legs for her daughter's head. It was there, but also a lot of blood. When she raised her hands, she could see it traveling between her fingers and gliding over the marks on her arm. Ink and blood. She had known they would be a powerful combination.

The engravings on her arm were an idea that had come to her in her sleep. If she believed in gods she might have thought it some kind of divine inspiration. Her plan had to work. The leather that the Gauntlets and Strop were made out of was essentially skin anyway, and it also pleased her that she would never be separated from the runes again. Not even the Wrayth could take them from her now.

She had hidden her plans so very well from her captors. Luckily they cared little for the Deacons once they were impregnated, and did not examine the women. In fact, they only ever came into the cells to deliver food. The blank stares of the peons were her protection. If any of the elder Wrayth had bothered to examine her, they would have seen the marks she had carved in herself. The quill and ink pot had been in her belt pouch, and she'd hidden them in her cell for months.

Caoirse knew all the runes, but she'd only been able to carve three into the skin on her arms before the ink ran out. Voishem, Seym and Pyet. It was probably best that she'd only managed those. Her Active power was minor, and she'd be acting as a conduit for Daughter's.

Daughter. That was the only name she would give this little creature, until they were safe; until she could tell if the Wrayth had made something horrific or miraculous with her, and if either of them would survive. Naming things was of great importance, and something she dreamed of doing in the sunlight. She missed sunlight.

It was time to find out what Daughter was. Her body was telling her to move, to push and uncover the truth. Everything went still, perfect and still. She felt open and alive, poised for a perfect moment in this darkness. Caoirse pushed, feeling her whole body open, and bright white light flashed behind her eyes. Then Daughter lay in her hands, not twisted, not malformed. Beautiful. She stared up at Caoirse with tiny, bright blue eyes, while her new mother cleaned her with the least stained cloth she had in the cell. Daughter had a beautiful crop of reddish hair, and, as if knowing the situation they were in, didn't cry.

The desire to nurse her was intense, but Caoirse resisted it. If she lay back and coddled Daughter there would be no *going back. The Wrayth would find them both there, and take her baby away to whatever fate it had planned. Then there would be no escape for either of them, and what they would do with Daughter could only be a nightmare.*

She swiftly tied a thread she'd worked loose from the sheet about the umbilical cord, and sawed it free with a rock she had sharpened over long months for this particular purpose. Finally she waited for a time, until she had birthed the placenta.

Then she carefully wrapped Daughter up in her sheet. The little girl wriggled a little, but her eyes never left Caoirse's. The once-Deacon had to smother back a sob. She took a moment to compose herself and to put all the pieces of her plan together one final time. So many things could go wrong—not just the Wrayth stopping her. A Sensitive using an Active power could burn out like a snuffed flame, or up like oil thrown on fire. She was not familiar with the runes, and they could turn and devour her.

Yet it was the only way. She had to warn the Order that this was happening; that not all their Deacons that went missing were killed. She could do this. One last time, Caoirse went over her plan.

First, Voishem to get her out of the cell, then Seym the Rune of Flesh to give her the strength to run. She'd race to the right, out of her cell; that was the direction all the women came from, and she remembered coming that way from the strange tunnel. The gleam of weirstones had been the last thing she recalled. If the tunnel had taken her far from Delmaire then it could take her back there. Then to the Abbey, if Seym would carry her that far. If any Wrayth got in the way or tried to stop her then she would use Pyet on them. She smiled grimly. Maybe she would use the cleansing flame on them anyway.

Gathering up Daughter, she called on the child's power. It was so much more than she could have expected. The rune's power scampered up the marks on her arms, and it was like pouring liquid lead into her veins. Her muscles spasmed and it felt like her eyes would burn out of her head. So much pain, but she couldn't afford the time to stop and feel it. For the Order's sake. For Daughter's sake.

Caoirse held up her hand, trembling and thin as it was. Voishem made the world pale and insubstantial. She liked that. Clutching Daughter in the crook of her arm, she stepped forward and out into the corridor.

Raed was watching Sorcha, who had only just placed her hand on the bloodstain, but he was also keeping an eye and an ear out for anything coming along the corridor. She'd said Aachon was near, but he heard no reassuring pistol shots or sounds of victory to tell him that this assertion was true. He wished Merrick were here to tell him what was going on with Sorcha, and perhaps to provide a little level-headed sanity to this situation.

It couldn't have been more than a minute since Sorcha touched the blood before she let out a tiny gasp and slumped back. It was only his hand on her shoulder that kept her from falling over completely.

Her fingers clutched onto him, and then, most remarkably of all, she buried her head against his chest. Just for a moment, even considering the dire place they were in, Raed spared time to cradle her head there, stroking her hair and making noises of comfort.

"She got away." Sorcha pulled back, wiped tears from her eyes and looked up at him. He had never before seen that expression on the Deacon's face; true wonder. He wanted to kiss her even more now; to make her eyes stop crying, and her chest stop struggling to find breath. This was not Sorcha—at least not the Sorcha he knew.

"Who got away?" he asked gently.

The Deacon gestured to the blood on the floor. "My mother. Caoirse. She was here, the Wrayth were breeding me from her. Just like those other poor women." She swallowed hard. "By the Blood, this was where I was made, in this horrible place!" She spun about abruptly and dry retched into the corner of the cell. It was a miserable sound, as if she were trying to purge her body and soul.

Raed sat back on his heels and rubbed her back softly. He knew better than to question what she had learned from the blood: the Order was the authority on such things.

Eventually, she collected herself, wiped her mouth on the back of her hand and glanced over her shoulder at him. Raed looked around. *So this was where you were born?* It hardly seemed like the place for a powerful Deacon to come into the world.

"That's why I am powerful!" Sorcha shook her head, and seemed not to notice that he hadn't spoken at all. It unnerved Raed no end, but he didn't bring it up. The Deacon looked as though she was already tottering on the edge of complete collapse. She was so much thinner than last time he'd seen her, and the large circles under her eyes told him many more things than she would ever say.

He waited in silence for her to explain. The distress across the Bond was something he could feel, like a foreign substance in his body. Something about the Rossin being so close to the surface had made him aware of the connection like he had never been before. Raed was not entirely sure he liked being conscious of it, especially in this situation.

Sorcha clenched her hands on the folds of the cloak he wore. "It's why the Bond is so strong between the three of us, don't you see? Even what happened with the Prince of Chioma's gift. It's because I am partly made of them." She stared at her hands with such fixation and such fury that he was worried she might start tearing at her very flesh. "I am part of their bloody breeding program—whatever they were trying to make, they made me along the way!"

He was familiar with her despair and rage. Far too familiar. The Young Pretender had gone through all those emotions himself when he first realized he was cursed. He knew how deeply destructive thoughts like that could become.

Carefully, Raed laid his hands on hers, swallowing them up. "They might have made you, but you are not their creature. Your mother gave birth to you, she loved you enough to get you out of this place. You are hers too. Don't forget that."

It was a lesson Aachon had often repeated to him when he feared there was nothing but the Rossin in him.

Sorcha held his gaze for a moment, and he tried his very best to project safety, kindness and understanding across the Bond. He wasn't sure if he was doing it right, or even doing it at all, but after a second or two, she nodded.

"You're right."

"Say it again." He smiled softly. "I love it when you say that."

Her short laugh was brittle, but at least sounded like her. "Don't get cocky, Your Majesty. I'll hold myself together until we get out of here, then fall apart in a heap you can enjoy picking up."

Getting out of here. Raed let out a slow sigh. "And we must stop Fraine too," he reminded her as gently as he could.

Sorcha met his gaze. "We will—but first let's get to Aachon. His head will implode if I don't bring you directly to him."

They went out into the hallway once more, and Sorcha slipped her hand into his. They were both fragile and weak right now, but even if that had not been the case Raed would still have enjoyed that little gesture. She had said she would not leave him again, and the Young Pretender appreciated that. As they left the cells and moved deeper into the nest, he felt very vulnerable.

"I confess," he whispered into Sorcha's ear, "I wish I was not doing this naked. That's the real problem with the Rossin, I never have any cursed pants or boots."

She turned and kissed him, lightly at first, and then more passionately, clutching him for a moment tight against her. She was smiling against his mouth a second before they parted.

"It is good to see you, Raed," she muttered, "and I don't care how few clothes you wear." She was trying to hold off what was going on around her, and what she had learned, and yet she was still aware of him. The prickly Deacon he had pulled out of the ocean the previous year had not escaped unscathed from all they had been through. But then, none of them had.

"Take me somewhere you and I can explore that further." It was a boastful thing to say, because the Rossin inhabiting his body for nearly a week had eaten away any strength he'd had before. Raed thought it was perhaps only pride and stubbornness keeping him on his feet and moving. If there was any fighting or running ahead, he didn't know what he would do—probably just lie down and try and gain Sorcha some time.

The Deacon up ahead was peering around a corner. Her head whipped around, and she fixed him with a baleful glare. "Don't you even *think* about doing any such thing!"

That damned Bond was going to take quite some getting used to—and he had no time to learn the skills to hide his thoughts. "Chivalry used to be all the rage," he grumbled.

Sorcha poked him with her finger, then pulled him close so that they could both peer around the corner of the hallway. It made quite the impression. With the new closeness of the Rossin, Raed felt more and saw more through the Beast's eyes, but there was a difference. The geistlord did not linger overly on visual details; he was always more concerned about the sounds and smells.

What to him had only been a pile of stinking, yammering humanity looked quite different to Raed with his own eyes. It looked, to put it bluntly, like an orgy. He'd never been to one himself, but there had been plenty of books in his father's library on many subjects that an impression-able boy probably should not have gotten hold of.

Men and women, covered in the mud and dust of their shadowy nest, were piled in the great room. All were naked, all were touching, writhing. Many of the females looked to be in various stages of pregnancy, but that apparently did not stop them. Men, women, all in one groping, licking, grinding mass. However none of their eyes were focused on each other, but rather at some distant unseen point.

"What are they doing?" Sorcha shook her head as a frown deepened on her forehead.

"You don't know?"

"Raed, I know what they are physically doing," she replied with an arched eyebrow. "However I studied as long and as hard as any Active, particularly when it came to the kinds of geists I might run into. This makes no sense."

A thought scuttled across the surface of his mind; one that was not his own. *This part of the Wrayth mind is solely consumed with pleasure. It doesn't have a higher function.*

"I can see that," Sorcha rubbed her temples. "So you are saying that the Wrayth functions like a beehive, with different parts doing things? Like some parts of it working the limbs, remembering to breathe, while other bits plot and scheme?"

You're getting it now.

It was hard for Raed to decide which was the more unnerving; that Sorcha was plucking thoughts from him, or that those thoughts were in fact the Rossin's. Strangely enough it appeared when the Beast was actively thinking his own thoughts it went unnoticed by Sorcha; she just assumed they were the Young Pretender's thoughts. It was all a nasty muddle.

"Seems a little too much like pleasuring yourself," he added, more to have something to distract her than anything.

"It gets so dull after a while. Maybe that is why they brought in the female Deacons."

"Oh no, these bits of the Wrayth had nothing to do with that. That was a real plan, with a purpose—we just don't know what that is . . . at least yet." She pointed to the far side of the wide room. "Aachon and your crew are coming up through the drain over there. We should help them. I don't think this part of the brain is conscious enough to be bothered with us."

Carefully picking their way across the rocky floor, but still sticking to the edges of the room, they reached the grate. It was, like everything else here, made of stone, but Sorcha used her long knife to lever it open. Both of them had to yank it away however.

Aachon and the dozen *Dominion* crew who emerged from inside the pipe were a sight for sore eyes. Mud and other unmentionable filth were caked all over them. They stood blinking, wiping the muck out of their eyes, and taking in the undulating bodies of the Wrayth mind with more than a little slack-jawed incredulity.

"I am sure," Sorcha said, trying to draw away their attention, "you wish at least one of you had taken me up on my offer."

Aleck, the tallest of the crew members, was rubbing the small of his back. Crawling and crab-walking through the muck of the Wrayth fortress could not have been fun for him in particular. "Remind me of that next time."

Aachon insisted on flicking as much filth off himself as he could, before embracing Raed. It had been months since the Young Pretender had seen his first mate, and he was damned if he was going to stand on ceremony. He grabbed him roughly and hugged him, quite lost for words.

"My prince," Aachon stumbled out, "it is good to see you alive and well—though somewhat lacking in the clothing department." Then he swung a rucksack off his back, and proceeded to pull out pants, boots, shirt, a pistol and most remarkably a stout leather tricorne hat. He had even thought to bring a second sword.

"Familiarity certainly doesn't breed contempt in your case," Raed exclaimed, and clasped his friend's arm. "It only makes you much better prepared." The rest of the crew members let him dress before roughly shaking his hand and slapping him on the back.

After so long apart, Raed felt like he was back among family again. Yes, family—the only real one he'd ever had.

"I am sorry to do this to you, old friend," he said, breaking into their moment of congratulations, "but we cannot leave just yet—though I do yearn to climb into a sewage pipe with you. Fraine and Tangyre are here, and we must get my sister away before she creates bloodshed in the Empire."

Aachon and Sorcha exchanged a puzzled look. "Are you suggesting," the first mate growled, "that the Wrayth have them prisoner?"

By the Blood, it was hard to have to say the words, but they all deserved to know, and more importantly they couldn't go charging around the Wrayth nest not knowing who their enemies were. "No, I am not. They are here of their own free will." He clamped his hand on Aachon's upper arm. "Tangyre Greene has been poisoning Fraine's mind for years. My sister is trying to drag Arkaym into civil war to gain the throne for herself."

"It will be civil war," Aachon whispered. "Thousands will be killed. Thousands of innocents."

"Not if we get her away from here." Raed glanced back at the writhing human bodies behind them, full with the influence of the Wrayth, now part of its twisted mind. "We can't let her be used."

"I agree, my prince, we cannot."

Raed appreciated Sorcha was quiet at his side. He ploughed on. "I last saw Fraine up in the top levels. I think that is where the higher-functioning parts of the Wrayth mind are. They were drinking blood, and my sister was making some kind of pact with them."

A mutter ran through the assembled crew members—it was not something that anyone would expect of their royals—but they hefted their weapons to show that they weren't about to back down either.

His first mate nodded, his hand clenching around his weirstone. Then as his eyes fell on the wall behind the mass of fornicating Wrayth, they widened. "Look at that, my prince. Most interesting don't you think?"

It was a formation of weirstones set in the wall. It described a circle just a fraction taller than a man, and inside the circle it was completely dark. Sorcha jerked back from it, and even the crew members jostled sideways when they saw it. Aachon was the only one that seemed fascinated by whatever it was. "It appears to be some kind of transportation device, by the cantrips worked in with the stones. But I can't quite understand—"

"Don't!" Sorcha yanked the first mate's hand back before he could touch the blackness. "Merrick encountered something like this underneath Chioma. There is no way of knowing where it might take you."

She glanced at Raed. "This is what my mother used to escape once she got out of the cells."

"Mother?" Aachon's interest was now obviously piqued.

Raed knew they couldn't stand around arguing; at any moment the Wrayth could become aware of their presence, and then there would be no chance to stop Fraine. He threw his hands up in the air. "We'll talk about that later. For now let's concentrate on finding my sister and getting out of this damned hive. This weirstone device isn't going to help us do that."

"I could have the answer, Captain." Jocryn called them over to the wall a little farther on. "Look at this."

It was the shaft that the Rossin had fallen down. Naturally the Beast had not taken much notice of the thing the man was pointing out, for it was a set of pulleys and gears made of wood and brass, and anything without flesh was of no use to him. However, the first mate smiled broadly.

"This is quite ingenious." Aachon was pointing to a switch on the wall, a kind of small brass lever. It was set into the wall, and although currently in the middle of a vertical groove, looked like it could be slid, up or down. Waving his hand like he were some kind of magician, Aachon moved it into the up position.

They all leapt when a jangle of chain and a rattle of gears started. Raed stuck his head farther into the shaft and observed something descending toward them. Hastily he pulled back. Within a few more moments the large box had descended. The side of the box facing into the room was open, and the interior was large enough for at least ten people to stand comfortably in it.

"With a fortress this large, and levels extending both above and below ground it makes sense," Aachon explained, seemingly quite pleased with himself. "I have heard the tinkers of Supo have been working on such a thing. I believe they call it a riser."

Sorcha shook her head. "Geistlords working with weirstones *and* tinkers? Whatever next? I lie down for a little bit and the whole world goes mad."

"We can use this to get up to the top levels?" Raed asked, and when Aachon nodded, he felt their chances improve a little more. "But how will we find Fraine? As I already discovered, this place is huge. They took my map and it's not particularly easy to navigate."

His first mate pulled out his weirstone and peered into its blue surface. "I know you will find it hard to believe my prince, but you still share a bond with your sister. A bond of blood is a powerful thing."

"I know that myself," Sorcha muttered, glancing back down toward the cells.

Raed squeezed her fingers lightly. He knew she was going to struggle with what she had discovered here, but he was impressed she was not falling apart. Deacon training still held firm apparently.

"Fraine has forsaken the bond of family," he muttered,

"but it is nice to know it will still be of some use." Raed was the first to step into the riser. "Now, let's go stop a civil war while we can."

Sorcha, Aachon and the rest of the crew followed him in. Tangyre was going to have a very nasty shock, and he was going to enjoy seeing her expression a great deal.

SIXTEEN

Plans and Patterns

Zofiya dreamed of her time in Delmaire. It was a pleasant dream—one without any sign of her father. She held Kaleva, a toddler, warm, soft and giggling in her arms. They sat in the sun on a warm stone bench in one of their father's palace courtyards, totally alone. The thick smell of honeysuckle and roses had almost made her giddy. She was wrapped in such happiness that she struggled to hold on to the sensation.

Then Kal had slipped off her lap and ran toward the fountain. As she watched, the water flowing in it had turned to blood, and she—unable to move from the bench—had cried out to him to stop, but he wouldn't. He just kept toddling toward the danger, arms outstretched, laughing and crowing to himself. Her cries made no difference to him.

It's a dream! A dream! She screamed to herself, trying to wake herself before her brother reached the deadly pool and tumbled in.

Zofiya struggled to regain consciousness—as if it were her life that was at stake, not Kaleva's. She only knew that she didn't want to see the end of the dream.

Finally, her own shouts woke her. When she realized she had made it from the dream world and opened her eyes, she was disappointed.

The Grand Duchess Zofiya was still a prisoner. The cruel device was pushed back against the wall, but its needle and tubing still ran into her arm. At least though, she was now mercifully alone. She lay back and pulled experimentally at her bonds—but there was no give in them. Carefully she considered her options. The links were strong and she couldn't really put all her weight against them, since her legs were bound too. However if there was a way to lubricate them she would perhaps be able to fold her hands and slip out of them. She'd always been flexible, and if she sawed back and forth, enough of her own blood might do the trick.

Zofiya flicked her head and strained her eyes to look around the room. Freed of the influence of whatever potion they'd given her, she could make out that she was definitely in a cellar. Against the wall were some implements that looked like hoes and shovels, and the smell of dirt filled her nostrils. It had been a far more pleasant environment in the dream.

However, one thing was obvious; they hadn't expected to kidnap her so soon. Her falling into bed with Merrick had just been a fortuitous event for them, and so they had apparently had to make hasty arrangements. This could play to her advantage should she get at least her hands free. Considering del Rue's physical attributes, Zofiya hazarded she might be able to get the best of him. No telling how weak she might be if they kept her here too long and under the ministrations of the device.

So yes, it had to be soon.

Zofiya began to work both of her wrists within the confines of the chain. Without drugs, it was going to be very painful. However, she'd only just started when a door opening somewhere in the shadows alerted her that she'd run out of time. Hastily, Zofiya slumped back on the bed, glad at least that she'd not hurt herself too much yet.

Del Rue came in whistling from the other room. She could hear his boots shuffling through the dirt of the floor, and made note of how long it took from the first door opening until he entered her room. Only six seconds. She tucked that information away, just in case she needed to run in the dark.

"How is my little princess this morning?" he asked conversationally. When she did not answer, he sighed dramatically. "Come, come, you are awake, so let's not play these games. I have other, far more interesting ones for you."

Zofiya turned her head and looked at him, keeping her face carefully blank. "I am sure you do, but what if I don't want to play them."

He shrugged. "That is neither here nor there." He set down a jug of water on the stool just out of reach of the bed, then a plate bearing a wedge of cheese and some bread.

Zofiya's mouth watered, and she ran her tongue around the inside of her mouth. She hadn't eaten much at the party, and nothing at all after with Merrick in her room. She didn't know how long it had been since then.

Del Rue busied himself with the device, filling up several empty containers that were part of its inner compartments. As he worked he whistled, though his back was to her. "My, you have taken quite a lot of houndsbane and myrwood." He glanced back over his shoulder. "Very impressive really."

The Grand Duchess' short laugh seemed to catch him off guard. "Obviously you don't know anything about the Delmairian Royal Court. All of the King's children are exposed to small doses of poisons throughout their lives. It's an occupational hazard that everyone lives with."

He frowned at that. "How very inconvenient, but I do have some other tinctures that are quite rare and most likely will do that trick." He snapped shut the device's housing. "I'll have to send out for the ingredients though." He didn't look at all impressed at this delay to his plans.

"Sorry," she said, her voice full of mock distress, "I do hope I haven't upset your timetable."

A bright and terrible light flashed in his eyes: a glimpse of something that Zofiya was fairly sure could not be human. The shadows around him seemed to grow deeper, and his words when he spoke boomed in the tiny cellar. "I was inclined to be kind, but now I see that would be wasted on you."

He snatched up the food, and stalked away, slamming the door behind him. It was, the Grand Duchess considered, like dealing with a very dangerous child.

She was having a hard time keeping up with his moods, and it was impossible to know how to approach her captor when he flip-flopped so often. Zofiya had known more than a few conspirators and traitors in her time and handled them easily. It was obvious to her that struggling against him was not working in any way, yet she could not find it within herself to soothe the man.

Hearing the final door to the cellar bang shut, Zofiya turned her eyes upward, back to her bindings. She didn't know how long her father's paranoia with the tinctures all those years ago had bought her, but she would assume it was enough. She began to yank and pull on the chains in earnest. Blood flowed as she set to with grim determination.

The Grand Duchess had no way of telling how long she tugged and pulled on her arms, sawing them back and forth against the rough metal, but eventually she felt her right hand slip. The pain was making her breath come in short gasps, and she shook her head trying to clear the spots that rose before her eyes.

She folded that palm as best she could and readied herself for a final tug. She knew she mustn't scream, because she had no idea where her captors were. So when she pulled, Zofiya bit down on her own lip. Every muscle concentrated on that right hand. She tensed her legs, bracing herself against the bed, and then yanked hard.

   The skin tore, the hand felt like it was being crushed in
a vice, but she didn't give up. Finally, the hand slid free
with a liquid pop that seemed very loud in the chamber.
Zofiya allowed herself to lie there for a minute and let the
pain wash over her. Then cautiously, she raised her arm to
examine the damage. Despite having felt quite the con-
trary, she still had a hand. The skin was torn, bleeding and
starting to swell without the constriction of the cuff.

   Yet she could not cosset her hand, now she had it free. It
had work to do. The first order of business was get herself
disconnected from the vile machine. She would have loved
to have knocked the thing to the floor, but again that would
make far too much noise, so she pushed it away on its
wheels. Now able to twist about and get some leverage, she
made quick work of the bed, bending the strut and getting
her left hand loose. After that, her feet, tied with rope, were
quickly freed.

   Zofiya sat up quickly, and immediately wished she hadn't.
Her head was swimming and it took a long moment for her
eyes to focus. This new point of view took a moment to get
used to. There was only one way in and out of the room, a
simple wooden door. Taking a moment to rip up a sheet, the
Grand Duchess bound her wounded wrist and examined the
place for a weapon of some kind. Nothing bladed was
present—that would have been far too lucky—so she yanked
out one of the struts from the bed, and swung it experimentally a few times. It should do in a pinch, but feeling like she
was, the target would have to be slow moving.

   Testing the door, Zofiya found with some surprise that
there was no lock. After taking a breath, she pushed it open
a fraction and glanced in. This next room was as dimly lit
as her own, and so, crouched over, she crept in. The smell
was the first thing that hit her, actually stopping her in her
tracks. It was the odor of urine and excrement, and not just
a fraction, but a considerable buildup. She'd been on cam-
paign with her father as a young woman, and despite the

joys of traveling with the King, she'd still been exposed to the more visceral side of life in a camp. However in a closed space, on top of her already fragile condition, the smell was so overpowering that for a second she had to choke back her own bile. She held her shirt over her nose and went on.

A single lantern hanging from the wall lit this room's prisoner. He was restrained, but not as she was. This old man sitting cross-legged on the floor was collared around the neck with a chain running from a fixture on the wall. The opposite side of the room was where this poor creature had been forced to defecate. It was a state that Zofiya would have been outraged to have any of her dogs in—let alone a man. After she conquered her disgust, she took another step into the room.

Zofiya glanced around, making absolutely sure that they were alone.

"Are you all right?" she whispered, bending down toward him, though the smell lower down was no fresher. The man did not acknowledge her presence, merely continued what he was doing.

The floor they stood on was dusty and strewn with straw, as a house in the countryside would have been. This debris of dust and wheat was what fascinated her fellow prisoner. He had sorted out the larger pieces of stalks to one side, and piled them behind him, so that what lay before him was a clear surface. He was drawing.

Zofiya tilted her head and stared as he worked. They were not words, but symbols. Despite the peril of the moment, the Grand Duchess circled around him to get a better look. She had never seen anything like it. These were curved interlacing strokes, elaborately curled and curiously beautiful. As she stared, she thought she could make out a couple of shapes she recognized; two runes she'd last observed on the Gauntlet of Deacon Sorcha Faris.

Crouching down, she addressed her fellow prisoner once more, "Old man, what are you doing?"

He continued on as if she were less than a shade in his perception.

Not used to being ignored in any shape or form, Zofiya grabbed him by the shoulder, and gave him a little shake. "Do you want to get out of here or not?"

His eyes now darted up to meet hers. They were perfectly clear pale blue, like looking into a sparkling mountain stream, but they were not focused on her. She noted how his hands still traced the symbols in the dust. "You are here." His voice was sweet and light for such a wizened-looking man.

She glanced down to where he was tapping. She couldn't see her name, her personal sigil or anything else, but a shiver ran up her spine. It was completely illogical, but she felt that he was right. Somewhere in the twists and turns he had mapped out, the little Princess of Delmaire and the determined sister of Kaleva was sketched.

Zofiya shook her head; maybe it was the blood loss and whatever del Rue had pumped her full of. A thought followed soon after. If her captor had seen fit to capture this old man as well, then he had to have some real value. It would undoubtedly be bad for the Empire and her brother.

Rising, she hastily examined the man's restraints and immediately saw that he'd been here a lot longer than she had been, and was far better secured. The bolt that fastened his chain to the wall was sturdy and screwed into the beam of whatever house they were in. Turning her attention to the other end, she accidentally stepped through the old man's creation.

He immediately stopped, like a puppet whose strings had been cut, staring at the floor without saying a word.

"No time for this," Zofiya muttered to herself, while tilting his head forward. "This has been on a long while hasn't it, old sir." The flesh on each side of the steel collar was covered in scars where his neck had rubbed against it and then healed.

Nothing in this room was going to break this piece of

the blacksmith's art, nor were her bare hands. For some reason, tears sprang to her eyes at the thought. Ridiculous that a man of such short acquaintance could bring such emotion out in her, but Zofiya wanted to protect him. He reminded her of the quiet nuns of Hatipai in the temple in Delmaire—the ones that had never realized they served a geistlord. She pressed her hands around his, for a moment stilling his reconstruction of the design on the floor.

"What is your name?"

He looked up at her with those incredible eyes. "Rati-mana," was all he said, before returning to what he was doing. As if that was enough explanation of everything.

She had to go. Del Rue or one of his cronies could return to check on her at any minute. "I will send someone back for you, Ratimana. As soon as I am back with my brother. I promise."

He did not glance up, not even when she reluctantly walked toward the far door. Zofiya glanced back once, but he still drew on. Many times in her life the Grand Duchess had wished for some of the talents of a Sensitive Deacon, but never more so than now. Something about that old man suggested he was more than he seemed. She would send her best Imperial Guards back to retrieve him, and a brace of Deacons just to be sure.

The next door was also unlocked, the final chamber in what she guessed had to be a root cellar of some house somewhere on the Edge of Vermillion. This one was unoc-cupied and much larger. The first thing she saw that raised her hopes immediately was a set of crooked stairs leading up. Scrambling up them proved to be dangerous as they lurched most alarmingly, but Zofiya reached the top, and felt a grin spread on her face. A pair of cellar doors.

She pushed on them. Then when that did not work, she applied her shoulder. Nothing budged. Taking a calming breath, she examined them more closely. With her finger-tips she traced the outline of the doors. They seemed sturdy, and the gaps were packed with dirt and rocks.

As she sat back on her heels, Zofiya realized that the cellar door had been most effectively sealed shut on the other side by a thick application of rocks and dirt. How were del Rue and his minions coming and going through?

Carefully Zofiya climbed back down the stairs and set about searching the rest of the room. It was larger than the other two, but not big enough that another entrance could be effectively hidden. She'd given up on stealth now. Desperation and frustration were growing. In her nightmares she had dreamed of her brother caught in a situation like this—but never herself. All those years of putting his safety first, and the worst thing she'd imagined was getting killed. Being turned into a pawn in someone's grand game had never figured. Perhaps she needed a larger imagination in the future. Depending on what that was.

She reached the far side of the cellar, and found only a narrow tunnel. This looked freshly constructed, because the brick walls on each side were ripped apart. Holding her broken bit of bed frame before her, Zofiya followed it.

The air in the tunnel suddenly became very close, and her skin began to itch frightfully. One summer in Delmaire she'd spent an uncomfortable hour by the lake while her father examined the latest addition to his river fleet. For three days after she'd itched to the point she'd wanted to rip her own skin off. This moment reminded her uncomfortably of that one. Every part of her body wanted her to stop moving forward and just go back. Maybe that cellar door wasn't as blocked as she thought. Maybe she hadn't checked all the corners of the last room thoroughly enough?

These thoughts made no sense, but felt so compelling. She'd been exposed to magic before, she knew the signs, so Zofiya kept plowing forward, one foot in front of the other.

The end of the short excavation ended in strangeness. An oval was described in the dirt, as tall as Zofiya was. It was outlined with the gleaming opalescence of tiny weirstones. That could not be good. Still she had a feeling this had to be the way del Rúe was traveling. When she was within a few feet of it, she extended her hand cautiously.

The surface was icy cold like she'd plunged her hand into a lake, but after only an inch, it did not yield any further—no matter how hard she pressed. She had to get to Kaleva. He must be turning Vermillion upside down to find her. What was he imagining happened to her?

However as Zofiya stood there thinking those things, hand still clamped to the surface, the darkness began to resolve itself. The Grand Duchess frowned and peered closer. Was she imagining it, or could she actually see Kaleva? His face was coming into focus in the darkness.

His expression was one however that she had never seen on her brother before. He looked angry; not just slightly annoyed, but truly and deeply angry. It reminded her of some of the expressions she had seen on the faces of men about to go into battle. Her father had some island folk that went into a maddened state before heading into a fight. The bulging eyes and clenched teeth had frightened her as a child, and seeing a similar look on her brother's face was worse.

"Kal!" she shouted, keeping her hand on the surface, lest she break whatever magic was allowing this to happen. "Kal, I am here!"

He didn't move at all, so not even a whisper of her scream was getting through. Then the scene around the Emperor began to make itself known, and she saw him. Standing at her brother's side was del Rue. Zofiya howled again, trying to pound her way through the barrier with her other hand. She even kicked at it, but nothing broke.

Taking a long breath she bottled her frustration back inside her, and concentrated instead on what was happening on the other side. It looked like the interior of one of the aristocratic chambers in the palace, and she surmised that this was the room del Rue had been given. It was luxurious, more like something a visiting Prince could command rather than a minor noble.

Kaleva was speaking to del Rue, waving his finger and pointing in a totally uncharacteristic manner. Zofiya's stomach clenched. She hated seeing her brother like this, and most especially knowing that she was the cause of it. Abruptly she had an idea.

Cautiously she pressed the side of her head against the surface. One side of her face grew numb, and her ear felt like it might break and fall off, but she was able to make out faint noise from the other side.

". . . and the Arch Abbot says he will not hand over that cursed Deacon for questioning." Kaleva's voice cracked with rage. "I never should have let them take him in the first place."

"You were in shock, Your Imperial Majesty. You cannot blame yourself for what happened then. What is important is what happens now." He gestured Kaleva to sit, and after a moment the Emperor did. "Have you given any further thought to what we discussed yesterday?"

"The Pattern?" Her brother looked distracted.

"I have been warning you, Imperial Majesty, for months, about the perils of this Order you brought with you." Del Rue pressed. "Now the man responsible for your sister's disappearance is safe behind the skirts of the Mother Abbey."

"It wasn't him!" Zofiya then screamed her brother's name again, but he made no gesture to suggest he had noticed it. Her hands clenched on the surface, but she could not look away.

"But they have rid Arkaym of the geists, and been very useful to—"

"Darling." A voice from outside of the range of the tunnel made itself known by cutting off the Emperor, and Zofiya immediately recognized it. The Empress was apparently also present. "You yourself said it was the Arch Abbot of the Order who was the one that conspired to destroy Vermillion last year. We cannot forget either that the Deacons who you sent to Chioma, only a season ago, returned with my home in flames and my father slain. Now, to top it all off, they have taken your sister."

Kaleva shook his head, glancing down at the floor. Zofiya knew that gesture from times past. He was coming to a hard decision. He was making his mind up with the poison of del Rue dripping in his ear. She pounded on the surface that stood between them.

"Much like the old Native Order, this one has fallen prey to avarice and power." Del Rue leaned in closer to the Emperor. "You can always summon more Deacons from your father's domain if you like. The Order of the Eye and the Fist is not the only one in the world."

"You must think of your people!" Ezefia came into view, stunning as ever in an Imperial scarlet dress, and sat next to him, resting one hand on his knee. "It is about their safety as well as your own." She made a sharp gesture, and one of her ladies appeared, carrying something on a cushion. With the care the lady-in-waiting displayed it could have been made of glass. Whatever it was however was a mystery, since it was covered with a blue piece of velvet.

"You got the Pattern from the vaults, my love," the Empress cooed. "You must know what needs to be done."

Zofiya sunk to her knees, keeping her face and hand pressed to the surface. "Kaleva, no! Whatever they are doing, turn away. Please!" She yelled it toward him, as if he could hear her by some kind of Deacon Sensitivity. If only they'd been twins, or born with the power. Too late now to hope for that.

Kaleva took the cushion from Ezefia's lady, set it on his knee and then drew back the covering. The Grand Duchess ceased her wailing and looked. It was the most beautiful thing she'd ever seen—and it was not the first time she'd seen it. Two pale blue marble tablets, about as long as her forearm, rested before her brother. A filigree of writing was carved into them, and soft blue light ran from the lines. From her angle she could not see what the words were, but she could remember from memory. The ten Runes of Dominion and the seven Runes of Sight. She'd last seen the Pattern, though she'd never heard it called that, on the wharf in Delmaire, just before they sailed for Arkaym. She recalled the Arch Abbot handing them to Kaleva reverently, and offering them up as a symbol of trust between the Order and their Emperor.

Back then she'd been too busy organizing her troops for the largest sea journey of any army in history to take much notice of what the Order did. As far as she knew he'd placed it in a box and sent it to the vault with all his other treasures.

However now, just looking at them, Kaleva's face blanched. His hand hovered a few inches above them, but did not dare to touch the stones. Even del Rue and the Empress were silenced for a spell.

"The inscription is indeed lovely," del Rue said, wetting his lips, "but if Your Imperial Majesty can see beyond that . . ."

"Think of Zofiya . . ." The Empress glanced up, locking eyes with del Rue.

Kaleva cleared his throat. "What do I do?"

The Grand Duchess was riveted, unable to move or say anything; trapped on the other side of the barrier and rendered impotent.

"One must simply break it." Her brother must have been too foolish or perhaps too enmeshed in del Rue's machinations to notice that the older man was leaning forward, and his eyes were hard stones fixed on the Emperor.

"Snap it? It's that simple?"

Ezefia smiled and simpered, as if she were asking her husband to pass the salt, rather than destroy a partnership that had brought Arkaym back from chaos. "You are the Emperor, and it is your right."

"No, no, no," Zofiya muttered under her breath. "Don't be an idiot, Kal! Think for yourself . . . please . . ."

Her pleas dissolved in the ether and never reached her brother. Kaleva straightened in his chair, and then leaning

forward took up first the Runes of Dominion and then the
Runes of Sight, and then simply by placing them against
the low table before him, bent them in half and broke them.
The snap of the fragile stone echoed in the room and in the
corridor Zofiya watched from.

Zofiya found that she was holding her breath, but there
came no rumble of thunder or shower of geists. Nothing.

Del Rue's grin could not have been bigger. He looked as
though he had fallen in a pit of gold and then been showered
with naked women. The Empress too appeared delighted.

Meanwhile the Grand Duchess could barely hold back
her rage. Kaleva! She loved him, and he was a fine Emperor
when it came to day-to-day things. Handsome, kind, but
the flaw in him had reappeared. That thread of weakness in
her brother, the desire to please that their father had fos-
tered in all his sons, had now come to the fore. It would be
his people that would suffer for it.

All three rose to their feet, leaving the broken remains
of the Pattern lying on the table. No longer gleaming with
blue light, they were reduced to mere shards of rock.
Utterly unremarkable.

"Now we can go gather the Guard and besiege the
Mother Abbey." Kaleva smiled bleakly. "I shall have that
Deacon and answers to what they have done."

"The Presbyterial Council and the Arch Abbot are the
ones to be held accountable," del Rue said nodding. "It is
not the fault of the everyday Deacons that they followed
their orders."

"I shall be merciful," Kaleva said, as he walked out
from view, followed by his conniving Empress.

To think, Zofiya thought grimly, *I was once happy he
chose her, and thought her a sweet girl. That man has
twisted her somehow.*

Del Rue closed the door on them and strode toward the
portal.

Zofiya swallowed and backed hastily away down the
tunnel. She only had a dubious piece of wood to defend

herself, but she would damn well give it a try. Taking up a position to one side where the tunnel opened up into the larger cellar, she marshaled her remaining strength and waited, stick held ready. If she was able to get in one good blow on his head, she might have a chance to overpower him. Just what she would do after that was a question that could wait until he was lying at her feet.

She heard del Rue's footsteps crunch on the dirt as he came toward her, and she let out a soft exhalation in preparation. Then she stepped around the corner, yelled in pent-up rage and frustration and drew back her weapon to strike.

However, before she completed her downswing, green fire enveloped her. It did not hurt, but she could feel the little strength left in her limbs drain away. When her captor withdrew the flames of Shayst, she was left limp on the floor, having trouble gasping for breath, and at the point of crying tears of despair.

She heard his words drop on her like hail. "I am a master of both Sight and Dominion, silly girl. Did you think I wouldn't feel you standing there waiting for me?"

He rolled her over with the point of one boot and stared at her with all the chagrin of a disappointed parent. "My little miss Grand Duchess. Whatever have you done to yourself getting free? I am going to have to clean you up or that wound could get quite infected."

She didn't have enough energy to reply to him: not a sneer, not a clever remark, not even a groan of pain. He scooped her up easily into his arms and began carrying her back the way she'd come.

"Never mind," he commented, "we shall start at the beginning again and all will be well."

SEVENTEEN

Silent Lesson

It was not a day they left him alone; it was much closer to a week. Twice a day a mechanized door would open at the rear of the Silence Room, and a plate of food would be behind it. Merrick would eat the bland repast, huddled in the corner of the room, and wonder why exactly he bothered.

Sorcha was long gone, far away, and who knew if she was well or not. Zofiya too was gone. All he had was the company of the darkling. Hearing it whisper into his brain was not comforting, and the longer he was here the more her words of vengeance and distraction were starting to make sense. Merrick was terrified that he would give in to the shadows, and become like her.

He missed the life he'd had before Sorcha disappeared: the cautious smile of the Grand Duchess, the smell of the liniment they used in the infirmary and the wonderful sense of communion in the Devotional first thing in the morning. He held on to those memories and fell into their embrace as a way of escaping the stillness.

So when Kolya Petav opened the door to the Silence Room and whispered, "Deacon Chambers," it took Merrick a long moment to realize that he was not hallucinating. Kolya had been nothing but a distraction and an irritation to him in the last few months, driving Sorcha into apoplexy with his stubbornness about giving her up as a partner. Now that he was standing there, holding the door open, he looked nothing like Merrick remembered.

His blond hair was askew, and his calm expression quite evaporated; the man who was technically still married to Sorcha had a clenched jaw and wide eyes. Even Sorcha's rough temper all those months ago had never made him look like this. "Come with me," he said, his quiet voice the equivalent of a shot in this particular space. He glanced around the room even though it was patently empty. "Quickly, we've got to get out of here."

Merrick climbed slowly to his feet. Perhaps this was some cruel kind of test by the Arch Abbot, or maybe Deacon Petav was working with the Emperor. "Get out of here?" he asked cautiously, craning his head to see if there was anyone behind Sorcha's former husband.

"Yes." The other Deacon actually stepped in and tugged on his arm, an entirely too familiar gesture—especially within the Order. "Now!"

"I take it I am not being released by the Council." Merrick didn't need his Sensitivity to discern the nervous flicks of Kolya's eyes, or the way his hand was clenched tight on the doorframe.

"Indeed not." His fellow Deacon gestured him into the narrow stairway. "Follow me quickly."

Two Sensitives escaping from within the Mother Abbey itself was an impossibility, so ridiculous as to be laughable. Merrick stopped, folded his arms and shook his head. "I'm not quite sure what has come over you, Deacon Petav. I appreciate the sentiment and your effort, but this is a foolish course. We can't just walk out of here, and I wouldn't want you to—"

"I believe right now we can," Kolya said somberly, and

held up his Strop—at least it should have been his Strop. It was the same thick piece of leather, but the runes carved in it were completely destroyed. Merrick stared at it blankly, not quite understanding for a long time what he was seeing. The sharp edges where Kolya had once marked the symbols were wrenched apart as if subject to a tiny gunpowder explosion.

The shapes were broken and rent, and the personal sigil that would have sat between the Deacon's brows was blasted clean on the rock that should have held it. Merrick's stomach twisted and he found his throat trapped shut. He couldn't breathe. By the Blood, this had better be a hallucination.

"How . . . what . . ." was the best he could manage through his abruptly dry throat.

Kolya too was blinking and now Merrick saw that he was holding on to the doorway for real support. The older Deacon was shaking. "We don't know. No one knows, Merrick. However now is a very fine time for one insignificant Sensitive to make himself scarce in the confusion."

That in the midst of this crisis Sorcha's former husband would think of helping her new partner was hard for Merrick to believe. "Shouldn't you be helping the others of our Order instead of getting me—"

"She asked me to help." Kolya went on, now pulling Merrick physically with him.

"Sorcha?"

Choking back a laugh, the other Deacon shook his head. "No, not Deacon Faris. Someone else, someone with dark hair and eyes in my dreams. I ignored her for the last week, but then last night she came and insisted that tomorrow something terrible would happen to you. That this would be the only chance to get you out and safe."

Merrick pressed his eyes shut, but he could still see her. Nynnia. The woman he had fallen in love with, lost, found again, only to lose her for good. On the Otherside, she apparently had not forgotten him either. One of the Ancients, the Ehtia, she still had access to more information than anyone in the mortal realm.

"I cannot let anything happen to you." Kolya's lips pressed together in a white line. "And I take my oath to my fellow Deacons very seriously. More seriously it seems than the Arch Abbot."

Deacon Kolya Petav could have no way of knowing about Nynnia. "But why should you trust some woman in your dream?" Merrick probed.

The other Deacon's eyes drifted away. "Because I ignored her advice once and lost something very precious to me."

Merrick nodded, understanding all too well about lost chances. He would not embarrass his rescuer further, and so followed him quietly out into the stairwell.

"Do you have a plan?" Merrick whispered, tugging up the hood of his cloak.

"Not really," Kolya said, flashing a wry smile over his shoulder, "but then Sorcha always accused me of not being spontaneous enough, so this is a good time to work on it."

It was his idea of humor—Merrick understood that—but considering the seriousness of what he was saying it was poorly timed. Still, he was not about to turn his back on his rescuer.

Reaching the top of the stairs, they entered the Devotional. Deacons of all kinds were there: some were slumped in the pews sobbing, others clustered in groups yelling at each other, while more still ran here and there. No one was taking any notice of anyone else—including two Sensitives trying their best to remain invisible. Merrick tentatively reached for the Bond and his Center, but he already could feel what awaited him.

He had thought the Silence Room was terrible, but at least he had known that if he went outside beyond its weirstoned walls, everything would be normal and as he had left it. Only Kolya's hand against his back kept him moving in this new, far more terrible silence.

His eyes however were taking it all in. They passed a young Active, wrapped in her blue cloak, who was cradling her Gauntlet like a wounded baby. The runes were destroyed just as Kolya's had been. Tears streamed from her eyes and she was rocking back and forth.

"I feel lucky," Kolya whispered, "that thanks to Sorcha's stubbornness I do not have a Bond to lose. Not a new one at least."

It was a strange thing to say, but everyone appeared to be looking for comfort where they could find it.

"Where are the Presbyters?" he asked as they hurried, as discreetly as they could, down the length of the vast stone building.

"In Council. Mournling has gone into deep meditation and no one knows where Arch Abbot Rictun is. Everyone is in disarray." They had reached the end of the Devotional and passed out into the courtyard.

When Merrick made for the gate, Kolya caught his elbow. "Not just yet. Your little dream friend told me of something else we must get in the library."

Merrick was so dazed that he allowed himself to be bundled toward the library. The light here was bright and clear, but everything else was foggy. "How are the runes gone? How can that be?" he muttered under his breath, but none around him seemed to have answers.

Kolya pulled open the doors and they hurried into the dim recesses of the library. Merrick had spent many happy days here as a novitiate, and later had come here to have questions answered, or just to have a little silence and peace away from Sorcha. The librarian, Stoly, was young but dedicated to her charges. She was also a lay Sister, wearing the gray, and so would not be affected by the loss of Gauntlets or Strop.

Still when the two men burst in, they found her seated at

her desk, hands before her, staring into nothingness. Kolya pointed off toward the back of the hall. "The book I want is back there. Stoly, may I?"

She waved one hand distractedly at him without making eye contact. "Whatever you need, Deacon Petav," she said softly.

While Kolya strode off, Merrick decided to wait for a moment. He had never seen the librarian like this, but then this was a day of confusion. Pulling up a chair, he sat down next to her and touched the back of her hand.

She glanced up as if he had shot her. Her green eyes were brimming with unshed tears, and she brushed at them distractedly. "Deacon Chambers? Oh, by the Bones, Merrick!" Now her hand clenched around his.

It was so strange to have the librarian touching him when Stoly had always been so self-contained and almost aloof. Yet, she was also a woman of knowledge, and he knew at this moment that they needed knowledge, so he did not disentangle his fingers from hers. They were all looking for reassurance wherever they could find it after all.

So he clenched her fingertips tightly. "What has happened Stoly? The runes destroyed? How is that possible?" He would have thought maybe a few of his colleagues might have come here for answers. His time in the Silence Room had perhaps prepared him better for all this.

In the thick but somehow comforting quiet of the library, he could hear Kolya moving around, walking among the tall stacks of books, parchments and tablets. But what did any of that history matter if the Order was broken? Merrick swallowed hard on his own despair.

"The Pattern," Stoly murmured. "It has to be the Pattern."

The younger Deacon's head flicked up, and he stared at the librarian. "The Pattern? I've never heard of such a thing."

Stoly leaned back and closed her eyes. "You would not

have. It is a secret for the Council, and of course, for your humble librarian.

"When the first Deacon made the first Gauntlets and Strops, there was a Pattern he followed; a recipe you might say, for how to use the runes to wield the power of the geists. Every Order of Deacons since then has made their own Pattern after each new schism. When the Order came to Arkaym they swore fealty to the Emperor, and as part of that oath they handed over the Pattern." She looked up at Merrick and shook her head. "No one thought it was anything more than a ritual. A sign of trust—because why would the Emperor destroy the Order?"

Merrick leaned back in the chair and closed his eyes, but no matter what he did he saw del Rue's satisfied smile. How long had Zofiya said that poisonous man had been working on the Emperor? How many hours had he devoted to twisting Kaleva's opinion of the Order of the Eye and the Fist? And how hard had he laughed when Merrick fell into bed with the Grand Duchess?

He loved the Order. It had given him control and strength in a world where he thought he would never have those things. Now, the grim truth was, it seemed that he had assisted in its destruction.

"We have to hurry." Kolya appeared out of the stacks, a leather-bound and rather dusty book under one arm. Merrick and Stoly jumped at his sudden arrival.

She might be traumatized by the day's events, but she was still a librarian. "Where did you get that?" she snapped.

Kolya actually glared at her—the first time Merrick had seen any sign of anger from the mild Sensitive. "Do you think now is the time to argue about such things? Need I remind you what is happening?"

Stoly glanced between the two men before slumping back in her chair. "Take what you want, Deacon. I hope it helps—as if anything can now."

Apparently this latest crisis had roused something in even Sorcha's former husband and partner. Merrick wondered what she would think of that. In fact, he wondered what she would be thinking right at this moment when her Gauntlets were gone. She was older than he, and couldn't even remember life before the Order.

I should be with her, he thought miserably, *instead of here with Deacon Petav.*

He barely had time to thank Stoly before Kolya pulled him out of the library. "They will be coming to get you from the Silence Room soon enough. Who do you think they will throw to the wolves for this?"

Together, heads down, hoods firmly in place, they walked as quickly as they dared toward the gate. Merrick didn't hazard a look up, but by straining his ears, he was sure he could make out more organized sounds coming from behind them in the direction of the Devotional. Despite himself, he picked up the pace.

They reached the postern gate. Two lay Brothers were still there, but they were talking to each other and not taking much notice of anything else. They wouldn't stop two Sensitives leaving when the whole Mother Abbey was in turmoil.

They wouldn't, until a voice called out. "Close the gate!"

Merrick and Kolya winced, and spun around. It was indeed Arch Abbot Rictun, with the rest of the Presbyterial Council trotting to catch up to him. All of them were making quick time toward the two Sensitives.

Merrick spun around, and contemplated running for it, but the lay Brothers had heard their leader and shoved the lever to bring down the portcullis. Hearing their councilors, all of the confused and frightened Deacons in the area began to gather around Merrick and Kolya. It was incredible. These were his friends, his colleagues, his classmates but now their expressions were dark. Everything they had known and relied on had been taken away, and they were looking for answers—and scapegoats.

Rictun, the handsome, tall Arch Abbot, now looked haggard and angry. "Come back to the Silence Room, Deacon Chambers."

Merrick swallowed hard. "There hardly seems to be any reason for that. I think I would like to pursue my own investigation since I am the one accused of stealing away the Grand Duchess Zofiya."

"We cannot allow that." The Presbyter Secondo Zathra Trelaine tottered forward. He was a tiny bundle of scars and wrinkles, and his voice was soft, yet when he spoke every Deacon, Active, Sensitive and lay Brother listened. "We must surrender you to the Emperor if we hope to rebuild the Gauntlet and the Strop." He pointed straight at Merrick, and the young Deacon flinched.

Once, the gaze of the former Presbyter of the Actives would have been terrifying. The man had stood in the center of monumental powers and commanded them all. He'd banished and destroyed more geists than Merrick could imagine—yet even he was willing to throw the young Deacon to the Imperial wolf to get his powers back. If that was even possible.

He ran his eye over the throng of his fellows. Some met his gaze with grim determination, but many of them glanced away, staring at their toes or at the dark clouds gathering above them. He couldn't feel a Bond with any of them, except—oddly enough—with the one at his back. Kolya was the only one to remain at his side.

The Deacons were still as dedicated and disciplined as he knew them to be, but the loyalty he'd felt a part of was gone. He really was alone.

However, he still had to find Zofiya, and he couldn't do that from a prison cell.

"I didn't think weapons would be necessary," Kolya whispered to him, "but now I wonder if I should have—"

"No," Merrick replied sharply, "I will not strike down any of our own."

The crowd now advancing on them, however, did not

look like they shared his misgivings about violence.
Among them, Merrick spotted another face. This one did
not look angry or distressed. Deacon Garil Reeceson instead
looked broken. Merrick wondered if the old Deacon had
foreseen all of this coming to pass.

They were all operating without the usual information
they got from their Centers and their Sensitivity, and they
were all frightened by what had happened. Some of the
Deacons facing him had been raised as children within the
safety of the Order.

Merrick knew he couldn't allow himself to be taken.
Del Rue would win—and with very little effort.

"I'm sorry," Merrick whispered, "I am so sorry."

And then deep within him, beyond the training of the
Order, the spark ignited. Somehow, without the strictures
and constraints learned in the Mother Abbey, Merrick's
wild talent found him. It was a smoldering ember that had
been waiting to be blown upon. With a cry, Merrick let it
out. All of his discipline and control was swept away; he
had no way of directing or holding it back.

The wildness fanned out among all of the Order gathered in the courtyard, and then spread from there to wrap
itself around the Mother Abbey itself. It pierced all of them
through, whispered that everything they held dear and
believed in was wasted. Then it howled into their deepest
souls that these most important things were lost, and they
were utterly alone. Nothing remained.

Merrick was the calm center in a storm of broken dreams,
but he was as lost as they were. When he opened his eyes,
swaying slightly on his feet, he was the only one still standing. Everyone, from high-and-mighty Presbyter, to lowly
lay Deacon from the infirmary, was curled up on the pave-
ment, their arms clutching their knees and their eyes wide
and staring.

He had done this before, brought low the crowds outside
the Imperial prison in Vermillion so that they could escape
with Raed. They had been people who were bent on rip-

ping a good man to pieces, and he'd easily turned their despair at the death of the Arch Abbot against them. The wild talent had left them crying in the streets. That was one thing, but this was another altogether.

These were Deacons of the Order, his friends and colleagues, and he had turned them to terrified children.

"What have I become," he said, running his hand through his hair, and looking around in despair. "There's no going back from this."

Yet this outrage would be for nothing if he did not recover Zofiya from the Circle of Stars and stop whatever plan they had set to running within the Empire. He took Kolya under the arm, and helped him to his feet. The application of his touch was enough to shake him free of the talent's grip.

He looked up at Merrick with undisguised horror. "How . . . how did you—"

"No time," the young Deacon barked in return, "we have to get out of here while we can." Now it was he that was tugging his rescuer along. Together they levered the gates open and stepped over the curled forms of the lay Brothers that guarded it.

Out on the street, everyday folk went about their business, chatting, bartering and completely unaware of the great and momentous events occurring behind the Mother Abbey's walls. The sudden and dark thought flashed through Merrick that they would know soon enough. When no Order stood between them and the predations of the geists, the citizens of the Empire would feel the bite of the undead once again. They had lived under the protection of the Deacons for years, and had almost forgotten what their lives had been like before their coming.

Soon, they would be reminded.

Merrick's hand tightened on Kolya's shoulder. "I hope you had a plan that involved more than us just standing on the doorstep of the Mother Abbey."

The tall blond man blinked, still shaking off the effects

of the talent on him. "I had a few ideas." He pulled two brown cloaks out from under a nearby cart, and hastily handed one to Merrick, before taking the second for himself. "Follow me, we're going to the Edge."

They stripped off their cloaks of the Order, but could not bear to part with them. Instead, when they donned the rough common ones, they tucked the bundled green cloaks under their arms. Pulling up this new and unwelcome hood, the younger man turned to follow Kolya.

It didn't matter where they went, today's events would haunt them both forever. No amount of running was going to change that. Merrick could only hope they would be able to find Zofiya and fix everything before it was irreversible.

EIGHTEEN

Strife in the Family

The riser rattled and jerked its way up the shaft interminably slowly. Sorcha stood as tall as she could manage—though her mind was in tumult. She was trying to be calm, as an example to the crew. In truth, she'd never had much to do with tinker's devices. They were almost as secretive and insular as the Deacons.

Merrick had told her plenty about the Order of the Circle of Stars, and how they had melded weirstone and runes to their own purposes. She could only hope that they wouldn't add in tinkering to that mix. As if to emphasize her thoughts, Aachon's weirstone flared, creating an eerie glow that set everyone's faces into odd masks.

The Deacon shook her head. She was becoming quite fanciful. The disturbing thought followed; had her mother been fanciful? No, no, no! She would not consider that right now. She would not think about going through the Order's records looking for a Sensitive Deacon called Caoirse, or finding some long-lost relatives she knew nothing of. At least now she was aware of where she came from, and had a hint about her past. What that could mean would be truly something to consider once they got out of here. Merrick would be able to help with that.

Without thinking, Sorcha slid her hand into Raed's, tightening her fingers around his. The Bond between them strengthened her resolve. She had one of the men she needed in her life, the other she would get soon enough.

Luckily the riser reached the top level with a shuddering lurch before she could think any more distracting thoughts. The crew unsheathed their weapons and primed their pistols. Aachon held the weirstone in one clenched hand, and jerked open the ironwork doorway with the other.

The crew spread out through the corridor in silence—which there was already plenty of. Sorcha swallowed. Raed had accurately described the place: silent as the grave. With a short nod to Aachon, she took her place at the head of the group, and then, closing her eyes, let her Center fly ahead of them. The fortress still vibrated with geist energy, and it was no surprise. The Wrayth must have used their powers to create such a strange and ominous building, because it was stretching every natural law to its utmost. The interior was not something human builders could have imagined or even attempted.

Now that she was within those walls, she could begin to make out the individual parts that made up the Wrayth. Those below her, the peons, only interested in fornication and pleasure, were like a low hum, something that insects might make as they went about their work. Here, higher up, she could make out other, more definitive presences. These were more focused, and even more lacking in humanity than those below. Yet they did not appear solely as geists to her vision. It was a confusing mixture, especially since deciphering the unliving was properly a Sensitive's role.

She shook her head, and let out a muffled sigh. "This is far more difficult than I thought," she confided in a whisper to Raed, "and Merrick makes it look far too easy."

"What about Fraine and Tangyre?" he said. "You could feel them more easily, perhaps?"

Sorcha considered. She had never met Fraine in person, but she had a brief contact with Tangyre Greene. From recollection she was a tall woman, who had seemed friendly enough, though concerned about Raed's welfare. She was obviously an impressive actress. Bringing the image of the captain into the front of her Center, she levered it wide and concentrated on just finding one normal human in the nest.

Cautiously, Sorcha opened her eyes and pointed to the first junction up ahead. "To the right," she intoned, and then, to demonstrate the courage of her own convictions, she took the lead.

The Wrayth, for all their cunning in kidnapping Deacons, and controlling their own little corner of the west, were not at all sensitive as those in the Order were. She could taste no panic or concern in those nearby.

So, in a somewhat circuitous route, she took them around the higher-functioning Wrayth, toward where the hot glow of the humanity of Tangyre Greene burned. Finally, they reached a chamber she felt was safe to usher them into. Her energy was guttering low, and she stumbled into the half-light of the room. Raed was there to smoothly slide his arm under hers and hold her up before anyone noticed. It certainly would not do to have the crew begin to doubt their Deacon.

"They are behind here"—she tapped the wall, but not pulling away, enjoying a little of his strength and a great deal of his nearness.

"The Rossin tells me you are right," he whispered into her ear, and she almost jerked away in horror.

Instead her blue eyes held his hazel eyes, communicating without any words her dismay. His tiny smile was regretful. Behind his gaze, she could read the great cost he'd been laboring under since she'd last seen him. If the Rossin had risen to a higher place within the Young Pretender's being, which he would have to do to speak directly to Raed, then her lover was in great peril.

And he knew it.

She wanted to ask him a thousand questions about the geistlord in his head, but here and now was not a proper place to let them fly free. Instead she clenched her hand around his arm. She hoped it conveyed what she was thinking and how determined she was. *I'm not giving up on you.*

As she stepped away, Sorcha cleared her throat. "There are three Wrayth presences in the room with Tangyre, as well as another human—that is most likely Fraine."

"Then let's just go in there, kill them all and retrieve the Princess." Jocryn was quite a bloodthirsty man—especially for a cook—still the cleaver he used as his main weapon looked well up to the task.

Raed appeared ready to take the advice of the man who'd cooked him breakfast for years aboard the *Dominion*, when Aachon raised a hand. "May I suggest we wait a moment? Much as I would like to get the Princess back, we might be better served to find out why she came here."

"To begin a war," Raed growled. Sorcha began to wonder if the Rossin was not nearer the surface than was safe.

"Surely not just that, my prince. Tangyre is too cunning a woman to bring her charge here—within reach of the Wrayth—for only that reason." He turned to Sorcha. "Could you not use Voishem again to listen to what they are saying?"

She glared at him. Trained as he was by the Order he knew full well the runes and what they could be used for. She did not appreciate being backed into a corner in front of the crew and Raed like that. "The real world is muffled and strained while under phase conditions with Voishem, but yes—I suppose I could try that."

"I need to hear this too." Raed's jaw clenched, a muscle twitching spasmodically. "Can you let me listen in as well?"

This was going to strain her strength even more. Voishem was a tough rune to master even when in perfect health, and Sorcha had just got out of a sickbed she'd been in for months. However the look on his face told it all; he needed this.

This was his sister. His kin.

His traitor.

Sorcha swayed slightly on her feet. It was imperceptible to outsiders perhaps, but a great display of weakness for a Deacon. The Rossin. The Rossin had spoken across the Bond.

She was sure of it. The voice was certainly not Merrick's or Raed's, and it thrummed with power and hunger. Her mind flashed back to the few moments she remembered in the ossuary under the city of Vermillion. They had made something, the four of them. Only a few recollections remained, but the overriding one was power. The Rossin was unfettered power, and untamed hunger.

Once that had been part of her, and now it was very close again.

Raed was looking at her expectantly, but he obviously had no idea that his Beast had spoken to her. He was waiting for a reply.

"Yes," she said haltingly, "I can manage that."

Quickly, before she could change her mind, or the Rossin could speak again, she took his hand in her Gauntleted one and, with the other, activated Voishem. Then she tugged him into the stone with her.

His terror raced along the Bond. It was certainly not an everyday occurrence to be part of a wall. Well, it was not exactly being part of the wall, more like slipping into a half state where the wall and body did not exist. Without training from the Order he wouldn't know that however.

Sorcha could not even see Raed, but she could still feel him holding her hand. Her fingers were locked around his, and she had no intention of letting go. A Young Pretender buried in a wall would be of no use to anyone.

The space around her was pale and insubstantial, outlines of strata in the rock, and undulations in its formation. Sorcha had never really stood still while using Voishem like this; most folk did their best to get beyond solid objects as quickly as possible. She pulled Raed along with her toward the other side.

She'd never used the rune for eavesdropping, but she discovered by virtue of placing her body near the surface of the rock and turning herself sideways, she was, if she concentrated hard enough, able to hear the words.

"The blood is good," a sharp, bright voice spoke. "It is a tie between us and your fine royal self. You can be sure if you play us false you will feel the repercussions." Though she could not see her, Sorcha just knew there was a smile attached to that pronouncement. "However there is also the treaty to sign—while blood is good enough for us, for others of your kind words mean more."

Raed jerked in her grasp, but Sorcha held him firm where he stood.

"And we get the trick of the weirstone tunnels?" Tangyre's voice sounded nearby. "Our forces will be able to travel through them to wherever we want?"

"It is to all of our benefit that the Emperor is toppled. He and that Order of his have kept our hive confined to the outermost west. With the agreement"—the faint sound of nib on parchment echoed through the stone—"you leave us everything west of the Tanderline ranges to do with as we will."

"Indeed," came a younger, lighter voice. "The west was ever a thorn in my grandfather's side; wild, few people and fewer resources."

"Then whatever we do with it will not bother your new Empire. We can send you on your way to begin your great work."

Sorcha had heard enough. She wrenched Raed and herself back with her into the room with the crew in it and doused Voishem from her Gauntlet. For a moment she stood gasping, bent over, hands on her knees, trying to control the shudders that ran through her body. She could only dimly make out Raed telling Aachon and the rest in a low angry voice what they had overheard.

"With these transportation tunnels," he was saying, "all the outposts of the Empire could be easily overrun. No fortress or city will be safe from them."

Sorcha, finally mastering her own dizziness, stood up. "Only the Order has kept the Wrayth confined to Phia. I cannot see how they expect this to work." She reached out, and propped herself against the stone wall, conserving what strength she could. "As soon as they start appearing, the Mother Abbey will gather its Deacons and storm this whole accursed fortress."

"Yes, they could," Aachon grudgingly conceded, "but we don't have the time for them to arrive. We have to get the Princess out of here now."

"They must be planning to reach their next destination using these tunnels." Raed glanced around at his crewmates. They were toughened fighters, but he only had these few. Sorcha glanced to Aachon and jerked her head to the corner.

He took her subtle hint and followed her over to a place just out of earshot.

"I am near the end of my strength." Sorcha knew there was no point concealing it from the first mate; he would be able to feel that through the weirstone. "However, if you can find a way to give me a little more, I will be able to help get Fraine back."

Aachon looked down at the weirstone, as if weighing it—perhaps he actually was. "I could," he murmured, "but the stone only has so much to give before it must replenish itself. In fact, it could be destroyed if I misjudge it."

"So could I." Sorcha met his eyes calmly. She would rather die than return to that dreadful prison of her own body. It was a feeling that she now knew her mother had shared—in a very literal sense. "The question is, how badly do you want to stop a war in the Empire? I know you care little for Kaleva—"

The first mate raised his hand. "I have no love for your usurper, Deacon Faris, but neither do I wish innocent people to suffer needless war over who wears the crown."

"Then we have an accord?" she asked, head tilted, eyes narrowed on him.

"Yes." The corners of his mouth twitched, as he rumbled, "I would never have guessed that I would be fighting to protect the usurper."

"Life is full of strange twists and turns we never see coming." She glanced back at Raed who was conferring with his crew. The Young Pretender was a turn in her path that she found both terrifying and delightful. "He believes that civil war is not the way—and I know you believe in him."

"He doesn't even want the crown," Aachon said, a deep frown folding his forehead. "It belongs to his family by rights, but he has never wanted it."

Sorcha stared at Raed a moment, trying to imagine him on the Vermillion throne, dispensing justice and commanding the Order of the Eye and the Fist to protect his citizens. It was not a difficult image to conjure up.

"Perhaps the best man for the throne is the one who wants the power of it the least." She whispered so low that Aachon did not catch her words.

The first mate was instead examining the swirling weirstone, searching for flaws in it perhaps. He sighed. "I will try my best with this." He wrapped the stone in one sleeve end with a smooth, practiced gesture. "Now tell me your plan to achieve this rescue."

Sorcha smiled at him. "Merrick is the one with plans. What I have, Aachon, is power. Do you think I am quite spent?"

Aachon's eye ran her length, examining her as he had the weirstone. "We shall see I suppose."

Despite the moment, Sorcha laughed. If her Sensitive were here she just knew he would have been unimpressed.

Kolya led Merrick into the Edge of Vermillion. "Just to be sure we're not followed," he hissed.

Both of them, as Deacons, were particularly familiar with this, the least attractive and prosperous part of the capital city. The scent of the Edge greeted them long before they saw it. It was the odor of a swamp: rotting things, marsh gases and desperation. To make matters even more enjoyable, the clouds above finally provided the rain that had been threatening all day. The two men pulled their inconspicuous cloaks of muddy brown tighter about themselves and splashed onward through deepening puddles.

They slipped over one of the fifty bridges that led from the islands that made up the better parts of Vermillion to the shore of the lagoon. Only a few of these bridges were reliable; the main ones were maintained by the Imperial City. The others were creaking things that had been put up by denizens of the Edge: smugglers, cutpurses and servants who worked deeper in Vermillion and wanted a way to get there more easily. The bridge Kolya chose was made of slippery, rotting wood that seemed in imminent danger of falling into the water and taking them with it.

Luckily it held long enough for two Deacons to cross. Deacons? Merrick clenched his fists as he followed Kolya into the blue gray mists of the Edge. Could they really still call themselves that, now that the runes were overthrown and every Strop and Gauntlet rendered useless? It was enough to make many turn back to the little gods in despair. He wondered if the news had filtered out to the citizens of Vermillion yet, and how long it would take the geists to make a return.

As if he was thinking the same thing, Kolya slipped Merrick his own Strop, hidden by the large sleeves of their cloaks. It felt good to have it back, but it felt like a lifetime ago that it had been taken from him in the Grand Duchess' bedroom.

The younger Deacon ran his thumb over the runes, broken and stretched as they were. No power remained in there. Through a tight throat, Merrick managed, "Thank you for bringing it Deacon Petav. It is a very kind gesture."

Kolya nodded grimly. "A bit of a pointless one though." They walked on through the rain a little farther, the older

Deacon looking back over his shoulder every now and then. Then he grasped Merrick's elbow. "Do you think if we recarved the runes, perhaps on the other side of the . . ." His voice trailed off as they shared a look. "No, I didn't think so either."

They were silent for a while after that, like rudderless ships adrift on the ocean. Merrick had never felt like this before, and it was something that he could not allow to stand. He finally tugged Kolya into the lee of a pair of huts. It was the kind of place a cutpurse would have waited for his prey, but luckily the rain had driven even thieves indoors.

"What was the book you took from the library? Will it help us?" he demanded.

In this light, the elder Deacon's face was terribly gray. He shrugged. "It doesn't really make sense."

"Let me see," Merrick demanded. The other Deacon held the book awkwardly between them so he could see the cover.

The title read, *Saints of the Order: Tales from the Darkness.* Merrick tilted his head. It looked rather like one of the books that all first-year initiates were given to read. Most such tales were of a dubious nature, since in the dark times after the Break there had been little time for record keeping. Still one was nearly universally accepted; the first Deacon was the progenitor of the line of Rossin Emperors, and a mythical boy who had risen from nothing and disappeared back into nothing.

Interpretations of other founding tales had led to the schism where different Orders split off. The Order of the Eye and the Fist had grown and flourished since that time, but many others had fallen by the wayside. The real mistake had been believing the Order of the Circle of Stars had been among them.

"And the dark-haired woman in your dreams said to get this from the library?" he asked doubtfully.

Kolya nodded while water ran down the hood of his

cloak but missed hitting the book. "She was most insistent."

For a moment the rest of the world ceased to mean anything to Merrick. All he could think about was the woman. Nynnia.

"And this was hidden?"

"Indeed." Kolya touched the book lightly on the cover. "In a secret compartment at the very bottom of the history section. I don't know how long it has been there."

The words were barely out of his mouth when he felt it. It was cold in this little spot just off the street, but something freezing touched his shoulders, as if an icy hand was pressing on his flesh. Both Sensitives looked at each other with horror. By Kolya's wide eyes, Merrick knew he was experiencing the same.

"A shade," the younger Deacon said, his breath coalescing before his eyes. Every inch of his skin was prickling and running, and his heart racing in his chest. "Yes, a shade for sure."

"I can't even see the damned thing"—Kolya flailed his arms around, as if that would help. "I hate being this blind!"

Merrick raised his hand. "Be quiet! Listen!"

For a moment, the sound he only faintly discerned was drowned out by the rattle of the rain on the nearby roofs, then he heard it; two words repeated. He thought of the spectyr that had brought Sorcha her vision of Raed's peril and set them on the path to Chioma.

It was frustrating being without his Center, but he heard the words, though it sounded like a distant conversation muffled by walls. *"Ratimana . . . Vashill . . ."*

Merrick frowned. The first was the same name he had heard in the Silence Room, the second was also familiar.

"What can it mean?" Kolya asked, head tilted.

Merrick took a long breath. He shouldn't have imagined that Nynnia would give up on him. She and he still shared a connection that had nothing to do with the Bond or the

Order. She might be lost to him, but she was the one who had gone to a great deal of trouble to be born into the human world, just to help stave off the Murashev. She was still watching him.

"I don't know who or what this Ratimana is, but the widow Vashill is someone Sorcha and I helped a few months back." He pulled his borrowed cloak tighter around himself. "We need to head to Tinker's Lane and ask the delightful lady a few questions."

"Tinker's Lane?" Kolya tucked the book away, and glanced up and down the alley. "That's back toward the center of the city? There are probably Deacons and Imperial Guard out looking for us."

"What other choice do we have? It's night now and this is our best chance." He clapped Kolya on the shoulder. "Let's try and think of it like an adventure."

Kolya shook his head and smiled. "Now you are sounding like Sorcha, and that doesn't make me feel any better."

Merrick laughed. "I am sure she would appreciate that."

They circled back through the Edge, and found a slightly better bridge to cross over. Since they were fugitives from the Order, they kept their hoods up. When they crossed back to the islands, the clouds cleared and the rain gave up making them miserable. Vermillion was drawing into evening and the stars were leaping to life in the sky.

Merrick much preferred looking up than taking any notice of the city. The moon and the stars had always been a mystery to him. However, he should have been able to understand everything about the people and things around him—yet he was blind.

Kolya also appeared depressed. After the excitement and rush of escape, the reality of the situation was beginning to sink in. As they passed the Street of Tailors, the older Deacon finally broke their silence. He stepped closer to Merrick so that they would not be overheard.

"What if the Order cannot be fixed?" He asked the question that had been burning its way inside the younger

man. "What will happen to Arkaym without us to deal
with the geists? We'll be thrown back to the dark times."
Kolya shook his head. "I joined the Order to make a difference."

"The Pattern," Merrick replied. "The librarian said
something about the Pattern. If the Emperor did something
to it, maybe it can be repaired or remade."

"We don't even know what it looks like," Kolya said
miserably. "The Presbyters and the Arch Abbot would
know, but we can hardly go back and ask them."

Merrick shot him a look, but the other Sensitive did not
even pretend to notice. Widow Vashill had been an awkward client, and it was in her house that Sorcha had encountered the shade that eventually took them to Orinthal.
However, when they returned to Vermillion, Merrick had
been left with very little to do.

So he'd checked up on their only real geist case in the
capital. Widow Vashill had been glad of the company, and
so he hoped that their unexpected nighttime visit now
wouldn't come as a complete shock.

They kept their nondescript hoods up and stayed to the
less populated streets, trying to keep out of anyone's attention. However, when Merrick heard his name hissed from
an alleyway he did turn reflexively. Another cloaked figure
beckoned to him, and before Kolya could stop him, the
younger Deacon went toward it.

The Imperial Guard would not have lured him, merely
snatched him from the street, and the same went for the
Arch Abbot. When he got closer, Merrick relaxed a little. He
recognized instantly the rather distinctive nose of the person
standing in the shadows. Leonteh Norin had been the last
person in any of their shared novitiate classes to ever raise
his hand. The gangly redhead lad from Vermillion was also
the smartest in the class. He'd become an Active Deacon
days before Merrick left with Sorcha for the east.

Now he was standing in the darkness of an alleyway,
behind a pile of refuse from the nearest public house. He

was not wearing his blue cloak. He locked his right hand around Merrick's offered one and grinned. "By the Bones, it's good to find you Merrick!"

"You were looking for me?" It seemed strange that any of the Order would want anything to do with him after using his wild talent on them.

"Well, everyone is looking for you," Leonteh replied, "but some of us for a different reason." He stepped back and another half dozen Deacons revealed themselves in the shadows. Merrick recognized a couple of them from his class, but the others were older. Tighon Murn was even older than Sorcha.

"What's going on?" Kolya, finally unable to contain his concern, joined them. "Are you going to drag Merrick back to the Abbey?" His hand actually went to his sword hilt.

Leonteh could not have looked more offended if he'd tried. "No! Some of us left just after you did. The Arch Abbot should never have considered handing you over to the Emperor."

Tighon Murn shook his head, his dark eyes distant as he contemplated what they had come to. "We are an Order of brothers bound together by our work. Even Kaleva comes second to that."

Merrick swallowed hard, remembering his history. The first Order and the first Deacon had not lasted long. Schism after schism fractured it, until there were more than twenty Orders. Every break was a peril for normal folk, and it had been generations since there had been one. Eventually, the Orders realized that they had a greater calling.

Had he inadvertently caused a new schism? The cold claimed his belly again.

"It's not just us." Leonteh took him by the arm, looking nothing like the prankster boy he'd been only a few years before. "About thirty Deacons took the chance to get out." He revealed a plum-sized weirstone in his hand. "We set off to find you, before the Arch Abbot shut and barred the gates. I'll tell the others we found you and that the dark lady was right. She said—"

Merrick closed his classmate's hand over the glow of the stone. "What do you mean?"

"The dark lady." Leonteh looked back at his fellows. "We all heard her last night. She told us that whatever happened, we had to stay with you. She spoke to us in Ancient and showed us a dire path that would swallow up the Order forever unless we followed her instructions."

Everywhere he went Nynnia had smoothed the way for him. However, whatever she was seeing from her vantage point on the Otherside, he was not.

"She said the gates would be locked in the Order," Kolya interrupted, "and they were locked and barred as they never have been since we came here." He turned to Merrick. "If she wants us together, then we should be together."

He trusted her. Even people who had only seen her once in their dreams trusted her. Merrick sighed and realized he would have to believe in her too, because that was all he had at this moment. He smiled hesitantly at Leonteh. "Tell them to meet us at Widow Vashill's establishment in Tinker's Lane—but let them know to come in small groups. We don't want to attract attention."

While his classmate raised the weirstone and did just that, Merrick gave the others instructions. He and Kolya set off, knowing they would follow in dribs and drabs. He hoped the widow had plenty of food and water, because tonight she was going to get some very unexpected guests.

NINETEEN

Loyalty and Challenge

The crew formed up behind their captain with grim faces and primed pistols. Sorcha and Aachon took the front positions. Surprise was the only advantage they had, and she was going to use it the best she could. Standing by the door in the dark chamber, the Deacon could hear the footsteps of the approaching people they had just listened in on. Sorcha took a long, steady breath.

The tang of the weirstone's power was the only thing keeping her upright and functioning, but it tasted flat, coppery and chill compared with Merrick. She was pining for his strength and good sense, and as soon as she could, she was going to drag Raed back to Vermillion to find him. If they survived of course.

With that thought, Sorcha took a step into the corridor and spread her Gauntlets wide before her. She only had a brief instant to take in the people before her. Tangyre was there, her arm guiding a shorter, younger, blonder woman before her, and Sorcha thought Fraine looked very little like her brother. Behind were three more women, but with

bone-white hair and skin. In them, the Deacon could feel
the flicker of the Wrayth, lying just under their skin like a
serpent.

They glanced up, and it was not her imagination, something in their eyes told her they recognized what she was.

If they saw anything about Caoirse in her, she was
pleased. Like her mother she would teach them a thing or
two about Deacons. She didn't spare them a word as she
darted forward, slipped between Tangyre, who was now
reaching for her sword, and Fraine. She made no introduc-
tions. Instead she kicked out hard with her left leg, con-
necting with the younger woman's knee; she sent her
sprawling to the ground with a surprised grunt.

Then Sorcha summoned the rune Deiyant. It blazed like
white lightning on her palm as she pushed forward toward
the line of women. The power of the Gauntlet filled the
confined space of the hallway with a massive explosion of
air. Like a geist moving furniture, Sorcha used Deiyant to
toss the bodies of all before her. They were chaff in her
way. As a Deacon she'd never done such a thing to humans
before and wasn't sure she dare examine too closely how
good it felt.

Raed and his crew sprang from the shadows and
scooped up the stunned Fraine before anyone could scramble up off the floor. She screamed and kicked furiously, but
Raed disarmed her, and there were more of them than one
outraged Princess could manage. Sorcha saw the cold light
in Raed's eyes as he grabbed her by the shoulders and
jerked her to her feet. He bound her hands before her with
sharp efficiency.

Aachon and Sorcha took up the rear while the rest of the
crew bundled their captive away with them, back the way
they had come, toward the riser.

It seemed like a dangerous apparatus to make their
escape, but it was all they had. They would have to trust it
since Sorcha could not phase all of them through the walls.

"Nicely done," Aachon commented as the riser continued its ascent. "We should be able to summon Captain Lepzig with the weirstone to pick us up from the roof."

"You're all dead," Fraine spat, straining against Arriann who had taken stern control of her. "I'll have the Wrayth slit your throats just like I ordered done to your crew members in Chioma."

The men and women who heard this glanced at Raed in undisguised shock. This was news to every one of them, including Sorcha. If what the Princess said was true, the Deacon could understand why the Young Pretender would keep it from them at least until they were beyond the nest.

Aachon drew back his hand, as if to slap the Princess stupid, but then at the last moment held his blow. "They died for their captain as we all would. He's earned our respect over many years. How many can you say would do that for you?" His voice was wracked with choked-back rage. It was the most emotional the Deacon had ever seen him.

Sorcha could understand; broken loyalties and conspiracies had almost destroyed her beloved Order. She touched his shoulder. "She isn't worth it."

Raed stepped between his sister and his first mate. "Enough, Fraine. I don't know what you gave up to the Wrayth, but this isn't the way to revenge yourself on me—bringing a whole Empire to the very brink of civil war."

"Brink?" Her smile was chill. "Brother, it has already begun."

The truthfulness of that statement could not be tested right then, because no sooner were the words out of her mouth than shots rang out above them. Many shots.

Instinctively everyone ducked down, but the bullets were not aimed at the people. They rained down against the top of the riser like hailstones.

Aachon grabbed Sorcha's hand. "Guards above are trying to shoot out the mechanism for the machine. We have to stop them!"

The Deacon looked at him as if he were mad. She

understood the risk, but she had no way of targeting anyone. Her Sight was not that accurate without Merrick and
she had more chance of killing them all with a misplaced
blast of Pyet, than she did of halting the assault on their
transportation.

Apparently the Wrayth had what they needed from
Fraine, because they were showing scant regard for her
safety. Tangyre must have had no say in the matter either.
However, Raed, perhaps out of habit, had covered his sister's body with his own. Not that it mattered.

For just then, the shots had their intended effect. The
riser lurched from side to side like a ball on a string, and
the sound of groaning metal filled their ears. The passen-
gers had nowhere to jump to escape, and Sorcha could think
of only one mad chance. Spreading herself on the floor she
shouted, "Hold on," to the crew.

It was perhaps an unnecessary piece of advice. The
chain above finally snapped under the assault, and the riser
began to do quite the opposite; it began to fall like a lead
weight back the way they had come. The sensation of her
stomach trying to force its way into her throat was a new
one to Sorcha, and it was accompanied by a feeling that she
was almost without any weight. In other circumstances
that might have been enjoyable, but since she knew they
were all about to be crushed to death at the bottom of the
fortress it took away much of the fun.

She had enough time to glance sideways at Aachon, and
scream, "Everything! Now!"

The weirstone flooded her with power and then shattered. It filled the inside of the riser with tiny crystal shards,
and the sound of Aachon's wail of outrage. However, since
everyone else was screaming it was lost in the din.

Pressing her Gauntlets down on the floor, Sorcha summoned Aydien, the Rune of Repulsion. Now the riser was
filled with screams, broken shards of weirstone and a flood
of blue light. The Deacon added her own howl to the mix,
just for good measure.

Her eyes blurred as she held on. The rune had never been used for this, that she'd heard, but she could think of nothing else. Everyone screamed as the riser bounced against the sides of the shaft. Its descent seemed relentless and to go on for the longest time.

Then blue fire exploded around them, wiping out—for a moment at least—thought, consciousness and hope. Sorcha felt, rather than heard, the riser shatter all about them. It broke and flew into as many shards as Aachon's weirstone.

That seemed to be it.

Then reality found her again; found her shaking her head free of weirstone shards, and tossed not too far from the bottom of the shaft. Staggering to her feet, Sorcha yanked off her Gauntlets and tucked them with numb fingers into her belt. There would be no use for them now.

It took another few moments before she found Raed, climbing to his knees. In celebration, she planted a kiss on his lips, while he was still looking around bemused.

"Are we all getting that treatment?" Balis was pulling a dazed-looking Fraine to her feet, a trickle of blood from a cut on his head staining his cheek. The sharp thought that if the young Rossin had died in the accident things might have been easier, passed through Sorcha's head. Immediately she felt terrible for such callousness.

Aachon climbed out of the shaft, over the remains of the riser. His glove was covered in the dust of the lost weirstone and his expression pained. Still he was moving, and Sorcha took that as a very fine thing.

The Deacon did a quick head count, and smiled. "I think I've found a new use for Aydien," Sorcha coughed on her own pride. Every one of the crew members was there, alive. Perhaps not exactly undamaged—but still alive.

"No chance of the rooftop then," Raed said, wiping dust out of his eyes. "So I guess we get to try this infernal tunnel instead."

No sooner were the words out of his mouth than a low groan began to rumble out of the tunnels behind them. The

peon level Wrayth were struggling to their feet, their naked
bodies covered in the debris of the crash. Many of them
sported far more horrific injuries than those that had taken
the tumble with the riser.

"Aachon," Sorcha whispered, as a peon with a large
slice of metal buried in his shoulder began to orientate on
them, "how quickly do you think you can activate the weirstones of the tunnel?"

The big man shook himself, and his eyes took a spell to
focus on her. How long had the first mate been using the
weirstone he had just lost, she wondered. Its loss could signal more damage than they could afford right now. However he still had far more experience with weirstones than
she did—especially considering she couldn't stand the
things.

The vacant eyes of the peons were unnerving, especially
as they came ambling toward them. The crew formed a
rough circle around Aachon and Fraine, close to the tunnel.
The Princess remained still, head bowed and her expression
unreadable.

Raed, standing next to Sorcha, blade drawn, chuckled.
In this dire situation he actually chuckled. "You know, my
dear Deacon, one day I would like to court you properly.
You know . . . without the geistlords, the angry goddess or
the nest of hungry Wrayth."

Sorcha considered what sort of strange world that would
be. "Damnation, that sounds like a lovely dream, but I will
take whatever I can get."

The peons were assembling in a mob that would certainly overrun them eventually. She was reminded of the
gathering outside Vermillion palace that she'd had to deal
with. That had been the beginning of her journey of dis-
covery. She hoped she didn't have to kill any more folk
than she had that day. It looked unlikely at this point.

Still, possessed by either geistlord or geist, the result
would be the same. Briefly she considered doing what she
had in Chioma, acting without Sight. But she was drained

of her own strength now, and without the support of Aachon even worse than blind. Yet . . . all these people—including Raed—were relying on her . . .

"I can still use my Gauntlets," she offered. "It's just without Aachon and his weirstone . . ."

"No," Raed replied firmly, "you can't do that again. I saw it once. Not again, Sorcha."

"We got plenty of blades," Frith pointed out cheerfully. "No need to worry yourself."

The peons surged forward. They might be naked and weaponless, but there were an overwhelming number of them. It seemed cruel, but Sorcha and the others had to protect themselves. She did not wince as her blade found flesh.

Small mercies meant there would at least be no shades made here today, since the peons had already succumbed to a geistlord. The crew all hacked and slashed, avoiding grasping hands, and charges by the thick mass of naked limbs and bodies. It was brutal butchery, but it was that or be pulled down into the chaos.

They managed to protect Aachon as he turned his back and tried to make sense of the tunnel that was their only chance of escape. Sorcha was no fool with a blade, but she was not as good as Merrick, and she found herself falling back step-by-step.

"Aachon," Sorcha shouted over one shoulder, "we can't keep this up all day."

"I need you!" came his curt reply, and she stepped back to find out what was going on. His fingers were running over the weirstones, each about the size of an eyeball, embedded in the wall. "I cannot see how to open this."

Sorcha tried to block out the sounds of battle at her back, and the imminent threat of becoming part of the Wrayth breeding program, and concentrate on what she was seeing. From time to time she wished she could go back to the novitiate and tell her younger self to study a little harder. Merrick would have, once again, been a welcome addition to this moment. How Aachon expected her to know any more about this was a mystery. He'd worked and examined weirstones more than she ever had, and it was specialist Deacons that tuned the stones for the Emperor and his military.

However useless it might be, Sorcha did at least try. She saw that it was not just weirstones, there were cantrips and things that might have been runes too. All of them were wrapped around each other, and the stones, like a braid. Whatever the Wrayth had done to create these things was complicated and required blood—probably their own.

The same blood as yours.

Sorcha jerked her head up as the words filled her mind. She couldn't tell if they were from the Rossin, or from somewhere deeper; somewhere that she had just discovered.

"By the Blood," she muttered, for the first time realizing the irony of that statement.

The sounds of battle behind her faded away, and she turned back to see if the crew had dispatched all the peons. What she in fact saw changed everything.

The peons had backed away from Raed and his people and parted to let others through. Tangyre Greene was striding a few paces behind the assembly of tall women and men. They had milky white complexions and dark eyes that the Deacon had seen before in the possessed. Though these walked with none of the clumsy, shattered gaits of the shambling mob she'd fought outside the gates of Vermillion. They were under far more severe control.

"Keep trying," Sorcha hissed to Aachon. "I'll see if I can gain us some time."

The woman in front was a lovely thing, like a statue carved out of alabaster. She held lightly in her fingers a brass chain that ran down to, and was attached to, a collar. This was in turn tight around the neck of another woman. She had long blonde hair to cover her nakedness but that was all.

The Wrayth woman stopped short of the outstretched swords of the crew and examined them as if they were bugs beneath glass. "I am Iuhmee. Set down your weapons and you will be allowed to live." Her gaze flickered to Raed. "Some of you may even find our company pleasurable."

"I would rather die," the Young Pretender growled. "Your women are not my type at all."

The corner of one of her lips quirked at that. "Many say that . . . at first. Eventually they come around." Her eyes flickered to Sorcha, and that calm mask of the Wrayth was broken for an instant. "What have we here?" It seemed like a genuine question.

A wave of sighs passed through the assembled peons, and two of the first women's companions, those not on chains and with the same dark eyes, stepped up closer.

"A hybrid?" The tall, heavily muscled man among them tilted his head in an alien gesture that made Sorcha's skin crawl.

"One of ours—but how?" the third commented, a note of excitement in her voice.

"Only one ever escaped." Iuhmee grinned. It was a gesture that Sorcha was sure she was copying, rather than actually experiencing. It made the Deacon's skin crawl. "We never knew what she made with us."

The Deacon had quite enough of being talked about as if she were not there. She knew, just knew, deep in her bones that she was her own person, not some monstrous creature.

"My mother made me!" She shouted it so emphatically, that even the Wrayth stopped conferring among themselves. "I am what she was—a Deacon, and proud of it. I have sent thousands of your kind back to the Otherside. You will be no different."

"Sorcha," Raed murmured at her side, but she didn't acknowledge him. She was busy facing the black eyes and cool regard of the geistlord that had forced her mother to bear her.

"So many of you Deacons have thought us that easy." Iuhmee pointed at Raed. "Ask the Rossin how difficult we are to banish. We have found the perfect way to survive in this world. No one body holds us. The death of one of our number does not diminish us in the slightest. We are immortal and unstoppable." She smiled, showing rows of perfect, sharp teeth all at once.

Sorcha felt her fingers grow numb, while her vision blurred. She would much rather have been having this conversation with Merrick at her side, and after a couple of weeks to regain her strength. However, it was what it was, and she had never backed down in the face of a geist before.

"Give us back Fraine!" Tangyre had apparently had enough talk. She pushed forward from the back of the press of Wrayth. "You had no right to take her." Her face was set in a red mask of anger—such as a mother might when her child had been snatched away.

However her rage was nothing next to Raed's. As Sorcha melted back to the tunnel entrance to examine it as quickly as she could, he stepped forward, bloodied blade held before him. "You poisoned her and forged her into your own cursed weapon! I won't let you use my sister to destroy thousands upon thousands of lives. I won't."

That's good, Sorcha thought as her fingers darted over the braid of weirstones and cantrips. Behind her, dimly, she could hear Raed and Tangyre yelling at each other, but all of the Deacon's focus was in front of her. Somehow her own mother had figured this out—else Sorcha would have been born in the Wrayth nest. An image flashed in her mind; her own tiny infant hand pressed against the stone by her mother's. The Wrayth within her responded.

No sooner had she remembered that than one of the weirstones shifted under her fingertips. For a second the stone was not hard and resistant, but smooth like water. Sorcha glanced at Aachon, but he merely shrugged, distracted by the continuing arguing over Fraine.

So Sorcha was on her own. Concentrating, she pressed harder on the stone, and closed her eyes. A memory darted up, like a fish from the depths of her unconscious. She had done this before. Her own hand, so very tiny, held against the stone by her mother. A child only a few moments old, she had moved these stones before.

Now, behind her lids she could see a town built in a mountain of gray stone. Shelton. It was a city to the northeast of Vermillion. Lovely people with the most atrocious thick accent. She'd dined on land crab there, steamed over an open fire. She could almost taste them now.

Ripping her fingers free of the stone, she found another. Lisle, a dreary little town of the Apotol desert inland. Kubmagahwe, a city built on the confluence of three rivers, in the southeast of Arkaym. Andis-Most-High, the capital city of Delmaire, where she had studied in the novitiate. She could hear the great bells in the town squares and smell the ocean.

The Wrayth had indeed mapped out many places all over the world. They had only seconds to escape, yet she did not want to be stuck in a distant city that could take weeks to get away from. So she searched on. There it was! Vermillion, the city of the Emperor and the Mother Abbey. The taste of the roasted chestnuts, and the sound of the tide pulling on the lagoon. She had not been gone that long, but she swore she was homesick.

"Raed." She spun around, and only then realized her mistake. She had called attention to herself and what she was doing. The Wrayth had been watching the verbal sparring between the two captains with some amusement: the kind an owner of a dog pit might have while watching two puppies preparing to fight.

Their dark eyes flicked up. The Wrayth might be proud of the invulnerability that they had achieved by spreading their power among so many hosts, but it had been bought at a cost. Unlike the Rossin, or any other geist Sorcha had ever fought, they were not sensitive to what was happening in the ether. They were blinded by looking out so many human eyes and ears.

It was a handy thing to realize.

"Stop them," Iuhmee hissed, shooting out her hand. The peons were fast, but Tangyre was faster. She drew her sword and charged at Raed.

Sorcha slammed her hand down on the stone for Vermillion, and slid it upward, away from the clutter of other stones at the side of the tunnel entrance. It moved smoothly toward where the great eye stood at the very top of the curve, and then clicked into place. The darkness the braiding encompassed resolved itself from oily barrier to the simple shadows of a corridor lined with bricks.

"Get Fraine through," was all that Raed had time to shout before Tangyre reached him. Aachon scooped up the screaming, howling Princess and shoved her into the corridor. The line the crew held buckled and bent under the now-coordinated surge of the peons. They turned back to their Prince, but he was no longer there.

As Tangyre, her scream of outrage rising above the chaos of the Wrayth, leapt through the press of peons, Raed shimmered. Flesh twisted and turned, bent and was made anew, as the Rossin thrust himself out into the world. Blood was in the offering, and he was there to claim it.

Raed's clothes were torn from him and his sword dropped heedlessly away.

"Get through," Sorcha bellowed to the stunned crew members, and in the face of the Rossin they obeyed her without question. The heat of the great cat filled the room as he spun and ripped peons down with tooth and claw. The Deacon scrambled and grabbed up her lover's tossed-away sword, catching a glimpse of Tangyre Greene's face.

It had gone from savagery to horror in an instant, but it was too late to turn back. The Rossin, his jaws and teeth already stained with blood, snarled at her, then let forth a great booming roar that reached even the primitive brains of the peons in the thrall of the Wrayth. They scuttled back

in terror. Sorcha watched transfixed as he bunched himself
and sprang at Tangyre. It was terrible and mesmerizing at
the same time.

Her sword flashed, cutting across the chest of the cat,
but it was a glancing blow that only served to enrage him
further. He twisted and landed atop her with both paws.
The sound of breaking bones rose above the cacophony of
howls from the Wrayth. It was hard to say if she was still
alive when the Rossin bent and engulfed her head with his
jaws. Sorcha still watched, even when they closed with a
snap and ripped it free. He chewed, cracking the skull of
Tangyre Greene once contemptuously, before spitting out
the remains.

"By the Bones," Aachon breathed behind her, his voice
tinged with awe. He must have seen the Beast many times
before, but there was something about its strength in the
sea of Wrayth chaos that demanded reverence.

As if in acknowledgement, the Rossin let out a roar that
pumped up from his huge chest, echoed out of his jaws
and filled the nest of the Wrayth completely.

Sorcha could barely feel her heart beating in her chest,
but she had the sense that her mouth was dry. She was
aware that she stood on the other side of the tunnel, one
hand on the stone that was the connection to the fortress.
She needed to shut the passage down, but Raed was there,
somewhere within the pumping heart of the Rossin.

The huge feline head turned toward her.

Wait.

Sorcha had spent all of her remembered life fighting the
geists, but when this one asked her to hold, she did just
that. The peons and higher slaves of the Wrayth scattered
as the Rossin leapt toward her. Vaguely she could hear the
people behind her, including Aachon and Fraine, scrambling backward in a vain attempt to get out of the way.

Sorcha remained transfixed.

The Beast passed through the portal to the other side.
The Deacon closed her eyes. He smelled of warm fur and

blood, and his muscular flank pressed against her. In a half daze she moved the Phia stone out of position in the braid, and then, wrapping her fingers about it, plucked it from the wall entirely. No more Wrayth would be coming through this entrance.

For a moment no one moved or spoke. The only sound was the low rumble deep in the chest of the Beast that filled the tunnel with his bulk. Without Merrick at her side, she knew she had no chance of holding the geistlord back. If she was to die, then Sorcha would at least feel that which would take her. Under her hand the fur was warm and thick, the kind of coat that a rich lord would have loved to decorate the floor before his fireplace with. Sorcha buried her fingers deeper within it.

The Rossin swung his head around, those golden-flecked eyes fixed on her with an intensity that held her still. She knew what a mouse felt like when pinned to the spot by a house cat.

This means nothing. You are still nothing.

Then the muscles under her hand began to shift and move with the powerful magic of the geistlord. Within a heartbeat she was standing with her palm against Raed's chest. He was breathing rapidly, staring at her, completely naked. More for her own sensibilities than his, Sorcha took off her cloak and, for the second time that day, draped it around him. Neither of them could speak for a while.

"Welcome back my prince," Aachon said, giving voice to the horrified faces of the crew, but Sorcha saw that his hands were trembling where they were clenched on his jacket.

Raed glanced back at the tunnel, worked his mouth once, before managing to get out, "Where are we?"

"Vermillion," Sorcha breathed. "Back to the capital."

"I couldn't even move them," Aachon whispered in a tone that approached awe as he indicated the weirstones in the tunnel. "How did you do that?"

Her mother. The Wrayth. All the answers clamored in

her head, but she let none of them out. Instead she shrugged
and tried to divert his attention. "Lucky I guess. Let's get
to the Mother Abbey as soon as we can. I can protect Raed
from—"

And then the world was ripped away from under her
feet. Every nerve ending sprang alive, and she cried out.
Sorcha didn't feel the ground come up and hit her, but she
found herself lying on the floor, staring at the feet of everyone else. Her mind felt scrambled and madness seemed to
be the best course. Her breath struggled in her throat, and
she felt the Bonds, all her Bonds to the Order spin away
from her.

"Sorcha!" Raed was on his knees, helping her up. His
grip on her felt like it was happening to another person.
"What's happening? Are you all right?"

She didn't answer him, but brushed him aside so that
she could get to her Gauntlets. Pulling them onto her lap,
she stared at them, unbelieving, uncomprehending. Yet,
there it was.

No power flowed through the leathers, and the runes
were broken and blasted. Devastated. The Gauntlets that
she had worked with so much care and precision were
ruined. She could vividly remember sitting in the sun in
the courtyard of the Mother Abbey of Delmaire, etching
the first rune, Aydien, into the leather with great care. It
had been her proudest moment—and now it was gone.

She looked about, searching for answers in the walls, in
the air, in the fabric of reality. Finally, she turned to Aachon.
"What can it mean?"

The first mate stared at the Gauntlets, and shook his
head. "I really don't know."

On the floor, Fraine began to laugh. Soon she was gasping for breath. Apparently she was enjoying Sorcha's horror just a little too much. "The Deacons of your Order are
done for."

Before Raed could stop her, Sorcha threw herself atop

his sister and shook her by the shoulders. "What do you know? Tell me, or by the Bones I'll smash it out of you."

It took Raed and two crew members to pull her off Fraine. "Sorcha!" Raed grabbed her hands. "Sorcha! She's just goading you. Shouldn't we go to the Mother Abbey and get help from there? Surely they know what's happening."

Sorcha swallowed hard, and then closed her eyes. It was hard to focus, impossible to find her Center. Garil was back at the Mother Abbey; he had sent her away because he had known that she would heal if the Fensena could find her. Had he seen this too?

She nodded. "I'm sorry. Yes, you're right, Raed."

He put her arm around him and led her along the tunnel. The others followed in their wake, carrying the still-giggling Fraine along with them. Despite her mirth, it was a somber procession.

TWENTY

Shadows of Bones

As they moved along the corridor, Raed felt Sorcha shiver like a horse about to give up after a long run. She was hanging on by the thinnest of threads, and he kept his arm around her as if that could hold her together. He even found himself murmuring, "It's all right, it's all right . . ." but she didn't say anything at all in response.

Fraine had finally and thankfully ceased her giggling and was silent between the two crew members. Now and then she lapsed into choked sobs. Tangyre Greene had been undoubtedly the most unwavering point in her life. Their father was no one to pin childish hopes and aspirations on. He was a cruel coward of a man who blamed his mistakes on everyone around him. Then the Rossin had killed their mother, and Raed himself had been sent to sea at a young age.

However his sister's tears did tear at him. Tangyre had been his friend too, until the moment he'd realized her deception. Though Captain Greene had been a clever woman, he doubted that she had constructed these alliances with the geistlords Hatipai and the Wrayth by herself. Someone else was moving the game pieces. Someone he'd very much like to meet face-to-face.

They had walked for maybe half an hour, before the brick tunnels of what had to be the sewage system of Vermillion broke through into another area he recognized.

Sorcha did too, for her head jerked upright and she stammered, "The White Palace."

The boneyard of the city was buried beneath everyday citizens' feet. It was naturally an eerie place, with all the bones arranged in patterns and stacks around them, but even more so when seen through the veil of memory. It was here, two seasons past, that he had been part of the being made up of himself, Sorcha, Merrick and the Rossin. They had battled the Murashev for the city and all the citizens in it. Raed reminded himself of one vital fact. They had won.

Raed had only spotty memories of that time, but when he looked into Sorcha's eyes he caught flashes of it. The power and the rage that they both had experienced while melded with the Rossin. It still called to them both.

"Strange isn't it," she said with a twist of her lips, "that the last time we were here we were all-powerful . . . now look at us."

He glanced back, and saw what she meant. Only a few of his crew members remained. Aachon's weirstone had been destroyed, as had Sorcha's Gauntlets. The only thing he had to show for the pursuit of his missing sister was the fact that Fraine was with them. However, even that was not the joyful reunion he had once imagined.

Sorcha touched his face, a stroke along his chin. "I have to find Merrick, but . . ." She stopped and caught her breath before going on. "But how am I to find him?"

Raed had never seen her like this, and while he loved that she was ready to show him her vulnerable side, the larger part of him was distressed by it. Brushing a lock of her red hair back behind her ear, he said as soothingly as possible, "He'll be at the Mother Abbey of course. Let's go."

Aachon checked the tightness of Fraine's binds, and

Raed overheard what he said to her. "My princess, we are going aboveground, and it would be best if you do not cry out. You, like your brother, have a bounty on your head."

She clamped her lips shut, but her eyes gleamed angrily. Raed knew his sister was lost to him—there were just some places a soul could not come back from—but he knew that he would still try to reach her. Maybe the clever, all-seeing Merrick would have some ideas.

They climbed up through the mausoleum doors that Sorcha directed them to and out onto the streets of Vermillion. Raed pulled up his hood and Fraine's—though she glared at him for this consideration. However as soon as they were out in the fresh early evening air, he felt something else apart from the chill. It was the Rossin, close to the surface, and he was relishing in something he tasted on the breeze.

They are gone and we are all unfettered.

Raed did not repeat the words to his companions, because he immediately knew what that meant. He didn't need to have it explained—he could feel them out there. The geists were stirring.

Yet when he shot a look at Sorcha he knew she didn't feel a thing. So he urged them on through the streets of Vermillion, across the gilt bridge that was strangely calm, and to the Imperial Island itself.

His crew tried to hide their awe as best they could. A few of them had been with him last time they were in Vermillion, but the Imperial City always impressed, with its canals gleaming under the moon, and its vast network of lamps on every street. By rights, the crew of *Dominion* should be coming here as heroes, not as thieves in the night, but Raed had long ago learned that life did not necessarily give people what they had earned.

Still, it was what it was. Raed gestured to Aachon, and they broke up the crew into three smaller groups, so as not to draw the attention a small mob would. However all of them strolled as casually as they could toward the same goal.

It was quiet out. The fancy residences on the lower slopes had many lights burning in the windows, but there were no carriages about on the street. Sorcha kept her hand in his and would not let him go. Truthfully, it was a comfort to him as well. In this crumbling world, he would hold on to Deacon Sorcha as tight as he dared.

He squeezed her hand, and she looked at him with a smile that made everything seem all right, even if it were for just a second.

It was as if Fraine took this as a cue. She'd been quiet for a long spell, but then, just as the crew that held her was taking in the sights of Vermillion, she moved.

Raed heard Aleck yell, and then shouts from the rest of the crew members. Aachon reacted first, darting—with surprising speed for a man his size—after the fleeing Fraine. Raed spun around to see Aleck clutching his nose, which was spurting blood down his shirt.

"Sorry, Captain," he choked out, "she's got a pretty good uppercut."

They should have bound her hands behind her. "Stay here," the Young Pretender shouted to Sorcha, before joining Aachon in the pursuit. He told himself they should be able to catch her easily enough; she didn't know the city that well.

They chased her down an alleyway, and then another with low-strung laundry. "Fraine! Wait!" Raed bellowed uselessly after her, but the only glimpse he got of his sister was her white shirt disappearing around another corner.

Raed eventually passed Aachon, who was puffing and panting, but still gamely kept on. Ahead came a vague rumble of noise, and one that the Young Pretender was very familiar with; it was a mob.

"By the Blood, Fraine!" he shouted, as ahead he could see the entrance to the street. Fraine shot a look over her

shoulder, victorious and enraged. The rumble of the crowd
was nearby, and now he could identify screams and howls.
Something was driving these people, and if Sorcha had lost
her power, then he could hazard a guess what was loosed in
the city.

Raed caught a glimpse of his sister, outlined against the
chaos. She looked into it, the tumble of arms and legs, and
the bodies already falling to the hard stone.

Fraine stepped out into the street with a cruel grin in his
direction. The mob swept her up, hundreds of terrified people running for their lives in one direction. Aachon held his
arm, but Raed did not go into the street. He swallowed hard
and stared into the maelstrom of panic. He could see,
thanks to the Rossin, the faint wisps of geists darting among
them, driving the crowd to greater frenzy and panic.

They came nowhere near him though—the geistlord so
near to the surface kept them back like flame in a wild
animal's eyes. The mob passed as quickly as it had come,
moving on and leaving a trail of dead and injured in its
wake.

Raed had to know. With Aachon silent at his back, he
walked out onto the street, his boots occasionally slipping
in blood and gore, until he found her. Looking down at his
sister, her limbs spread at odd angles, her eyes wide and her
lips still stretched in a mad grin, Raed felt his world con-
tract.

"She did this deliberately," Aachon said, but bending
and draping his own cloak over her. "My prince, you should
not—"

"Enough," Raed held up his hand, feeling his insides
turn to lead. "You're right, but she is still my sister." He
picked her up and carried her back to the group.

The crew glanced between the first mate and their captain in utter shock. Sorcha's jaw clenched. Raed deposited
Fraine's still-warm body into the arms of Arriann. The
young man swallowed hard.

"You know your way back to the ossuary?" Raed croaked

out, and when Arriann nodded he continued. "Take her back there, then come find us at the Abbey. It is fitting that my sister should lie in the boneyard of our ancestors. Be quick about it."

The young crew member dropped his gaze away from his captain's and turned to do as bid.

Sorcha started forward, "Raed, I—"

"Not yet." He held up one finger sharply before her. "This will be for later." He'd always known that trying to stop Fraine might mean her death, but he had never imagined she would choose to take her own life. That was a specific kind of pain.

"To the Mother Abbey then," he said, and turned back to their original course.

They didn't have to walk far up the hill to see what else was wrong with Vermillion. Sorcha stopped, absolutely still in the middle of the road, and stared.

Raed was not a Deacon, but he also felt the shock of what they were witnessing. The Mother Abbey stood as it always did, with the Devotional towering behind the walls, and the cluster of lower buildings around it only glimpsed over the top of them. However the gates were shut, and no lay Brother guarded the outside this time. Ranks of Deacons in the blue and green lined the walls. They were armed. It was immediately obvious why; lined up outside the gate were ranks upon ranks of Imperial Guard. They looked like red toy soldiers lined up at their master's bidding.

Indeed, the Emperor must have emptied their garrison, because it looked like all five hundred were outside, at attention.

They were not attacking the Mother Abbey that Raed could see, but they were most effectively blockading it. Sorcha took a step forward as if to try and simply walk through the lines, but Raed grabbed her shoulder.

"Don't," he hissed to her.

When she spun around on him, he could see the glint of

panic and rage in her eye. This had been a dire day for her; learning how she was conceived, losing her Gauntlets and now seeing her Order put under virtual siege. A weaker person would have crumbled under such an assault. "I have to get in. By the Bones, I have no love for the Arch Abbot, but he is still my superior—"

"Look at these!" Raed snatched her Gauntlets from her belt and brandished them in front of her face. "Have you ever heard of the runes being destroyed like this? I had the best education my father could provide, and I can tell you I never have!"

Aachon was also gape-mouthed and staring at the quite unimaginable scene. Raed knew his first mate concealed his disdain for the Order, but by the expression on his face, he too was at an utter loss.

Luckily, all of them standing around staring in slack-jawed horror was not going to attract any attention, because there were plenty of other folk doing the very same thing. The citizens of Vermillion clustered in the shadows of nearby buildings, whispering among themselves as if afraid the Guard would turn on them.

Since no others of his crew were quite capable of movement or thought, Raed took it upon himself to find out what he could. A huddle of three older women seemed the best pick to approach. Two were wearing the long aprons of fishmongers, and smelled appropriately, while the third had the look of some old streetwalker well past her prime. They were obviously not residents of the Imperial Island, but must have trekked from other parts to observe proceedings.

He sketched a little bow, though in these circumstances it was perhaps a little over the top. "Excuse me ladies, I've just come in from the countryside, and had a message to deliver to the Arch Abbot. Do you know what is going on here? Is it some kind of ritual?"

"Ritual!" one growled. "Not like one I've ever seen, and I'm born and bred in Vermillion."

"The captain of the Guard demanded the Deacons open the gates half an hour ago," a second, with a kindly face, spoke with the hushed tones of one in the know and more than willing to share. "They said something about being traitors."

"Never liked them Deacons," the third offered, "but they did protect us. Now there is a rumor going around all their power is gone."

"They deserve it though—taking the Emperor's sister right out of her own bed and all!"

Raed couldn't quite believe what they were saying. He was no friend to Kaleva, or his sister, but he had saved the latter's life once. That tended to stick with a person.

He put on his most winning smile. "Forgive me, lovely ladies. But I have been long from Vermillion, and had not heard this news."

"Really?" The fishmonger with a face like it had been struck with a fry pan, glared at him. "Living under some kind of rock were you?"

The streetwalker however flashed him a grin, almost devoid of teeth. "The Order took her last week. Snatched from her own room, and she hasn't been heard from since. The Arch Abbot there won't give up the Deacon that did it neither."

"You don't happen to know the name of that particular Deacon do you?" A deep part of the Young Pretender twisted—like he'd eaten something rotten.

"I do," the second fishmonger said, waving the stump of her index finger. "Made me laugh and all . . . something like chamber pot I think."

By the Blood, it could only be one Deacon. "Could it have been Chambers, perhaps?" Raed ventured.

"Oh yah, that's it!" two of the ladies piped up, while the third deliberately turned her back.

The Young Pretender smiled. "Thank you for your kindness gentle ladies."

The streetwalker actually reached around and pinched

his backside as he made to go. "I'd love to do you a quick one right here," she shouted after him, "but this looks like it's getting interesting real soon."

Raed half backed, half leapt away, before striding back to his companions. He put his hand on Sorcha's shoulder, and leaned in close to her ear. "I am sorry to tell you this— but I think what has happened to you has happened to all of the Deacons."

She sagged against him, and he would not have given her the terrible news about Merrick, but she needed to know. She glanced up at him. "There's something else too, isn't there?"

He swallowed. "Yes, yes there is. According to that huddle of gossips, last week your partner was accused of kidnapping the Grand Duchess."

Sorcha looked down at her feet, her jaw working from side to side, and her grip on his arm tightening. "I knew he was going to the palace just a bit too often, but I can't believe he was stupid enough to kidnap Zofiya—and besides—why would he want to?"

It did seem ridiculous. Merrick was far too clever a young man to do anything so mad. Yet, he had been quite deeply in love with Nynnia and then had her snatched away. Had he set his sights on another unattainable woman?

"I don't know," Raed shook his head. "It doesn't make any sense. But then"—he swept his arm to encompass the whole scene before them—"none of this does."

"The runes destroyed," Sorcha repeated under her breath. "That is even more unbelievable."

Perhaps she'd been hoping it was just herself that was affected, and when her colleagues examined her Gauntlets they would have an answer. It was not to be.

That was the final straw. She had been through too much, and her energy was sapped beyond words. Sorcha slumped against him, staggering on her feet like an injured horse. Raed swiftly picked her up, cradling her against his body. She was terribly thin and light. In comparison, he had more energy than he knew what to do with. The Rossin had eaten well. He could have carried her for hours.

Sorcha's head lolled against his chest. "We must get inside and find Merrick," she gasped. "I need him but I can't feel him anymore." Her eyes were so glassy it seemed she might cry. He wouldn't blame her.

He is not in there. The mouse has escaped his trap. Perhaps he gnawed off his own paw.

The Rossin was almost purring, and very near the surface now.

Can't you feel him? He is a part of you, as much as he is a part of her.

When the Rossin pointed it out—full of strength and vigor—Raed could. The Bond Sorcha had created had always been such an intangible thing to the Young Pretender. She'd spoken of it, and he knew it existed, because she had found him in Orinthal with its help, but he'd never been able to sense it. Until now.

It was a pull, the direction of all things. Perhaps this was what migrating birds on their way south for the winter felt. Raed twisted his head back and forth feeling the unusual nature of this awareness.

The Rossin was helping him. Just why he would do that was another impossible question to answer.

"I can feel him," he whispered, and Sorcha, still held in his arms, stared up at him in undisguised disbelief and relief. "He is not in the Mother Abbey. He is in the city, not far away." Raed kissed the top of her head. "Let's go find him."

TWENTY-ONE

Old Friends and Industry

Sorcha was enjoying being carried by Raed. It was the only enjoyable thing about this whole day. Even though the Order was in ruins, the Grand Duchess abducted from her bed, and the whole world seemingly falling down around them, she would take comfort in small joys. The Young Pretender's arms were strong, and though he smelled of sweat and blood, underneath she could detect his warmth.

For just an instant she imagined retreating to a cabin in the forest somewhere. No Order. No Emperor. Then, reality reclaimed her. She knew her nature; that would never be enough for her.

Still, it would have been pleasant to find a place, and expend the last of her energy with him. She'd dreamed of him while she lay in the infirmary, and gradually given up hope that she would ever be able to make love with him again. Now she was mobile and so was he, but there was no time.

Everything was as per usual.

Nestled against his chest, she did manage to keep one eye open as they traveled through Vermillion. They went

back across the Bridge of Gilt, which was her least favorite
of the city's many bridges, and traveled through the prosperous merchants quarters. Raed had abandoned stealth it
seemed, because he pushed through crowds of folk with
never a care, even when the hood of his cloak blew off.

She could understand why; there were far more problems in Vermillion tonight than one dispossessed Emperor.
Everyone was pouring out into the streets, as word spread
that a standoff was occurring at the Mother Abbey. Many
people were streaming toward the Imperial Island, which
seemed mad to her.

The whispers that passed them said that most were
expecting a show, but talked of not venturing too close,
lest there be a riot, or perhaps an explosion of rune magic.
Sorcha wouldn't have been surprised if they were looking
forward to something like a fireworks display.

Not many who they passed were raising words in
defense of the Order. Most were whispering about "their good
Emperor finally taking control," or "about time the Deacons were taken down a peg or two." Her ire finally began
to overcome her shock.

These were the people that the Order of the Eye and the
Fist had protected for years. They were the reason so many
of her brethren had laid down their lives. And yet, here
they were almost looking forward to its demise. Maybe the
Circle of Stars was right, perhaps the people of Arkaym
should be ruled over ruthlessly since they had so little
thankfulness for what was done in their name.

They circled through the Boulevard of Cloth Merchants,
and dodged the crowds on the Lane of Easy Virtue. Some
of Raed's crew spared a glance up to the brightly decorated
balconies of the ladies and lads of easy virtue, but fortunately all of them were abandoned. It appeared that even
those that made a living on their back had an interest in
tonight's events—enough to give up an evening's earnings.

Sorcha, as much as she loved the Young Pretender, was
beginning to doubt that he could feel the Bond between

himself and Merrick. After all, she couldn't and she was a trained Deacon. Not that that meant anything anymore.

Still as she was cradled in his arms, she did begin to feel a little stronger, and by the time they reached Tinker's Lane, she tapped him on the shoulder to be let down.

She frowned when she realized where he had led them. "Here?" Tinkers and Deacons went together about as well as oil and water.

Raed didn't answer, merely took her hand and led her farther down the street until they were outside a place that Sorcha recognized. It had only been the previous season that she stood outside this place with Merrick and Kolya. The sign still proclaimed, VASHILL—MASTER TINKER TO THE PALACE, while within, a single light flickered in one of the downstairs rooms.

Aachon and she shared a look, while the crew scoured the darker parts of the street for any dangers. Raed however was oblivious. He marched up the path and banged on the door.

The noise echoed down the silent roadway and made Sorcha jump. It was a very fine thing that the Imperial Guard was busy right now. No one came to his first knocking, and Raed was just about to try again, when the door popped open.

There in all her nighttime glory stood Widow Vashill. She looked no older or wiser than when Sorcha had rid her attic of the shade of her dead husband. Her face was just as welcoming now as it had been then however—that was to say, not at all.

"Oh it's you," she said, pulling her shawl around her and peering at Sorcha, while completely ignoring Raed. "I thought someone said you were dead."

"No, not quite," Sorcha muttered. "I don't suppose you have seen any other Deacons about have you?"

The old woman grinned, showing her vast expanse of crooked teeth, but rather than denying it, she instead stepped back and ushered them into the shop.

Sorcha kept expecting it to be some kind of trick, and a mass of Imperial Guards to rush out to carry them off to prison, but the widow gestured half of their company onto the lifting pallet.

"Not all of you," she croaked. "Next ride, or take the stairs." She looked delighted for some reason.

On the pallet, they sped up to the third floor, and in this large space, with the windows covered with dark sheets, Sorcha finally felt she had come home.

The room was full of Deacons. They still wore their cloaks, and there were both blue and green in evidence. A tight ball of emotion lodged itself in her throat, but it didn't stop her from racing over to them. It was hard to tell in the half-light but she would have said there were about twenty or more of them.

Lujia, Kabel, Sibuse, Elib . . . She began to lose count of the familiar faces that surrounded her. Then out of the press of people, the one face she wanted to see most of all, and feared she never would again, emerged.

"Merrick," she whispered, and not caring who was standing nearby, threw herself into his arms. He felt solid and real, and he was hugging her back just as hard. She had to slap him on the back several times before she was convinced she wasn't imagining it.

The Bond between them though was silent, and that loss was an ache inside her that felt like a wound. She kissed him once on each cheek and squeezed him again for good measure.

His brown eyes were gleaming with delight, and his curly hair was even more unruly than ever. He blinked at her as though he thought she might disappear. "By the Bones, Sorcha! I can't believe it! You're all right." Then she realized why he was blinking: he was trying to hold back tears.

"Yes," she said, giving him a little twirl. "Not quite myself." She patted her skinny hips and held out her rail-thin arms. "Still, nothing that a good few weeks of eating won't help."

"So long confined to a bed," Merrick marveled, "and yet that is all? You're a miracle!"

That brought Sorcha back to reality with a thump. He didn't know. Without the Bond he wouldn't know unless she told him. That was a bitter thought indeed.

To cover her confusion, she gestured into the crowd and Raed managed to squeeze his way through. Merrick let out a delighted yell and grabbed him into a hug, before ending it with several hearty slaps on the back. Such a display from her young partner was quite endearing.

"I hear you've been causing quite the stir," Raed commented. "Kidnapping Grand Duchesses and igniting a feud with the Emperor himself!"

"He did no such thing." Kolya emerged from the back of the crowd, his usual calm demeanor showing signs of cracks. "However, I got him out before Kaleva could torture him into confessing to something he didn't do."

Sorcha looked her former partner up and down, reevaluating him. "No one was there to help Merrick?"

"Not a soul," the Deacon himself responded.

Sorcha did not voice her disappointment that it had not been Garil that aided him. "Thank you," she said, turning to Kolya, and genuinely meant it. "You did a very good thing with every chance of punishment for it."

He blushed and looked away; their shared past made things awkward between them. However compared to what had happened to the Order, it now seemed very trivial. Sorcha shifted from one foot to another for a second.

"Yes," Merrick broke through the moment of tension. "The Emperor is not really himself at the moment. He's been keeping rather bad company."

She was certain there was more to that comment than was first apparent, but the Deacons were more important to her right now. "How did all of you get here?"

"We found each other out on the street, and we could hardly just wander around with guards out there too. This was the best place I could think of to bring them." The other Deacons were once more settling on boxes and the floor, talking among themselves. Merrick glanced around before lowering his voice. "Many of the Order were either outside the gates when they closed or escaped beforehand. Everyone here is appalled at what the Arch Abbot is doing . . . or not doing."

"An understatement," Kolya offered, "but the Emperor is not what he once was. The loss of his sister has quite unhinged him."

The Deacons nearby nodded their agreement. Sorcha glanced back at Raed who looked like he might never smile again. He had lost a sister, and she hoped he could survive that. Looking around further, Sorcha saw that every one of her colleagues was nursing a set of ruined Gauntlets or Strop like a broken limb. She was not going through this grief alone, but that didn't make it any easier.

She took Merrick by the elbow and guided him into a slightly less-occupied corner. "What really happened between you and the Grand Duchess? I know you were attracted to Zofiya, but—"

"You heard everything I said to you in the infirmary?" Merrick blushed. It was amazing he was still capable of that after all this time with her.

"Yes, and it was a good thing too, I got into a couple of situations where your experience was very useful." Quickly she outlined what she had seen in the nest of the Wrayth. Since it was Merrick, she spared no detail—even including what she had found out about her own heritage. The only detail she kept to herself was the deal with the Fensena. That seemed of little importance at this moment—and her partner would only fuss. So she lied a little and said Aachon and the weirstone had helped her remove the curse.

He sat down quickly on a box after that. "Well"—he cleared his throat before going on—"the story behind your conception explains many things about you, Sorcha. The strength of the Bonds we made, as well as your ability to survive Hatipai . . ."

"And perhaps why Rictun hated me, even from the novitiate," Sorcha conceded. "He was never able to explain it, but something about me irritated him."

"I always assumed it was your—" Merrick stopped suddenly, and she smiled.

Luckily, Raed saved the young Sensitive from further pain, when he wandered over.

"Have you got out of him what happened with Zofiya?" he asked mildly, as if they had all the time in the world.

Merrick flushed again. "There's not much to tell. After Sorcha disappeared I went to the palace with the intention of getting the Grand Duchess to secure an airship, so I could pursue her."

"I'm sure that was the reasoning," Sorcha murmured, thinking of the sly looks the Imperial sister had been giving Merrick even on the way back from Chioma. She was experienced enough to know when two people were attracted to each other—even if one of them was second in line to the throne of the Empire.

Her partner ignored her jibe and went on. "Zofiya had been having some concerns about a minor noble, del Rue, who was being taken into the Emperor's confidence in a deep and puzzling way. When I met him, I realized he was the man I had seen in the tunnels in Chioma—the man that tried to take my mother."

Sorcha clenched her hands into fists. "When I was laid out you told me all about that—that they were of the Order of the Circle of Stars?"

Merrick nodded bleakly, while Raed frowned and asked, "But that Order was destroyed generations ago . . ."

"Apparently not," the young Deacon said. "They're not really as dead as we thought. They still want the Empire for their own. Your grandfather's attempts to have them wiped out forced them underground—but they never left."

"They're responsible for all this. Ulrich. The White Palace. Chioma." Sorcha leaned back on the box, and stared at the ceiling for a long moment.

All three of them considered the implications, but it was Raed that gathered his thoughts quickly enough to ask, "Well then, what can we do to stop them?"

"Find Zofiya," Merrick replied swiftly. "The Emperor might become a little more reasonable with her back at his side, and perhaps we can fix what he has done to the Pattern."

"The Pattern?" Sorcha blinked.

"Apparently there is a master Pattern for all the Gauntlets and Strops of the Order, and it was held in trust by the Emperor. It was a form of surety that we would not run amok and steal his throne as the Circle of Stars tried to. The Pattern's destruction is to blame for the failure of the runes." Merrick absentmindedly rubbed the length of the Strop between his fingers. "I don't know what it looks like, but maybe it can be repaired somehow."

Raed snorted, but held his tongue. This was all new information to Sorcha, but she believed what Merrick was saying; her partner knew a great deal more than she, even if he had been in the Order for a much shorter time. Book learning was not her forte, but then that was why they were partners; to be a strong team.

"So, if we know that this del Rue took the Grand Duchess, then how do we plan on getting her back?" Raed asked, his eyes staring at a distant point.

Merrick seemed to come to a decision, folding up his Strop and tucking it away quickly into his pocket. "He must be using the weirstone tunnels to pass back and forth between the palace and wherever he is keeping her. Very convenient since he doesn't have to worry about guards or walls."

"He could just be using Voishem," Sorcha offered.

Her partner shook his head vehemently. "No, that rune doesn't make you invisible, and he wouldn't risk being seen. Besides, he's constantly at the palace. He needs a way to pass around easily and without drawing comment. The Wrayth's tunnels would work best."

"So," Raed said, standing up and brushing off his jacket, "you are going to say that we have to break into the palace and without the help of your runes?"

"Why don't you choose something hard?" Sorcha groaned, thinking with longing of Voishem, now lost to her.

"We are not completely without resources, some of us have a wild talent or two." Merrick would not meet anyone's eyes, but Sorcha felt a surge of pride in her partner. She'd been outraged when first partnered with him—now she wouldn't have it any other way. "Now, I don't exactly know how well I can control whatever it is, but it is a weapon we can use . . . at least until we get the runes back."

Raed nodded. "It has to be done, so let's get to it. The longer Arkaym is without the Order the more geist activity will increase." He walked back to Aachon, pulled him away and began to talk to him quietly. The first mate listened and nodded. As he did, his face became even grimmer.

Merrick, watching them, looked just as despondent. Sorcha laid her hand over his. "We'll find a way back. We have to, and besides"—she nudged him—"you at least have some kind of power. Without my Gauntlets I am nothing."

He shot her an appraising look. "With what you have told me, I don't think that is necessarily true."

She flinched and would have yanked her hand back, but he twisted his and held on tight.

"You can't ignore this, Sorcha." His brown eyes were stern in the dimly lit room. "Think of the Prince of Chioma; he too was a product of geistlord and human. The Wrayth are trying to make something with their breeding program. Maybe they already have what they wanted and they just now found that out."

She stood and looked down at him, still holding her hand. "Once the Order is fixed, we'll send back a Conclave of Deacons to root the Wrayth out. Until then, we have plenty to occupy ourselves with."

In the way of Merrick, he did not argue. It was push and back away, with him—forever testing her boundaries and demanding more of her. Now he had found one, and he left it up to her to see if she was brave enough to cross it. Sorcha pressed her lips together and glared at him.

"Come on then," he said, with a shrug. "Let's go find the right Deacons to infiltrate our Emperor's palace."

She twisted her mouth. "I suppose you will insist on Kolya?"

Merrick assessed her for a moment. "Would you mind if I did?"

She shrugged and glanced over to her former partner. "If you think he will be useful, then that is fine with me." In the moonlight, she realized she had never looked closely at Kolya—not since he'd recovered from the geist attack outside the palace. In all the time she'd spent angry with him, she had forgotten much of the good about him. She'd married him for a reason, not just for convenience. He had reminded her of that by helping Merrick.

The young Deacon's hand rested on her shoulder. "I don't think Kolya should come, not for this . . . but perhaps he can guard those left behind. I know he is a fine shot."

"Yes," she agreed, "he is indeed."

Merrick squeezed her arm. "Then come meet the others, and let us find what we can among the remains of our Order."

TWENTY-TWO

Things Never Foreseen

Merrick crouched next to Raed in the shadow of the garden wall and felt the weight of a rifle in his hands as some kind of desecration. It was not that he had never fired a gun, or wielded a sword, but the fact was that it had never been his first line of defense—Sorcha always had been.

It was a miserable evening to be out. Rain had started to fall and clouds had covered the moon, so that the only light in the Imperial Square before them was from the torches atop the wall. Raed had commented it was good weather for a sneak attack, and while Merrick could see that, it didn't lighten his mood.

On the other side of Raed, Sorcha was also armed, and looked about as happy as he felt. Behind them were three pairs of Deacons: Leonteh and Quannik, Murn and Natylda, Lujia and Sibuse. All of the Deacons had left their cloaks of the Order behind at Widow Vashill's home. The rest of the group was made up of crew from the *Dominion*. At this point, they were far more useful than the members of the Order. Merrick knew Murn and Natylda well, as both had tested against him in the practice arena, but the older pairs were a mystery to him. They had claimed competence with a rifle, but that remained to be seen.

Kolya had been left in charge of the remaining Deacons; a steady and dependable rudder on this madcap ship. All of the things Sorcha had found boring about him nonetheless made Deacon Petav an excellent administrator.

Exactly what Raed felt about all of this was impossible for Merrick to know, without the Bond. It also made focusing on the path ahead that much more difficult. He found his thoughts wandering away from him, dwelling in dark corners and conjecturing everything.

While he did that, Sorcha pulled out a set of binoculars and focused them on the postern gate of the palace. Apparently she was not having the difficulties that Merrick was laboring under. The Emperor's palace was not built to withstand sieges of any kind, with sprawling gardens and elegant white stone walls. However the inner fortress was older, and had crenellations and battlements that had seen war in the centuries past.

"Only a light guard tonight," Sorcha whispered over her shoulder. "I guess we can thank the Arch Abbot for that."

"We'll need every mercy and good turn we can get." Raed checked his pistols for what had to be the second time. "Now where are this del Rue's apartments in the palace exactly?"

Merrick pointed to the east wing. "Third floor. Not quite on the same level as the Emperor himself, but very close to it."

"And are we just supposed to shoot the guards to gain access?" Aachon growled. Being without a weirstone had not improved his mood any.

However, there mightn't be a need for it—not if Merrick's wild talent worked. He hoped it would; these were guards that the Order had worked with, and he knew many of them by name. He'd hate to have this terrible week culminate in slaying those that were in fact on their side.

"No," he snapped rather forcefully. "Let me deal with

this." Then, before any of them could argue or stop him, he darted out from the shelter of the building and toward the gate. As he reached the point where he wasn't going to be pursued by his friends, he slowed down, and strolled toward the palace as if he were in fact expected.

His heart was pounding, and at any minute he expected the guards to shoot him. It was a very tenuous and vulnerable position. Without the comfort of the Bond, and with the knowledge that it might never come back, he felt as though he were stepping out into space with no surety that there would be anything under his foot when he put it down. This was the spot where, last year, Sorcha had fought a geist-powered mob, and Kolya had been badly injured. This was, then, in reality, where his adventure had begun. It was fitting.

As Merrick approached the gate, he was very glad that he had left his cloak, folded reverently in the Vashill attic, behind. Two guards stood by the gate, while another two were talking with each other in the guard post. He could discern nothing particularly alert about them, but then without his Center he couldn't be sure of anything.

"State your business," the guard standing in the shadows barked. He was holding a staff with a weirstone the size of his fist embedded in the top. Merrick knew its purpose; to summon more guards if needed. In the flickering lantern light he recognized only one of them, but couldn't recall his name. They were on nodding acquaintance from when Merrick was coming and going at Zofiya's insistence.

The young Deacon's heart began to race. He had no time to mess about; he had to use his wild talent and quickly before he was in turn recognized. The trouble was, he really had no clue about what he was doing.

"I said, state your business," the guard reiterated, taking a step forward. Out of the corner of his eye, Merrick saw the others shifting, turning and beginning to wonder what was going on.

Panic started to surge through Merrick's body, and he

became aware how foolish this was. They might not think immediately that he was a Deacon, but he was a man, unannounced at the gate in the middle of the night; a night that the rest of the guards had been summoned to do battle with the Order.

Within, he groped furiously for the talent, but that meant Merrick was nearly incapable of doing anything else—such as replying to the guard's challenge. He caught sight of one of the men raising his rifle to his shoulder.

What feelings would guardsmen have foremost in their mind? What would they respond to? Merrick pushed down deep, letting their emotions wash over him like a river of confusion. One trait was shared by all of them: dedication to their duty.

It was not like it had been outside the prison, or in the Mother Abbey, where emotions were already running high and easy to tap into. These were calm, centered individuals, but they shared this one thing. Merrick's talent reached out, wrapped itself around that and twisted it.

When he looked at them, their eyes were gleaming with intensity, and they listened to him, though he could not tell what they were seeing. Still, the words that came out of his mouth rang with command. "Your Emperor needs you, report to the Mother Abbey immediately!"

They swayed slightly, caught in the breeze and influence of his wild talent. Merrick could feel his heartbeat banging in his throat, certain that he was about to be shot down. The guards' eyes flickered from side to side, as if seeking something that did not exist. Then they snapped to attention and marched from their post like windup children's toys. Merrick stood alone there for a moment in the rain, feeling light-headed with his hands shaking just a fraction.

"You'd make a fine general." Raed and the others had run up quickly to him as soon as the soldiers left. He gave Merrick a sharp little nod.

Sorcha caught his elbow, lending him physical strength

even if she could not offer him anything else without the
Bond. "Well done," she whispered, "but pace yourself—we
may need that power again."

He nodded and, gathering himself, followed after, as
they all slipped in through the gate. The pleasure gardens
beyond were gray and smothered in low mist. No lantern
light punctured it and nothing moved. Yet, Merrick couldn't
shake the feeling that something was hovering just beyond
the perception of his eyes.

Aachon and Raed led the way, with the crew and the
Deacons taking the rear of their little assault force. Even in
his worst nightmares, back in the novitiate, Merrick could
never have imagined he would be helping the Young Pretender to the throne break into the palace.

Raed knew the way through the palace, and led them to
a side door. Obviously his father had made sure his son
knew everything about Vermillion, including the layout of
the royal lodgings. What he probably hadn't taught his son
was lock picking. Merrick shot Sorcha a glance over the
Young Pretender's back as he bent and worked the door
open. She shrugged, as if to say he was just as much of a
mystery to her.

They slipped inside the quiet palace. A building like
this should not be silent. Merrick's skin ran icy cold. As he
passed the halls and the doorways, he recalled their visit to
another royal home in Chioma, as well as the death and
disaster they found there. The religious riots that Hatipai
had stirred up were unlikely to be repeated here, but he had
the feeling that the Circle of Stars was waking with far
more wide-reaching consequences. What they would find
in the Vermillion palace terrified him.

They padded down corridors and should have met at
least servants or guards, yet it was as if the residents of the
building had all vanished. Merrick longed to investigate
the matter, but caution held him back from opening doors.
They had to find del Rue as quickly as possible.

At last, the group reached the carved and gilt-worked

main stairwell that led up to the top floors of the building.
Barely had Sorcha put her foot on the first tread when cold
enveloped them. Merrick saw her breath outlined against
the flickering lantern, as if she were outside in the depths
of winter.

He might not have his Sensitivity, but any citizen of the
Empire knew the signs of a geist appearance. All the Dea-
cons, including Sorcha, automatically drew together in a
circle. Raed spun around, his eyes wide like a feral animal.
His connection with the Rossin had to mean he felt the
Otherside in a far more visceral way than any of them.
Merrick was almost jealous of that.

"Something is coming," he growled, as his eyes darted
around the stairwell.

"The Rossin!" the young Deacon hissed, suddenly
aware that they could be swallowed by the Beast that lived
inside Raed if a geist made a sudden appearance.

"Don't worry" was the only thing the Young Pretender
had time to say, before the geist made its presence felt in a
more powerful way.

Vermillion was bound to have many memories and
echoes of people who had lived in it for nearly a thousand
years, and every Deacon was taught how dangerous such
old places could be. That was why the palace had been the
first building that the Deacons had cleared out when Kaleva arrived to take up his mantle of Emperor. Now it
seemed that work had been quickly undone.

While the group looked upward in increasing horror,
lights filled the dim stairwell. Groups of gleaming rei orbs
spun on each other and floated down the staircase toward
them. The smell of old roses clogged Merrick's nose with
an almost funerary scent.

The crew shrank back, but the Deacons, acting on training rather than good sense, did not. In fact, Merrick felt
Sorcha step forward. She was too used to taking the lead in
these matters—even when she was no more powerful than
the sailors.

They were so fixated on the oncoming undead attack
that no one—not even Merrick—noticed Raed shrug off
his clothes behind them. The only thing that made them
turn was the chorus of indrawn breaths from the crew
members, and then the massive feline bulk of the Rossin
was shoving them out of the way.

Merrick stumbled back feeling the heat of the great cat
and its thick fur brush against him. He should have been
killed instantly by the Beast—probably before he even
realized it—and yet he remained breathing. The truth was
immediately apparent that something had changed with
the Rossin. The geistlord was in control of himself and in
control of his hunger for blood. What exactly that could
mean he could hardly identify right in this moment.

The geistlord filled the corridor, blocking out the lantern light and somehow smothering that from the rei. The
group of Deacons and crew held their breath. As if sensing
this, the Beast turned and looked back at them in contempt,
his golden-flecked eyes flicking over them. Aachon was the
only one capable of movement. He bent and picked up his
Prince's clothes, folded them precisely and draped them
over one arm. The other humans stood fixed to the floor as
if nailed there. It was as good a response as any; Merrick
knew that the pistols and swords they carried would be no
use against the Rossin.

After a long moment, the Beast let out an exhalation of
air, as if disappointed with the whole situation before him.

The rei spun around on themselves faster and faster,
then fled in the face of the threat like a cloud of insects that
could fly through the walls. It was the only thing to do;
consumption was an inevitability when confronted with a
lord of the unliving.

The Rossin padded up the stairs and then paused. The
Beast turned his head and regarded them. It took a moment
for them to understand he was waiting for them.

Merrick swallowed hard. "We should all be dead." His

whisper stated the obvious, but he felt it needed to be
pointed out. They were all moving into uncharted territory.

"I, for one, will take what mercies we can get and sort
out the mystery later," Sorcha said, leading the way up the
stairs. The others followed quietly in her wake. Merrick
took his place next to his partner, while Aachon acted as
guard at the rear.

Following the geistlord so close that he could hear the
constant low rumble in the Beast's chest, Merrick nonetheless had the urge to grab hold of the lashing tail. He thought
of his father's favorite saying: "When you have a tiger by
the tail, it is best just to hold on." This was certainly a situation that more closely matched that than anything he'd
ever thought to find. Though the Rossin was far worse than
any tiger could possibly be.

The upstairs rooms and corridors were as deserted as
the downstairs ones. Twice, Merrick caught the glimmer
of the pale shape of a shade out of the corner of his eye, but
they blew away quickly, as frightened of the geistlord as
the rei.

"The residents are surely hiding," Sorcha said under her
breath to Merrick. "Everyone remembers what it was like
before our Order came. They must be terrified of what is
going to happen."

"A perfectly justifiable concern," Merrick replied. "But
hiding is not going to save them from geists."

Those who could must have fled to their own city
houses, or perhaps to their outlying country estates. Behind
these doors would be servants, the foolish, the brave or
those who had no other choice. His concerns for them were
great—these were, after all, the people who he'd been
sworn to protect.

It was not just the Order that was falling apart—it was
the mechanism of the Empire itself. Only it, and the Deacons, kept the population safe. Del Rue's plans were ripen-
ing faster on the vine than even he could have expected,

and Merrick could only hope that would mean the conspirator would make mistakes.

Clinging to such hopes was all the young Deacon had at this moment. He glanced up and realized the Rossin had come to a stop, like a very fierce bloodhound. He now stood, glaring at the humans, silent.

"What now?" Natylda asked her partner Murn, in an aside. It was certain she was feeling the same disconnect Merrick and Sorcha were. Asking something of one's Sensitive in this kind of situation was very strange.

Merrick shook his head in sympathy, but replied for Murn. "We have to go in . . . but carefully."

The group looked around, but Raed and his skills were no longer available. Finally, Aleck of the *Dominion* bravely dared to creep up next to the geistlord, withdrew his own picklocks and began working on the door. He couldn't help looking up occasionally though, as if to reassure himself that he wasn't about to have his head bitten off.

"Everyone has always assumed the Rossin is just a Beast," Naleni, the youngest of their crew members, said, her eyes gleaming with interest. "Perhaps there is something more to him than—"

Sorcha, having had enough of this banter, pushed her way past the petrified and befuddled, and opened the door with the far simpler method of kicking it hard. Vermillion's palace doors were not made for security, and the wood around the lock shattered after two blows. Reaching in, she slid back the lock and flicked the door open. She smiled at Aleck, who was staring at her with some concern.

Merrick couldn't help it—he let out a little laugh. In all this madness some things remained constant; his partner's temper was one of them.

"Sorcha!" Aachon snapped. "By the Blood, could you be more—"

"What?" she retorted. "This del Rue is going to know we've been here anyway, and the longer we stand in the corridor the worse it is." Then spinning on her heel she entered the room.

Aachon shared a look with Merrick. "Deacons are supposed to have more control," he muttered, before slipping in after the Active Deacon. The Rossin waited by the door, his golden eyes tracking each human that went past him, like a wolf might count sheep.

If there were any traps, magical or mechanical, in the room, Sorcha apparently was going to trip them all just from sheer rage. Her recent trials had not changed her that much, and her partner was very glad of it.

After a moment, the humans were able to ignore the Rossin and concentrate on the search. However, no matter how many drawers they opened, or how thoroughly they turned over the bed, the room looked like nothing more than any other stateroom in the palace.

"Strange how very few personal items are here." Aachon pulled one of the watercolor paintings away from the wall. It was so tiny that it could not have disguised a tunnel, but the frustration in the first mate's voice was obvious.

Merrick knew how he was feeling. "Not an image of a loved one," Merrick agreed, "any letters, or even any kind of distinguishing clothing." He tossed the piles of folded white shirts onto the floor.

"It's like he doesn't live here at all," Sorcha grumbled, throwing herself backward onto the bed in a curiously childish manner.

"Almost like one of our cells back at the Mother Abbey," Sibuse mused. He pressed his dark hand over his eyes as if to wipe away the whole situation.

"That would make sense," Merrick began, "as he is—"

"Merrick!" Sorcha half sat up on the bed. "Merrick, do you remember the marks on the Priory ceiling in Ulrich?"

The cantrips, incantations and curses had hung over him for a long time, so he'd had plenty of opportunity to study them. Quickly, the young Deacon took up a place on

the bed next to his partner. It was such a wide piece of furniture that Aachon was able to do the same. The crew and
remaining Deacons had to make do with craning their
necks. Even the Rossin padded to the bed, sat down and
peered upward.

"Truly beautiful," Merrick breathed, for a moment in
awe of the artistry.

Most ceilings in the palace were painted, with land-
scapes or scenes from history, and this one was as well. It
showed the first Deacon, Saint Crispin, making the original bargain with the geistlord—the very one that sat like an
immense house cat at the foot of the bed. Merrick wondered what the Rossin would make of the depiction he was
looking at. It was impossible to tell through those great
yellow eyes.

The first Deacon was shown as a handsome hero, golden
hair flying in the wind along with his green and blue cloak.
The Rossin was a hovering black shadow, having not yet
taken full form, though he had gleaming red eyes and
ethereal, shadowy arms, which were reaching out toward
Crispin. Merrick tilted his head. It was strange, but in the
streaming depictions of wind and smoke there appeared
to be another figure, lightly sketched, but definite, there
behind the Rossin.

"I hardly think it is coincidence that del Rue picked this
room for his own." Sorcha glanced across at her partner.
"Do you?"

Merrick wriggled uncomfortably. "Maybe there was
something he found comforting about it."

He was so busy examining the image that he almost
missed the one thing they were looking for, and when he
did see it, he felt an utter fool.

The medallion directly above the bed was indeed decorated with weirstones and cantrips. It looked new. It looked
handmade.

He pointed to it, "Sorcha, is that—"

No sooner had he done so than his partner was leaping up.

"Get off the bed," she barked, shooing Merrick and
Aachon off the bed and the others away, like a child scattering chickens. Briskly she ordered them to help her swing
a chest of drawers onto the bed, which gave her enough
room to climb up and touch the ceiling.

Merrick shivered as she pressed the stones. Sorcha had
always been very loud in her dislike of weirstones and
those that meddled with them.

"Sorcha," he cautioned, "that stone-and-cantrip mix
looks dangerous. You shouldn't be . . ." His voice trailed
off as he observed her eyes go suddenly blank, and he had
the feeling she was somewhere very distant that he did not
like. However, just as he was about to pull her down and
damn the consequences, the stones under her fingertips
became suddenly fluid. As they all watched, she shifted
them around.

Her voice was slurred slightly when she spoke. "I see a
tunnel to a great castle." She paused and moved the stones.
"Now a boat by a beach, but this one is not used very
often." Now she frowned. "This one . . . this one very much
more so."

They all watched, even the Rossin, as she pushed one of
the stones around to lie on some other portion of the frame.
The space described by the circle shifted, becoming a soft,
gray section of wall, rather than a painting. It looked
remarkably like a group of shades shifting and dancing
with each other. Then it resolved itself into a dark corridor;
disturbingly commonplace, though in an incredibly odd
place. Sorcha looked down at Merrick, and he almost
swore in shock at the blank, eerie look on her face. For a
moment, she was an utter stranger.

Sorcha cleared her throat and that woman thankfully
washed away. "This leads to a dark cellar." She held out her
hand to no one in particular, and it was Tighon who took it.

Merrick took it from him and pressed his hand briefly over hers, and then turned back to the rest of the group. He also despised giving his partner so little of his attention, but he only had a little to give.

In his heart of hearts, Merrick knew he should have pushed her, demanded to hear every detail of what she had discovered about herself, but she had been right—it was not the time to examine too closely what they had in the here and now. There was very little of it to look at, and under close scrutiny it might evaporate.

He replicated Sorcha, and climbed up on the dresser. "I have to say, this hardly seems the best way to enter a portal."

It was Aachon who had the answers. "Cantrips, weirstones . . . who knows what the Circle of Stars has at its disposal. I can't see this del Rue climbing on furniture either."

Sorcha jumped up to join him. "Looks like we'll have to lever ourselves in there." She reached upward.

She didn't get far; without any warning the Rossin suddenly sprang from the bed and into the maw Sorcha had opened.

Both Deacons cried out as the great cat knocked them flying. Merrick tumbled backward while Frith somewhat awkwardly caught Sorcha before she fell off the bed altogether.

For a moment it was all a confused tangle of arms and legs. When Merrick finally had helped Frith and Sorcha disengage, the Rossin was long gone.

"The portal works," Aachon commented dryly, as he examined the space the geistlord had disappeared into. Then he climbed up their makeshift ladder and toward the portal. The burly first mate had no problem pulling himself up and into the portal. The weird moment when he switched from vertical movement to standing in a horizontal corridor was abrupt. Merrick and the other Deacons had seen many odd things, but the crew members whispered among themselves.

When Sorcha went to take her turn, Merrick jerked her back. She shot him a look that could have melted metal, but he hissed under his breath, "Wait a second."

The crew and Deacons, in various states of eagerness, clambered up, and helped each other through the most unusual portal. Then it was just Merrick and Sorcha alone in the room.

Able to speak his mind for the first time since reuniting with his partner, the younger Deacon knew he still only had a few moments. "Do you know how far away this is taking us?" he jerked his head toward the portal.

She shrugged. "I cannot tell that . . . it could be somewhere in Vermillion or somewhere even in Delmaire."

Merrick swallowed. It wasn't as if they could rely on the Order for support, so moving far from the Mother Abbey should not have bothered him . . . yet it did. He thought of the tunnel he'd last encountered the Circle of Stars in and it did not provide any comfort.

"Just don't get too far away from me," he said, squeezing her shoulder.

Her eyes surveyed him, but she nodded without challenging him about this sudden clinginess. "I will try."

"And be careful," he added. "I can't feel you through the Bond right now, and I hate that. Just know I am a person that cares about you, and we all need to come out of this alive."

Her hard expression softened to one of vague amusement, and she cupped her hand around his cheek. "These are not the times any of us can take care, but I will do my best not to implode before we get the Grand Duchess and the Pattern back."

Her partner sketched a bow before her, gesturing toward the portal. "I will take that. Now up you go."

He watched her go, saw her arrive, and then knew that this was his turn.

Wrapping his hands about the lip of the dark portal, Merrick pulled himself up and into the unknown.

TWENTY-THREE

Between the Jaws

The geistlord landed softly in the darkness of the cellar and inhaled a great whiff of air. That was the wonderful thing about a body; it brought him so much more information than when he'd been a creature of ether—or even worse, in between, trapped in Raed's mind.

Immediately, he knew that the cellar was full of old things, a dead rat or two in the forgotten corners, the scent of rusted metal, and somewhere, the odor of humanity.

However, there was nothing like the smell of another geistlord—which was what the Rossin had been hoping for. The cat's huge head swung from side to side and his annoyed growl filled the space. He'd been aiming to catch one of his kin by surprise, and devour them before the humans arrived to spoil things. The Rossin had hoped all this might be another geistlord's doing, setting himself up as ruler in the guise of a god, as Hatipai had done. It was a favorite ploy, and one that might have suited the great cat, if he'd been clever enough to devour said geistlord. He would need all the power and strength he could gather in the days ahead.

Much as he hated it, his future lay with the humans—at least for now. He'd had to stomach much worse—especially in the early days—but it was galling to have to put up with their company after all this time. He would abide them for a while, and see what the winds of change brought him.

So as the rest of his human retinue scrambled through the portal behind him, the Rossin concentrated on the one scent that rose above those of earth and metal. It was no geistlord smell. It was most definitely human. However as he drew the air through his nostrils and over his tongue, the Rossin let his mouth open a little. A drone of a growl began in his chest as he began to sort the mix of odors out.

When the geistlord finally did, the realization of what he had found took him by surprise. It was not anything he would have expected.

Two scents; both were vaguely familiar—but one of them in particular had his full attention. It was the Tormentor. The one who had cheated him and cast the Rossin down into the depths of the family that belonged to him. The geistlord had spent generations lost in the state between life and death . . . unable to form into anything while the heir of the family continued to be born in Vermillion. It had been a thousand years before rule turned into legend and they bore a child beyond the city.

Somehow the Tormentor had not died but had cheated death. It had been a thousand years, but the Rossin's rage still burned. It was lucky indeed that the Deacons were currently unable to read him through their Bond. They might have sensed his plans. The hatred was so deep-seated and ancient that even their pitiful senses would have been able to discern it.

While the geistlord digested this stunning new reality, the Deacons and the rest of the ragtag crew scrambled into the cellar, trying to be quiet and yet making a racket that disturbed his sensitive hearing.

For relief, the great cat padded to the door. He didn't need to sniff to ascertain what was behind it; the smell of overripe, unhygienic human filled his nose. Generations and hundreds of years in an animal's body had changed the Rossin's perceptions of many things, but one thing that had not altered had been his impression of people. As far as he was concerned they were sweaty, undisciplined, foul creatures—good for little except for providing blood.

What he detected behind the door did not change his mind in that regard, nor did it make him anything like hungry.

When Sorcha came to the door, the Rossin stepped back and let her open it. Her reaction was most amusing. The Deacon staggered back a couple of steps, clapping her hand over her mouth.

"By the Bones," she gasped to the little Sensitive behind her, "I think something died in here."

Humanity's sense of smell was not that accurate. Still when they went into the room there was much excited yelling, but no sign of the enemy. They had missed him by some little time. The Rossin could smell his odor lingering in the corners of the room even over the smell of excrement.

When the mortals finally emerged from the cell, they were dragging a sorry excuse for a man. Even among humans he would have been dismissed as refuse. They must have broken him free, because he had the end of the smashed chain still secured about his neck. He was covered in his own filth and wearing only the barest of clothes.

The Rossin was about to dismiss him as merely another worthless scrap when he stopped and narrowed his eyes on the pathetic creature.

The smell of excrement masked the man's real scent, and it was probably meant to do that. A hot anger began to grow in the Rossin's chest. He knew this man—or whatever he had claimed to be.

The cat's massive claws clenched in the dirt, and he almost leapt upon him there and then. The Maker glanced at him from under a matted crown of hair, but said nothing.

There was no flicker of recognition for the giant cat glaring at him.

It was greatly worrying that the Tormentor and the Maker would be in the same place—though they were often together in the early days, the geistlord thought they had fallen out. The Rossin crouched down on the floor and waited to see what would happen.

The humans were all chattering among themselves. They offered the Maker water and food; one of them even gave up her cloak to hide his near nakedness.

"What's your name?" Sorcha asked as she gently tried to wipe away some of the grime with a handkerchief. It was of little use; the dirt went all the way through as far as the Rossin was concerned.

The Maker looked up at the Deacon and recognition flickered on his face. So even he saw it—the change in the Deacon—but he was sensible enough not to point it out. As always, the Maker was a cunning creature. Instead, he worked his jaw a little, and whispered, "Ratimana."

The Rossin tensed. The foul man had not bothered to change his form nor his name—even in all these years. It was no wonder the Circle of Stars had been able to find him.

The Sensitive Deacon, Sorcha's favorite, jerked. "I know that name. It is the one Nynnia told me to seek out." He looked the filthy human up and down, and his confusion was easy to read. "But why?"

"Not all gifts shine," the taller, older Sensitive, the one who smelled like old books and frustration, said.

"Did you see her?" Merrick bent down and asked their new companion. "The Grand Duchess? A woman with dark hair, very beautiful. Was she here?"

The Maker did not answer for a while. His gaze was now leveled at the Rossin. The flicker of cunning in the man's eyes drove the great cat mad with anger, but he had lately learned to temper his rage.

He noticed that the Maker, as was his nature, had been

busy creating. Limited by resources trapped in this cellar
he'd not had much to work on apparently. A broken sliver
of wood was the only thing he'd been able to find, and he'd
drawn a pattern on it in blood.

Still it was a thing of power, and the Rossin snarled at it,
causing all the humans to jump in their skins in a most
pleasing manner. However, he did not leap on the man, a
supreme act of will. The Maker was not his friend, but the
Deacons would need him, and without them the Rossin
knew his chances at destroying the Circle were not good.

At first Sorcha and Merrick flinched away from what
the Maker held up. After all, it reeked of blood and excrement like everything about this twisted remnant of humanity. After a moment, however, they looked more closely at
what he had made. They began to see the truth of it.

The old man had made a pattern of swirls on the wood.
The designs were intricate and interwoven in incompre-
hensible ways so that even the Rossin could not follow
them all. That was the art of the Maker, something that the
great cat could not understand, but had at one time needed.

"Are those—" Sorcha paused, wetted her lips, and then
went on. "Are they runes?"

The young Deacon leaned forward, careful not to touch
the piece of wood. "I believe so, but I don't understand the
designs around them. Perhaps . . ." His voice trailed off.
"Could this be . . . a Pattern?"

*Really, the humans were incredibly slow. Ratimana, the
Patternmaker, the liar and oathbreaker. Another geistlord, but trapped in a broken, aged body.*

As if he could hear the Rossin's thoughts the old man
glanced over his shoulder. A flicker of a cruel smile passed
over his lips revealing his dark, broken teeth. Time had not
been kind to that body of his. He turned back and looked
up at the Deacons. "The Patternmaker they called me. The
first of your kind. The very first."

He did not tell him the history of the Circle of Stars. He
did not dare.

I need them, the Rossin reminded himself, the rumble of anger barely contained in his chest. *And they need him . . . for now.*

The great cat folded himself onto the ground and tried not to think too much about past betrayals. Let the Deacons put their trust in the Patternmaker. It did not matter to him, but someday there would be a reckoning.

"Have you tamed the Rossin then?" Ratimana pointed a crooked finger at the great cat. "Dare you turn your back on such a cruel creature?"

The Rossin snarled at the geist in a man's flesh, incapable of doing anything else to register his displeasure. Time had not taken away any of the sly, devious nature of Ratimana.

"The Rossin is here with us, and his own creature. We hold back his rage, but he is still what he is." That Merrick had certainly learned to lie as well as many older Deacons. It was quite impressive.

The Patternmaker looked away and nodded. He did a very good impression of an old human. It brought out the protective instincts of those around him.

"The woman," Merrick pressed, his scent growing hotter by the minute, "did you see her?"

"Took her, took her away," Ratimana muttered. "Broken and made again, they took her to the Abbey. They have the Emperor on his leash and mean to slay every last Deacon."

His words stilled the cellar.

"He means to bring down the Order altogether?" one of the other Deacons, the one that smelled like dead roses, asked in a whisper. Her head was shaking back and forth.

Yes, it was certainly hard for those of the Order to believe what had happened to them. The divisions were, however, what the Rossin delighted in. The schisms and infighting among all the Orders was bliss to him—like the warm carcass of a recent kill. If he could not slay the Maker or the Tormentor then he would enjoy this.

"If he has convinced, and tortured Zofiya into saying

our Deacons kidnapped her—then the Order is done for."
Merrick sunk onto the floor, desperation coming off him in
delightful palpable waves.

"And there is no way we can defend ourselves without
the runes," one of the sweet-smelling Deacons whispered.

"Then we must defend the Order with words," Aachon,
that great man-mountain, broke in. "We must go confront
the Emperor and show him the duplicity of del Rue."

"What a fine idea," Sorcha snapped. "We go in with
guns blazing and a hungry Rossin at our sides and see what
happens? Or shall we perhaps save the Circle of Stars the
trouble and just slit our throats now?"

The argument devolved into a shouting match. Even
Deacons, usually so controlled, gave themselves over to
the desperation of the moment. The Rossin would have
purred if he'd been able.

That was until the Patternmaker staggered to his feet
and held aloft the item he'd been making. In the dimness of
the cellar the words began to glow with soft white light.
The Rossin remembered the first time he'd seen such a
thing, the first time he'd taken form, and begun this journey in the physical realm. It was not necessarily a pleasant
remembrance. The great cat lowered his head and growled.

The Deacons immediately stopped their yammering,
which was a great relief to his ears. Instead they turned and
looked at the ugly, broken little man, holding above his
head the thing they wanted. Power.

None of them had ever seen a rune Pattern before, but it
was the physical representation of all that they used every
day so thoughtlessly. The secret of it was kept away from
the majority of their Order, lest the vulnerability be revealed,
but it was how the power they stole from the Otherside was
channeled into their foci.

It was the Patternmaker's gift, and the Rossin had
helped him create the first one. Now he was forced to watch
as the Deacons clustered around Ratimana like foolish
moths. The smell suddenly did not seem to matter to them.

The Rossin saw that there would be no blood right now, and decided he did not want to watch what had to happen. He'd seen it once, and that was enough. He would return when there was killing to do. Let the foolish mortal Raed deal with this.

The Young Pretender came back to his body and tried to realign his brain. It felt different hearing and seeing things through the Rossin's eyes, and it left him with more than a bad taste in his mouth. His blood surged with rage, and it took him a long time to look at the Deacons without feeling the need to beat them to a bloody mass.

"Raed?" Sorcha and Aachon approached, finally noticing that the massive bulk of the Rossin was gone. They smelled of the man who the Rossin had identified as the Maker.

"He leaves you now, just like that?" Aachon asked as he handed Raed's clothing back to him. It was one advantage of this closer connection with the Rossin; the ability to know when the change was coming had saved him plenty of pieces of clothing and personal belongings.

"I think he was too disgusted to stay," Raed replied as Sorcha helped him to his feet. Across the cellar, the Deacons still surrounded Ratimana—including the fascinated Merrick. "Something about that man distresses him. Sorcha, I think he actually has met him before."

She gave him an odd look, as if she wasn't quite sure if it was he or the Rossin saying these things. Not that he was entirely sure himself half the time now. "He can help us, Raed. He says he can make a temporary Pattern so that we don't go into the Abbey with nothing."

"How can you trust him though?" He leaned forward and grabbed her shoulder.

"He is the enemy of the Circle of Stars," she said jerking back from him, "and that is enough for right now." He couldn't understand her look of disappointment and outrage as she strode back to join the group around the Patternmaker. It was a perfectly reasonable question.

"To have power snatched away is no easy thing." Aachon's hand spasmed closed, around the space where the weirstone had once been. "When I was cast out of the Order, it took many years for me to find peace. Do not judge them too harshly."

They watched as the Deacons talked excitedly to the Patternmaker, who stood in the middle of them grinning from ear to ear. He didn't speak much, but he held what he had made high, showing three or four runes.

Aachon understood the nature of Raed's silences after so many years. "We are down to very few choices, my prince. It is trust him, or watch the Empire fall into war and the geists overrun the land."

Put to him that succinctly, the Young Pretender sighed. "By the Blood, this reeks of wrongness, but I see your point."

They both cautiously rejoined the group. His crew gave him little nods of recognition, but the Deacons didn't even look up—so entranced were they by the newcomer. He was the sole focus of their attention.

Sorcha was crouched down in front of Ratimana, holding her arm out before him. "Can you work runes here, on my flesh?"

Just where she had got that idea Raed did not know for sure, but it chilled him to the bone. He wanted to stop her, wanted to say something, but what could he say to her to change her mind? He was still getting to know Sorcha, but there was one feature of her personality that had stood out about her from the first moment they met. She was the most stubborn, determined person he had ever come across.

Either he went along with her, or she'd do it anyway and he'd be left alone to wonder about the outcome. Better that he, and the Rossin, were there to assist. As hard as it was to do, he managed to keep his silence.

Two of the Deacons helped the old man to his feet as he nodded. It looked like the gesture alone might knock him down. His eyes raked over them. "Yes, I can do that, but there will be consequences."

"And, what would those be?" Merrick was at least a small voice of sanity in all this.

Ratimana ran his tongue over his lips in what Raed interpreted as a calculating gesture, as his hands clenched on the piece of broken board, which still gleamed in the darkness. Finally he admitted, "Not sure. Could be many things."

The Deacons drew closer, but there was no fear on their faces—it was expectation. They were trained to die to defend normal folk from geists, and Raed knew very well that there were few old Deacons. They were used to taking risks.

Sorcha glanced at her colleagues and then held out her arm. "Do your best and we will do ours."

Slowly but surely, the rest of them rolled up their sleeves in an echo of her gesture.

Sorcha looked at Raed. "You best come up with a plan and soon, because you will soon have your weapons." Such conviction should have reassured him, but a feeling of dread consumed him as thoroughly as the Rossin did.

TWENTY-FOUR

Coming Home

Sorcha was glad to be the first to go under the Pattern-maker's hand—one that she noticed shook just a fraction. She wanted to make sure that this would work, or at least not kill her before any of the other Deacons tried it. The perils of coming up with the idea herself—or at least stealing it from her own mother. The image of her carving the runes into her flesh was now about to become very real.

The Patternmaker had no ink, no time to get any, and so he had used what was to hand. It seemed appropriate that the scrolls and turns of the runes were painted on her in dirt and her own blood. As Ratimana worked on her, Sorcha thought of her mother. Had it been childbirth in that dire place that had killed her, or had it been the runes themselves? Perhaps her daughter was about to find out firsthand.

Raed, Aachon and the remains of the *Dominion*'s crew stood to one side and watched. The Young Pretender had his hand covering his mouth, and in the dimness of the cellar his hazel eyes were dark, with only a fleck of gold gleaming in them. Sorcha did not speak to him however.

As the Patternmaker carved into her arm, the pain swelled, so she concentrated on the Young Pretender. The ease with which he flickered between Raed and Rossin was alarming, and she knew he was hiding something from her. Something had changed.

By the Bones, if they survived this, there would be a conversation between them that would not be gentle. If they survived.

As the Patternmaker finished her right arm, and moved on to her left, she looked across at Merrick.

The Sensitives would also have to bear their runes on their arms, but in addition Ratimana would have to sketch the third eye and their sigil between their eyebrows. It would be a disturbing effect.

Ratimana's breathing came harder as he worked the final marks on her forearm: the design of Deiyant the half moon, bisected by two horizontal lines. It took something from the old man, and his strength, to do this, she now realized. Yet all concern for him was washed away as he drew the final Rune of Dominion on her arm, Teisyat. Abruptly she was suddenly aware of the Bond again.

Sorcha gasped, squeezing her eyes shut before tears could escape her and she was embarrassed. Merrick was there, in her head, a warm, calm influence that felt like a lodestone in a world of turmoil. Even if he couldn't feel it yet.

Then she perceived Raed. He had never been able to feel their Bond as the Deacons experienced it, but his head came up now with dawning comprehension.

He had indeed been hiding something. Fire burned in him. Before, when she had looked at Raed through her Center the Young Pretender had blazed sliver bright in the ether. Now however, he was red-hot, like a bubbling cyst of lava that should not be in this world. His ease with the Rossin had been bought at a great price.

Sorcha swallowed back her outrage and her despair. This man had somehow claimed a slice of her soul, and yet he had done something that endangered his own. All the other Deacons' eyes were on her. Soon enough they would see what she saw, though they wouldn't be able to understand it as she did—or quite so intimately.

The fact was they needed the Rossin and couldn't afford to question his, or his host's, motives. Sorcha sighed. The fact was, they might all be dead soon anyway.

"Quickly," she gestured to the Patternmaker. "We all need this."

The Deacons lined up, excitement and trepidation etched on their faces. Sorcha stood by and watched grim-faced as he worked. Despite the shaking of his hand, he knew what he was doing and was efficient at it.

When he was done with the Actives, he moved swiftly on to their partners. The runes carved on their faces gave the Sensitives an appearance of rage that she'd never seen on their usually calm countenances. On Merrick it made him appear wrathful and older than his years.

Now, finally he was able to feel what she had. The Bond flared fully alive between them. They didn't touch, but they grasped each other's minds across the distance.

"These will fade." The Patternmaker slumped back on his heels and glared up at them. "Proper ink will make proper patterns. Dirt is not enough."

"If we ever have time," Sorcha assured him, "we will get you proper tools. For now this will have to do." She stared at him a moment, realizing what he had given back to them all. "Thank you," she added finally.

She'd made up her mind about one thing however: the Order would not die in this stinking cellar. Walking over to the weirstone portal, she laid her hand on what she'd come to think of as the keystone at the top of the circle. It flared to life, and there they were looking at del Rue's bed in the palace.

"Aachon," she said, folding her newly dyed hands before her so as not to smear the designs, "I want you to take the Patternmaker to safety. Get out of the palace and go to

Widow Vashill's house. If we do not return, the future of the Order—if there is any—is in your hands." To the old man she said, "Carve their skin too, properly. Make of them the semblance of an Order again."

Aachon's brow furrowed as he shot a glance at the still crouching, still foul-smelling old man. "Where my prince goes I go. I cannot—"

"Dear friend," Raed broke in, his mouth twisting into a bittersweet smile, "there is nothing more you can do for me, but you can do so much for the Order. They protect the people of Arkaym so much better than I do, and all my family has ever been in recent times is trouble."

The first mate shifted from foot to foot, trapped by old loyalties and realities. "If you died, my prince, I would have failed."

Raed's laugh was short and pained. "If I die in service of the Empire and its people, then that is my fate. I would rather that than live this life of running and losing. You know how ill it has suited me of late."

Aachon's hand clenched a few times, as if he would be glad of a weirstone and a reason to wield one at the side of his Prince—but eventually he nodded.

"And take the crew with you," Raed added. He turned and looked at each one in turn. "Your deaths with us would be needless. I have already had too many friends die for me. This is my last order: go live, be as safe and well as you can be."

He shook each of their hands in turn, and then embraced them whispering a few words into each ear. Frith at first would not look at him, but eventually gave up with a sharp sob. Aleck looked as somber as a funeral mourner.

Aachon bowed slightly. "I know you will bring honor to the name of your family, my prince."

Merrick sketched an elegant bow to the first mate, a strange gesture in such an ugly place. "My mother and young brother's rooms are on the floor below del Rue's rooms in the palace. I fear the Emperor might think to use them against me, or they might fall prey to a geist. I would owe you a great debt if you can get them to Widow Vashill's where there is at least some chance of safety."

Aachon studied the young man seriously, before giving an equally broad bow. "I give you my word on it."

Raed then clapped his arms around Aachon, and the two men embraced while the Deacons watched impassively. Sorcha couldn't say anything because there was a strange lump in her throat. Merrick was looking down at his shoes.

Then the crew members took their leave, and leapt through the portal, bouncing somewhat ridiculously on the bed. Aachon waited for Ratimana to go before him.

First the old man placed the board in Sorcha's hands. The new Pattern. It was a flimsy thing, ripped from a crate discarded in someone's cellar, yet it was now the most important thing to the Order. She held it in her hands and gazed upon it in wonder, mixed with a little fear.

"Remember which you are; the Eye or the Fist," the old man cackled, before turning and leaping through the portal.

Aachon favored the remaining group with a piercing look, as if fixing them in his memory, before giving a curt bow to all of them in turn. He followed the Patternmaker through the tunnel.

Then it was just Raed and the Deacons in the chamber. The Young Pretender sighed and straightened as if a burden was settling on him. "Now what? There is no portal into the Mother Abbey I take it?"

"No." Sorcha smiled, but did not touch him. Instead she ran her finger over the keystone. "Not yet."

Naturally del Rue had not dared to make a portal into the Mother Abbey while all the Deacons had their runes. Nor did he probably wish to show his own power to the Emperor just yet, considering he was playing the wily advisor and Kaleva was enraged by the Order. It would not do to have the Emperor turn his wrath on him.

However, Sorcha was starting to understand the weirstone tunnels. Someone had to have made them, and every time she used them there was a feeling that something was also opening up inside herself. Her mother, after all, had given birth to her with this sole purpose in mind. If anything was engrained on her psyche it was the tunnels, since she'd only been a few moments old when her mother had taken her through one. Perhaps, she realized with a jolt, that was why she had always so disliked weirstones.

Cautiously, she placed her fingertips on the keystone once more and the image of the grand bed in the palace wavered and disappeared. She was going to change the place these weirstones knew with one she knew and remembered. In the darkness underneath the Mother Abbey, she, Merrick and Raed had found a world that had belonged to the Circle of Stars: a long stretch of tunnels and underground passages where they kept their darker creations. The possibility matrix and the tunnels that led to secret escape routes into the city had been destroyed—at least according to Arch Abbot Rictun. However she thought of the great room with the stalactites and the stalagmites. That had been there an eternity, and surely had not been easy to bring down.

Holding that image tight in her mind, she pressed forward into the weirstone. The images of her mother flashed again, what she had seen and felt. The Wrayth, the geist-lord that had ridden in her biological father as he made her, was there too. She didn't want to think about or acknowledge that part of her being, but it was there and allowing her to do this. She pushed harder into the borderlands of the Otherside itself. The realm of the geists knew nothing of time or space—Merrick had journeyed into the past with Nynnia's help from there. It would take not much more than that to bend the Otherside toward the Mother Abbey.

It surprised her; the strength of her own will, and how pliable the stone was. The drawing of two points together felt suddenly easy. Behind her, Sorcha heard Merrick gasp and the whispers of her fellow Deacons echoed around the cellar.

With a shake of her head, she looked through the weirstone tunnel to the familiar underground chamber. She recognized that soft blue light. "These are tunnels under the Arch Abbot's rooms at the Mother Abbey," she explained. "Merrick and I found them a year or so ago. The secret door should hopefully still be there."

Raed looked at her, and it was almost as if he was seeing her for the first time. "That's quite something."

She merely smiled, and then to demonstrate her faith in her own abilities stepped through the portal.

On the other side it was as chill and damp as she remembered, and lit by the same odd blue light from the moss that grew in the caverns. Before she could get too maudlin about the changes that had been wrought on her life since her last time down here, Merrick stepped through, followed by Raed and the rest of the Deacons.

Deacon Natylda looked about in amazement. "All this lying under the Abbey, and no one ever knew it was down here?"

"Well, some did," Raed whispered. The place seemed to require whispers. "The Arch Abbots of your Order probably found it early on."

Before anyone could comment further, Merrick spun about. "I have to check something," he said, and darted away from them, deeper into the field of stalactites and stalagmites. Sorcha had a good idea what he was up to.

Raed opened his mouth to speak, but she forestalled him. "We'll give him a moment." While they waited, she decided that she had no desire for this del Rue, or any of the other Circle of Stars Deacons to come up behind them. It was surprisingly easy for her to wrap her fingertips around the keystone, and pull it loose. It was the most effective way to lock the tunnel. Raed was staring down the passage keeping an eye out for Merrick, so he wasn't there to notice her slip it into her pocket.

Her partner didn't take long to come back to them. A
grin was on his face. "You might not like Rictun, Sorcha,
but he did what he said. The possibility matrix and the tunnel to the outside canal are all gone. Looks like they pulled
down part of the ceiling to block both."

"I don't think Rictun is working with them." Raed drew
his pistol and examined the powder for dampness. "Just
that he is the wrong man for the job."

Merrick's mouth twisted, and along the still fragile
Bond, Sorcha felt his rage like a streak of poison. "No, it
has most certainly become clear that it is the case."

"Regardless there is only one way out of here," Sorcha
said, turning toward the stairs. "Let's not give the man any
more time to destroy the Empire and the Order."

She led the way, feeling the dampness under her boots,
and slipping now and again on the stairs. It was, as Merrick
said, apparent that no one had been down here for some
time. They climbed for a little bit in utter silence, but the
flickers of emotion around her were in chaos. It was hard to
trust this new way of doing things, especially when crafted
by a crazy, dirty old man. The new Pattern, tucked into the
back of her pants, felt like ice pressed against her skin, and
she was terrified of slipping and breaking the fragile piece
of wood with her backside. That would be a graceful end
for the Order right there and then.

Merrick, climbing behind her, chuckled—even though
she had not said anything. Sorcha shot him an angry look
over one shoulder, and it actually made her feel a little better. Things felt more real with their partnership intact. The
Bond was still strong, even if the runes felt a little unstable.

Finally they reached the last stair, and above Sorcha's
head was the closed circle of stone that should lead into
Rictun's chamber. She turned back to Merrick, and caught
the faint impression of Raed's face behind him. "Here's
hoping the Arch Abbot is not asleep right now. Merrick,
you did this last time."

Her partner smiled, then pressed his hand against the

smooth surface and whispered one word in Ancient, "*Taouilt.*"

"You always were the better scholar than I," she murmured into his ear, as she watched the stone begin to move. They had to go back up a little as the stone steps slid out from the wall. Sorcha led the way into the Arch Abbot's private bedchamber.

She let out a little sigh of relief. Rictun was not at home, though five small oil lamps were burning in his chamber. She padded around the room investigating while the others clambered out of the tunnel. The last time she had been there, it had been Hastler's room, and as sparse as a hermit's abode. Now it was cluttered with all kinds of little gleaming objects. She couldn't help but grimace as she saw a Harthian coil of gold made into a representation of the little snake god Histo. Such things had no place in any Abbey, since the Order had given up religions nearly a thousand years ago. Also the lush wall hangings were displays of wealth she did not care to see from her Abbot.

Merrick stood at her side and looked at what she was eyeballing so angrily. "It's not a crime, Sorcha. He is still allowed some possessions of his own."

She hated it when Merrick reminded her of the truth. So Sorcha grinned rather grimly. "You might be right, but let's say we try and find him instead of his possessions."

Merrick's eyes slid away from her, and she sighed just a little as he shared his Sight with her. By the Bones, she had missed it. He offered his Center and she took it. The world unfurled before her, like an unrolled map, and her senses were flooded with light; every sound filled her ears, from the ants scurrying on the floor, to the cooing of the doves sleeping in their nests under the roof. Without her partner as her anchor she would have been swept away.

Every creature that lived came alive in her mind, and so it didn't take much to find the other Deacons. They were all in the Devotional, and such a gathering burned as bright as ten signal fires in her vision. They were all there; every single one of them, even the lay Brothers.

That cannot be good. Merrick's voice in her head was sweet, even when it carried bitter words.

And the Emperor? she responded.

Look, he's there too. And more. His Center directed her attention. Yes, there was the Emperor, the dull red pulse of command running through him, but there, to his right, was someone else. For some reason it was hard for Merrick to concentrate on the person. The color of his presence kept changing from gray to a flickering gold, and then to something else, something woven and dangerous.

That's him. Del Rue. Merrick's outrage flooded her. *He has almost given up hiding his true nature. Deceiver. Conspirator. And look he has her.*

Yes, Zofiya was there, but her etheric appearance was dire and strange. Like her brother, the shreds of power clung to her, but they were run through with a gleam of gold. It was impossible to taste her emotion among all that confusion.

Merrick brought her back to reality with a jolt, by the simple method of hauling back his Center. He looked around at the three other pairs, and his voice was grim. "We must form a Conclave to stand any chance against del Rue."

"Sounds impressive," Raed muttered.

The others were struck dumb for a moment, but Deacon Lujia voiced their concerns adequately enough. "A Conclave can only be made by the Presbyterial Council. None of us have any experience with forming one and . . ."

Her voice trailed off, and Sorcha jerked around, in something verging on horror. She'd just caught the tail edge of it; Merrick's wild talent working on her fellow Deacons. Despite everything that they had been through together, she never would have thought he was capable of doing such a thing to members of their own Order.

Her eyes locked with his, while Raed stood by, completely unaware. She should have said something—reprimanded him at the very least—but then she saw the effect on the others. Calmness washed over them, and all doubt and fear drained from their faces. Although she didn't know much about Conclaves, she knew one important thing—they forged Deacons into one unit with one purpose. Merrick was doing that very thing.

"I know how to do it," her partner said softly. "The Conclave will be strong, and we will prevail."

The look he turned on her was harder and darker than any she'd seen on his face before. She did not like it. *Thus a unit is made,* came his reply.

Many times Sorcha had wished that her young partner would grow up a little, but now that he was doing it, she found it deeply disturbing. She knew he was right, that things were dangerous, and that they had to work together, but to twist their own brothers in such ways felt wrong.

Some things you couldn't walk away from unscarred. Some things there was no going back from. The chill of the Pattern against her back grew deeper and more profound.

Merrick was no fool; he knew about consequences and had decided to take them on. So Sorcha stepped back to observe what he would do next.

He did it all far too easily. He held the rune Kebenar before him, the one that showed the truth of a situation, and wove it between them. Something else was in there though, the strand of his wild talent binding them, calm and determined, to him.

It was similar to creating a Bond, but he was a Sensitive, not an Active. Yet there he was combining their powers, their runes and their spirits together. It was a beautiful and terrifying thing to watch her young partner create a Conclave.

When he was done, Merrick turned to her. His shoulders sagged a little, and she could feel the darkness in his soul was a little deeper than before. Sorcha couldn't untangle her feelings of pride and fear however. He was much changed from the raw recruit of last year, full of hope and honest dreams. She would have seen him keep some of that in his life—but it was obviously not to be.

"It wears us all down in the end," Raed muttered, though she could not tell if it was in response to her thoughts. "This has to be a fool's errand. What can we accomplish by facing this del Rue?"

Merrick's smile was bright.

"Everything," he replied. "Del Rue is dangling us all like puppets from the shadows. He moves us about to achieve his aims. So tonight we drag him kicking and screaming into the light and expose him for what he truly is. Everyone in Arkaym should know the danger, and that the Order of the Circle of Stars has returned. The time for subterfuge is over."

Raed held his gaze for a spell and then dipped his head in consent. "As always you show your elders the truth of things, Merrick." He went to the door. "Shall we be about it then?"

The Deacons, as one, nodded. Sorcha opened the door, and gestured Merrick out into the light.

TWENTY-FIVE

An Unholy Enterprise

Merrick, with his Conclave at his back, walked down the corridors that seemed now very unfamiliar. Though he led the way, his heart was racing. His own body felt lighter and more insubstantial than even the Bond with Sorcha. The emotions of so many people in his head distracted him. The strands of the Bonds he had crisscrossed and tangled within him, and he felt as though if he let any of them slip he would be lost.

He had made a Conclave. Something only the Presbyters did, and yet he had gone and done it. Now he held the lives of seven other people in his hands. One wrong move and they could all forget to breathe.

Sorcha's confusion and disappointment hammered away in the corner that he had shoved his primary Bond. A Conclave was a serious matter, and few of the Actives knew that it was Sensitives that formed them. He was, from recollection, right now acting as the nexus of the Conclave. He would be the only one to retain complete memory of proceedings during the event. It was one of the many secrets the Sensitives kept to themselves . . . that and the nature of the final rune of Sight.

By the Bones, he hoped he wouldn't have to use that as well tonight.

Merrick, through effort of will, pulled together his scattering thoughts.

It was a short walk from the Arch Abbot's rooms to the Devotional, but it felt like an eternity to get there; so many feet, so many breaths and so many thoughts to filter and make as one. He was suddenly given a great appreciation of what Actives went through every time they used their runes. His skin burned and his eyes watered, but he was giddy with the feeling. It was like walking a tightrope with a deadly fall on each side.

As they reached the end of the corridor to the Devotional, he paused at the great ironbound oak door. The sound of voices was coming from the other side, but not as many as he would have thought, and he could tell that the flame of del Rue's attention was now directed at them. He'd naturally been aware when the Conclave was formed; there was no other rune activity within the whole of the Abbey after all. So because of that, they burned like a signal fire on a moonless night.

We can't allow him time to respond. All we have is surprise, Merrick sent along the Bond. *We have to move now!*

Sorcha's blue eyes fixed on him with total trust. She nodded, and he opened the door to lead them into the Devotional.

Merrick had never seen the whole congregation of the Mother Abbey assembled anywhere before. The great vaulted space of the Devotional was full to the brim with his colleagues. Hundreds of Deacons, a virtual sea of brown, blue and green cloaks lay before him. Every wooden pew was filled, and they had taken up the aisles as well. If it had been a theater production it would have been a grand night indeed, Merrick thought, somewhat strangely.

Then he noticed the rest of the gathering was not just Deacons. Taking up the apse section at the front of the Devotional was a good number of armed Imperial Guards, and in their middle stood the Emperor, his sister and a smiling del Rue. Before them in turn, disturbingly on their knees, was the entire Presbyterial Council, from the Arch Abbot to the ancient Presbyter Mournling. All were bent in supplication—some to greater degrees than others. Merrick's spiraling thoughts alighted on how another Order had once been slain for not showing the correct level of penitence to some horde-leading warlord. Was this what was going on?

"There they are, the traitors!" Del Rue's voice echoed in the vast space of the Devotional and all heads turned as one to them.

Merrick's mind was occupied with holding the Conclave together, and he felt as though he was trapped in amber. Sorcha was luckily not so encumbered. She smiled and stepped down the nave as if she were out for a stroll. "I think you are not familiar with our way of doing things here. The Devotional is for our Order, not yours. I believe you gave it up when the people of Arkaym had enough of your cruel endeavors, and the Emperor outlawed you all."

The Emperor did not flinch, but a wave of whispers ran through those assembled. The Imperial Guards had not yet raised their rifles, but they looked ready to at a moment's notice.

Merrick finally had enough of a hold on the Conclave that he was able to study Zofiya. She stood, silent at her brother's side, but her eyes did not meet his. Through his Center he could see she was not the woman he had shared a bed with a little over a week ago. Del Rue had broken her—something that he would have never thought possible. Through his Center, the Sensitive could see a gleam of gold on the bright scarlet of her soul. It was a stain that had not been there before, and it sickened him. How had del Rue managed to tame the determined royal so quickly? Merrick liked knowing about his opponents, their strengths and weaknesses—or at least being able to research them. By hiding and destroying all information on the Circle of Stars, Raed's grandfather had done them all a great disservice.

Del Rue ignored Sorcha's barb, instead pointing to Raed standing behind her. "Look, she has brought the Young Pretender with her, Imperial Majesty. Proof that the Order is conspiring against you as I said."

Kaleva spun around, his face contorted with rage. Merrick knew then what the golden stain was. The strain of del Rue's influence on him was subtler than in the Grand Duchess, but it ran far deeper—and he had no time to work on it now.

"If you recall, Your Imperial Majesty," Raed said to the man who occupied the place he might have occupied, "last year, I risked my own life to save your sister. This, I hope, means you will let me speak before you shoot me dead in this place of sanctuary."

Merrick held his breath. Killing people in the precepts of the Mother Abbey was forbidden, because it was highly likely to create a geist—not that he expected the Circle of Stars to care much about that. Del Rue's eyes narrowed on the Young Pretender, but perhaps the threat of the Rossin stayed him from doing anything rash. Meanwhile, the Imperial Guard shifted in their ready position—not enough for a normal eye to tell—but the Deacons saw it. These guards, even if they had not been there, still knew what the Order had done for the Empire. He could only hope that would give them a moment's pause.

Given this brief moment, Merrick considered using his wild talent on the room, but there were too many conflicting emotions between the fear of the Deacons, the Emperor's burning rage and the confusion of the guards. If he picked the wrong one to amplify then he could trigger a massacre.

"This man calling himself del Rue is no friend to the

Empire." Raed's eyes flicked over the Imperial Guard and the Deacons, trying to hold their attention.

While he did so, Merrick began examining the Grand Duchess. Zofiya had a great strength of mind—very similar to a Deacon in fact. If he could just find a way to free it a little, she would do the rest for herself. Dimly he felt Sorcha's frustration begin to bubble up. The idea of guards in the Devotional was an abomination to her, and he couldn't hold her in check forever.

"He's a traitor, a conspirator and the one actually responsible for your sister's abduction." Raed gestured at the Grand Duchess in an overly dramatic fashion. "In fact he is one of the Order of the Circle of Stars, the very Order that my grandfather's father cast down for trying to overthrow the Empire once before." He pointed up into the massive vaulted ceiling, making all of the assembled look up to where the hacked-off faces on the statues, even now, hung above them. Out of the corner of his eye, Merrick saw an unsettling smile light on del Rue's lips. He had not looked up nor did he make any protestations that it was not true. He was very confident.

The Presbyters, forgetting they were powerless, rose to their feet in shock. Most looked horrified, but Mournling had the appearance of one who had dreaded such a day and was now seeing it come to fruition. Arch Abbot Rictun opened his mouth a few times, as if he wished he could find the words, but nothing came out.

Sorcha, we will need to move quickly and soon. Merrick blasted the image of what he wanted to do along the Bond. She flinched slightly, but then gave him the tiniest of nods in response. Underneath the sleeves of her cloak her hands clenched.

"And I am to take your word against the word of a member of my aristocracy?" Kaleva threw back his head, filling the Devotional with cracked and mocking laughter. "You are the Pretender to my throne, and now you think to claim it. Guards, take this man into custody immediately!"

His soldiers looked relieved to have something to do that was not a move against the Deacons. Raed was the sole enemy they easily recognized among those who had so recently been allies.

Now!

At Merrick's command all the Conclave of Deacons stepped out wide from behind him, spreading between the pews in a disciplined move that even the most practiced military men could not have emulated. The Actives raised their hands and Yevah, the Rune of Fire burned on their skin. In the Conclave so much pain was only compounded— they all shared it, but it did not stop them. The rune was burning through every muscle and sinew—or so it felt. The temporary designs the Patternmaker had created barely held together, and they had to concentrate twice as hard to keep Yevah in place. Yet they did. Merrick felt triumphant, for without a Conclave, this would be impossible. He also knew, without Sorcha there would be no strength in the rune. Merrick felt her like an iron rod in the group; a core they could all grasp onto.

Despite the difficulties, a sheet of summoned flame erupted between the mass of Deacons and the Imperial Guard. The soldiers flinched back from the unholy fire, and their shock was perfectly understandable. No one had ever used runes on humans. Not in all the history of the Order of the Eye and the Fist. However it was a time of change and chaos. All the rules were gone now, and his small band of Deacons was making its own. For a brief moment Merrick reveled in that freedom.

The Deacons, those still without powers, rose to their feet turning to those who held the rune before them. A few smiled broadly and cheered to see that at least some of their colleagues had regained power. Others hid their faces in shame. At the front, the whole Presbyterial Council looked up as the wide length of flaming shield reflected in the stained glass windows in shameless beauty. Merrick caught a glimpse of another face in the crowd, the weather-beaten visage of Deacon Garil Reeceson. He merely nodded to Merrick, not exactly happy with what he was seeing, but not surprised either.

"This meeting is a sham. He gathered you all here to kill you!" By some trick of the moment and acoustics of the building, Sorcha's voice boomed down the whole length of the Devotional. "Get out to the stables, my brothers! Leave Vermillion while we still can! We shall find each other after!"

Merrick felt his partner's plan like a hard pebble in his mind, but there was no time to examine it. It was enough she had some idea of how they could survive this. The Presbyterial Council members, who had all looked so powerful to Merrick, now appeared fragile creatures, but several of them did in fact turn to do as Sorcha suggested. Melisande Troupe had her arm around the elderly Trelaine. Her eyes locked with Merrick's for just an instant.

Not everyone heeded Sorcha's warning. Some brave Deacons stayed to fight even though the Order had no weapons on them, while others just looked confused and stricken by indecision. Those who did turn and flee from the Devotional kept to their training and did not panic. Even as they ran, they reached out and helped one another. Merrick's pride in his fellow Deacons surged, and he set his jaw, determined to give those who could escape the best chance possible. They would have to hold the attention of the Emperor and his guards for some time for that to work.

As confusion began to take hold, del Rue finally showed his true colors. With a shake of his head that made him look like an angry bull, he raised his hands. They were covered by the thin calfskin gloves that Merrick had observed previously. When he whispered something to them however, the runes on them became visible. Such fragile objects should not have been able to contain and control even one rune.

One man with no Sensitive? Sorcha's heady delight in violence rushed through the Bond. *Let's end this while we can.*

Merrick, struggling to hold the Conclave together, would have urged caution, but by then it was too late. Sorcha drew her sword—actually drew her sword—and strode forward.

In response, del Rue summoned Shayst. The green flame of the rune was impossibly fluid as it wrapped around their shield and dispersed the power like a child blowing out a candle flame. He didn't need a Sensitive. He was like the Arch Abbot—a wielder of both Active and Sensitive powers. No wonder he was so sure of himself. He was everything he required!

Each Deacon had in him the seeds of both Active and Sensitive, but to find one with equal strengths was incredibly rare. Merrick should have been able to see that immediately—that he hadn't, made the young Sensitive wonder just what this conspirator was. Only an Arch Abbot should have that ability, but this enemy was more than that. While his butterfly thoughts chased that particular fear, del Rue flexed his fingers in his far-too-thin gloves.

Kaleva's eyes bulged and he staggered away from the man who had just revealed himself as a Deacon. The conspirator's weeks of work began to tangle around and trip him, because the Emperor was now horrified by any kind of Deacon power. Del Rue didn't notice at all. He was lost in the mad delight of wielding power. His face was set in a mask of joy as he summoned Chityre to him. Lightning bloomed in the highest reaches of the Devotional, dancing from pillar to pillar and illuminating those powerless Deacons still fleeing the building. The whole building rang with the sound of thunder.

Tighon had the distressing thought, which filtered across the Bond as stones groaned, that all the Order's work to repair this beautiful building was about to be undone. It was so hard for Merrick to keep a clear mind in Conclave with all these new chaotic thoughts darting about.

Deiyant! Sorcha's voice was like a shout in his head, rising above the rumble of the yammering of the others.

She called for the rune that wielded air, often called the push rune, but he didn't have a moment to think. He acted. The Conclave raised its hands as one above their heads, and the amber glow of the rune flashed out around them. The pews around them flew up, wrenched from their places and thrown up, just barely above their heads.

This all happened in one long heartbeat, just as the lightning came down among them. The Devotional keened again, like a ship caught in a storm, and in fact did seem to list. Then one of the two front pillars of the asp cracked and toppled, bringing down a portion of the ceiling.

Like a mast, Merrick thought dimly to himself, as the Conclave buzzed in his head. Something impacted him in the chaos, but it really didn't seem to matter. For a time, his world was entirely comprised of stone, dust and rubble.

Reflexively, Merrick held on to the Conclave. When finally he could make sense of the world, he found himself lying at the edge of a pile of stones, coughing up dust, with his ears ringing.

Sorcha was lying sprawled across him, but she was miraculously alive, though bleeding from a wound to her head. Staunching the blood with one hand, she yanked Merrick to his feet with the other.

His ears were still useless, but he heard along the Bond. *Tighon is dead.* She really didn't need to tell him that—he could feel it in the Conclave. One had fallen away, and with him Natylda his Sensitive. Merrick glanced to his left and saw her screaming and trying to dig him out of the rubble, even though all in the Conclave could feel his loss. Thanks to Sorcha there were not as many Deacons buried beneath the stones than there would have been otherwise, but they could still all feel them; injured, broken, dying. Even as Merrick's Center flooded him with information, he felt in that moment a man's life go out.

The Devotional was now groaning and creaking, still shuddering with the terrible wounds it had taken. The sheer weight of bricks and stone could not hold forever.

Some distance off, Merrick spied del Rue pulling himself out of the dust. He was completely unharmed, but the young Deacon spotted his one chance. Del Rue was concentrating so hard on finding a way to destroy the Conclave, that for a moment his mind was vulnerable and unprotected. Merrick wrapped his mind around the rune Aiemm and cast it at him like a javelin.

The Rune of the Past consumed the young Deacon as he saw through del Rue's eyes. No, not del Rue: Horris, Cristin, Melloir, Hjan. Hundreds of names, places and memories rolled over Merrick, until only one remained. Pulled back from the ocean of the past—Derodak. Merrick plunged down desperately after that name.

The world was new, and he was an Ehtia; a creator of magic and machines. Like Nynnia, he had fled with his people to the Otherside so that the world might not be destroyed by the geists that hunted the Ehtia after the Break. However, also like Merrick's lost love, he had chosen to be born back into this world with many of his powers stripped away—but not for the fine and good reasons that had motivated Nynnia.

A world he felt had failed him. A world he now wanted to control. He had lived too long, been too many people: first Deacon, Emperor, saint, rebel and destroyer.

"Derodak," Merrick whispered to himself. It literally meant "the first" in Ancient. The Conclave was forming around him again, seeing what he now saw, the real person behind the mask that was del Rue.

However, they were not alone. Kaleva and his remaining guards could now be seen through the clearing dust. The ceiling high above still held, and the stones had only wounded a few of them, yet the Emperor's rage was reaching apoplectic proportions. The calm leader Merrick had been introduced to was long gone. His etheric presence was pulsing, indicating he'd passed the point where sanity had any hold on him. All the bonds that held him, his sister, his love of the Empire, his determination to be a good ruler, were blown away under the assault of so much chaos. Derodak had done his work well and had now pulled the trigger.

"Demons are trying to kill me!" he screamed. "Kill them all! Whatever it takes." The Imperial Guard needed no urging to take action. They'd been witness to many unleashed powers this day, come close to death themselves, and were now ready to unleash some of their own.

Merrick, scrambling to hold all the straining powers of the Conclave together, saw their rifles come up, and called again for Aydien. The blue fire ran widdershins around the Conclave, dancing off flesh and lancing out. Bullets zinged around them, even as the power of the rune pushed back against the guards, sending them flying like chaff in all directions. Still some of their aim held true, and Leonteh and Quannik crashed to the ground, choking on their own blood. Horror and disbelief flooded the Bond, and the rest of the Conclave threads began to unravel between them. He only held Lujia and Sibuse with himself and Sorcha now. It was barely enough to be called a Conclave now.

The Imperial Guard kept firing, but underneath Merrick heard the sound that he had been fearing: the growl of the Rossin. In all of this, they had forgotten Raed. He had stood with them, but apart, and now whatever control the Young Pretender held over the beast disappeared. Merrick had known it would happen eventually. Perhaps, if he was honest, it was the reason they had brought him with them. The Rossin was always the wild card in the deck.

Raed shared a look with Merrick and Sorcha, his hazel eyes already turning to gold, but he had no time to remove his clothes or spare them a word.

The great cat leapt into existence, snarling, and ready to do what his nature dictated. He glanced once at Derodak, shook his head and then sprang among the guards. The sound of their screams was painful for Merrick to hear, but they had opened fire on the Order.

However once he had cleared the Devotional of soldiers firing at them, the Rossin did not turn back. A rear guard of soldiers tried to keep firing to cover their Emperor's escape, but the Rossin pursued. The scattered remains of the Conclave could do nothing to stop him.

Keeping his head down, Merrick saw with great disappointment that Derodak was untouched. He rose from among the bullets and debris, still with that damnable smile on his lips, and held out his hand to the Grand Duchess, who took it. She looked no more than a piece of furniture, still Merrick felt relief wash over him.

Del Rue took no notice of her however, instead focusing on the Deacons. "How very unexpected of you, Faris and Chambers! Looks like you've managed to cobble together something akin to a Pattern—so you must have found him then?" His brow furrowed. "How did you do that though, I wonder?" His eyes drifted to Sorcha, piercing her through with Sight. "Something we did not count on then . . ." He did not appear afraid, but rather intrigued; as if Sorcha were merely a piece he had to fit into his game board.

Being examined so, did not improve Sorcha's mood. Merrick felt her raise her hand, but even in the Conclave he could not hold her back; she was far too strong for that.

She plucked Pyet from the ether, screaming in rage and pouring fire down upon Derodak like some mythical dragon. The heat was so intense in the confined space that Merrick, Lujia and Sibuse staggered back, falling to their knees. Merrick thrust his face into the crook of his arm so that he might have a chance to breathe. It felt as though every hair on his head was going to catch fire. They were all going to die. Against the flame, all he could make out was the outline of Sorcha. Her skin was wreathed in blue flickering lights that wrote out the runes on her flesh. High above them, the stained glass succumbed to the heat, and then it was raining red-hot molten drops—blues, greens and reds—down on them all.

Merrick was going to have to use Ticat on her, the last-resort rune held by the Sensitives. By the Bones, he didn't want to, but if she didn't stop he would have to.

Sorcha! Come back!

It was a near thing, but somehow she pulled herself back. The flames died away under her command. What was left behind was a scarred and pitted Devotional that would never be the same again. The smell of burned wood and stone filled the survivors' nostrils.

Sorcha herself was sobbing, shaking and staggering on her feet. Yet out of it all, emerged Derodak, only the hem of his cloak singed, with one arm still around the pale and staring Zofiya.

He glanced once to his right, and smiled bleakly seeing the Imperial Guard fleeing before the Rossin, taking the Emperor with them.

"Kaleva was always the weakest of the siblings, but luckily I don't need him anyway"—Derodak shrugged—"I have his sister." With that, he grabbed Zofiya by the arm and pulled her in the opposite direction her brother had run. Merrick realized none of them could use Voishem, because of the protective cantrips worked into the walls of all the Abbey buildings to prevent geist infiltration.

What exactly his plan was, Merrick couldn't fathom, but Sorcha spun on her heel, her eyes wild with rage. "We can't let him get away or we might never find him. By the Bones, come on!" And then not waiting for his reply, she vaulted over the tumbled rock and chased after him.

Lujia and Sibuse were bleeding, injured, still capable of movement but not much else. The Conclave was broken. Merrick fixed them with a sad gaze, realizing they could well be the only members of the Order still capable of using their runes. He wasn't sure how much that mattered now, but there was the faint chance it did. "Get out of here, and go back to Widow Vashill's. You've done all you can here." Then he turned his back on them and followed his partner into the dust and confusion of the end of the Order.

TWENTY-SIX

Alliance and Victory

The Rossin ran, following the guards out of the building and out onto the cool grass. It didn't matter where they were; he tore them apart with great relish. Human blood was so much more satisfying than anything the Wrayth could give him; primal and run through with fear.

Behind him the Devotional of the Order began to crumble in on itself, a great rumble of stone and masonry falling to ruin. That it was the Deacons tearing it apart was a delicious irony. He leapt clear of the dust cloud and with a bunch of his hind legs ran a literal circle around the guards. They saw at once that they could not outdistance him here. Instead they huddled around their Emperor, who had drawn his sword and waited, all foolish confidence, for the beast to approach. Many had made the mistake of thinking him some overgrown lion or tiger that they could battle easily enough. He was more than that.

The Rossin knew the time had come to reveal himself to this latest in a long line of foolish Emperors.

The guards took potshots at him, but the bullets had about the same effect as beestings would have. He kept relentlessly stalking toward them, his golden-flecked eyes locked on Kaleva, Emperor of Arkaym.

Yet he did not spring upon them, as he could have easily done. Instead the great cat sat down at the outer edge of their circle and waited. Eventually they ran out of ammunition. He could smell the salty tang of their fear on the breeze. The Emperor's was no different than any of the other men's.

That was when the Rossin chose to speak. "Do you know me?"

The surprise on the humans' faces was almost comical. It had been an age since the great cat had spoken into the world. All thought him a dumb Beast, but like all geistlords he was more than capable of it. Before he had nothing to say. After all, why would a wolf talk to sheep.

Kaleva, perhaps not the total fool the Rossin had taken him for, straightened. "Yes," his voice wavered more than a fraction. Good, a little fear was an appropriate response.

"Then are you prepared to beg for your life now?" The great cat could feel Raed trying desperately to understand what was going on, but the geistlord stuffed him down deeper, where he would be able to see nothing. This was secret business he would not yet have the Young Pretender aware of.

The Emperor's eyes were wide and frightened—just like all prey. "Perhaps," he said, taking a stumbling step back. "If there is anything you want from the Empire, maybe a—"

"I can take most everything I need," the Rossin snarled, showing his vast expanse of teeth, "but I want something from you."

The Emperor froze, perhaps sensing the scent of a deal in the air. His eyes darted to the crumbling Devotional, and the Rossin knew what his tiny thoughts were; there was now no Order to protect him from the geists. "What . . ." He stopped and coughed up some of the dust that was in the air. "What can I do for you?"

He was so weak, and this moment so easy, that the Rossin would have laughed, had he been in the mood. However seeing his old Tormentor had not put him in a good mood. That ancient foe was moving pawns on the table, so now it was time for the geistlord to do the same.

"It is what I can do for you," he growled. "I will be willing to serve your new line of Emperors as I did the old one. I gave them power and prestige that was not questioned for nearly a thousand years. I will lay the family that bears my name low for you . . . for a price."

The Emperor's eyes gleamed. "What would that be?"

"There is an object, a trinket I gave the first of my line, that lies at the heart of the palace. It is the one place in this realm I cannot go. When the time is right you will fetch it for me."

"Is that time now?" Kaleva swallowed hard.

The Rossin tilted his head up and examined the stars closely. "No, not just yet . . . but very, very soon." He fixed his gaze on the human before him. "Do you agree? Have we a pact?"

The mortal did not even hesitate. The words were barely out of the Rossin's fanged mouth before Kaleva, Emperor of Arkaym said, "I do."

The essence of one was now bound to the other. It was not yet as strong as a Bond of the Order, but it would grow with time. They still had a little of that. The Rossin would have purred, if he could.

"However, if anyone finds out I made a deal with a geistlord—" Kaleva paused and stared pointedly at his half dozen men who were beginning to look at him with genuine horror. It was an easily fixed problem.

The Rossin unleashed himself upon the remaining guards and cut them down in bloody swathes where they stood. He was as swift as a desert wind, and just as unforgiving. When he turned back to Kaleva, his muzzle was covered in scarlet and gore.

"Do you see how things are with me in your service?"

The Beast was, after so long in the human realm, a consummate liar.

The Emperor nodded, the look of befuddlement never leaving his face. He could not understand why this was happening or quite what it meant. Perhaps the Tormentor had done the Rossin a grand favor; messing with the Emperor's mind and soul made him very easy to manipulate now.

"Then go," he snarled, "and await my call."

Kaleva, the Emperor of Arkaym, turned and ran like a child dismissed from school. The Rossin watched him, while licking the remains of the Imperial Guard from his mouth. The pieces were nearly all assembled, but for now he would feast.

The great cat dropped his head, and began to devour the soldiers who had given their life for a worthless leader.

The Mother Abbey was being reduced to rubble. The runes that had been unleashed were pulling it apart—everything that the Order of the Eye and the Fist had stood for was falling down around her.

The horror of that remained distant to Sorcha—put away for examination at another time. All she knew was that it was no longer the place she had loved and grown accustomed to; now it was merely an obstacle. She could feel the ends of her hair burning, and hear the scream of stone tumbling behind her as she ran up the nave in pursuit of del Rue—now revealed as Derodak. The structure, once punctured, could not hold itself upright, and the loss of the columns sealed the Devotional's fate. The night sky was visible through the once soaring roof, and it was framed in green flames. In the screaming recesses of her mind, Sorcha knew the Order of the Eye and the Fist would never come here again, and for that she would make her enemy pay. She ran harder, pumping her arms, and leaping as best she could over broken pews and piles of still-sliding stone.

Dimly, Sorcha realized Merrick was trying to keep up with her, but she summoned Seym, and drew strength from the Rune of Flesh to power her pursuit ahead of him. Her partner would only try and stop her, and she would not let that happen. She scrambled after Derodak with the intensity of a lion on the chase, but this was no gazelle she was chasing.

Ahead, Derodak must have also summoned Seym because he was carrying Zofiya along with him. She was a limp bundle in his arms, and she was no lightweight, since she was no shrinking Court beauty, but a warrior in her own right.

They reached the edge of the devastation, and now she could see, through the smoke, Deacons riding out of the burst-open gate. The Breed horses, beloved by the Deacons, were carrying the last of them away from the destruction. She wished man and horse well. Perhaps equine grace would be all that would remain of her Order.

"Derodak!" Sorcha barely recognized her own voice, cobbled as it was out of human, Wrayth and rune. Whatever she was, and however she had got here, it no longer mattered. She was stripped bare and raw.

Her enemy heard that, sensed it, and despite everything, could not contain his curiosity. He turned around, and what he saw made him throw Zofiya to the ground as casually as a bundle of laundry. He actually ventured back a few steps and looked Sorcha up and down.

"Most incredible," he said admiringly. "I did not think the Wrayth could do it—but here you are."

"Sorcha!" Merrick, finally having caught up to her, appeared over the top of the rubble, covered in dust and bleeding from many small cuts. He glanced between the two of them and a frown creased his forehead. Even he, the Sensitive of all Sensitives, could not quite understand what was passing between them. Still, he held out his hand. *Come back . . .*

The yearning and love he put into that plea were heard

by Sorcha, but did not move her to action. His kindness and good soul were very far off, and directed at some creature that she could never be again. Sorcha didn't move. Derodak took up her whole vision.

"What am I?" she whispered and only he seemed to hear her question. Sorcha stepped nearer and circled the man as if they were dancing some strange alien steps.

Through her shared Center the man was an enigma, and yet as fascinating as the night sky above. She felt if she kept looking she might fall into him, and not be anything at all.

"You are . . ." He pursed his lips and stopped himself from continuing. Instead he said, "Why don't you come with me and find out? It could be most interesting."

Merrick had run to the Grand Duchess, and was crouching over her still form. What he found, Sorcha did not know, but he hauled her into his arms and backed away from the other man. "You can't have either of them."

Derodak laughed at him. "Have the girl, I am done with her. She served her purpose when she pointed the finger of accusation at your foolish Order. I have better things to occupy myself with now." He tilted his head and regarded Sorcha with a small smile playing around his lips. "I don't think I will even need Vashill's machine for you."

Sorcha felt herself the center of his attention, and in the state she now occupied she liked it.

When he opened his palm, she saw three gleaming weirstones rested in his fingers. He held out his hand again. "Come with me. I am the only one who can understand what it is to be you, and I can teach you many things."

He threw the stones down on the ground and immediately the triangle they described began to shimmer. It was as if the earth herself grew soft at his touch. With awe, Sorcha realized he was making a tunnel before her very eyes. Not just redirecting the stones as she had done, but bending the Otherside to his will.

Sorcha moved toward him. His words made sense. She

did not belong with human or Deacon. She was something else, and Derodak would show her what that was.

As she did so though, she felt the Bond with Merrick suddenly burn bright. She would have turned to tell him to let her go, but the young Deacon was faster than she would have thought possible.

He too was more than he seemed, and Derodak had failed to fully grasp that. As Merrick threw himself at Sorcha, he gathered up all the emotions around him. Every feeling of loss, despair and fear that hundreds of Deacons had felt that night. An accumulation of lost dreams, battered determination and the best of intentions, all brought to nothing. It was a terrible night, like few others in history, and Merrick was there to use those feelings for Sorcha's benefit.

His wild talent channeled all of them, and directed them at Derodak. The man had many shields. Sorcha glimpsed how many years he had worked to protect himself against runes of all kinds, but this talent was not a rune, not hard-won from the geists. It was a totally human power, and consequently one Derodak was not fully prepared to repel.

Derodak howled, as those emotions poured over him like a tidal wave, battering at him in an almost physical fashion. He twisted back and forth, trying to escape them, but they were not runes and he had no defense. Sorcha knew he had grown chill living so long, insulated from his own mortality. These feelings cut to his core like the sharpest of knives. His own talents crumpled under their weight as he clawed at his own face.

At last, desperate to escape, he activated the weirstones and, stepping into the triangle, disappeared into the earth. It was the last thing Deacon Sorcha Faris saw for a little time.

When she finally came back to consciousness, it was to find herself cradled in Merrick's arms. He was weeping, while Zofiya, completely unconscious, lay a few feet away.

Sorcha touched his face. "I certainly hope those tears are because of what you just did, and not for me."

He brushed them away, and smiled crookedly at her. "Yes . . . that's what it is . . ."

Together they clambered to their feet. Sorcha surveyed the devastation while Merrick went to tend the Grand Duchess. Fire had spread to the other buildings, and she knew that come morning the Mother Abbey would be but a smoldering memory.

Merrick returned, half carrying Zofiya. She looked pale but was coming around. When she found out what had happened here, Sorcha was sure there would be hell to pay.

"What now?" Merrick asked, though he could now see the seed of a plan she'd been mulling over since they found the Patternmaker.

"First we regroup at Vashill's . . . then we go our own way." Sorcha sighed and put her shoulder under Zofiya's arm. She could already feel Raed in the city, back to himself and heading in that direction. They had much to do.

"We have work to do," Merrick muttered. He probably didn't even realize he had done it, but once again her young partner was stealing her thoughts from her head. Strangely now, it was a comfort.

The Bond held her together for now. Later would come soon enough.

TWENTY-SEVEN

Scattered Remains

The widow Vashill's house had not been a good place to stay, and Sorcha had moved the remains of the Order on as soon as they had all that could be gathered. Vermillion was a shaken city, full of panic and disorder, and fallen into utter chaos. With no force of Deacons to fight geists, they were coming back. *Vermin can always tell when the cat of the house dies.* Sorcha recalled her beloved Pareth telling her that—but she had never thought it was a warning for Deacons.

Then there was the Emperor to deal with. He had survived somehow the destruction of the Mother Abbey, but lost none of his blind and foolish hatred of the Order. The Deacons had no doubt that he would come looking for them as soon as he regained control. After only two days, they got word he was hunting former members of the Order down.

So the Deacons and their companions filed out of the city in small, unremarkable groups, and formed up, once on the road, beyond sight of Vermillion. They marched for many days, covering their tracks and checking the ether as they went. Half of them had managed to take Breed mounts, and they carried what few provisions that they'd scavenged. The sooner they got into the hill country the better.

By the fourth day, everyone, man and horse, was exhausted, dirty and at the end of their tether. Sorcha gave the order to make camp off the road at the foot of a thickly wooded hill, and it was there finally that they were able to take stock of what had survived the mad escape from the city. They could also eat.

The Arch Abbot was not among them; dead or captured, it was impossible to know. Three of the Presbyters had however managed to escape: Thorine Belzark, a battered Melisande Troupe and most surprisingly the elderly Yvril Mournling. They were the most shocked of all of them, and barely spoke to each other let alone anyone else. Merrick commented that they only needed some time.

None of them could be sure how much of that they had. Sorcha sat in the grass and finally forced herself to count who was not with them. Garil was not among the ragtag group of leftover Deacons, but the stark raving Pattern-maker was. Kolya had quietly taken up a place within the group, but kept to himself. Lujia and Sibuse, battered and bleeding, proudly took up guarding the rear of the caravan, since they still had some faltering runes at their disposal. The Patternmaker's marks were, however, fading. A dozen of the crew of the far-off *Dominion* were still with them, along with a silent and brooding Aachon.

In total, sixty people, some once Deacons, some not, surrounded her on this grassy spot in the late autumn sun. It was not large enough a number to be an army, but not small enough to pass easily unnoticed.

"So then," Raed said, dropping down to sit with her, "are we all to become outlaws and live in the forest?"

He laid the back of his hand tentatively on her knee. Along the Bond, his pain sang, but it was tinged with just the slightest hint of hope. She put her palm against his. "Perhaps, or perhaps something altogether different. I have been thinking on a new Order, one with all the strengths of the old one, but with none of the weaknesses."

She took out the thin piece of wood that the Pattern-maker had created in the cellar. The lines were disappearing from it as mud and blood lost its power. Soon enough, it would be useless.

Tracing her fingertip over the fading script, she whispered to him, "Do you realize this is the longest we have spent together without being chased since our time together on the airship?"

His laugh was low. "Here's to a little more time then. I don't think we are the only ones who would appreciate it." He jerked his head to where Merrick and Zofiya were tucked under a tree, talking in low voices. For a moment Sorcha considered them. The Grand Duchess did not look so grand as she once had, but she was smiling, despite the situation. She was the kind of woman who could bounce back from even Derodak's treatment.

"I hope they can find some happiness," she said softly, "but unfortunately we cannot give that to them. And there is more . . ."

This was going to be the hard bit. She looked off into the distance and shared with him what she had heard from one of the scouts the previous day.

"The Wrayth have bred themselves another girl—one that looks something like your sister, and they have raised her in the west. Ten Princes have already defected to her banner."

She knew that he had worked so hard to stop war washing over Arkaym—sacrificing much to the cause—and yet there it was. Sometimes no matter how hard a person strove, it was not enough.

He looked down at their intertwined hands. "You know, when my mother died under the Rossin's claws, I thought that was the worst thing that could ever happen to me. Now I am not so sure. Fraine never really had a chance to be a normal person . . . a good person."

Sorcha reached up and pulled his head down to rest against her shoulder. She wanted to give him some comfort. She wanted to have some time to cherish what little they'd been able to salvage from the destruction. That mattered more than food or rest.

She'd hunted in these woods, and she knew them very well. Standing up she held out her hand to Raed. "I've got something to show you."

A frown creased his brow, but he got to his feet and allowed himself to be led away from the others. His faltering steps told her that he too was tired.

When they had gone a few minutes from the crowd, into the dappled shade of the forest, he smiled. It was a small hunter's hut. Not much but woven walls, and a timber and fern roof. It was the kind of place where a lone traveler might find solace for a spell while tracking game.

Sorcha led him to it, unlatched the simple door, and when he was in, closed it behind him. Raed let out a long sigh, and cradled her head in his hands as they leaned against each other, forehead to forehead.

She traced the line of his cheek, and kissed his lips softly. Part of her was afraid that this spell would break and they would be flung apart again. Another part was fearful that they might find their feelings not what they thought.

"You are a good man, Raed," she said to him, while her fingers unlaced his shirt, "and we all make our own choices in this world."

He kissed her palm, and then ran his tongue up the inside of her wrist and around her arm, following the curve of the fading runes. He had probably already guessed what she meant to do, and she loved that he had said nothing of it.

They dropped back to the bed, which was merely a pile of heather covered in a blanket, but it felt as good as an Imperial piece of furniture.

"We don't have long," he breathed against her skin.

Sorcha nodded, knowing that they must move their ragtag group on soon, but she did not stop undressing him. "But we have enough time," she replied, somewhat shakily, as his lips descended on her.

It could not be the passionate romp that they'd shared on the *Summer Hawk*, or even the fumbling delight of their time in Chioma, because they were simply exhausted. However it was its own special moment.

When at last they had sated themselves, kissed, and murmured and reacquainted themselves with each other's flesh, they left the little hunter's hut and returned to their companions.

Soon enough they were moving again, heading west once more, toward a series of caves Merrick knew of. Here at least they could make fires, have a little hot food, and everyone could get some sleep.

It was in these caves that Sorcha decided to finally reveal her plan to Merrick and Raed—though both of them, connected so strongly to her through the Bond, already guessed at it. However, she wanted to say the words and tell them because they were her closest companions. They deserved that, and so much more.

It was a long, hard road she was setting them on, but one guided by the past.

Her partner, young and battered though he was, still managed to raise an objection to her plan.

He shook his head. "Sorcha, you can't know if this worked for your mother or not. She most likely died, and that was why you ended up in the Order. It could have been this process that killed her . . ."

He was right—she knew that. She'd only seen one vision of Caoirse in the nest of the Wrayth, and she knew deep down that she had died somewhere and somehow shortly after. Still she would not be put off. "It was far more likely to have been childbirth in that dreadful place that did it, and we have to try to get back some of what we've lost. The Empire needs the Order. We all know that."

Her blue eyes held his brown steady for a long moment.

Raed stood not far away and remained silent on the matter. Another reason she was falling in love with him—even on this longer acquaintance. The Young Pretender did not try to make her what she was not, or bend her to his will.

The Pattern is gone, and we need the Order. Without them we've lost Arkaym.

She pushed the words toward him, but Merrick did not hear them through the fading rune. Sorcha had been complaining and worrying about having the young man in her head ever since she'd made the Bond. Now, it was the thing she wanted most in the world.

"Besides, if this works we can find the Circle of Stars' Pattern." She grinned at him wickedly. "Once we do that, we can teach them how dreadfully uncomfortable it is to have that ripped away."

"At least let me go first." Merrick glanced over at Ratimana sitting ready and waiting in the corner of the cave. The old man had been cleaned up some, but his eyes still glinted with madness.

"No." She said it as kindly as she could manage, but maybe a little of the old Sorcha came out in the command. "I am Wrayth—at least a part of me, and like the first Deacon I must be the one to take the risk."

It hurt to admit to that part of her, but Raed was there. He understood. He had lived his whole life with a geistlord inside him, so whatever little portion she had, she could also make peace with. At least she didn't have one talking in her head.

She kissed the top of her partner's head. "I always wanted to be a saint," she whispered into his ear. "Let me have that chance."

This statement, said so very seriously, made him burst out into unexpected laughter. When he had recovered himself, Merrick snorted and shook his head. "When I first saw you, that was what I thought. That woman will be a saint one day."

Sorcha grinned, masking her own lingering concerns, and then stripped off her shirt, quite unconcerned about her nakedness before these men who had seen everything about her. She even pinned up her hair so that the Patternmaker would have nothing to distract him from his work.

Ratimana waited for her, seated on the floor, legs crossed, looking relaxed and at peace. It was amazing what the application of a little water and soap could do for a person. He smelled a thousand times better than he had in that dank cellar. He was a gift from Nynnia, yet another person she had underestimated in her life. Now it was time to learn some lessons and trust herself.

She sat down and held out her bare arms to the Patternmaker. "What do you think?"

Ratimana ran his firm, practiced fingers down from her shoulders to her fingers. "I think," he said, his eyes fixed on nowhere, "that there is room for each rune from here to your wrist. Your sigil you must carve yourself, into your palms."

She swallowed hard, feeling a trickle of sweat begin to form along her temple. "We'll do that last then."

The Patternmaker nodded. "Then I shall begin with Aydien on your right shoulder." His fingers slid over the instruments they had gathered for him: a pointed comb, a container of black ink and a little hammer.

Merrick came and sat down on her left, while Raed took up a place behind her. Sorcha looked across at her partner. His gaze was as steady and true as it had ever been.

Then she leaned back and felt Raed's hands rest lightly on the nape of her neck. His grip was warm and constant. The other hand she held out to the artisan who stood ready with the tattoo hammer.

The Deacon's voice when she spoke was firm. "Let us begin then."

TWENTY-EIGHT

Unseen Fangs

In the darkness of the night, after the exhausted Deacons slept, the Rossin took Raed's shape. The Young Pretender was standing at the entrance to the cavern, watching the misty forest, while his thoughts roamed over what he had seen that evening. He barely had time to realize that the geistlord was on him, before he took over.

Ripped clothes and outrage would be all he'd have to remember of the moment, as the Beast stuffed him down deep into his own consciousness. This conversation was something that the Rossin would rather keep from him.

The air was chill, and the great cat's breath stained it as he padded into the woods. He had not gone very far before a coyote's howl sounded. The Rossin's head swung up as he made a great bellowing roar in response and then sat under a twisted willow tree to wait.

The Fensena came to him, padding through the under-growth. The coyote's eyes gleamed in the moonlight, and he was as the Rossin remembered, lanky, shaggy and rather disreputable looking.

Even on the Otherside the Fensena had been useful. He'd specialized in working his way into other geistlords' favor and then bringing them into the Rossin's reach to become fodder. The coyote dined off the leftovers of the great pard, and now it seemed that he would do the same again.

Well met, my Lord, the coyote said, laying one paw forward and bowing over it. The Fensena was always very well mannered, but behind that courtesy was a sharp-toothed grin. Even the Rossin knew it paid to keep an eye on the creature.

Whose shape do you wear tonight, coyote Prince? The Rossin pressed the words into the mind of his fellow geistlord, but allowed a low rumble to take up residence in his chest. If any humans wandered across this strange scene they would be surprised at this meeting of beasts—at least until they were devoured.

A simple shepherd. The coyote's tongue lolled from one corner of his mouth. *I killed his dogs and bit him as he was running for home.*

The Fensena did tend to burn out his hosts rather fast. It was a similar method to the Wrayth and the Rossin, but far more likely to attract attention. That was why the coyote kept moving.

It was no simple chance that they had found each other while Raed was traveling to Phia. The Fensena had always possessed the ability to locate the Rossin—like real scavengers that shadowed lions on the plains. The Young Pretender had never even heard the coyote following him, but the Rossin had sensed him. It had been many hundreds of years since they had seen each other.

You are indeed mighty. The cat licked his paw with studied indifference. *Preying on the strays of this world.*

It is one way to survive. The Fensena was unmoved by his jibe.

You survive on my sufferance, the Rossin said, with a growl, *remember that. Your fate and mine are tied together.*

Indeed, the coyote observed slyly, *but as of yet, neither of us is up to confronting Derodak. His is blood that is long overdue to be spilled.*

The cursed Ehtia had grown strong in this world, learning his lessons better than any geistlord could have. He'd also amassed followers that spanned the whole world. It was not surprising that the Wrayth had thrown its lot in with him.

He will eventually bow before me, as will all creatures of this world. The cat's golden-flecked eyes fixed on the Fensena. *Have you secured what I tasked you with?*

The coyote flopped down on the ground and yawned as if the whole affair bored him. *Indeed, I have taken all precautions to get you what you want, my lord. The Deacon is bound to me by way of a favor, and I have procured for you the answer to your vexing question.*

The Rossin's eyes narrowed. *I can no longer dwell in the darkness of this half life. Especially with the Rossin line having been whittled down to just one heir.* He did not need to point out that when the line died out there would be nothing anchoring him to this world.

Yes, and it is such a surprise considering they started off so prolifically. The Fensena ran his tongue over his muzzle. *The death of the sister is most worrying for you I am sure.*

The great cat flexed his claws. The coyote had not been reminded of his power for a long time. Perhaps it was nearly due again.

The Fensena must have felt the change in the air, because he whined and flopped down on his back. He presented his soft belly to show he still remembered his place. *Luckily, I have found a way for you to never have to fear that again.*

The Rossin's ears swiveled about. *What have you discovered?*

The monks of Illus have made quite the study of you. Their library on the northern plains has unparalleled vol-

umes on you and your history. You should be quite flattered at all the attention. The coyote wriggled from side to side, like a dog seeking flattery. He got none from the Rossin though.

Were they flattered by your meager attentions then?

The coyote's wide smile would have frightened mortals to death. *They gave me what I wanted: instructions on how you can take the Young Pretender's life for your own. It will not be easy, it will take time, but it can be done.*

The great cat lifted his head and inhaled. He smelled smoke, blood and saltpeter coming from a great distance and from all directions of the Empire. *War is brewing and that will occupy the mortals' attention to my benefit.*

The Fensena rolled to his feet, his cunning eyes fixing on his fellow geistlord. *The doing of this will require the help of the Deacons. Are their attentions going to be diverted as well?*

The Rossin also rose to his paws and glared down on him. *She loves him, and she is trying to remake what was broken. That is more than enough to keep her away from my work.*

He didn't answer for Merrick. The Sensitive Deacon was a problem, one that would have to be taken care of eventually. He was too clever by half, and saw far too deeply for the Rossin's liking.

Follow us, the great cat commanded, as he prowled from the clearing. *Observe and obey, and when I come to my full power, you may have the scraps.*

As he made his way back to the sleeping Deacons, the Rossin did not check to see what the coyote did—he was already thinking how fine it would be to walk the world with impunity once more. The Empire—or what remained of it—would learn to fear and respect the will of the Rossin. Only then would everything be as it should have been from the very beginning.

Born in New Zealand, **Philippa Ballantine** has always had her head in a book. A corporate librarian for thirteen years, she has a bachelor of arts in English and a bachelor of applied science in library and information science. She is New Zealand's first podcast novelist, and she has produced four podiobooks. Many of these have been short-listed for the Parsec Award, and she has won a Sir Julius Vogel Award. She is also the coauthor of the Ministry of Peculiar Occurrences novels with Tee Morris. Philippa is currently in the United States, where her two Siberian cats, Sebastian and Viola, make sure she stays out of trouble. Visit her website at www.pjballantine.com.

Yasmine Galenorn

SHADED VISION

AN OTHERWORLD NOVEL

It's the night before Valentine's Day and the D'Artigo women are preparing for their friend Iris's wedding. But when Delilah and her sisters get word that the Supe Community Council has been bombed, things get really ugly. The evil coyote shifters—the Koyanni—are back, and Newkirk, their new leader, has joined forces with a group of rogue sorcerers. Just when they think things can't get worse, the demon lord Shadow Wing sends in a new front man, and life *really* goes to hell…

galenorn.com
penguin.com